To Marianne an...

Merrybegotten

with love and best wishes

Fiana

MERRYBEGOTTEN

Fiona Williamson Pearson

Kennedy & Boyd

Published by
Kennedy and Boyd
an imprint of
Zeticula
57 St Vincent Crescent
Glasgow
G3 8NQ

http://www.kennedyandboyd.co.uk
admin@kennedyandboyd.co.uk

Text and Line Drawings
Copyright © Fiona C. Williamson Pearson 2004

Cover photographs, of *Sheep Crag from Fair Isle*,
and *Sunrise from Fair Isle* © Dave Wheeler 2004

Fiona C. Pearson asserts the moral right to be identified as the author
of this book.

*This novel is entirely a work of fiction. The names, characters and
incidents portrayed in it are the work of the author's imagination. Any
resemblance to actual persons, living or dead, is entirely coincidental.*

ISBN 1-904999-03-4 Hardback
ISBN 1-904999-04-2 Paperback

To my three wonderful daughters,
Franki, Gabrielle and Jazz.

Acknowledgements

Many Thanks:

To my supportive family, my husband, Keith, and our daughters,
Francesca, Gabrielle, and Jasmin.

Huge thanks to Craig and Elaine Pritchett for their support
and encouragement and for Craig's invaluable help in getting me into
print.

A special thanks to Dave Wheeler, meteorologist and photographer,
for his wonderfully evocative cover photographs of Fair Isle.
Dave is also the person behind the Fair Isle website:
www.fairisle.org.uk

To Sigurd Towrie for his superb Orkneyjar website:
www.orkneyjar.com
and for his knowledge and wisdom willingly given on all things
Orcadian.

To Anne Cooper, Cathy Sharp and Deborah Spry
for taking me on my first trip to Orkney – day return in a six-seater
plane!

To my readers and supporters, Freda Markham, Helen Hazell, Peter
Baines, Julie Boothman, my sister Pam Munro, my cousins Liz
Molloy, Patt Jackson, Moira Leask,
and my aunt Joan Cochrane.

For help with my research, I would like to thank Catherine Cuthill,
Marion McLeod, and Fiona MacNab, Anne Slater for her copy of
George MacKay Brown's book 'Greenvoe',
and Alison Fraser of the New Kirkwall Library and Archives.

George R. Gray, Adrianne Leask and others at the Orkney Family
History Society
www.orkneyfhs.co.uk

Bruce Benson, Tony Gott and others at the
Shetland Family History Society,
www.shetland-fhs.org.uk

Sam Harcus, Development Officer for Westray and Papa Westray
www.westray-orkney.co.uk

Philip Welch of the Scottish Islands Explorer magazine:
www.scottishislandexplorer.com

And to the many other lovely Orcadian people and descendants of
these parts
for their invaluable help.

Fiona Pearson,
July, 2004

Glossary

Ain hame: own home
Auld: old
Bairns: children
Bannock: flat oatmeal cakes baked on a griddle
Biddie: body, person
Broonie: a traditional Orkney oatmeal gingerbread
Caddie: motherless lamb
Ceilidh: Scottish social gathering for dance to fiddle music
Close: narrow, covered passageway or alley between buildings
Coo: cow
Croft: a small farm with arable land
Disnae: doesn't
Dwam: daydream
Faider: father
Fou: drunk
Girnal: food store
Geo: like a small fjord
Guid: good
Haar: sea mist close to shore
Hogmanay: Scottish New Year's Eve
Howdie: midwife, untrained. Also refers to a person who lays out the dead, prepares bodies for burial
ken: know
Kirk: Scottish church
Ling: a fish (type) caught around Orkney
Merrybegotten bairn: illegitimate child
Midder: mother
Ne'er-do-weel: waster, never-do-well
Nor' Wast: the North West, ie Canada and the New World
Peedie: little
Pinny: an apron
Pownie an geeg: pony and trap
Roo: method of loosening and collecting longest wool by hand from sheep
Scattald: common pastureland for the rough grazing of sheep and

cattle
Sixern: open fishing boat rowed by six men
Speug: sparrow
Truncher: food platter
Twa: two
Up-Helly-Aa: a Viking festival held in Shetland to this day
Voe: small fjord or inlet
Wuber: weaver

In Chapter 13: Ella

Scottish Grace by Robert Burns:
Some have meat and cannot eat
And some will eat that want it;
But we have meat and we can eat
And so the Lord be thanked.

In Chapter 16: Twin Arrivals:
Here's tae us, an' wha's like us. Gey few, and they're aw deid – mair's the pity! :

Here's to us and those like us, damn few and they're all dead – more's the pity!

In Chapter 38: Toasts to the Future
May a moose ne'er leave yer girnal wi' a tear drap in its e'e.
May yer lum keep blithely reekin' till yer auld enough tae dee;

May a mouse never leave your food store with a tear drop in its eye.
May your chimney keep smoking happily until you are old enough to die.

Contents

Map
of Orkney

Fair Isle

Papa Westray

North Ronaldsay

Westray

Eday

Sanday

Rousay

Stronsay

Shapinsay

Kirkwall

Mainland

Hoy

South Ronaldsay

Part 1

1

Stonybrek, 1859

Fair Isle was bathed in autumn sun. A lone guillemot soared idly in the cloudless sky. Reflected in its dark eyes were the dazzling highlights that ricocheted off the sea's choppy surface. The high-wheeling seabird drifted into a wide spiralled descent and the Isle's treeless landscape loomed into its bird's eye view.

Inside the crofts and cottages that were scattered across this remote island preparations were being made for the expected return of the fishermen, who had been away at sea for over a week. With their return the predominantly female and child population would be redressed. The women waited for their husbands, fathers, sons, setting aside their farm work, their knitting and mending, to prepare hot meals for their all-important breadwinners. The livelihood and survival of all the inhabitants depended on their fishermen, men who in turn were dependent on the sea.

But Hellen Williamson of Stonybrek had something else on her mind.

Her solitary figure stood close to the western cliffs. As often happened in these parts, it took only moments for the weather to change. Hellen was the first to notice the brooding menace roll in from the north-west. She watched as the sun bravely punched holes in the shroud of cloud and sent down shafts of sunlight to dapple land and sea with flickering and fading undulations. The wind intensified and waves raced towards the cliffs, exploding against them in high-flying jets of vivid spray. Fair Isle merged into one dark entity with its surrounding water as an impenetrable barrier of storm clouds formed between sun and turbulent sea. Like a heavy grey blanket, the ominous sky dropped over isle and sea and the elements raged and thrashed beneath it.

The jagged and indented coastline is proof of centuries of assault by the weather. Constantly ruffled by breezes or battered by gales, Fair Isle is a small eruption on a vast seascape. Barely four miles long and half as wide, it is a mere blip of an isle sitting alone like a stepping stone between the archipelagos of Orkney to the south-west and Shetland to the north-east. It is readily overlooked on a map, hidden under a stray fingertip or lost to the eye in the blue print deluge of sea.

Hellen Williamson hunched her shoulders and drew her shawl more tightly around her. She narrowed her eyes against the flying droplets of sea spray carried on the wind and peered far beyond the jagged inlet that lay before her. She scoured the sea's panorama for a sighting of the *Zetland Breeze*. The *Zetland Breeze*, along with other local boats, was due to return to Fair Isle as soon as its haul of fish was off-loaded at Kirkwall harbour in Orkney. On board was Hellen's husband, Andrew.

As the guillemot entered the woman's world, its tranquil flight was shattered. The increasing cacophony of the storm forced the gull to seek shelter in the nooks and crannies of the western cliffs. Its battle towards the cliffs caught Hellen's eye and she decided to follow the bird's precedent by seeking shelter. She made her way back up the slope to continue her vigil from the doorway of Stonybrek.

"Come along, come along, Zetlan' Breeze, where *are* ye?" her words, spoken aloud, were snatched away by the greedy wind.

This was to be the day of Meg's conception.

Hellen frowned up at the dark sky then dropped her eyes back to the horizon where she caught a transient glimpse of a distant object disappearing behind the swell of a wave. She focused upon the spot until she saw the sight that was as familiar to her as an old friend. The *Zetland Breeze* rose briefly up onto the crest of a heaving wave, then once more vanished just as suddenly behind the rolling walls of seawater as it was tossed mercilessly towards the harbour.

She hurried inside Stonybrek for one last check to satisfy herself that all was spick-and-span for Andrew's homecoming. Taking up the poker, she gave the fire a prod, invigorating ribbons of passive flames to leap into life with crackling protests. Returning to the doorstep, she fixed her gaze on the approaching boat. Her cheeks were glowing with the fire's warmth – and with anticipation. She longed to greet Andrew and embrace him the way she used to do – before their family tragedy.

The *Zetland Breeze* was near enough for Hellen to see the figures of the fishermen on deck as they endeavoured to control the boat's aberrant actions whilst steadying themselves against the buffeting of the waves. Andrew Williamson stood at the bow. Hellen could distinguish him from his fellow crew by his tall stature and blonde hair. Andrew gazed out through a heavy veil of sea spray towards his homeland, the land of his ancestors. Stonybrek croft was a welcome sight, nestling as it did in a dimple on the hillside. It had been eighteen years since he and his father began building it for them as newly-weds, Andrew then twenty-five and Hellen Leslie just seventeen years old. The croft was to be ready for them within months of their wedding, but due to an unexpected turn of events Stonybrek at one time stood more like a forgotten ruin.

Conversation between the men on board the *Zetland Breeze* was made nigh impossible over the thundering noise of the sea and wind. But this was of no matter as each man was lost in his own thoughts, each contemplating the welcome from their family. Auld Jack Stout dreamt of his first home-cooked meal for nearly two weeks and licked his chapped lips, lips that were over-exposed to salt spray. Nineteen year old Ronald Brown was still trying to decide which of the two bonnie Wilson sisters he should ask out to the dance on Saturday, a dilemma he had been wrestling with the entire trip. Samuel Eunson deliberately stubbed the toe of his boot hard into a deck rail post, vexed at the thought that the fishing trip was all but over. For Samuel life on the open sea held more attraction than life on land. Any hardships endured at sea were insignificant compared to those created in his cramped cottage, overrun by his ever-growing family and ever-expansive wife.

Marriages on Fair Isle were for life. If a young romance failed people couldn't glibly say that there were plenty more chances of romance, or "plenty more fish in the sea" as they would in other parts of the world. Men were not in plentiful supply in this remote and sparsely populated isle. Many left to seek work in the alluring 'Nor-Wast', Canada and in America, as whalers, merchant seamen or fur traders, further depleting the existing meagre supply of eligible men. But there were literally "plenty more fish in the sea" – an abundance of fish; cod, haddock, ling, and swaithe swam in bountiful supply in the not too distant waters. Fishing was the principal occupation, the main income. Fish was the staple diet and frequently mentioned in conversation. The lives of the Fair Islanders revolved around fish as surely as the fish revolved around the Isle.

Andrew could make out the figure of his wife Ellen standing in the doorway. To Andrew she had always been 'Ellen'. He watched from afar as she struggled with her untamed hair given a life of its own by the relentless wind. Too far out to sea to distinguish her facial expression, he was yet cheered to see his wave returned. It was sufficient to know that Ellen was waiting and watching his return.

Hellen was an optimist by nature, but for two long years a deep sadness had changed her. Her depression was rooted in the tragic death of their only son. A tiny, premature offspring, he had lived a matter of minutes, if he had lived at all. There had been no time to give him a name, let alone christen him. Their only son and the only baby not to survive. Hellen withdrew into herself. She retreated into an impermeable shell to wallow in her grief. After the tragedy, life became mere routine and tasks were carried out with a dull heart. Smiling was no longer a natural reaction, more a physical impossibility for her. Interaction with her three daughters had been minimal and her loving husband was emotionally left out in the cold, forced to suffer alone his grief at the loss of their son.

The *Zetland Breeze* anchored safely in the harbour, its haul previously off-loaded at Kirkwall. The fishermen on board alighted like drunkards, belying the fact that they were all cold sober. The sea had been rough for most of their passage and they needed time to find their land legs once back on terra firma. By the time Andrew reached the path to Stonybrek he was in his usual stride and able to withstand the force of the rain-splattered gale that tore down the hillside against him. Hellen was grinning, impishly grinning, and watching him with long-awaited, seductive eyes.

Andrew stepped inside his cosy croft and dropped his kit bag to the floor. Hellen flung herself at his drenched body and laughed as she fired rapid kisses at his salty, sea-spayed face and tugged at his wet clothing. Over and over she told him how sorry she was and how much better she felt, that she would make amends for the past two miserable years. In those few minutes together she spoke more than she had in any one week of the last two years. Her words spoke volumes to Andrew. He realised her depression had truly lifted.

For two years her greetings to him had been scant and factual. "Take yer boots aff, Andrew," or "Fish an' tatties will be ready soon enough". But today there was *no* welcoming aroma of fish and potatoes. At that moment the absence of tantalising cooking smells seemed superfluous for Andrew's heart was hungrier than his stomach.

"Ellen, are ye pleased tae see me?" he teased as she clung and hung lightly around his neck. He had forgotten quite how light she was, light as Shetland fairy folk.

"Wheesht!" she said, placing her finger over his lips.

No other words were spoken until the consummation of a frenzied tumble of passion and laughter taking them across every available surface of their small and humble home. Inside the walls of Stonybrek the fire crackled and danced as if enjoying and encouraging their mood of abandon. Outside the storm ragged noisily, and yet noiselessly for Andrew and Hellen.

And thus the seed for Meg Williamson's existence was firmly planted that day.

At the schoolhouse on the other side of the island, Hellen and Andrew's three daughters were preparing to walk home after studies. Only the two older daughters, Barbara and Agnes, were scholars at the school, but the teacher, Laurence Mather, allowed Anderina to also attend. She was a headstrong child and would take it upon herself to follow her sisters to school most mornings, yet would sit quietly in a corner of the schoolroom and play with a pencil or coloured crayon. In the Williamson household there were no pencils or coloured crayons, nothing of wonder such as those.

Barbara, Agnes and Anderina would long remember the sight of their mother that day as she hurried across the hillside towards the school. Dissipating storm clouds scudded overhead, parting suddenly to illuminate Hellen's dishevelled figure in a ray of sunlight. Her face was flushed and she was short of breath as she told her three daughters of their father's safe return. Laurence Mather also noted Hellen's mood change. He could not remember a time when Mrs. Williamson had exuded such energy and enthusiasm.

Hellen's uplifting change in attitude filled her family with new happiness and the day she announced that a new baby was expected was a turning point for the Williamson family of Stonybrek.

2

Gyaain Trang Taegidder

It was a Fair Isle Christmas Ceilidh that brought Hellen and Andrew together. Engrossed in the frenzied music of the fiddlers Hellen clapped her hands and tapped her feet, her dark wavy hair bouncing around her shoulders. Her blue dress had been seen on previous celebrations, worn in turn by her older sisters, but to Andrew this hand-me-down looked pristine. Through fleeting gaps in the throng of merry dancers Hellen became aware of his tall blonde presence and fixed gaze upon her from across the hall. Their eyes locked, her heather-colours falling deeply into his fathomless blue pools. The memory of that moment was frozen with them forever.

But their romance did not begin until after the festival of Up-Helly-Aa.

Hellen was the sixth of eight children born to Grizel Irvine and Jerome Leslie. Grizel worked for the local weaver, or *wuber*, as one of a small team of blanket makers. She was also a knitter, as were all the women and girls on Fair Isle. Day in, day out, women knitted highly acclaimed Fair Isle jumpers and cardigans with intricate and distinctively patterned yokes. The renowned soft wool of the indigenous sheep was collected not by clipping, but by 'rooing', whereupon the longer wool of the previous year was loosened by hand and the whole length of wool was pulled out. This allowed the new wool to grow through below the old. Some women made very fine shawls of almost gauze-like delicacy, each weighing only a couple of ounces and taking many months to complete. Women's hands were never idle. These items, along with knitted socks and gloves, were traded for goods with passing ships.

Everyone helped with the rearing of sheep, which grazed across the scattald, or common pastureland, of Fair Isle and also on the top of Sheep Crag, a tall steep stack of rock standing proud off the eastern coastline and covered in nearly ten acres of lush grazing land. The

Crag's near vertical sides deflected the wind upwards, creating a peaceful environment for the grazing sheep. The men had an age-old system in operation concerning the utilisation of this seemingly inaccessible pasture. There was a way to climb one steep side to reach the top and then to haul one another up with the aid of chains. Sheep were raised and lowered by ropes; raised in the springtime and lowered in the autumn.

Jerome Leslie was a fisherman, farmer and trader. More than one occupation provided more than one means of making a livelihood. Depending on weather and season men would join forces to complete any necessary task at hand. Primarily they were fishermen, either joining deep-sea fishing fleets, or fishing local waters in small two man yawls or sixerns rowed by six men. But an eye was constantly kept on the sea's horizon for passing ships, which provided trading opportunities not to be missed. Ships from all over the world passed by Fair Isle in order to avoid the treacherous currents and maelstroms of the Pentland Firth; ships from Norway, Russia, Holland, Denmark, whalers from Greenland, and ships destined for the Canadian Hudson Bay Company. For their crew, away at sea for months on end, the luxury of fresh chickens, eggs, vegetables, were eagerly sought. On sighting a ship the Fair Isle fishermen would row out, their yawls laden with fresh produce as well as knitwear, blankets and hosiery. More frequently than not, the ships' captains gave permission to board. Trading was the highlight of any day and bartering when different languages were involved rarely presented a problem. They would exchange their island produce for items not known or grown on Fair Isle, Dutch cheeses, Danish salamis, Russian vodka, dried foods, fruits, clothing or tobacco.

Before their marriage Grizel and Jerome, as a young betrothed couple, had followed the Shetland Island's custom of 'bundling', whereupon a courting couple were permitted by their parents to spend nights together in the girl's bed – so long as they were fully clothed. Although this strange practice would seem to result inevitably in immorality, this rarely happened, perhaps due to the complete lack of privacy within communal and cramped sleeping quarters of small cottages.

The fresh air and wide heather-clad pastures proved to be the undoing of Grizel and Jerome's good intentions. On a sun drenched afternoon shortly after Jerome's return from a long haul fishing trip, he and Grizel threw caution and 'bundling' to the wind. Their privacy out on the moorland was vast, their liaison only interrupted from the clear blue sky above, where high-flying gannets, guillemots and kittiwakes squawked raucously. Grizel's pregnant outcome provoked no chastisement from either the Irvine or the Leslie families. To the community, they were as good as wed and her pregnancy merely proved that as a couple they could make babies and produce a family together, a positive sign for a lifelong relationship. The ability to produce children was deemed a most important factor in the success of a marriage. Grizel and Jerome went on to produce seven more children.

The start of the romance between Andrew and Hellen was more intense. After the Christmas Ceilidh their working lives at opposite ends of Fair Isle kept them apart, absence making their hearts grow stronger. At the end of January Andrew sailed with the other young men to Lerwick in Mainland Shetland to join in the annual traditional Viking festival of Up-Helly-Aa. Festivities there included nightly fiery torch-bearing processions and the rolling of lighted tar barrels across hillsides. Routine life of fishing, farming and trading would not resume until early February back on Fair Isle by which time Andrew's thoughts were filled with Hellen. And on the far side of the Isle, Hellen's daydreams reverberated around Andrew.

Andrew Williamson was a fisherman and trader, like his father before him and his father before that. Robert Leslie, one of Hellen's elder brothers, frequently fished with Andrew and after fishing trips Robert often invited Andrew to his home for supper. The Leslie home was nearer to the harbour and it was no trouble to Grizel to feed one more when she already had ten to feed. Grizel made sure that Andrew was seated next to Hellen and she would watch the young couple as if they were two of her cooking pots, catching their first simmering bubbles of romance. Shy smiles and furtive glances did not go unnoticed by their hopeful matchmaker.

The meal the family ate together was usually baked haddock or cod with stovies, which were potatoes cooked in the oven. The meal was served on two trunchers with the stovies on one platter and the fish on the other. Before apportioning the dinner, Jerome as the head of the household, would say a Grace over the two platters:

"Oh Thou who blest da loaves and fishes,
Look down upon our two poor dishes,
And tho' our tatties be but sma'
Lord grant dat dey may fill us a'."

A family pause for reflection would follow, interrupted as if in ritual by the eldest son John muttering under his breath: "And dat will be a miracle." A characteristic of the Shetland dialect was the persistent use of "d" in place of "th". After the grace the family would raise their heads from prayer to embark on the serious business of filling their bellies.

Before long Andrew Williamson and Hellen Leslie were known to be 'gyaain trang taegidder' or 'going out together'. As soul mates Hellen and Andrew were well matched, but their appearance together made for a somewhat odd couple. Hellen was around five-foot tall with dainty, elfin features and a mass of dark wavy hair, while Andrew was over six-foot tall and wore his Nordic blonde hair long and sleek to his shoulders. Hellen was free-spirited and spontaneous. Andrew was calm and methodical. Attraction of opposites, Jerome said.

Weddings were a grand affair on Fair Isle. Andrew and Hellen's wedding day was carefully chosen. The moon would be new on the night of the twenty first of June 1841 and following superstition this would ensure good luck to newlyweds. Robert Leslie and Andrew went from house to house bidding the inhabitants of Fair Isle a welcome to the celebrations. Friends and neighbours contributed to the wedding feast, donating sheep for roasting, fresh vegetables by the sackful and home-baked bread and cakes. Hellen's wedding gown, again a hand-me-down previously worn by her elder sisters, Babs, Merran and Jane, was too long to fit Hellen's smaller stature, and alterations had to be made.

After the marriage ceremony in the Kirk, the congregation formed a wedding procession and as they walked to the community hall some of the older women threw pieces of broken oatcakes over their heads for good luck and a blessing. A piece of oatcake placed under pillows the night after a wedding would ensure good dreams and good fortune. At the hall the wedding feast was laid out and local fiddlers gathered in readiness for the long night of nuptial celebrations. A traditional duty for bride and groom was to offer a drink from the Bride's Cog to each guest. The Bride's Cog was a circular drinking vessel, handcrafted from staves of light- and dark-hued woods and held securely by metal hoops with two long upright handles jutting up from the brim to use as handles. The Cog was full of a potent mixture of warmed ale and stout added to whisky, rum, gin, brandy and port with sugar and mixed spices stirred in. Andrew and Hellen carried it from guest to guest and the celebrations soon became wild and frenzied as foot-tapping music played until daybreak, when the wedding breakfast was produced to sustain flagging revellers. Midsummer on Fair Isle meant that the night remained as day, its clear skies not dark enough for stars to shine.

Andrew and Hellen's wedding night was the first they had spent alone together and neither set of parents had proffered any advice. Previously Andrew's father had made one awkward attempt to give his eldest son a talk about sex, 'man-to-man', but after mentioning "men's ardour rising" as he put it, he came to an abrupt halt, unable to explain or to continue. His wife, Barbara Brown, who like Grizel Irvine was known by her maiden name according to local custom, asked her husband if he had talked with his son and when he nodded, drawing deeply on his pipe, Barbara said "Guid!" and that was the end of the matter. Hellen was also left guessing as to what was in store for her wedding night, Grizel having previously dismissed her daughter's questions with a "you'll get tae know all in good time, lassie!" The tales told by Babs, Merran and Jane, her teasing sisters, were surely too amazing to be believed.

Stonybrek was far from completed, due to pressures of fishing and farming duties, therefore a snug corner of the attic of the Williamson home was made ready for Andrew and Hellen's wedding night. It was to this secluded spot that they managed to escape as their guests continued to enjoy the wedding festivities in the hall. The absence of the central characters went unheeded as the eating, dancing and wild fiddle playing continued for family and neighbours, and whilst most of Fair Isle was noisily enjoying the nuptial celebrations, Andrew and Hellen were noisily enjoying their first lovemaking. They gave in to sleep as the first light of dawn crept under a gap in the attic door.

Their slumber was broken by a loud tutt-tutting from the door of the attic. Barbara Brown's large frame was silhouetted by the midday sunlight that showered over them from the attic's diminutive doorway. Andrew's mother stood solid, big hands on big hips; stocking knitter and mother of six, she was making a stand before her eldest son and his wife of one day. Tutt-tutting until they woke, she proceeded to scold them as if they were children late for school, asserting one last moment of matriarchal control over her firstborn, a power lost to her the preceding day to Hellen, his new wife, her usurper.

"Canna be havin' a day awa' jist 'cause yer been gettin' married..." Her words trailed off as she suppressed her smile and turned towards the attic ladder. She left the attic muttering about there being work to be done.

But the honeymoon period was soon to be arrested in dramatic manner.

3

Yawl Adrift

A few months after the Williamson wedding, the community was shaken to its core by an unprecedented violation against two of its Islanders. The crime was seen as an outrage to everyone. The perpetrators were foreign seamen who sailed onto the horizon on a beguilingly bright, sunny afternoon and could not resist taking profit from an offered opportunity.

From high coastline rocks, ten-year-old Sinclair Wilson was engrossed in catching the fry of coalfish. The surrounding stillness was suddenly interrupted by shouts of alarm from far out at sea. Sinclair looked up and saw a large cargo ship in the distance. Beside it, unmanned and untethered, he saw his Uncle Andrew's two-man fishing yawl bobbing and rolling uncontrollably. Squinting and shielding his eyes against the sun, he noticed that on board the huge ship the crew was moving erratically and amongst the turmoil on deck he recognised the distinctive flaxen-headed figure of his uncle. When the ship began to sail away, leaving Andrew's abandoned yawl in its wake, Sinclair realised that Andrew and his yawl had been forcibly parted.

Earlier that fine morning Andrew Williamson and Robert Leslie had set out to fish in coastal waters. Their day's intentions included trading with passing ships so Andrew's yawl was well stocked with fresh, island produce. Two ships sailed on by keeping a steady course at full steam ahead. Some captains kept strict destination deadlines that allowed no time to trade. A third ship slowed and the captain gave permission for Andrew and Robert to board. They appeared to be in luck – or so they believed at the time.

A rope ladder was dropped to their yawl from the side of the ship. Andrew tossed a sack of vegetables over one shoulder and grabbed hold of the trussed legs of a live hen as he began to climb. Robert followed, similarly laden. As Andrew glanced up eagerly to the deck above, he felt a trickle of unease ripple down his spine.

The faces of the waiting crewmen appeared furtive, excitable, and as he stepped on deck a feeling of menace hit him; it hit him just before the first punch was thrown. Andrew reeled, his hands still struggling to hold onto the sack and the panicked, clucking hen, while other crewmembers reached over the side and grabbed Robert by his shoulders, hauling him up on deck beside Andrew. Shouts in a foreign language resounded in their ears as they were overpowered and roughly grappled to the deck by several crewmen. Outnumbered, they were soon trussed up like one of the chickens they had come to sell. Bruised and baffled, Andrew realised in horror that he and Robert were being 'impressed'. To add insult to injury, the crew emptied the contents of Andrew's yawl on board, before the yawl was cast adrift, and scrapped over the pairs of knitted gloves and stockings that were strewn about the deck. Cabbages and carrots rolled riotously about and the vivid splash of broken egg yolks smeared the wooden planking.

The crime was the transgression of the ship's captain. Before his ship neared Fair Isle he had realised he was two men short of a full crew. By their request for permission to board these two hopeful traders presented him with an opportunity he was unable to resist. He thereby instructed his crew to form an impromptu Press Gang.

In previous times during the years Britain was at war with France press-ganging had been rife along the east coast of Scotland. Many British seamen volunteered to fight at sea, though many more were impressed into the service of the Royal Navy. The Navy knew that the hardy seamen from the northern isles and the coastal ports of Scotland were fully competent in handling boats and well acquainted with the complexities of sails, knots and splices. They were favoured prey because they 'knew the ropes' and could cope with just about anything the seas might throw at them. Able-bodied seamen were in constant demand. This kidnapping continued around the turn of the nineteenth century as a means for passing ships to obtain a full complement of crew at low cost. Under cover of night many drunkards were absconded from outside quayside alehouses at Scottish coastal ports. They were easy prey for the Press Gangs. Men would awaken from their stupor to find themselves far out at sea and if they refused to work they were often unceremoniously thrown overboard.

No one had been impressed or kidnapped from Fair Isle in Sinclair Wilson's lifetime although he had heard stories told of such occurrences. In panic, the boy dropped his catch into the water and raced over the rocks to raise the alarm. Within minutes farmers on the hillside and fishermen near the shore knew of the abduction, but to no avail. The ship carrying Andrew and Robert had disappeared over the horizon. Although their forlorn and empty yawl was retrieved from the sea, there was nothing that could be done to rescue the two young men who had occupied it. The yawl, stripped to the wooden planks by the pirate crew, cruelly divulged no evidence of their existence. The remaining Fair Isle fishermen knew that Andrew and Robert, plucked from the seas around their homeland, might never be seen on the Isle again.

Sinclair was despatched to tell the new bride of her husband's abduction. He was later to say that it was one of the worst tasks he had ever been assigned to do. When he began to relate his gibbering story, Hellen's body plummeted like a stone on her doorstep. With glazed eyes she sat there ungainly sprawled in stunned disbelief. Sinclair tried his best to support her back to standing for want of what else better to do for her.

News of the upset travelled swiftly around the community and islanders appeared from all directions to give solace and hope to Hellen. Everyone was shocked. Nothing like this had happened on Fair Isle for decades. Press-ganging was barely within living memory. It was something that belonged to folklore. The women wanted the men to act immediately but the men, collectively and pragmatically, knew that it was already too late. The cargo ship would be leagues away and Fair Isle had no ship to match its speed.

Hopelessness shrouded over Hellen like a darkening sky over the perfect sunrise of their time together. In one fell swoop her happiness had been annihilated and her life with Andrew scurrilously disunited. Although married life had just begun it seemed that it might already be over. Simmering anger within her rose at the thought of her husband and brother, no doubt kicking and screaming, forced into another existence – at best a life at sea amongst strangers. And for how long? Fear gripped her heart at the thought of what might have befallen them. Would she ever see them again? Plucked from the sea as if they were fish caught in a net and splayed across a deck to flounder. They would be lost souls gasping for air out in the world beyond Fair Isle that was unknown to Hellen. She shouted her anger across the open panorama to the disinterested sea beyond.

"De blagards, de pirates, who stole oor guid men frum deir homeland!"

Fury made her rant and rave at the calm and innocent sea. Its only response was to continue its relentless undulations and lap fawningly at the jagged rocks of the cliffs.

Feelings of desolation flooded over Hellen as tide washes over loose sand, leaving it hard and cold. She felt plundered. With her life so long entwined with his, she was now excluded and deprived of his company, no longer privy to his thoughts and conversation, perhaps forever. She thought back to how the day had begun, to visualise exactly how they had parted that morning and the precise words said to one another. These were all-important to her, now that she was left with only memories. Would she have only memories of Andrew? In her mind's eye she conjured up his every gesture and idiosyncrasy. She must not forget a nuance. She would keep him alive in her heart. Grizel and Barbara, as distraught mothers of the lost seamen, helped to share her plight. They supported and consoled one another. But Sinclair's recollection of the fight on board added to their misery and thoughts kept returning to unanswerable questions. Had their loved ones survived the abduction? If they refused to work with the crew would they be thrown overboard? But more poignantly, would Hellen, Barbara and Grizel ever know?

Days passed and turned into weeks, and the Fair Isle working routine fell back into place. The ease in which normality returned for everyone around her only added to Hellen's dismay. In the turmoil within her she found herself daydreaming of solutions, of straws to clutch hold of. She imagined a letter arriving from Andrew, a letter to say that they were alive and well and returning home. She imagined that on receiving this news jubilation would spill over Fair Isle like overflowing cream. Then she realised she had never seen Andrew's handwriting. In his life as fisherman and farmer he had no need for the written word. Whatever meagre writing skills he might have managed to retain from his school days were a mystery to her. Yet in her imagination he drew caricatures across the pages of his long letters. She visualised a drawing of himself and Robert, a black eye apiece, standing proudly beside a pile of battered and unconscious men, their captors. There was little else she could do but hold onto the belief that they would safely return to be reunited, so she resolved to keep herself busy with work in order to have something to show for her efforts when Andrew returned home. They said she worked like a woman possessed. She busied herself weaving baskets for carrying peat and collecting vegetables. She knitted cushion covers and whittled wooden cooking spoons from driftwood. Covertly she knitted a baby's bonnet. These special treasures of her own handiwork were carefully stored away.

Until the day of the abduction, Andrew had worked in spare hours from fishing with his father, Andrew Williamson senior, on the building of Stonybrek. His father, who refused to work on without his son, treated the void that Andrew left behind like bereavement. With all progress halted indefinitely on Stonybrek, it looked increasingly dilapidated, more like a ruin than a future home. Although Hellen's own hands were itching to have a go at dry stonewalling, she was forced to bide her time as this would wreak havoc against tradition. But Hellen wanted to make her mark on her prospective home, determined that it would be her home someday, and set about cultivating the strip of land to one side of Stonybrek. She planted vegetables and grew a fine harvest crop of potatoes, turnips and cabbage. These were mostly superfluous to the Williamson family consumption, so she bartered produce with neighbours for items the family did need. The four sheep and one cow, given by Islanders as wedding gifts, fattened well on the common pasture, the scattald. The cow yielded good milk with which she was able to churn butter, mostly for trading purposes.

The decrepit state of Stonybrek was an eyesore. Her brows furrowed every time she caught sight of its dereliction. To Hellen its state of neglect represented time standing still with her life on hold. Her father-in-law reacted as though a part of his life was over, a chapter closed. Hellen understood that the project had been a joint effort between father and son, a tradition to carry through, and that to complete it without his son would give him no satisfaction. But with constant optimism, she persisted in trying to persuade him how grand it would be to have the building work completed for the return of his son. His response was always deflating. He would shake his head sombrely, and look away from her out to the sea's constant horizon, despondently replying, "*If* he returns".

Hellen kept constant vigil over the circumference of sea around her homeland, searching for ships that might bring Andrew back to her. The sudden and enforced separation meant that she led the life of a widow. Wistfully she would watch from afar as fishermen set sail or busied themselves with work that Andrew would normally have been involved in; work that would have brought him home to her each evening. During the summer months everyone on Fair Isle was busy as they rallied to help cure the fish catches, splitting fish then pickling them in wooden vats or drying them over peat fires, ready for the landlord, their absent Laird.

Hellen's assumption that Andrew and Robert would return was not, however, the opinion of some of the eligible bachelors on Fair Isle. Most held out little hope of seeing either of the lost men again. The 'abandoned', sweet yet feisty Hellen began to appeal to many a suitor, who thought her too pretty to waste on a life of solitude. For a time she became nectar to the bees, but rebuked all advances and held true to her vows. No one came close to Andrew.

As the anniversary of Andrew and Robert's abduction loomed, versions of the story were retold and Sinclair Wilson was most in demand for his eyewitness account. Time moved on and another year slipped by with Hellen immersing herself in whatever work needed to be done for whoever might need help. Her speciality was to help with the lambing, especially in the care of any caddies, or motherless lambs. It was as she was nurturing one weak and tiny caddie lamb that she heard loud and agitated shouts from the cliffs. Wrapping the bleating lamb in rooed wool, she went to investigate the cause of the fracas.

A boat was approaching the harbour. It was the ferryboat from Orkney, yet no one was expected to call that week. Curiosity got the better of many of the Islanders, who stopped the work in hand to watch its arrival, shouting to one another across the scattald. Hellen's heart missed a beat as her hopes soared. Convinced that Andrew must be on board that ferry, she picked up her skirt and raced down the West Road towards the harbour, setting a pace for a throng of excited and inquisitive children.

4

Lost Souls

For Andrew and Robert the first two days of their captivity were spent in a daze, locked in the grumbling bowels of the alien ship. A huge cargo vessel, it was unlike any fishing boat they had ever sailed in before. Below deck they were unable to assess the direction of travel, the speed or distance covered and had little indication of weather conditions. A brief exchange with the captain, who spoke hastily in a foreign language, left them none the wiser as to his intentions for them. Their only means of communication was to glare their anger and indignation, but the captain was unconcerned. He had a job to do and they were merely cogs for his wheel. After the initial scuffle with the crew on deck, resulting in a black eye apiece, no further violence was shown towards them. They were brought watery soup or thin gruel to eat with a flat doughy sort of bread, the occasional chunk of dried meat or piece of strange tasting fruit. Crewmembers treated them with civility yet spoke in the same alien tongue as the captain and, when Andrew and Robert were eventually led up on deck, communication consisted of mimes and demonstrations in order to show what was expected of them. They could tell by the position of the morning sun that the ship was heading south, but without land in sight there was no way of knowing where they were, let alone where the ship was bound.

To plot an escape from their foreign captors whilst on the high seas was a useless ploy, yet at the first port of call both men determined to jump ship. Their plan proved futile. At the merest glimpse of land the crew bundled Andrew and Robert below decks and locked them into a storeroom. Twice the ship docked, took on supplies and set sail again before they were allowed back on deck. They constantly talked of ways to break free and return to Fair Isle from an unknown part of the world, yet they knew this would entail working passage on other foreign vessels with possible indiscriminate crews, unscrupulous captains and unknown destinations. Robert took in the hopelessness of their situation, seeing only an indefinite period spent in captivity. Andrew began to realise a reunion with Hellen was highly unlikely.

Work began to occupy their every waking moment as the days turned into weeks and they fell into their new routine with resigned ease. It was to be a long haul. Unknown cargo was yet to be loaded before delivery to an unknown destination. Andrew and Robert worked in a crowd yet in isolation. The language barrier proved insurmountable. Working on deck was second nature to them and without the intricacies of fishing it proved to be more straightforward than working the boats on the seas around Fair Isle, but this was no compensation for the life and freedom they had lost. Andrew knew that Hellen could only guess at what had become of them. There was no means of sending word to their loved ones back on Fair Isle to at least say they were alive, well and being treated as fairly as could be expected in a captive state. Both men began to wonder at their fate once their services were no longer required on ship. This thought fired a pact to jump ship and their opportunity arose unexpectedly.

After a day of clear skies and calm seas there came a dramatic change in the weather. It was twilight when land was sighted from the crow's nest, but within minutes every crewmember was too busy to march the two captive workers to the storeroom prison below. An ominous ambience merged with the imminent nightfall. Angry waves were swiftly gaining momentum and rising up high against the sides of the ship. All hands were needed on deck as the sudden storm encircled them, there, on some vast and heavy ocean far from Fair Isle.

The heavy red sun dropped like a stone into the sea's horizon before storm clouds won their battle to blanket the sky. The dark ink of night became more cloying with the thickness of shrouding cloud. In no time a gale raged, and confusion reigned on deck. Water hit the men from all angles, high waves crashing above them and sidelong sheets of rain drenching and weighing them heavy. For over an hour the crew fought to keep control of their ship. Visibility was lost and strength sapped. Orders from the captain were impossible to deliver with shouts being carried off in the wind. With waning stamina men grabbed and held onto whatever came to hand as their struggle to keep the ship on course turned into a battle to keep it afloat and ultimately a fight for survival.

A sudden cacophony, screaming even above the deafening din of the elements, heralded the triumph of the storm over the ship as the vessel was rammed onto unseen rocks. The ship shuddered and crew were jolted from safe holdings, some thrown headlong into the walls of deluge. A fixed resistance from beneath proved they had run aground. In the eerie, wild gloom of the moonless night the ship was marooned and taking the full onslaught. A huge gash on its keel sucked in seawater greedily and spewed it through the belly of the ship in torrents. Splinter by wedge the ship began to disintegrate under the persistent assault of wind and waves. It was every man for himself. Then the fist of the storm dealt its fatal blow by snapping the main sail mast in two as if it were a chicken wishbone and bearing it off on the gale.

Throughout the storm Andrew and Robert had kept within reach of one another. They heard the mast crack above them and decided to hold out no longer. Andrew turned to face his brother-in-law and grabbed him by his sodden shoulders. Long strands of dripping hair lashed across their bearded faces. The whites of their eyes shone luminously as they locked on to one another. Blurred and stinging with salt sea spray, Robert's eyes expressed a look, though fleeting in time that penetrated deep into Andrew's soul as a flash memory. There was pain and fear and something indefinable. Words were not needed to make the decision to jump overboard. They turned and struggled forward against the howling gale to what was left of the starboard deck rail. Together, simultaneously, the lifelong friends leapt, far out into the hell of the night.

As they flung their drenched bodies out into the black unknown beside the doomed ship, Andrew and Robert, their legs and arms flaying, felt suspended in time and space. Sightless in the impenetrable gloom, they had no indication where sea or sky met. Contact with one another was lost as survival instincts took over their adrenaline-charged bodies. It seemed an eternity as they waited for flesh to meet element with the hurricane raging all around them and with no assurance of a safe landing.

Both men were able swimmers, unlike many other fishermen of Fair Isle, who believed that death by drowning would be quick in their icy water and therefore there was no need to be able to swim. These southern seas were milder than those they had known. But swimming to shore was not an option in such tempestuous waters. Men were carried on the force of the incoming waves, powerless to help themselves. Some crew clung desperately to the riggings only to be crushed by the sea along with remnants of the ship. Others floundered and perished. Whither the two press-ganged members were alive or drowned was not a concern for any seamen who made it to dry land.

Plunging through seawater like a stone, the noises of the storm dulled in Andrew's ears by the mass of water around him. He felt his downward momentum slow and buoyancy take over. His head at last shot through the sea's surface, his mouth gasping in air. His ears reverberated with the resumed din as he struck out immediately to swim away from the creaking, cracking ship behind him. The swell of the waves carried him towards land and on a fall of one wave he touched ground and he was able to stride through the water. It felt like sand beneath his bare feet. Soon he was in the surf, the angry sea behind him though all around him was awash in black ink. No light fell on the scene. Only sounds and senses surrounded him.

It was then that pain overtook him and he became conscious of every muscle in his body, and every muscle was aching. Every inch of skin seemed to sting or burn. His breathing was weak and laboured. He sank to the ground exhausted yet tried to haul himself away from the rage of the sea. Lying prone in the darkness, he waited for some strength to seep back into his body. To one side he heard the surf crashing against rocks. He turned his body painfully to the other side and saw shapes silhouetted in the distance further inland. They resembling tall palm trees, but Andrew had to rely on his memory of schoolbook pictures. There were no trees to speak of on his homeland, where seeds had a hard time implanting themselves in the consistently windy weather. He wondered if this land could be an African coast.

"Robert!" he shouted, his weak voice swallowed up by the wind. "Where are ye, Robert?"

Exhaustion took hold yet he was dimly aware of the occasional muffled shout and distant scream from other shipwrecked victims in the vicinity. Drifting in and out of consciousness, the last thing he heard that day was the ship's death throes, its annihilation against the rocks, the cracking and crashing of ship's timbers mingled with the turmoil and clamour of the retreating gale. The storm began to dissipate after claiming full destruction of Andrew and Robert's prison. "The wrath of God…" thought Andrew as he plummeted into unconsciousness.

Andrew was roused by the feeling of heat penetrating his damp clothes. A strong sun was beating down onto his aching body and over his closed eyelids, where grains of salt lay caked around his lashes. Cautiously he opened his eyes and winced with pain at the bright sunlight that flooded in. Pain screamed at him from all over his body. His skin was covered in bruising, and salt from his lengthy submersion in the sea aggravated his flesh wounds, making him fully aware of their exact location. Transcending the pain, his survival instincts took over. The foreign captors might be lurking nearby. He raised himself onto an elbow and looked around before drawing on all his strength to drag himself over to the undergrowth at the top of the beach to find somewhere to hideout until he could assess his situation.

But he need not have been concerned. All was still and peaceful. The only sound to be heard was that of a gently lapping surf across the idyllic beach where he found himself to be. It seemed incredulous that the worst storm he could remember had given way to this glorious morning and contemptuous that such a storm had occurred in such a beautiful place. The aftermath and evidence of the night's devastation soon became apparent. Debris from the cargo ship could be seen strewn across the scene of beauty and Andrew noticed the occasional beached and lifeless body. There appeared to be no other living person around. Only birdsong.

"Robert!" Andrew shouted. "*RO-BERT?*"

Andrew thought that he might be sleeping in the undergrowth, trying to recover from the ordeal or he might have set off inland, unable to locate Andrew. But as Andrew searched the length of the beach close to the tree line he soon came to realise that few, if any, of the men on board ship had survived the night. As he turned to leave the beach something very familiar caught his eye.

Floating gently back and forth in the gentle sway of the high tide line was a shirtsleeve, the check pattern of which Andrew would have recognised anywhere. It was the check pattern of Robert's shirt – but it was no longer attached to his shirt. Andrew moved closer – then recoiled in horror. Robert's arm, amputated at the shoulder, was still inside the floating sleeve.

Aghast, Andrew fell to his knees on the sand. Through narrowed eyes reluctant to see, he looked upon the familiar fingers, now swollen and lifeless. With such an injury Robert would not have been able to swim. And the blood loss would have been too great for him to survive. Robert must surely be dead.

Sweating under the scorching rays of the foreign sun, Andrew searched frantically amongst all the debris and the undergrowth for his lifelong friend, alive or dead. Several yards out to sea he saw more flotsam and jetsam from the shipwreck drifting towards the shore. In contrast to the surrounding darks and browns of broken wood, the sharp blue and red check of Robert's shirt shone out. Andrew waded out, the morning's gruesome discovery imprinted in his mind. Yet still he was unprepared for the shock of seeing Robert dead. His lifeless body, face down, rising gently with the swell and flow of the rhythmic waves. Washed in by the tide, Robert seemed calm and at one with Nature. Andrew sighed so deeply he thought his lungs would collapse.

Sinking below the sea's surface beside Robert's body Andrew rose gently to position his friend across his shoulder. He carried him up the beach to a secluded spot inland beside a meandering stream, where he dug into the hard baked soil with planks of wood from the ill-fated ship. That previous night both wood and bodies together had been broken and tossed ashore by the sea. Andrew placed Robert's body in the grave. He stood a while, trying to remember prayers to recite. In this foreign place, so far from their homeland, he wanted to give Robert as decent a funeral as he could muster alone. Then he sat beneath the trees, locking into his memory, into the fathoms of his mind, Robert's final resting-place that he may, one day, be able to describe it in detail to Grizel and Jerome, and to Hellen. If he was ever to see them again. But no sooner had the despondent thought overtaken him than a new determination took hold. What good could come of his life if he didn't strive to make it back to Hellen and to Fair Isle?

Once more he looked around to check that no other survivor had him in his sights. He made his way to the sea's edge to wash his many flesh wounds in its healing, stinging water. Most of his clothes were in tatters. One leg of his trousers had been ripped away just below the knee. He tore the other leg off at the same level. His navy wool waistcoat, last night heavy with seawater, felt tighter and had sprung several holes. His check shirt was open at one shoulder seam and its meticulously hand sewn, collarless neckline was somehow frayed by the force of battering wind and sea. His feet were bare, his leather boots gone. Before the night's rapid descent he managed to salvage two reasonable shoes from the flotsam and jetsam. They were odd, but they were roughly the right size, one slightly larger than the other.

The occasional fish jumped from the now calm sea. Unseen animals and birds chirruped and rustled deep amongst the trees. Although Andrew drank thirstily from the stream, hunger stayed strangely at bay. Although his body felt pain, his mind was numb. It gave him no satisfaction that he appeared to be the sole survivor. The longed-for escape, the achievement of freedom, were cold comfort when he found himself alone, having lost his closest companion. He was unwilling to leave Robert under the ground of this unknown territory and it was a daunting thought – to make his way alone to Fair Isle from this unknown place. He was a fisherman, a navigator, a seaman – not a land traveller or an explorer. He had no experience of travel overland. Fair Isle could be walked from one end to t'other in a matter of hours.

Mentally and physically drained, Andrew summoned the will to venture further from the beach. Under cover of nightfall, which was a sudden darkening like a snuffed candle, he roused himself and left the scene of devastation, making his way through undergrowth and forestation.

The sound of voices ahead of him made Andrew freeze. It was

the same foreign language of his captors. He was not the only survivor after all. Swiftly crouching out of sight in a dense thicket, he kept still and silent. A man's scream pierced the still air, startling birds in the trees around Andrew. The birds, though mute in fright, flapped in panic and trawled awkwardly up into the air as if woken from a heavy sleep. Andrew heard the raised voices of at least two other unseen men. It seemed an eternity before the muffled voices faded further inland. Andrew remained in hiding until he heard birds returning to their night perches on the high branches around him. Venturing warily forward, his way was heavily obscured by the dark of night. A moonlit sky appeared only at the tops of the trees directly above him. Weak rays of moonshine filtered lazily down around him but illuminated little and he found himself scrambling through the unknown, his wounds constantly scratched by the surrounding, untamed vegetation. If the unseen foreigners were still in the vicinity at least the dark would conceal his whereabouts, but Andrew's bungling gait was disturbing wildlife to the left and right of him. He decided to keep to a shoreline route, hoping that by daybreak he might have come across a port.

But sleep got the better of him and he dropped where he stood. He awoke just before dawn to find he was close to a more open terrain and further inland than he had hoped. Yet he needed to travel overland rather than by sea, wanting no further risk of being made a slave on board a ship. After travelling inland for a while he set a northerly route by the sun.

He drank water from flowing streams, but weakness forced him to rest a lot. On the third day he was walking easily through light vegetation when he heard the sounds of a fire crackling and smelled the unmistakable aroma of meat cooking. Ahead of him above the tree line he saw a plume of meandering white smoke. Cautiously he approached the spot, keeping hidden. Through concealing branches his eyes alighted upon a series of small huts made from branches and grasses bound by what looked like dried mud. A few dark skinned people wearing colourful cloths moved around the area. A woman walked gracefully, balancing a basket of fruits on her head. A man with his back to Andrew squatted by the fire, slowly turning the handle of a giant spit upon which the blackened, meaty carcass of a large pig or a hog rotated, filling the air with its tantalising smell. For a moment Andrew was unaware of the small, staring boy, who stood only feet from him. Without fear the boy called to his father, jolting Andrew from his dwam. But before he could be afraid of the consequences of the little boy's actions Andrew was being helped out into the bright light of the clearing. The people, jabbering in an even stranger tongue, remained straight faced yet friendly and gentle towards him. They stared but seemed strangely unfazed by the presence of a shipwrecked mariner, so much so that Andrew wondered if shipwrecks might be a common occurrence along this coastline. They pulled him encouragingly towards the object of his desire, the delicious smelling meat. He was fed handsomely, eating more than he had ever done at one meal, whilst nodding his gratitude and smiling his praises to his saviours.

No news preceded Andrew's return. All his efforts had gone into travelling home as quickly as possible. He would therefore arrive on Fair Isle unannounced and unexpected. A wariness stirred within him. What would he find on his return? Would Hellen have waited for him? Would she have remarried, thinking him dead? Perhaps she'd had a baby with another man…he couldn't bear to think that way. As a reunion became imminent Andrew took stock of his appearance. He looked down at his ill-fitting clothes, fresh and clean as they were. His hair felt damp with sea mist and lay limply across his head.

The island grapevine was set in place the moment Sinclair Wilson looked through his family spyglass and caught a glimpse of the approaching ferry through the patches of rolling mists. There, looming out at him from the centre of the magnified lens, Sinclair espied a longhaired, blonde yet bearded man, who reminded him of his long lost Uncle Andrew. Sinclair, the last person to see Andrew's unjustifiable departure, suddenly realised that he was to be the first to confirm Andrew's return. Soon most of the islanders could see Andrew with their own eyes and this wonderful revelation rippled across the gathering crowd like waves to the shore. Surprise, delight, disbelief and an intensity of fervour heightened. Andrew Williamson, father of this lost son, was overjoyed at the physical proof before his eyes; that his first-born son was safely returning to the fold. Barbara Brown said she had never seen her husband so ecstatic, so out of character.

As for Hellen, she felt unbridled euphoria and her sheer delight warmed the hearts of all who witnessed it. As the ferry moored the cheering of the welcoming crowd was deafening. Andrew stepped boldly and proudly onto his native soil, amazed at his welcome. Hellen, who stood foremost on the quayside, flung herself into his outstretched arms. Bliss adhered Hellen to Andrew's body, locking them in embrace.

Barbara Brown was pleased to see that although Andrew's body looked lean and hungry, he appeared to be fit. The constant exposure to the high sun of foreign parts had tanned her son as brown as a nut. It was then that everyone wanted to know the inevitable – where was Robert. The community was deeply saddened that one of their fishermen had drowned off some foreign land. It troubled Grizel Leslie that his body could not be returned for burial on Fair Isle. In time a wooden cross with an inscription to Robert's memory was erected in the Kirk yard and he was given a proper Christian service on the first subsequent Sunday that the minister from Shetland paid his parishioners a visit.

The tales of Andrew's travels were infinitely the most newsworthy stories the Islanders had heard in decades. No one tired of hearing of them. The nightmare of his experience as he remembered it and had lived through it, became glorified and embellished into an unsurpassed adventure. Young lads doted on his every word. That small and remote population found it hard to relate to the experiences that Andrew talked about. They found his descriptions a continual fascination. To even imagine dark skinned people living in climates so different from their own was barely comprehensible. Andrew and Robert had sailed the high seas. They had been to unknown lands where the weather was intolerably hot in the daytime only to chill so drastically at night that they slept under frost-laden sails. There was nowhere remotely like Fair Isle on the other side of the world, Andrew told them.

And of the journey home, he talked little. The only means he had of knowing which direction he should take was to use his knowledge of the sun's position as no one that he met spoke a language he could understand. Begging passage on passing carts, Andrew travelled through hot, dusty regions with baked, dry landscapes. One old man offered his own straw weave hat to cover Andrew's sunburnt forehead and when they parted the man insisted Andrew kept the hat. Along the way he came across blue-robed travellers riding on camels taller than any horse he had ever seen; he was offered vegetables and fruits he had never before encountered. Fervently he drank in the differences between this world and his world that was Fair Isle. Yet he yearned all the more to be back on his homeland. With each day came hope. Each day brought him nearer to his goal. He covered long distances by hitching rides, which enabled him to rest his weary limbs.

So much time had elapsed since the day Andrew and Robert had climbed the fateful rope ladder of their future prison, the very ship now dashed to pieces on the liberating rocks. Andrew was probably half way around the world from their starting point. The hardest part to endure about this time spent away from the only homeland he had ever known was travelling alone with his conspicuous loss of companion. His resolve strengthened, however, the more he thought of Hellen. He hoped she would be waiting for him. He hoped she had been able to cope with his unknown fate.

Like most memories softened by time, any advantages of his experiences abroad were only obvious long after his plight was resolved. "*Whit disnae kill ye, will strengthen ye,*" - words of wisdom from his mother rang in Andrew's ears.

During his journey Andrew managed to earn a little money by occasional farm work. Although it was money he did not recognise, it bought him food in the country of its origin. His seemingly endless journey included a sea crossing from Africa to Spain for which he had money enough to buy passage. He encountered many people but was not able to strike up a conversation with anyone. He made do with a form of sign language and found he became quite expressive with this type of communication. A few times on his journey through Spain and through France he accepted long term work in return for his keep. He helped with harvesting or fruit picking for several weeks at a stretch, and spent time with the local people, eating with them, sleeping in cabins with a bed for each worker. When he moved on it was often on the offer of a lift on a wagon or cart. On the occasions he walked alone, often for miles on end, he picked berries to eat, scrounged crops from fields, and guddled fish from streams, which he cooked on an open fire or bartered for other food. Many people willingly shared their meals with him and generally he survived with a fair degree of pride, sleeping in outhouses or under trees – trees still being a thing of wonder.

On arriving at the English Channel, he whooped with joy for he knew he was only one country away from Scotland. His outburst made the other, briefly startled, passengers cheer with him. As he travelled the last part of his journey, through England, he continued to hitch lifts. Wherever he was dropped, at whichever town or village, he would ask for paid work. He helped to milk cows, deliver lambs, to carve table legs on a lathe, to weave baskets, and to groom horses. There was nothing Andrew wouldn't turn his hand to.

On his last lift on his umpteenth horse-driven cart he felt new strength surging through his veins with the knowledge that there were only two more sea crossings to go, one to Kirkwall in Orkney and one to Fair Isle, before reaching his homeland. Andrew's Shetland accent was recognised by the ferryman at Scrabster. The man was curious to know what had happened to Andrew, considering how tanned, lean and dishevelled he looked. So Andrew, with a straightforward and unassuming manner, told him his incredible tale and was intrigued by the man's reaction. Andrew found he was being treated like a hero and the ferryman insisted he should rest at his home that night. He ate a hearty dinner with the man, his wife and family, during which he was regaled to share his travel tales with them. He accepted a set of fresh clothing from the kindly couple; the trousers were a few inches short, the shirt too tight to button at the neck, but it was bliss to feel clean cloth against his weathered skin. After so long away he wanted to make a reasonable impression on Hellen. The following morning the ferryman gave Andrew free passage to Kirkwall, where another ferryman, on hearing Andrew's story, insisted on taking him free of charge to Fair Isle.

Although it was summer the weather around Fair Isle was, as ever, unpredictable and prone to heavy rolling mists as the warmer air met the cool mass of sea. As the boat sailed from Kirkwall a blanket haar enveloped the boat slowing its progress. As they neared the isolated Isle the mists began to roll and thin, opening up tantalising spy holes of his beloved homeland. Andrew's heart felt huge with longing and anticipation.

In retrospect, he would admit that his adventure had been the experience of a lifetime, but would hasten to add it was not one he would wish to repeat. It had been an interminable time, years in fact, to be away from his new bride.

5

Island Grapevine

Occasional ferries brought supplies, mail, or visitors to Fair Isle. Visitors were a rarity and a curiosity to the islanders. There was the occasional official from the British government, or travelling salesman hawking his wares, or small gaggle of ornithologists intent on studying and collating the antics of an amazing diversity of bird life that nested and bred on the predator-free Isle. The approximately four by two miles of isolated environment encapsulated a compact world of increasing interest to botanists and naturalists, eager to study the flora and fauna, taken for granted by the inhabitants. The ferries also brought news from the outside world.

The ferryman usually initiated the island grapevine and news found its way to all parts in no time. Anything and everything was newsworthy as nothing much changed from day to day. News from the other islands took precedence over world affairs. The explorations in Africa by fellow Scot, David Livingstone, the births of Queen Victoria's babies, or the start of the Penny Post in Britain, would take second rating to news of a local romance, a fishing accident, a shipwreck on Orkney, or a beached whale in a Shetland geo. News would also arrive by means of the yawls.

In 1850 a greater storm than had been experienced for many a decade raged across the northern islands. Everyone there was affected as no one could go about his or her normal chores. The men were unable to take to sea in their yawls and the gales prevented crop harvesting, piling of seaweed, and cutting and collecting of peat blocks for fires. Animals had to be kept in the byres. Thatch from roofs was ripped from its anchoring. All the islanders could do was wait indoors until the gales passed.

When the wrath of the winds wore themselves out, Auld Jack Stout and his two sons sailed their yawl to Orkney Mainland to pay a visit to Jack's only daughter, Mary. Mary had settled on Mainland after her marriage to an Orcadian lad. Jack was named 'Auld' since the time, some twenty years before, when he was only in his early thirties, his hair turned prematurely white overnight, giving him an 'old', or 'auld', appearance.

On the Stouts' return to Fair Isle Sinclair Wilson was waiting for them.

"Any news from Orkney den?" asked Sinclair. "Anythin' new happenin', Auld Jack?"

Sinclair helped the men to drag their yawl up the shingle beach. He wanted to be the first to hear any news from Orkney that was worth knowing – and repeating. Nothing could be said or done on Fair Isle that wasn't common knowledge in a matter of hours.

"Big news, Sinclair, big news," said Auld Jack with an air of intrigue.

"Weel, wha' is it den?"

"Dere's news from Orkney gaain' all roond the world, Sinclair," said Auld Jack.

"Weel, telt me what it is, Auld Jack. Get on wi' it!"

Sinclair Wilson's youthful impatience were no match for Auld Jack's craftiness, gained from years of experience in telling tales to their best advantage. Auld Jack liked to have an attentive audience.

"Whit's this? Ye've stopped pullin' da yawl, lad! Get yer back intae it!" Auld Jack shouted, seemingly indignantly. His sons saw the glint in his eye.

"Aye," taunted one of Jack's sons, "where's yer strength, lad?"

The yawl had to be safely beached as far from the high tide line as possible before Auld Jack would let Sinclair stop the task in hand.

"Och, man, yer teasing me!"

"Aye," Jack drawled and they all laughed.

"I dinnae want tae know anyway," said Sinclair feigning indifference.

Only when the boat was secured, nestling between bigger rocks at the top of the shingle, did Jack turn to Sinclair with a smile, ready to share his news from Orkney.

An amazing discovery had been made at Skaill Bay in Orkney

the day after the recent great storm. The raging winds and an especially high tide had unearthed parts of an ancient stone-built village. Sand and soil laid down over the centuries had entombed the dwellings of ancestors, preserving them for posterity, hidden underground at the top of the beach. Archaeologists excavating at the site, known as Skara Brae, had unearthed eight identical dwellings linked together by low alleyways. Stone dressers, beds & cupboards reckoned to be around five thousand years old had survived, buried within the snug circular dwellings that were built before the Pyramids in Egypt.

The township was thousands of years old, or "thoosands o' yaars auld," as Auld Jack put it, dating back to a time before Christ. As far as Auld Jack and Sinclair were concerned this was almost before the beginning of time.

Mary had taken Auld Jack and her brothers to visit Skara Brae. Hundreds of other people, many from other parts of the world, were arriving in Orkney to view the remarkable wonder. News reporters, artists, archaeologists and travellers had flocked to witness the findings. Newspapers were not yet distributed in Orkney, but reporters from around the world wanted to record the findings for their own country's readership.

The most plausible explanation for Skara Brae's undetected interment was that a mighty storm of similar ferocity to this recent one must have begun the burying process. Further centuries of high winds completed the job of entombing the ancient township and only a storm of the same ilk had managed to unearth it. It was assumed the people who once lived there had evacuated prior to its burial in the sands of time as no human bones were discovered at the site, only furniture, cooking utensils and pottery, preserved as if used only recently.

"Something aulder dan Auld Jack Stout, my, my!" said Sinclair with a hoot of laughter.

"Ach, away wi' ye!" said Jack, cuffing the lad playfully across his ear. "Aye an' dere's some mair news."

"Oh aye?"

The older man allowed time for his customary pause. "Mary is expecting a babbie!" Jack beamed with pride at the thought of his first grandchild.

"So – ye'll be a grandfaider den, Auld Jack – and ye nearly forgot to tell me!"

As they all climbed up to the track that led to their homes, it was Sinclair's turn to speak with an air of importance.

"I've got news, too," he said.

"Aye?" said Jack with a note of false indifference.

"Dere's a babbie due on *Fair Isle* as weel," said Sinclair as he walked on nonchalantly.

"Aye?" said Jack again, more eagerly this time. "An' whose babbie would dat be den?"

Sinclair cleared his throat and paused for effect. "Why, ma cousin Andrew an' his Hellen."

Auld Jack looked pleased and slapped Sinclair heartily on the back. "Weel, dat's welcome news, Sinclair, lad. I thowt tae mesell dey could be doin' wid a son aboot deir ain hame."

"Aye."

Jack was referring to the fact that Andrew and Hellen at this time already had a daughter and therefore, by his reckoning, they would be hoping for a son.

Hellen had been in her twenty fifth year before she started her family.

"Nearly an auld woman," Margaret Rendall had remarked at the time, having produced the first of her own seven children at the age of nineteen.

Being a naturally gregarious community the women preferred to congregate at one or another's croft to carry out their knitting or shawl making. They would discuss every nuance of every family on the island. The women sat, knitting needles clacking, tongues wagging. Some sat in tall back wicker chairs so designed to shield heads from the constant draughts. Others congregated around the kitchen tables on pews or stools. Often they rested their feet on footstools or wooden blocks to keep them from the cold mud-impacted floors. The continual lack of issue from Hellen and Andrew's union regularly came up in conversation though the wives did take into account that Andrew had been Shanghai'd on the southern seas during the first few years of their married life.

"It's not for want of trying!" Margaret would remark. The women could all remember the gossip in the months following the Williamson wedding and again after Andrew's return from his ordeal abroad. Any time that Andrew was not away fishing, the young couple would go missing, lost to the rest of the community.

Conversations pertaining to sexual practices usually reduced the women to much shared laughter, but it was strictly taboo for children to overhear such things. Yet out of curiosity as to the cause of all the hilarity, children would often appear, drawn from a game, and would be immediately despatched back to play on the pasture so that the outbursts of laughter could be resumed. But not all the women found the *risqué* chatter amusing. Old Jeannie Smith found the tittle-tattle much too embarrassing and would often interject under her breath, "Och, tisk, tisk, dearie me!" in a mortified tone every so often in the conversation. This only added to the general enjoyment of the rest of the women.

The discovery of two magazines of a sexual nature kept the women in absorbing conversation for weeks. The magazines were printed in a foreign language but a few pages bore pictures of unusual sexual positions. Unusual, that is, to the general populous of Fair Isle, but apparently carried out with regularity in this far off exotic region of the world. These publications had been found hidden under a water barrel near an outhouse belonging to the Jamieson family. The teenage sons of the Jamieson family were apportioned with the blame and were thereafter known as the 'wayward boys'. Their father had confiscated and destroyed the offending articles. That is what Mrs. Jamieson was led to believe, but copies mysteriously began to discreetly circulate amongst the older men.

"It must be a' dose new fankled positions dey young yins get up tae nooadays."

"It's probably too difficult to make a babbie when yer twisted intae dey funny positions."

"Aye, dey probably tried hingin' upside doon frae da roof beams!"

"Och, tisk, tisk, dearie me!" from old Jeannie Smith, who kept her head down, trying to concentrate on her knitting whilst blushing profusely.

Margaret Rendall whispered to her friend, Ursula, that auld Jeannie "wus just de sorta wummin to be caught hingin' upside doon frae de rafters; dey quiet types, eh?!" which set the two women into stomach hugging convulsions at the very thought. And the increase in hoots of laughter brought in an increase in curious children.

Needless to say, unusual sexual positions had nothing to do with any delay in producing offspring for Andrew and Hellen. To any enquiry Hellen would retort, "All in good time." But the first time Hellen experienced labour was not a good time. Her labour lasted over a day and in bitterly cold weather with flurries of snow swirling around the front doorway. Andrew spent the duration of Hellen's labour sweeping the snow from the front steps to keep them clear, in readiness for the stream of visitors that were bound to arrive after the birth. The island's unofficial midwife, or 'howdie', was Grace Jamieson, the mother of the 'wayward boys'. She and Barbara Brown were attending to Hellen's labour and as her labour progressed Hellen kept asking her attendants when the waves of pain would end. "All in good time, dearie," Grace would say, bringing Hellen's words back to haunt her. "Yer no' de first wummin to havin' a babbie, ye ken."

Their first daughter, Barbara, was named after the grandmother who attended her birth.

6

Daughters Galore

Crofts on Fair Isle were basic. Most had only two main compartments and were known as But and Bens. The But end was used during waking hours for cooking and eating and had an often central fireplace. The Ben end was the sleeping area, where the whole family slept, and this usually led directly off the But end. Beds were either recessed or 'neuk' beds made of stone or wooden 'boxed' beds, which efficiently conserved body heat.

The construction of boxed beds was an age-old craft in all Shetland Islands. They were traditionally built by the man of the house and handed down through the generations. Raised off the ground by sturdy wooden legs, the beds could be completely enclosed with two doors on one side. The handles were hand-size holes in the doors and these provided ventilation.

The Byre for the animals was usually situated to the front of the But End, either adjacent or attached to the main dwelling. Cows and sheep could be housed overnight in the Byre and during the winter months, they were kept there both day and night. The crofts and But and Bens were often built 'with the rig', that is, end on to the slope, which allowed for easy drainage of byre and stable.

Babies slept in the parental boxed bed until the age of around one-year-old when the baby would be introduced to the bed of its siblings. In most family homes, the norm would be three boxed beds; the parental bed, a bed for the sons of the family, and a bed for the daughters. The bed Andrew and Hellen slept in had been made by Andrew's great grandfather many decades before and the passing years had lent a glossy shine to the mellow wood. The one made for Barbara, and for any further daughters to share, Andrew had built himself.

Hellen and Andrew's second child was also a daughter and they named her Agnes. The young Barbara slept in a boxed bed to herself and Agnes slept with their parents until she was nearly a year old.

Hellen then introduced Agnes to "Barbara's bed", as Barbara called it. She laid Agnes beside her three-year-old sister and closed the ventilated door. Within minutes, the baby's incessant wailing from inside could not be tolerated and it was decided Agnes would be allowed to sleep in her parents bed for a while longer. But on each attempt to put her to sleep in "Barbara's bed" the same wailing and crying would occur and Barbara would complain that she couldn't possibly sleep with all the noise her sister was making. It did cross Andrew's mind at times that the wailing was out of character for Agnes, who was normally a very content baby. Four years went by before Agnes slept contentedly with Barbara in "Barbara's bed". It was coincidentally around this time Barbara began to interact with her younger sister, having previously thought of Agnes as a noisy nuisance. Unbeknown to Hellen and Andrew, when they had first put the one year old Agnes in "Barbara's bed", Barbara had unashamedly pinched and shoved her peedie sister, hoping that she would object, which she did with her wailing, and thus allowing Barbara to regain her territory. When the doors were closed on a boxed bed, no one quite knew what was going on inside. Barbara presided over this bed for more years than was necessary and it was always known as "Barbara's bed".

With Hellen's third pregnancy everyone was convinced that this baby would be a boy and they would name him Andrew as was the tradition for first sons to be named after their father. When another daughter was born they called her Anderina. Her name was derived from her father's name with the addition of "ina", a common practice of the time, resulting in names like Peterina, Alexina and Jamesina.

According to Anderina's eldest sister she looked "like a squashed hedgehog" when she was born. Barbara was unimpressed by babies, but it was the fact that Anderina's shock of thick dark hair stuck up in spikes around her misshapen head that contributed to Barbara's description. Hellen thought she looked like a baby troll. Agnes had wanted a baby brother and she soon lost interest in her new sister. The arrival of yet another daughter brought degenerative disappointment to Hellen and the unsaid feelings were subconsciously transmitted to the new child, who, throughout her life, had a vague feeling of superfluity. And the squashed-hedgehog look never quite escaped her. Her face also took on a consistently 'dour' expression. Anderina would never be as attractive as her sisters. The feelings of indifference and lack of bonding may have accounted for the self-sufficiency that Anderina found at a very early age. As soon as she could walk, her wandering instincts led her far and wide, keeping the rest of the Williamson family busy for much of their time searching for her. The moment backs were turned, she would disappear into a world of her own.

From her first pregnancy, Hellen had wanted to bear a son. Three daughters later, she despaired. A son was an important asset to a fishing family. Sons were needed to continue the main occupation of Fair Isle. When Hellen fell pregnant for a fourth time, she was utterly convinced this was her longed-for son. She reckoned she was owed a son and decided they would name him Jerome after her father. But during this labour the anticipation that she had expected to feel was strangely missing. This baby's delivery was awkward and she felt no joy when her howdie confirmed her assumption, "Ye have a wee boy, Hellen." Instead of feeling euphoric Hellen felt uneasy. One look at his purply-blue body confirmed her fears; he was tiny and fragile. The usual thrill given on hearing her newborn's yell of protest at the cold world into which he entered was denied her as tiny Jerome's lips lay silent. His wrinkled eyelids remained firmly closed. He was not destined to participate in their world. Weak and wizen as an old man, he faded rapidly and died – without a glance at his mother.

Long after baby Jerome's death neighbours could hear Hellen's low, anguished moaning, as she rocked her son's limp body in her arms. The atmosphere was bleak inside Stonybrek cottage, as bleak as the weather on that mid winter's day. Eventually, with an aching heart, Grizel tenderly prised the cold, lifeless baby away from her grieving daughter, saying under her breath, *"What the Lord giveth, the Lord taketh away"*.

During the months that followed, Hellen withdrew deep inside herself, barely communicating with anyone. Andrew was away at sea much of the time and the three Williamson daughters soon became self-reliant while their mother retreated into her shell of grief. The girls' independence worked against the family because Hellen found more time to prolong her mourning, and blaming herself for her obsession to produce a son. The depression put down sturdy roots inside her heart and it was to last two long years. At that time in their marriage, Andrew and Hellen were alone in different worlds.

A new and inspirational minister arrived to preach one Sunday in every month, weather and sea crossings permitting. He sailed by boat from Dunrossness Parish on Shetland. His uplifting approach to Christianity inspired Hellen to renew her faith. A very down to earth character, he had little time for sympathy or excess emotion. Being both unmarried and childless, he tended to look at life with a more focused approach than the people to whom he preached. He hadn't experienced first hand their hardships, bringing up a family on little income, being the breadwinner battling in rough seas and having no right of tenure to the place they called home. He wasn't burdened by their worries, but he endeavoured to share them and help with them as best he could. His uncluttered, orderly lifestyle proved to be an asset and he could clear his mind to deliver an uncomplicated sermon with his inimitable attitude. His parishioners had family support systems to uphold and worries he could only oversee though never fully comprehend. He made Hellen feel ashamed of her self-pity. He told her that she must concentrate on the living, not the dead. She saw her grief in a different light when she realised the selfishness in it.

Time, the great healer, passed slowly but Hellen saw her life from a more overall perspective. The depression began to lift and her pain began to ebb. It was the spring of 1859 before Hellen's fog began to lift. She awoke one crisp, clear morning with a crisp, clear mind. As her daughters dressed themselves ready for a day at school and ate their bannocks for breakfast, she watched the antics of the swooping seagulls. Her heart began to soar with the birds and the tired muscles of her face won a battle with gravity. Turning from the front step at Stonybrek's door, she smiled so sweetly at her three daughters that they were quite taken aback. Agnes liked the look of her mother's smile and smiled back. She ran to her mother, flinging her arms around her in the hopes of a cuddle. Hellen in turn swept the child into her arms and swirled her around the tiny cottage, knocking cushions from seats and wooden platters from shelves. Barbara's face began to soften, too, but Anderina did not take too kindly to this new version of her mother. On that particular morning, her usual and expected daily ritual of hair brushing and plaiting had not been performed. This was Anderina's special time with her mother. The mutual silence between them was bonding and personal. It was an essential start to Anderina's day. But that morning, Hellen postponed this favourite routine and in the interim the peedie girl had conjured up a foul mood.

Hellen's brooding over her dead son changed to a different kind of brooding; that of the desire for another baby, not as a substitute for their loss, but as a positive binding for her splintered family. She took responsibility for that splintering caused by her protracted and introverted mourning and this time her desire for another baby was backed by all the right reasons. All she wanted was a healthy baby, its sex was incidental.

On the stormy day when Andrew and the *Zetland Breeze* returned safely to Fair Isle, Hellen had been ready to prove her change of heart. And so it was that Meg was conceived.

At the time of Meg's conception, Barbara was twelve years old, Agnes nine and Anderina nearly four. Like their mother, all three girls had dark hair, but that was where the similarity between them ended. Barbara was tall like her father. Her hair was long and sleek and she wore it tied back at the nape of her neck. An excessively neat child, she seemed older than her years and took it upon herself to assert her position in the family. Barbara was the disciplinarian.

Agnes was quite a different child, chirpy and carefree, she was always on the go, active and busy. She liked to have her wild mass of chestnut-tinged hair flying freely and for this reason it was kept shorter than Barbara's, because it was wilder, like her spirit. Her bossy older sister constantly kept Agnes in check. "Stop yer fidgetting, Agnes!" or "Sit still, Agnes!" and "Fur guidness sake, will ye no be quiet, Agnes!" were phrases Barbara used every day.

Third in line was Anderina, the squashed hedgehog. Anderina set herself apart from her sisters, a self-sufficient child, she had no need for the company of others, siblings or peer group, who were usually for their part put off by her predilection for gloomy and wilful moods. Happiest in her own company and that of animals, she would never be one to suffer fools gladly – unless they were the four-legged variety. Every morning, Hellen would tightly dress Anderina's thick hair into two long plaits, which hung heavily and flatly over her shoulder blades. During this plaiting ritual, both mother and daughter would lapse into a dwam, or daydream, of their own private thoughts. The plaits were only released each morning, ready for immediate re-plaiting. It took Hellen very little time to complete this perfected task, but to Anderina it was special because it was the only time she had her mother all to herself. An incorrigible wanderer, this daughter was often away from home for hours, making expeditions over the hills or down to the caves and though 'lost' to her family, she was in control of herself. She could always be relied upon to find her way home, usually carrying a collection of shells or an apron full of wool pulled from the bushes or a wounded bird that she had found and wanted to nurse back to health. Her mouth was often 'pouty'; that was how Andrew described it, though an outsider to the family would call her expression dour. Even her own grandmother described her that way.

"Dat's a dour expression on yon yin's face," Barbara Brown used to say.

Hellen encouraged the marked differences in character in establishing her daughters' individuality. She took pride in her girls, but it was an unspoken pride. She was not known to openly praise them – "lest dey get too big for da boots". Andrew had quite the opposite attitude. He liked nothing better than to arrive home after days away from his family and see their happy faces light up when he showered each in turn with his compliments.

An aura for adoration of the new arrival was established well before baby Meg was born. She arrived in the first week of the hottest month of 1860 and proved to be both strong and healthy. Hellen's most precious moment was hearing the tiny gasp taken by her fourth daughter as she drew life-giving air into her lungs for her first breath. Grizel beckoned Andrew into the woman's world of childbirth and as he stepped through the front door of Stonybrek his latest offspring made her first cry, a sound much like a kitten mewing.

"Did ye hear da peedie soul, Andrew?" said Hellen, her eyes gleaming.

"Aye, I did, Ellen."

" 'Meg' – she said 'Meg' – did ye hear dat, Andrew?"

Hellen's excitement was infectious.

"It did sound like 'Meg', it did, Ellen."

"Aye, we must call her Meg, dinnae ken?"

Hellen would not be denied this, more a statement of fact than a question and Andrew would not dream of bursting the bubble of happiness surrounding her on that of all days. Although Barbara Brown had instructed her son that to follow the naming pattern of the islands the baby should be named after her maternal grandmother, Andrew knew Grizel had never liked her name and would not be offended by her latest granddaughter's own choice. He calmly replied, "Aye, Ellen, dat'll do weel."

On the next visit from the Minister of Dunrossness Parish, Shetland, this bonnie wee babe with golden wisps curling across her perfect skull was christened Meg. The Minister would only contemplate the twenty five mile sea journey from Shetland to Fair Isle if the weather conditions were favourable, which usually meant that winter-born babies were not christened until the early summer. This was not the dynamic young preacher who had instilled hope and future into Hellen, but his replacement, who was quite a different character.

Meg rewarded her family's adoration and was indeed a blessing to them. She was a happy child with head-turning looks. She had inherited her father's tall and slender stature, his handsome Nordic looks and his blonde hair. Her hair shone like the rays of sunshine that had spotlighted her mother only minutes after Meg's conception. With mischief in her eyes and a smile that was endearingly askew, she was easy to love. Anderina, who now had someone smaller than herself to care for, was an altogether more contented child when she was around Meg. Barbara was less inclined to boss her baby sister, because her naughtiness only made everyone laugh. Agnes treated Meg like a precious doll to be attended to constantly.

From the moment she took an interest in life, Meg chattered and burbled and beamed at everyone she came across. Grizel said she was the island's happiest, most beautiful child, a conveyor of joy, and believed Meg had an important destiny.

Little did they realise the consternation Meg would cause in later years.

Part 2

7

Fair Isle to Westray, 1866

For decades, the owner of Fair Isle had enormous control over the lives of the island's inhabitants. It was the factor of the owner who set the prices not only for their fish catches, but also for the household items and equipment at the only shop. The fish had to be cured and dried and the owner provided the salt for curing and the casks for fish oil. Fish oil amounted to almost half the total value of the catches. In plentiful supply, it was a most useful by-product and was used for lighting in the crofts. All the sea catches had to be sold exclusively to the factor at the Landlord's price, which was never generous. The proprietor also made considerable profit from the supply of produce to the Islanders. When the year's harvest was exhausted, which was normally around early Spring, the islanders had to buy their grain and other essential supplies at his inflated prices. An occasional floating shop from Orkney would dock in the harbour at Kirkigeo, selling everyday products and undercutting the factor's prices, but the owner would always endeavour to put a stop to this practice.

The rental of the crofts depended on the tenant's ability to go fishing and any absence was usually penalised. Sons were expected to take the place of grandfathers and fathers in the fishing yawls to perpetuate the system. Fishing was of prime economic importance. Their lives revolved around fishing and growing crops, tending farm animals, knitting hosiery and looking after children and older folk. The women contributed around a fifth of the rent and the men took every possibility to trade with the passing shipping to supplement their meagre earnings. Crofts enabled self-sufficiency in that the grain and vegetable crops that were grown, along with the produce from the animals, eggs, milk, butter, cheese, and whey, kept the families fed and gave them produce with which to trade.

Crofts varied in size but averaged about three merks, around six acres. As sons grew to manhood and married, subdivision of the land had to take place, but six acres was little enough for one family's survival and destitution often loomed, especially in families with many sons. In desperation, some Fair Islanders were forced to move away to Orkney, Shetland, Aberdeen, Inverness, or to emigrate to Canada or New Zealand. Others followed when they heard from their relatives about the better quality of life in far-flung places. Many left, never to return. The Isle could only ever sustain a limited number of families. From around the beginning of the nineteenth century when the population started to rise fairly rapidly, Fair Isle fishermen and their families were actively encouraged by the owner to settle in Orkney where the fishing industry was beginning to expand. In these communities, the inclusion of some hardy Fair Isle fishermen with their deep-sea fishing expertise would be a distinct advantage to the Orcadian fishermen.

In the early 1860s the crop harvests in Fair Isle had been poor and there was less farming land available to sustain the extending families. The owners at the time of Meg's early childhood were also landowners on Westray and Stronsay in the Orkney Isles, twenty five miles away. Andrew was offered one of these homes in Westray. Initially he was interested in the prospect of a new life and a better future for his family. With four daughters, who would not be following him into the fishing industry, he would have to plan their futures. They would be in need of husbands and prospective husbands were becoming few and far between on Fair Isle. But discussion on the subject came to a halt before it got started at Stonybrek, because Hellen would not contemplate such a move at that precise time. She was heavily pregnant, at the age of forty, with their fifth child. The offer was declined.

As the birth due date approached, the grandmothers of the Williamson offspring organised Hellen's midwifery care. They had taken this in turns throughout the births, Barbara Brown being the first to help deliver her first grandchild, the granddaughter who was given her name. For this sixth delivery both Barbara Brown and Grizel Irvine were to be in attendance, believing that, due to Hellen's advanced years in childbearing terms, this would most probably be her last baby. Grace Jamieson was told that her midwifery expertise would not be needed as Hellen said there would be too many women fussing around her as it was. Although both in their early seventies, Barbara and Grizel were active, healthy women and had seen many a baby into the world, their own as well as their many grandchildren.

A son, John, was born "in the wink of an eye", as Grizel would later recall. Summoned to Stonybrek by twelve-year-old Agnes, the grandmothers arrived just as he made a healthy protest to his new world. Like most women in Shetland around this time, Hellen had a speedy delivery without complications. This fact was attributed to the fit and active lives the women led, the heavy manual labour that women were involved in, sometimes carrying on their backs, kishies, straw baskets of fish or peat, which could weigh around fifty five kilos; widening hips and creating easy childbirth. John's trouble-free delivery came to the mother who had found it difficult to fulfil her dream of a son. He would carry on the Williamson name. He would carry on the fishing tradition.

But the passage of time would prove different to normal expectations. In the years that followed there would be four offspring in Andrew's lineage that were given the Williamson surname yet not attributed to John's descent.

The fact that crops on Fair Isle had been light and fishing poor in the past couple of years had precipitated a crisis among the inhabitants. John Williamson was not yet walking when the Stewarts again gave Andrew the chance of work, a home and a new life in Orkney. A croft called Quoylet had become vacant in Westray. This time he and Hellen considered the prospect. This would probably be the last time they were offered such a chance and in considering their daughters' futures in particular, they decided life would hold more opportunity in the wider community of Westray. Hellen was loath to leave Grizel, Jerome and her brothers and sisters. Westray was one of the most northern islands in Orkney, an archipelago consisting of around seventy islands though less than a third were inhabited. Grizel was all for progress and moving along with the new ways. She, too, believed Andrew's family would be better off on an island that was a part of a group, being more interactive than the remote, detached existence on Fair Isle.

Barbara Brown, however, was beginning to notice the first signs of senile debility in her husband. She discussed this with no one, worried that it might negatively influence her son Andrew's plans to start a new life. When the younger Williamson family did set sail for Orkney, Barbara said they would come to visit them soon, but she knew well enough that it was highly unlikely. It was only a few months later that Andrew senior lapsed into another world in which he talked about his wife, Barbara, as if she were somewhere else when, in fact, she was the very person he was talking to. He smiled at the kind old woman helping him to dress in the mornings and feeding him at meal times. He didn't recognise her as the woman he had known all his life, who he had married and who had borne his children. Soon Andrew was in no fit state to travel and by the time his eldest son and family had settled in their new home on Westray, Barbara was mourning the loss of her life time partner – long before he actually passed away.

Hellen and Andrew felt positive about the decision they had made for the betterment of their family. The voyage from Fair Isle to Westray was undertaken in torrential rain though this did nothing to dampen the spirits of Agnes and Meg. Their eldest sister Barbara remained calm, taking the upheaval in their lives in her stride. Anderina's mood, however, alienated her from the world of humans. Having spent her last hour on Fair Isle amongst her favourite Shetland ponies on the scattald she had had to wrench herself away to join her awaiting family, who were all champing at the bit to start their new life. Hellen assured her that Orkney had ponies, too, though perhaps not this distinctive breed.

The rain eased but the sea remained rough that day, so rough that at times when the boat hit a crashing wave the children's feet, much to their delight, left the deck as they were ejected into the air. The deck would then immediately rise, smacking the soles of their feet back onto it again. Hellen made sure they were all safely ensconced within the inner decks of the boat lest she lost one of her children over the side. After hours afloat, a sighting was made of the first of the Orkney Isles, North Ronaldsay. The skipper chatted to Andrew about the worst shipwreck ever recorded in those parts when, over a century before, a Swedish ship had run aground with the loss of some ninety lives.

With North Ronaldsay to starboard, they sighted the island of Sanday from the opposite deck, distinguished by its black and white painted lighthouse on its most north-easterly point. Meg stared for a long time at the smartly painted, candy-striped tower, little realising how prominently this lighthouse would feature in her future.

North Ronaldsay shrank away behind them as they sailed along the coastline of Sanday on course for Westray. The sea was calm when the much smaller island of Papa Westray loomed up through a veil of rolling sea mist to their starboard side. Meg gazed in wonder at the islands of Orkney scattered all around them, at the nearness of one to another, each within sight of other land. It brought home to her how very isolated their world on Fair Isle had been.

"Fair Isle must be on the edge of the world..." Meg said, more to herself than to any family member. Her words floated on the haar. Only Andrew had ever sailed over the horizon beyond Fair Isle. He alone knew how detached it was from the rest of the world.

The inhabitants of Westray knew to expect the family from Fair Isle. Small groups of Orcadian people ready to welcome the new family stood on the pier as the boat approached Pierowall harbour. The Williamson girls fell silent in awe, and with a mixture of anticipation and fear of the unknown. All were wide-eyed, except for Barbara, as the boat docked. People came forward and spoke kindly in turn to Hellen and Andrew. Several of the local men helped to transport the family and their belongings in carts to Quoylet, the empty croft allocated to them by the Laird of Westray. Quoylet was more spacious than Stonybrek and set high on a gentle hillside overlooking a wide sandy bay on the south-west of the island. Neighbouring women appeared at their door bearing gifts of fish, vegetable broth and fresh scones for their first meal on Westray. Hellen's anxieties vanished. She was soon to enjoy the company of many more neighbours than she had been used to at Stonybrek. As Andrew and the men moved their few items of furniture into Quoylet, Hellen took her family on a walk over the Ward Hill, the ground soft and wet beneath their feet, until they reached Logie's Store to buy their first groceries.

"Welcome to Westray, Mrs. Williamson," said Mrs. Logie in her high, cheery voice, dimples plunging in and out of her cheeks as she spoke.

Mr. Logie appeared through a door at the rear of the shop. He was shorter and more solemn faced than his wife yet approachable enough to shake hands with the Williamson children in turn. Each child began to relax and allow a glimmer of smiles to creep over their faces, faces shining with wonderment. The natives seemed friendly enough.

The Logies were also a contrasting looking couple in other ways. Her greying hair was thick and wiry, while his head was practically hairless. Her face was large and full of warmth, where his was pale and small featured. But they were the type of couple who finished off each other's sentences, having lived and worked together in their store for over two decades. They both took to Hellen and her family straight away. Mrs. Logie liked Hellen's bonnie smile and her neatly turned out and well-behaved children. She made a fuss of John and Meg; John, a bouncing babe, nearly too big to be carried but not yet toddling on his feet, and Meg, an impish-faced five-year-old. Anderina went missing before she could even be introduced and was found by Agnes in the Logie's byre, stroking their black Shetland pony of around nine hands in height. Mr. Logie explained that they had bought the pony for their sons to ride when they were peedie boys, but now their sons had outgrown the pony. He said they no longer had need of it, but that the Williamsons would need a pony, if only to carry peat from the peat fields, a fair distance from Quoylet.

Peat was needed as fuel to keep the home fires burning. The smell of burning peat gave every home its distinctive aroma, helping to disguise the smells from fish oil lamps and farm animals in the byre. Although most of Orkney and Shetland was covered in a blanket of peat, located deep beneath the heather, certain areas were designated as peat fields, where islanders went to stock up on their supplies.

Hellen showed an interest in hiring the pony. She said she would have a word with Andrew about it. Anderina's face lit up. The pony reminded her of all her beloved Shetland ponies that roamed over Fair Isle and in whose peaceful company she used to spend most of her time. For a child who rarely showed any form of enthusiasm, let alone delight, Anderina had both these emotions bubbling under at that moment. This was duly noted by her mother.

During their visit to the store that day, Mrs. Logie took the time to have a chat with Barbara. In conversation, Mr. Logie explained to Hellen that they had been discussing the prospect of taking on a shop assistant to help them out, but had as yet been unable to find the right young person to fit the post. Mr. Logie wanted more time to tend his vegetable garden. Mrs. Logie wished she had more time to bake. Mrs. Logie noted that Barbara possessed good sense and a confident maturity, and thought she would be just the kind of helper their shop needed. After a quiet discussion with her husband, Mrs. Logie announced that she would like to offer Barbara a job in their shop. The post would include accommodation in the servants' cottage, shared with another young girl who worked as a domestic servant in the Logie household.

This offer came at a perfect time. Barbara Williamson was seventeen and in need of employment. She had also outgrown the 'Barbara's bed', which was fast becoming much too small for all four of the growing Williamson girls to sleep comfortably within. Throughout the night Agnes constantly objected to being poked in her newly budding breasts by a sister's stray elbow. Anderina snored and Meg constantly wriggled, although most nights Meg crept into John's bed. There was more space there as John had a bed to himself, being the only son. Yes, Barbara was very ready to start an independent life and when she overheard Mr. Logie's conversation she took more of an interest in the shop. Having just set foot on Orkney her horizons were already widening. She was shown the servants' cottage at the rear of the shop and was pleased to note she would have a bed of her own. Three beds were set out, not the traditional boxed ones, but they had several blankets over them. The other girl in the cottage was called Williamina, the daughter of a William Stout. She was the same age as Agnes. It was agreed that Barbara would move in straight away, without any need to move into Quoylet.

Barbara was soon enjoying her new independent, working life and got along fine with Williamina. All the inhabitants of Westray used the shop to buy their groceries. In the ensuing weeks, Agnes often walked the mile across the hillside to visit Barbara. Agnes and Williamina became firm friends. When Agnes was sixteen years old, the Paterson family at the Powdykes Farm offered her a job as farm servant.

Living in Westray had not changed Anderina's predilection to wander the hills and she often appeared at the Seator family home at Ness Farm. She would boldly ask Margaret Seator, the farmer's wife, if she could help in any way. Soon Margaret noticed that this young girl had a wonderful way with animals, a natural healing instinct with her four-legged friends. She was an able, hard working girl and an asset to have around the farm. And so it was that Mrs. Seator asked Hellen Williamson if Anderina could live and work at their farm although she was only fourteen at the time. Anderina begged her parents to consent. They agreed. Their third daughter seemed to have found her niche in life, working with and caring for animals. Hellen felt proud that someone had found good qualities in Anderina, qualities that Hellen as her mother had not yet appreciated. Anderina was soon much sought after by neighbouring farms wanting her help when they had a sick animal. To all intents and purposes, she became an unqualified but expert veterinary carer.

Back on Fair Isle, as Barbara Brown had expected, Andrew senior proved too debilitated to ever make the journey to visit his oldest son and family on Westray. She awoke one morning to find him lying ice cold beside her, having died peacefully in the night. Andrew and Hellen insisted that Barbara came to live with them at Quoylet on Westray and this softened her heartache. All the months of strain and worry as she watched her husband deteriorate and fade before her eyes had exhausted her. At the grand old age of seventy-two, Barbara felt rejuvenated by the prospect of a new life awaiting her on a new island. She left Fair Isle for the first time to make her first sea crossing, her first visit to other shores. The three older girls all lived and worked away from home and so with only Meg and John living at Quoylet there was space enough for Barbara Brown. Quoylet would be her last home.

The 1871 Census for Westray was carried out in the early part of March. Two straight-laced and uncomfortably dressed government officials went all around the island taking down the scant details needed to produce a list of who's who of Westray in that particular decade. They required the name of the croft or home, the names and ages of all those living there and their relationship to the head of the family. The enumerators also needed to know the occupations of the inhabitants and the birthplace of each.

Many of the people on Westray at that time could neither read nor write well so the enumerators took down the details phonetically. Over the years this created all sorts of discrepancies in the spellings of occupant's names, as well as in the names of the homes. On one occasion 'Quoylet' became 'Quoylatte' and the name 'Ursula' became 'Orsilla' at one Census and 'Usilla' at another. The records were dependent on the individual transliteration of the official who heard the information. The enumerators were tolerated, sometimes fed and watered, by those who felt sorry for them doing what was considered to be a very wearisome government task.

Andrew and Hellen were finishing their breakfast when their intruders arrived. They didn't stay long. Hellen made sure of that. She told them what they needed and watched as they scribbled in their cumbersome, hard-backed binder.

Name, Age	Relationship	Occupation	Place of Birth
Andrew Williamson, 55	Head	Farmer & fisherman	Fair Isle
Hellen Williamson, 48	Wife		Fair Isle
Barbara Brown, 79	Mother	Widow/Knitter	Fair Isle
Meg Williamson, 10	Daughter	Scholar	Fair Isle
John Williamson, 7	Son	Scholar	Fair Isle

The Census recorded Barbara Williamson, twenty-two years old, when they visited the Logie family grocer shop, and Agnes, who was nineteen, with the Paterson household at Powdykes Farm. Anderina was listed as farmer's servant at Ness Farm with the Seator family. It was to be the last time the Williamson family were recorded living in the same area, albeit in different households. Future decades would show their dispersion.

Barbara Williamson was the only family member to leave and settle 'abroad'. She went to live in Germany after marrying Jon Muller, the eldest son of the only German man living in Westray. As a young man, Jon's father, Jacob Muller, had been shipwrecked onto the beach at Shingley Brae. Within living memory there had been nine or ten ships wrecked on the jagged rocks around Westray. The few survivors of Jacob's ship had eventually returned home to Germany with the exception of Jacob Muller. Jacob had fallen in love with the girl who had nursed him back to fitness and during his recovery he enjoyed the life the Orcadians led, fishing from the rocks, setting up lobster pots, weaving cloth, crafting wicker chairs. He and May Eunson were married and went on to have six children together, the eldest of these was Jon.

In her occupation of shop assistant in the Logie grocery store, Barbara had begun to notice that a tall, studious looking boy kept approaching the counter to buy some trifle or other. Folk called him the 'German boy' although he had been born and bred in Orkney. Barbara thought it a bit strange at the time that the lad was buying such trifles, but Mr. Logie said it was good business and she was not to bother about it. One day Jon bought a length of hair ribbon, a beautiful deep blue satin ribbon. Barbara had often admired this roll of ribbon when there was no one in the shop to see her. But the 'German boy' must have noticed because, no sooner had he bought the ribbon, which Barbara had carefully wrapped in delicate, crisp white tissue paper, than he handed the coveted item back to her as a present. Barbara had only ever been given a present by someone within her immediate family. She was overawed and embarrassed. But from that day, she began to take more notice of the smiling 'German Boy' and to pay special attention to her special customer. In the following weeks, she reacted quite out of character. Normally a down-to-earth young woman who stood for no nonsense, Barbara displayed suddenly acquired feminine wiles. When Jon appeared in the open doorway of the shop, she found herself shyly smiling. Barbara was in love.

Although Magnus Logie had seen it coming from a long way off he was marginally peeved when their romance began in full. It meant that the boy stopped buying his wares in such a plentiful manner. Jon merely waited for Barbara to finish her duties so that he could walk her home. They would walk over the heather or along the beaches. Occasionally there would be a Ceilidh, a gathering with local fiddlers and possibly an accordion player for dancing. From that time, Mr Logie noticed that Barbara was always in a dwam, head-in-the-clouds, and not concentrating on her work, but his wife would scold him, saying he shouldn't be so miserable in the face of romance.

"Can ye no mind when we fell in love wid each ither, ye daft man!" she scoffed. She told him her head had been turned by his handsome looks and his then full head of hair.

"Och awa' we ye!" he retorted as if he could never have been there. Yet he remembered all too well his once full head of hair, now much receded. Mere wisps of hair of undetermined hue trailed thinly at the nape of his neck.

Barbara married Jon Muller in the April of 1875, four months before their daughter, Elizabeth, was born. In that same year, Jon suggested they go to live in Germany. He was not cut out to be a fisherman and yearned to go in to business with a cousin he had in Frankfurt. After settling in Frankfurt, Barbara often wrote to say how much she was enjoying city life. She took up tailoring, using the sewing skills Hellen had taught her as a child, and became quite renown for her dress designs, which were sought after by high society ladies across the city. Elizabeth remained an only child. A one child family would be very unusual on the islands, but as Hellen had once remarked, probably the norm for city dwellers. Though this did make her wonder if her eldest daughter had a happy marriage and was driven to ask Barbara directly on one of her visits back to Westray. Barbara retorted that there was more to life than producing offspring and that Elizabeth was quite enough for them to concentrate on in their busy lives as business people. That ended that topic. Elizabeth thrived on her parent's individual attention. She went on to become a scientist in Frankfurt. Hellen had no idea what a scientist was, but hoped it made her granddaughter happy.

8

Barbara Brown's Dreams

For his mother's eightieth birthday, Andrew carved and put together a rustic rocking chair. Barbara Brown was delighted with it. She began to spend most of her time in the rocker, either knitting or napping with her knitting resting on her lap. The rocker was soon to be blamed for instigating the strange dreams that appeared to her.

During the day, Barbara often napped. So short were her naps that often no one in the family would realise she had fallen asleep until she suddenly sat bolt upright, eyes staring wide, reciting her dream with urgent rapidity. If no one were within earshot the dream would be reiterated to an empty room and soon forgotten by Barbara, who never understood the dreams that came to her. Many times someone would walk in to find her in this habitual state of anxious narration. She became a conveyor of strange and incomprehensible messages, given to her via dreams, and was unable to recall them unless reminded by whoever heard her recitals.

One dream proved to be a vague premonition although no one realised its implications at the time. She dreamt that she was struggling in darkness with a scabbed ram in angry mood bleating furiously and champing at her heels, which were caught fast. The ram's butting horns were only inches away from her body. She could feel his hot breath on her ankles as she struggled to free herself. She woke in panic and squealed in terror like a frightened child as she told the tale. It was not until a few days later that any connection was made and it was thought to have been a premonition. A neighbour's young son went missing close to nightfall and a search party was established. The lad was only three years old and the general feeling was that he would not have wandered very far. A deep ditch had recently dug to separate two flocks of sheep. This ditch was about half a mile from the boy's home. Night was rapidly falling as his rescuers approached the ditch, where they heard wails, like the bleats of a troubled sheep. The boy was found. He was frightened and sobbing and standing upright at the bottom of the darkening ditch with one of his feet wedged and stuck fast between boulders. There was no rabid ram, but his painful wails had sounded like one.

There was one particularly vivid dream that made Barbara Brown's family and friends feel decidedly uneasy. It came about on a blustery Sunday afternoon. After returning from the Kirk, Barbara settled into her rocker and began rocking herself gently. She dozed off and the dream that followed was more foreboding than any previous ones.

Andrew was the only family member in the room at the time of her awakening and therefore the only person to hear her immediate description. She told him breathlessly that she had seen an unmanned ship sail eerily up from the beach and over the fields. This ship passed Quoylet and knocked down part of the dyke to the side of the porch, directly in front of the window. The dream was short but the impact intense. It was widely believed in those times that a dream in which a ship sailed over dry land was a bad omen. Barbara related it to Andrew as if mentally reading another person's script. She had no idea as to the meaning of her dream nor did she see any specific connotation within it. No one wanted to make sense of her dream, because of the ominous implication of a ship uncannily passing over dry land.

A week later, Andrew went out alone to fish in his yawl. The sea had been calm and the sky only a little overcast, but he had not been out for very long when a thick haar descended, the type of haar described as a 'pea-souper'. An eerie silence accompanied the mist. All around Andrew was still and grey, drained of colour and tone. A tightening in his lungs unnerved him and he stood bolt upright in the yawl. He felt as if he was being stifled. The gently lapping waves under the sides of his boat sounded muffled. His feeling of unease, like the lull before a storm, gave way to a feeling of impending doom, which lay heavily upon him.

There was a sudden rush of water. He swirled his head around but wasn't able to see what was speeding towards him. The forerunning wave of a large shoal of seals tipped the boat sideways as if a bubble were bursting beneath him. Several silent seals darted past and under his yawl, seemingly as disorientated by the fog as Andrew was. Had he been seated he would not have fallen. But fall he did. Completely taken by surprise he lost his balance and toppled awkwardly into the starboard side of the boat. The yawl rocked out of control, breaking the stillness with its splashing sound. For a moment only, Andrew became precariously balanced on the edge of his yawl, staring directly down into the depths of the deep grey sea, wondering how it was possible that he could find himself in such a position. Next the equilibrium of the boat was lost and he was tipped over the side into the icy water.

Two fishermen on the high shoreline were mending nets. The haar was all around them and its silence engulfing, but an intensified grating noise arrested their attention. They simultaneously looked up from their work in time to watch the vision of Andrew's empty yawl mysteriously drifting out of the grey haar, out of the grey sea, and gliding eerily up across the shingle shore before coming to rest in front of them. Its discovery was the first indication of his accident and a search was hastily organised. For the second time in his life, Andrew had been forced to evacuate his yawl. On this occasion Andrew nearly drowned.

His washed-up and unconscious body was found, lying prone on the shingle. It took five fellow fishermen to carry his drenched weight up the slope and across to Quoylet. No one was sure if he were dead or alive until he spluttered out some seawater. Hellen found a faint pulse and worked at frantic speed to resuscitate his frozen body. She stripped him of his sodden clothing and covered him with blankets, then stoked a ferocious fire to blaze in the hearth.

But the essence of his being was fading and his condition worsened in the days that followed as rheumatic fever took hold. Everyone thought Barbara Brown's dream of the ship on dry land was surely a premonition of Andrew's near drowning, especially when the two fishermen on the shoreline described how his yawl had drifted eerily out of the haar to run aground. Hellen was gripped with foreboding. For his beloved Ellen, Andrew found strength for only one more smile.

Hellen and Barbara Brown took it in turns to tend to Andrew as the days became weeks. Three weeks later to the day, Barbara was mopping her son's sweat-beaded brow when Andrew opened wide his weary eyelids and looked directly into his mother's eyes. His look seemed to convey a devastating understanding as an inevitable dawning crossed over his troubled mind. Without a word, he closed his eyes. He had no strength for words. For three long weeks his eyes had remained closed to the world around him, only then to open with a look of complete hopelessness. Hellen was denied one last look into those tantalising, dancing pools of blue beneath Andrew's eyelids. He had closed his eyes for the last time. The following morning, Andrew died, wrapped in Hellen's arms.

On the day of his funeral, Barbara was to realise the further implications of her dream. There was not enough space to manoeuvre Andrew's long coffin through the dogleg entrance to Quoylet as its small porch was set at right angles to the front door. The only way to bring the empty coffin in to Quoylet, and ultimately back out when Andrew's body had been laid to rest inside, was through a front window to the side of the porch. In doing so, and in order to keep his coffin horizontal, several stones – to the very stone of Barbara's dream – had to be removed from the dyke wall in front of Quoylet.

Before the rheumatic fever Andrew had not had a day's illness in his life. The infection was probably a result of his near drowning, the doctor said. Andrew's lungs became infected and the fever took such a hold that it sapped his strength, reducing him in a short space of time to a wasted state. Hellen was devastated. She had always held out hope that he could beat the fever. She found it hard to believe that Andrew, so much a part of her, had left her forever and before they had grown old together.

Death normally took the very young and the very old. Andrew was fifty-two years of age. Those born and bred on Fair Isle were generally assured of a long and healthy life and rarely fell ill. The lifestyle of the islanders of both the Shetlands and the Orkneys, their diet of fish, seafood, fresh vegetables, and their never-ending endurance of the cruel hardships forced upon them by the rigours of the weather made for an intrinsically hardy race. Their longevity usually surpassed the populace of mainland Britain. Andrew's was an untimely death. The shock for his family was double edged; they were fatherless, and they were left without a source of income.

An impending threat arising from his death overshadowed the family's grieving for Andrew. The family had moved to Westray under the proviso from the Stewart landlord that the rent for their new home at Quoylet would be paid by the head of the household. Hellen felt the precariousness of their new situation. Although thankful that three daughters were now working and independent of the family home, she had still to feed and house her remaining two children and a dependent mother-in-law to consider. Meg was nearly thirteen and John only eight. The threat of eviction loomed over Hellen's fragile state of mind. The rent would be impossible to pay without the income Andrew brought in from fishing. To make matters worse, their attendant plot of land for growing crops and vegetables had not yet become fully self-sufficient.

John's reaction to his father's untimely death was particularly disconcerting for Hellen. The eight-year-old took on an uncharacteristic anger, a rage directed at his deceased father. He blamed Andrew for not fighting the fever, and for never teaching him how to catch lobsters in creels, and for not taking him, young as he was, out in his fishing yawl. He was in shock and in denial. He had loved his father's tales of life on the unpredictable sea, the constant hunt for fishing banks, the raging storms, the excitement and action. To John it was a life full of exploration where no two days were the same. He longed to grow up and become a fisherman. It was in his blood. But with no older brothers or uncles on Westray to teach him the intricacies of deep-sea fishing his future was in jeopardy.

After Andrew's funeral, the remaining Williamson family members called a meeting at which John's hopes were dashed. His mother, his grandmother and his sisters decided that he would have to take up a different trade. Their options on the matter did not include moving back to Fair Isle. Although they still had relatives living there, none had accommodation in their crofts for two adults and two children. Besides, making a living on Fair Isle was becoming more and more difficult and islanders were constantly emigrating and separating across the unknown world. Uncle William, the brother closest to Andrew, had long since settled in Kirkwall on Orkney Mainland with his family, but he worked on the docks and was no longer a fisherman. Hellen wouldn't hear of her only son moving away from home when he was still so young.

Faced with the prospect of losing their home, Hellen turned her mind to ways to pay the rent. Young as she was, Meg keenly felt a responsibility to support her mother at home at that time. Going to school was not something she would miss as she had read all the school books several times over and was bored with helping the less intelligent class members with their educational struggles. Hellen and Meg needed each other more than ever.

Meg had been particularly close to Andrew. She sorely missed his company, his wit and his love. She had presumed he would always be around for her as her protector and mentor. Bearing her grief silently and inwardly, the family believed she was coping, but a certain happiness ceased for Meg from the day her father was brought unconscious to the doors of Quoylet. It was a long time before happiness was reinstated.

9

The Bannock Business

For generations the Orcadian way of life revolved around the link between land tenure and the fishing industry. Crofters were obliged to be fishermen under threat of eviction by their landlord, the Laird. It was within the jurisdiction of the Laird of Westray to retrieve Quoylet from Hellen in order to house a fisherman and his family. Normally sons took over from their fathers as fishermen, but John, at eight years of age, was much too young. Hellen was painfully aware that their state of security at Quoylet had become perniciously precarious and feared homelessness if they were unable to pay the rent in full.

The night after Andrew's funeral, Hellen, Barbara Brown and Meg huddled around the peat fire by the light of the fish oil lamps and discussed what the future might hold for them. They tried to think of ways in which they might be able to pay the rent and Meg suggested that Hellen baked large batches of her special recipe bannocks to sell around Westray. Everyone who visited Quoylet was offered one of Hellen's freshly baked bannocks with a cup of buttermilk or tea. The quality and distinctive taste of these flat oatmeal cakes baked on a griddle was frequently remarked upon within the neighbourhood. They were different in both taste and appearance to those made in Orkney, their uniqueness attributed to Hellen's recipe brought from Fair Isle and handed down through the generations. Barbara Brown thought Meg's idea might bring in some income without too much outlay as the fire was always lit in Quoylet and milk to make butter was plentiful, therefore the only additional costs would be for oats and for packaging. Mrs. Logie sold crisp, white oiled paper in her shop that would be ideal for wrapping and Meg said she would design labels. It was decided to give her idea a try, and to get started right away.

Williamina Stout was behind the counter when Hellen entered the Logie's store the next day. She had been promoted and given Barbara's job after Barbara's marriage and subsequent move to Frankfurt.

Williamina's old job had been given to her younger sister, Esther. Mrs. Logie appeared from the kitchen as Hellen was asking to buy a large roll of their oiled wrapping paper. Curiosity forced her to ask Hellen's intentions for such quantities of paper and the new Williamson family business plan was explained. It was heartening for Mrs. Logie to see someone so recently made destitute exuding such enthusiasm, but it did cross her mind that this would mean competition for her own home baking. Hellen assured her that she would be solely specialising in the baking of bannocks and as Mrs. Logie never baked bannocks, only cakes, scones and scotch pancakes, she felt relieved and wished Hellen well in her new venture. She was showing Hellen templates of small white cardboard boxes, that they also had in stock, when her husband returned from the ferry laden with supplies.

He was told about the bannock baking idea and he stood rubbing his chin thoughtfully for several moments. Bewildered, Mrs. Logie looked at Hellen and shrugged her shoulders and Hellen looked at Williamina, who frowned. Esther came in from the back room and stopped short, wondering why such a silence had descended in the shop.

"If these bannocks prove to sell weel ….." Mr. Logie began,

"Aye…..?" said his wife.

"…then I wid…"

"Spit it oot, man! Whit would ye do?"

"I wid consider selling them in the shop – for a sma' cut, of course."

"Ah, there's a grand idea!" said Mrs. Logie, smiling in relief at his final explanation.

Mr. Logie came up with a marketing plan. The offer was too good to refuse. Mrs. Logie said it would be best to take orders so that stock would not go to waste. Hellen's business was off to a good start.

From that day their business began in earnest. Meg and John set about churning butter for Barbara Brown, sitting in her rocker, a large bowl and wooden spoon resting in her lap where she mixed the butter with oats and sugar. Hellen kept two griddles continually hot and baked batch after batch of bannocks. Meg cooled them on grids over every available surface within Quoylet. When they were ready for wrapping John assembled a few white cardboard boxes. Meg designed a simple notice to stand by the packets and boxes of bannocks in the Logie's store, which read "Ellen's Finest Fair Isle Bannocks," in memory of Andrew's name for his wife.

Customers at the Logie's Grocery were keen to try new produce and keen to support a friend in need. Soon the business was operating at full stretch with Hellen struggling to keep up with the demand, which included orders for other island grocery shops. Meg and John enjoyed being part of a thriving business and were thrilled by their first feelings of success. Hellen was proud of her young work force and knew that Andrew would have been amazed at his enterprising family.

News of Ellen's Finest Bannocks spread swiftly. Through its success the rent money was found and the depleted Williamson family held onto their home for a while longer. The threat of eviction, however, always hung in the wind. The trepidation and vulnerability that Hellen felt around the time of Andrew's death dissipated with each month that slipped by. She felt that through adversity she had been given a way to prove her worth in her new community. The business was not something she would have considered starting had Andrew been around to bring in the rent money.

Peter Harcus of Eday was one of six sons of the boatman who ran a ferry service between the islands. When Barbara Williamson worked at Logie's Grocery, Agnes often went to meet the ferry with her sister to collect supplies for the shop. On some occasions they delivered boxes of "Ellen's Finest Fair Isle Bannocks" to be sent to the grocer shop on Eday. Peter was always joking and fooling around, but his antics usually made Barbara roll her eyes in disdain. Agnes on the other hand seemed to be in tune with his humour and there was much laughter when they were together. She liked the way he continually tossed his curly red hair out of his eyes and how it flopped around his forehead like a pet creature at play.

On their first courting walk Peter took Agnes to his special place along the cliffs at the southern tip of Westray, where caverns that had been formed by the influx and reflux of centuries of pounding seas. At high tide and in tempestuous weather, the sea was forced along narrow crevices and tunnels in the rock to a great distance inland, where the force of the water would explode to the surface through holes of its own making. Seawater bursting forth and springing high into the air created a sudden and dramatic spectacle. When Agnes first witnessed this phenomenon she squealed and darted back from its soaking spray. Peter had received the desired reaction and soon they were in each other's arms.

Their favourite courting walk took them to a place they called the Witches' Cauldron, a place they had discovered together whilst walking on the cliffs. They had heard low rumbling and gurgling noises in the distance and as they climbed closer the noise became deafening. A precipice overhung what appeared to be an immense boiling cauldron of frothing seawater in a perpetual swirl, its noise continual and terrifying, stunning their ears. They discovered that they could walk half way around the top of the cauldron on high pillars and arches of solid rock. Agnes loved the drama created by the noise and force of the water, its power and urgency.

Orkney's landscape was generally less dramatic, consisting mostly of undulating slopes and not prone to steep hillsides or high cliffs, all with a noticeable absence of trees. The high winds that continually buffeted the landscape were a contributory cause for the general lack of forestation, making seed implantation difficult and spreading salty sea spray far inland. Some islands, lush green with grass and a purple haze of heather, looked like the backs of whales protruding from the dark sea.

Agnes married Peter later that year and before their wedding, Peter found himself a good job at Rapness Farm at the southern end of Westray, in the next bay to Quoylet. He and Agnes were allocated a home, a But and Ben, sarcastically named 'Rabbithall' due to its diminutive size. Rabbitha' as the locals called it, nestled amongst several other cottages for the farm workers. Peter had, with the help of his brother, built the wooden box bed, carving intricate corner designs on the side that he fitted with doors. It had taken him several weeks to complete, working mostly in the evenings. Knowing that this very bed would be handed down from father to son through the generations Peter took pride in its construction. He was not the eldest son of his family and therefore he would not inherit his parent's bed. Babies were born in quick succession to Agnes and Peter, one a year for several years, therefore two more boxed beds were made, one for their sons and one for their daughters. Each bairn inherited their parent's thick and wavy locks, some with Peter's red colouring and the others with the brown of Agnes's.

The ritual collection of annual rent from the crofters generally took place in the late summer months. Sometimes it was the only time the inhabitants of Westray saw their Laird. Rent collections took him to every corner of the island to view the state of his properties and their occupants and to discuss farming and fishing. His manservant and two other men in his employment usually accompanied him on horseback. The Laird's large and imposing frame was given added stature when he rode the highest and most handsome horse ever seen on Westray. He struck a formidable mien, a strong and forceful presence in natural command of any assembly and his workers would generally agree that he was a fair master.

Meg was fifteen when she took heed of the Laird of Westray for the first time. She and her family had heard the rumble of hooves across the land and gathered to watch four horses cantering up to Quoylet. The Laird was in the lead, conspicuous by his dark aura. Darkly clad, his black hair grew in thick waves like a sea in storm. It streamed horizontally back from his forehead as if constantly driven there by the force of some unfelt wind, which also appeared to have made his hairline recede slightly, creating a tall and noble face. Black sideburns grew to his chin. He towered above the assembled Williamson family grouped before Quoylet as he sat proud, mounted on his high black horse, its coat shiny as velvet.

Following closely behind the Laird was a thinner fair-haired man riding a chestnut mare. This man had a thinner nose and a distinctive, smooth moustache that covered his unusually long upper lip, hiding his mouth from view. Both ends of his moustache trailed to below his square jaw. His shoulder-length hair was the colour of cool wet sand yet his moustache was a lighter tone. Hellen was reminded of an illustration she had once seen of a Viking warrior. This was the Laird's right-hand man, his constant manservant.

Two servants on horseback galloped side by side behind these men. As they rode up the gentle rise the black tangled locks of one man streamed out behind him like the mane on his horse. His red haired companion sported a thick beard. To the wary tenants these visitors looked mean and menacing, but not to Barbara Brown, who had lived too long to be fearty of someone's appearance.

"Master of all he surveys," she muttered under her breath to Hellen as the Laird doffed his hat in deference to them.

"Wheesht!" retorted Hellen from the side of her mouth. She was still in fear of eviction and gave the straight-faced giant of a man as pleasant a smile as she could muster.

With her childhood behind her, Meg had evolved into a stunning young woman with a striking blonde beauty that turned heads. She stood taller and more slender than her mother, following more in Andrew's genetic mould. Her hair was loosely pinned to one side of her head as she stood balancing a basket of dark purple blackberries on her left hip. When the Laird's party approached Quoylet, Meg's slim young body and flaxen hair elevated her from her family's reception line. The gaze of the approaching riders was drawn towards her, mesmerised until within eyeshot, when they politely averted their eyes towards Hellen as the head of the household. The Laird spoke and exchanged the usual pleasantries with Hellen, while Meg watched him fixedly. So seldom did gentry visited their humble home that she was fascinated and impressed by the vision of this well-dressed man on his well-groomed horse. Her reverie was broken when the Laird pulled his horse up abruptly beside her. She was obliged to smile up at him in her own, distinctively askew way. His only response was to blink – as if to regain some infinitesimal loss of composure.

The Laird's right-hand man accepted the rent money and placed it inside a large leather saddlebag. He then wrote in a cumbersome ledger balanced on his saddle. The party of four turned their horses around and Hellen felt her breath slowly release as if she had been holding it in check since the men's arrival. But when the Laird haltingly circled in front of Hellen and slowly opened his mouth to speak, her sigh was quickly arrested. She stood motionless with bated breath once more, expecting the worst.

It took her completely by surprise therefore when he addressed her directly and said, "I'd like to congratulate you, Mrs. Williamson, on your fine baking. Very enterprising of you to start a business. I wish you continued success with your bannocks."

Hellen's eyes widened but she hid her amazement – unlike Barbara Brown, who whistled through her teeth.

"Praise be where praise due," were the Laird's last words to them as he thundered off over the land to the next croft. He left three Williamson family members standing aghast. The fourth was watching his disappearing figure with a flutter in her stomach and the merest suggestion of a smile flitting across her face, an awry smile she had inherited from her mother. A day at Quoylet had never been more interesting for Meg.

This compliment from the Laird reassured Hellen and her sense of relief made her quite light-headed. She felt her family was secure within the walls of Quoylet for a while longer.

The three other riders bid the family farewell and began to canter one by one after their master, though the bearded man held back for a moment. He leant over his horse's neck to speak to Hellen.

"He eats dem himself every mornin' so I hear," he said with a friendly wink as he galloped off to catch up with them.

"Weel, weel!" said Hellen in amazement. "Dat Laird's nae such a bad sort, is he?"

Two weeks after the Laird's visit, there became one less resident at Quoylet. Barbara Brown had been napping in her rocking chair all afternoon before anyone realised that she was not in fact sleeping. It was eleven-year-old John Harcus who tried to wake her when supper was ready. Gently shaking her by her shoulder, he watched in horror as, in response to his unsettling, his great grandmother slithered gently from her rocker and cascaded onto the floor in one rustling glide.

Later Hellen said that it was a grand way for her mother-in-law to die, asleep in her rocking chair, happily unaware of the Grim Reaper's approach.

The next summer Hellen's wariness of eviction returned. She dreaded the visit from the Laird, fearing that he might insist on reclaiming Quoylet for a working fisherman and his family. There would be nothing Hellen could do. Quoylet had housed a family of seven, small though it was, and now there was only Hellen, Meg and John living there.

One afternoon, as Hellen was busy about her chores she was surprised to see the silhouette of a solitary horse and rider loom up outside the open doorway of Quoylet. The vision instilled her with panic and she remained in the shadows, peering out into the bright sunlight at the rider. She recognised the Laird's manservant from the previous year. The man's droopy moustache still made him look like a warrior right out of an old Viking saga. Certainly to Hellen he felt like an invader; with or without a horned and armoured helmet, he was encroaching on her privacy and her precious property.

"Aye?" she said, frowning up at him and squinting against the sun as she emerged from the sanctuary of her home.

"I've come frae the Laird," he replied as he dismounted.

"Aye," she retorted, exasperated by the obvious.

But what he went on to say was not expected. He had come to offer Meg a position as servant girl at the Laird's Manor. The Laird, his wife and family lived in Westray Manor to the far north of Westray. The Manor was part of the largest farm, Black Bull Farm. The Viking throw-back said that the Laird's wife, who was expecting her third baby, needed another servant.

Meg overheard the conversation from the byre where she was milking the cow. An unsurpassed feeling of excitement arose within her as she stood up and walked out into the sunlight, where her gaze fixed on the horseman with his gaze fixed upon Meg. The 'warrior' waited patiently beside his mount for a reply. His horse had been given a good ride for waves of white steam were rising from her glossy flanks. Hellen and Meg locked eyes and a look of inevitability crossed between them. To refuse such a position might go badly with the Laird and cause repercussions for Hellen's tenure on Quoylet. The initial relief that this visit was not notification of an imminent eviction was then replaced by a feeling of entrapment for Hellen. She felt this offer was almost like a demand yet told the messenger they would think about it and let the Laird know. But Meg interrupted her, saying she had already given the matter thought and that he was to tell the Laird she would accept the post. Meg knew this had to be. A curiously eager anticipation spawned deep inside her.

"The Laird hopes she can bake bannocks like her midder" his words came from somewhere under his thick moustache.

"Aah!" Hellen retorted. "He dis, dis he!"

Like every mother, Hellen knew that her children had to forge an independent life for themselves and she was pleased that Meg had been offered a secure job with the Laird's own household. But she would sorely miss her cheery company and it would leave only herself and young John living at Quoylet, increasing their threat of eviction.

That night Meg slept little. The thought of working at the unimaginable Manor House for the most refined family on Westray, a new environment in surely affluent surroundings, excited her greatly.

Any remaining fears of sudden eviction were completely dispelled for Hellen a few weeks after Meg moved to Black Bull Farm. Agnes and Peter insisted that she and John went to live with them at Rabbithall. Agnes by then had five children, including twin boys born only a few months previously. At Rabbitha' Hellen's bannock baking could continue with Agnes's help to replace Meg. John would be given work to do with Peter on the seventeen acre Rapness Farm. For Hellen the blow of losing Meg's company was softened by the fact that she would once again share a home with Agnes and would be surrounded by her grandchildren.

Peter and a few strong neighbours manoeuvred Hellen's box bed into the But end of Rabbitha' as there was no room in the Ben end.

The living area was constricted by the presence of Hellen's boxed bed but otherwise the arrangement worked well. John would sleep in with his nephew, two year old Angus, in their box bed in the Ben end. The twins, James and George, still shared the parental bed. The Harcus daughters, Alexina and Peterina shared a bed. Alexina Harcus was shortened to "Xina" and Peterina was known as "Trina". The Harcus children were very young, born one after another, year after year. There would be nine children in total born to the Harcus family.

"Ellen's Finest Bannocks" were just as successfully baked on the fires at Rabbitha'. In fact the range was twice as wide and, with an extra griddle, twice as many bannocks could be baked in a batch. The smells of peat fires and fish oil lamps at Rabbitha' were replaced by the constant appetising aroma of toasting bannocks. The best were packaged and sold. Any broken pieces or misshapes were eagerly devoured by the children and animals. Nothing was wasted.

10

Rabbithall

The land between Ness Farm and Rabbitha' rose up from the shoreline like the back on a huge whale. On Sundays Anderina regularly walked over this rolling hillside to visit her family. Her favourite Shetland pony, Peedie One, usually followed her and it was not unknown for Anderina to also bring along a sick animal that she was currently tending, such as an orphaned new-born lamb wrapped for comfort in its dead mother's fleece. The Harcus children loved Anderina's visits and were especially excited to see what animals she had in tow.

For the Christmas of 1877, an eagerly awaited family reunion was planned. Anderina and Meg were to join Hellen, John, Agnes, Peter and their children for a Christmas dinner at Rabbitha'. Barbara would be the only sibling not to return. It was a long journey from Europe and travelling in midwinter would entail a predictably treacherous sea crossing. Besides, Rabbitha' would be bursting at the seams with Anderina and Meg to accommodate.

Anderina arrived two days before Christmas Eve with Peedie One harnessed to a small trap, which was piled high with farm produce, a Christmas bonus from the Seator family. This included a live duck, immediately allowed to roam free in the yard. Aunt Anderina brought two kittens for the children to look after; one was jet black except for one white paw and the other was a ginger stripe. The children named them Snowpaw and Kipper. The first name was an obvious choice but the children chose the second due to that kitten's penchant for kippers. It had been their first meal at Rabbitha' and this tiny kitten had demolished the contents of his brother's dish as well as his own. Agnes said they should have called him Gannet.

A letter from Meg arrived that day via a passing farmer in his cart. In the letter Meg said she would arrive on Christmas Eve and that the Laird and his wife had set aside a whole turkey for the Williamson dinner. This news caused much excitement. It meant that their old pig, Penny, would receive a stay of execution and that Mrs. Seator's duck would live to see more days. There was a special page in the letter written to John, who missed Meg more than he thought possible. There had only been the occasional letter from Meg since her move to Black Bull Farm. The following year these would become more scarce.

On Christmas Eve a horse-drawn wagon, owned by the Laird of Westray and driven by the now familiar Viking throw-back, trotted into the yard at Rabbitha'. Only one person in the welcoming party noticed Meg's initial steadying intake of breath before the customary smile lit up her lovely face and that was Anderina, standing on the periphery of the family throng and tuned to any nuances in her sister's behaviour. The transition from this uncharacteristic nervousness to Meg's usual happy demeanour was infinitesimal, but noted by Anderina, who was not one to show excitement on such occasions and had time to note the scene from the sidelines. She watched as the Harcus children jostled for position to get close to their Aunt Meg. She watched as Agnes began her usual gaiety-filled chatter before Meg had alighted, and she saw John quietly unload Meg's bag from the back of the wagon, knowing that his turn would come to welcome his favourite sister. Meg's moment of unease was gone before Anderina could attach much importance to it. She put it down to her sister's tiring journey, although later she would read more into that moment.

The driver helped Meg down from the wagon before taking hold of the trussed legs of the promised Christmas turkey, slaughtered that morning and ready for plucking. He carried it – the biggest bird the children had ever seen – into the But end and hung it on the first available hook from the roof. While the numerous inhabitants of Rabbitha' were noisily greeting and fussing over Meg, the Laird's manservant returned to his seat on the cart and, taking a hold of the reins, turned the horse around. His departure went unheeded except by Rookie, the Harcus sheepdog, who barked and bounced around the horse's front legs. The horse trotted on undaunted.

Meg also bore gifts. For Hellen she had hand stitched a heather-coloured, satin scarf and for John, she had knitted a neckerchief. She gave Agnes a box of handmade peppermint creams and Peter a white linen handkerchief with the initial 'P' embroidered in one corner. For the children, Meg handed out skipping ropes with carved wooden handles and spinning tops that made whistling sounds. Meg told them that many of the servants at Black Bull Farm spent their spare time whittling or carving wood.

The children busied themselves creating makeshift beds for John and the boys, who were to vacate their boxed bed for the duration of their aunts' visit. They would sleep on the dry hay bales in the corner of the byre to enable Anderina and Meg to have their bed, the 'boys' bed', in the Ben end of Rabbitha'. When it was time for sleep, Agnes took pleasure in saying to the boys, "Time tae hit de hay, lads!"

On Christmas Eve the adults congregated around the roaring peat fire for endless conversation. On Christmas morning the family put on their best clothes and made the trek across the hillside to the Kirk. The minister from the Mainland could not be there, but the elders nominated the hymns to be sung and gave the predictably God-fearing sermon and suitably seasonal Bible readings. The huge turkey had been roasting in the oven overnight, filling the home with its tantalising aroma. After their visit to the Kirk the brute was about ready to be carved and the children visibly drooled as the final preparations for the meal were set. The meal was eaten with relish.

Those four days were packed with chatter and fun with the children, who were allowed to stay up late with the adults and join in with any singing that went on around the fire. John made music by blowing along a comb wrapped loosely with a thin piece of paper. Peter accompanied him by clapping two spoons together across his thighs, his forehead, his bottom, anywhere that would make the children laugh.

Everyone wanted to know about the life Meg led at Black Bull Farm. No one else had travelled to the other end of Westray, let alone to the Laird's Farm. Meg told them that she was a servant to Isobella, the Laird's wife, but that she might also be asked to help with the milking, or with food preparation in the farm kitchen, and sometimes to prune roses. The family was very impressed by the 'pruning of roses' though they had no idea what she meant or how she would go about such a task. The children had never seen a rose. The work Meg enjoyed the most, she said, was looking after and playing with the Laird's young children and caring for the youngest, still a baby.

Like all good times, the few days they had together soon came to an end. Hellen had always marvelled at the fact that weeks of living a nonentity, a dull and insignificant existence, could pass by and be soon forgotten, never to be recalled, yet it took only a few precious moments of a particularly happy or special time to make an everlasting, indelible memory.

The Laird's wagon with predictably the same driver arrived from Black Bull Farm to collect Meg. Without alighting, the driver waited patiently in the yard, staring vacantly ahead of him, without uttering a word. His mission was obvious. There was no need for explanation. No one heard the wagon driver speak a word on either of the two occasions he appeared at Rabbitha' that Christmas. He might doth his cap to the ladies and children, nod to the men, but that appeared to be the full extent of his communicational skills. Hellen hoped that the other servants at Black Bull Farm were a cheerier crew. She was curious about the man and asked Meg what he was called.

"Dat's Seth," said Meg.

"Seth? Wha sort o' a name is dat?" said Hellen, who found it difficult not to turn the 'th' sound into 'd'.

"He's just Seth," said Meg. "And he disnae say much, midder, so dinnae ye be prattlin' on tae him!"

"A'right, a'right!" laughed Hellen.

Tall and slim, Seth's fair hair was flecked with red and Hellen thought he should have been called Rory, because he looked like a Rory. His distinctive appearance, strong jawline, long moustache, again reminded Hellen of Orkney's Viking invaders of the eighth century. He would have looked foreboding in a warrior's helmet. Yet out of Christian Yuletide benevolence, she went over to the cart and handed him a waxed-paper packet of "Ellen's Finest Fair Isle Bannocks", saying to him that she hoped his Christmas had been a merry one. She did wonder, however, if this man ever felt merry. He doffed his cap in passing appreciation. It was impossible to see if he had smiled through the thick undergrowth of his moustache, which was like hay in need of scything.

"Farewell auld Penny, I may ne'er see ye agin!" said Meg. "They will be eating ye soon, poor lass!"

By saying goodbye to the old pig, Meg made light of the panic she felt inside, the panic that was noted by her observant sister, Anderina. Before climbing the step at the front of the cart, Meg bade her fond farewells to everyone, which again seemed more poignant to Anderina long after the event.

Hellen wished Andrew had been there to share this particular Christmas. There had been more laughter than for many years and more food eaten than at any previous Christmas time. A time of plenty, plenty of love and plenty of sustenance. But Hellen had no inkling of how things would be a year hence. She was not to know that this was to be the last Christmas the Williamson family would spend together.

Over the following year, Meg's increasing severance with her family brought nothing but worry and bewilderment to Hellen. The strong bond they had all once shared was slowly eroded by the absence of news and her inability to visit them at Rabbitha'. More letters arrived from Barbara than from Meg and Barbara lived hundreds of miles away.

Meg did, however, manage to make an appearance on the day of Hellen's fifty-sixth birthday.

Alerted by the steady pounding of a horse's hooves in the distance along the dirt track, Hellen went out to investigate. She recognised Seth at the reins of the Laird's wagon. She recognised Seth before she recognised Meg, who sat hunched and shrouded in her cloak beside him. The wind had been blowing up a gale that morning and Meg arrived looking pale, dishevelled and cold. Her visit was short. She seemed distracted, explaining that there was much to be done at Black Bull Farm and that she must go back soon. Hellen worried that she was being over-worked but Meg assured her mother that everyone at the farm was just as work-laden.

Seth spent the time at Rabbitha' hovering around the yard and the byres as if lost for a worthwhile occupation, as if champing at the bit to return to Bull. Agnes said it was as if he was Meg's servant, waiting on her beck and call, which made them all laugh. Hellen asked if he was perchance sweet on her and Meg looked at her in mocking disbelief.

"Seth?" she said. "Naw, naw, he's got a string of admirers has Seth! He disnae need the likes o' me!"

They tried to tease her further about any sweetheart she may have at Black Bull Farm, but she hastily dismissed the query with a quick rise and fall of colour to her cheeks and joked that no one yet was good enough for her.

"Dat's the spirit!" said Agnes.

After Meg left, Agnes remarked that she seemed happy enough and was certainly looking well fed. Hellen had to agree with her second sentiment. But Agnes's life was completely taken up with the needs of her children, with cleaning and cooking, with the milking of cows, the rooing of sheep, the delivering of lambs, the churning of butter and the baking of bannocks and her all-important pastime, joking and loving with Peter. She was not in the habit of spending time in deep thought. If she had, she might have come to the conclusion that her sister's behaviour was somewhat out of character.

That evening as they sat at the fireside, Hellen voiced her anxieties about Meg. John had been working at the farm with Peter all day. Although Meg had said as she left that she would be going over to Rapness Farm to search out John and Peter before she returned to Black Bull Farm, neither of them had seen sight nor sound of her that day. John was hurt. He and Meg had always been close. This compounded Hellen's theory that something was amiss.

"Yer only frettin' as she didnae stay long," Agnes said.

"Aye, I only wanted her to stay fur supper wi' us, Agnes," sighed Hellen.

"'Course ye did, midder," Agnes gave her mother a hug.

"She didnae come to see me," said John, peevishly.

"She probably didnae ha' enough time, lad," Peter conjectured, drawing deeply on his pipe. This clay pipe had been a wedding present from Hellen and Peter enjoyed smoking it. Tobacco was the only extravagance at Rabbitha'. None of the family drank whisky now that Barbara Brown had passed away.

"Meg always used tae ha' time fur John," Hellen added.

"She might ha' gone tae look but couldnae find them," said Agnes.

John stood up suddenly and pushed his chair back, scraping it across the rough floor. The noise hurt everyone's ears, but the hurt was not equal to the one in John's heart.

"I'm awa tae bed," he said sternly as he headed towards the Ben End.

"Aww, dinnae be hard on her, John, ye know she loves ye," but Hellen was at a loss to explain Meg's behaviour.

John resolved that on the following Saturday, he would go on the long walk to Black Bull Farm to see Meg. He didn't need to worry Hellen with his plans. They had no horse and cart and to walk to Bull was too far for Hellen to manage. The only way Hellen could see Meg was if Meg visited them at Rabbitha', which was much too infrequent. John wanted to see for himself where his sister worked, to establish if she was happy there. Although she was three years older than him, he felt protective of her.

But John's plans were thwarted when his employer announced that Saturday was the Annual Agricultural Show in Kirkwall, an important day for all farm owners, and all the farm hands were needed to help. John was forced to postpone his plan and decided to visit Meg on the next big market day at Pierowall, which was in the north of the island. But this plan was also doomed for on the trip to the Agricultural Show, John met Mary Elphinstone, a pretty young farm servant who showed a keen interest in him. His growing infatuation for her soon took possession of his every waking thought and his best intentions for his sister were pushed into a recess of his mind. Years later, John would wonder if he could have altered the path of Meg's destiny had he fulfilled his intent.

Hellen did not see Meg again until the day she met William.

11

Anderina's Romance.

A fishing catastrophe took place that directly affected Anderina. Four fishermen in a small yawl were caught up in a sudden storm many miles from Westray. The gales carried their boat away. As dawn broke the following day, the empty yawl was found – washed up on one of the beaches. The Islanders went into mourning for the four lost souls. Two had been married men, Laurence Stout and Will Brown, who left between them, eleven children orphaned and two wives destitute. The other two were Laurence's seventeen-year-old son, Benjamin Stout, and Alexander Watt, a bachelor in his early forties. Anderina's personal interest in the accident concerned Alexander Watt.

Two months before, she had been called out to the farm of Mrs. Jacobina Twatt. Jacobina was an elderly widow, having lost her husband to the sea many years before, and she single-handedly ran a thriving farm. Her only son was a fisherman and was away at sea for much of the time. She had needed help with her small herd of cows and had taken on a farm girl to round them up and milk the cows every day. To the formidable Jacobina this girl had proved useless and was soon replaced by another dairymaid. But the same thing happened. The cows became 'truculent'; this was how she described them to Anderina. They refused to be rounded up and the poor old woman had to go out and do the job herself every time. Anderina recognised this trait in cows immediately, especially in small herds who had been looked after by one owner all their lives.

"Every byre has its leader," she told Jacobina.

"Aye, I've heard dat said," said Jacobina.

"Well, yer 'leader' has taken on a mood," continued Anderina. "She disnae like da change in her routine. She likes de same biddie to milk her every day. And dat coo, da 'leader' coo, she sets da mood for a' da ithers."

"Ye don't say!" said Jacobina, looking flabbergasted.

"Aye, I do, Mrs. Twaa......," Anderina's voice tailed off, because she just couldn't make herself say the word – Twatt. She thought it such an ugly word.

The herd's problem was solved by slowly introducing the farm girl, who was designated to be their regular milker, along with Jacobina, until the leader cow accepted the newcomer. Although Anderina had managed to sort out Jacobina's problem, she inadvertently gave the old woman a different problem during the following weeks. It concerned their family name.

During her visit to this farm, Jacobina's son had returned home from sea. He was a strongly built fellow, a good few years older that Anderina. In high spirits, he was especially pleased on his return to find a new woman on the farm. Anderina warmed to his joviality and they began to spend time in each other's company. Alexander and Anderina took to meeting and walking together – until she told him in no uncertain terms that she would not consider courting with a man whose name was Twatt, a name she would not bring herself to say. She quite simply detested the name. Alexander, like Anderina, had never been courting before and he was keen to please. He was very fond of Anderina and if this was what she wanted of him then so be it. After much thought and rubbing of his stubbled chin with his huge callused hand, he eventually asked her if the name 'Watt' was acceptable. Anderina said, yes, this was infinitely better. He was generally an unassertive man, quite easily swayed on most subjects. This was a character trait that Anderina would have found irritating, had they ever married.

At that time however, she merely enjoyed his company. He liked to do a lot of talking, which fitted in with Anderina's general lack of conversation. What Alexander saw in Anderina was probably to do with her attention to him and his admiration of her skills at caring and curing sick animals. He told a friend she had lovely hands. There wasn't much else one could say was attractive about Anderina, who was stout and plain with quite a dour expression. Her face had been known to light up into a smile on occasions when she was particularly pleased and when this happened, it always took people by surprise. Her face lit up a lot in Alexander's company.

At the time of the fishing disaster, on the day the unmanned yawl was found stranded on the beach, Anderina had been walking out with Alexander most Saturdays for about three months. Before that fateful day, they could often be seen walking for miles across the heather, usually with an animal of some description in tow, a ewe on a leash, a Shetland pony, or a skipping piglet. Jacobina Twatt did not give her blessing to this friendship, mainly because of Anderina's insistence on the family name change, which had horrified the old lady. Initially she had liked the girl and was full of appreciation at Anderina's diagnosis of the problem with her herd. But any goodwill had ceased when her only son announced he wanted to be called Watt, that he was no longer a Twatt. However, Jacobina's stubborn attitude was partly due to jealousy. Jealous of the fact her son, who she had thought would always be at home with her, was courting for the first time – at his advanced age.

And now, after the discovery of the wrecked and empty yawl on the beach, it looked as if Jacobina had lost both husband and son to the unrepentant sea, both bodies never retrieved. She began to wish she had been more welcoming to Anderina, because she could do with someone to comfort her now. As for Anderina, she came swiftly to terms with her loss, reverting back to her lonely life with the animals. Not that she ever felt lonely. It was only other people who thought of her as lonely. 'What would be, would be' was her attitude and it appeared that their union was not to be. She had however, been upset to think of Alexander drowning in freezing waters during a raging gale as was her caring nature, but as she could do nothing about it, there was no point in dwelling upon the fact. Life must go on. Hellen was upset for Anderina, having hoped that the romance might have blossomed into a proposal of marriage. She had taken to the great lumbering fisherman, who always carried a whiff of ling about him.

The poor destitute wives stricken by the disaster at sea took charity from their neighbours and survived on a thread. Life carried on as usual with everyone trying to recover from this blow to the community, the loss of four fishermen. But another shock lay in store for the beleaguered islanders at the end of August, four months after the sinking of the fateful yawl.

It was harvest time and everyone, with four men short at this vital time of the year, was hard at work in the fields. John Williamson was one of the men scything oats. As he stood up to stretch his aching back, his eyes were drawn out to sea where, on the horizon, the ferryboat was approaching. John pointed it out to his fellow harvesters and they all agreed that some very important passengers must be on board, because there was no ferry due that day. As it sailed nearer to land, the harvesters were able to identify the people standing and waving on deck. Their work came to an abrupt halt as they gazed out to sea in sheer disbelief. Only a moment before the fields had been a hive of activity, but now, one by one, the workers looked like they had turned to stone, standing in various degrees of astonishment as they each began to recognise the four passengers hailing to them from the deck. Jumping up and down was the 'ghost' of Benjamin Stout. The harvesters stared, frozen to the spot. Were they all having the same nightmare?

It was no nightmare. Benjamin, his father, Laurence, Will Brown and Alexander Watt, all now bearded and four months older than at their last sighting were sailing into the harbour.

Laurence Stout's wife was struck dumb with shock for nearly a day and his 'orphaned' children wailed, yelling that the bad ghost-man should keep away. Will Brown's wife had since taken up with another suitor, a widower with four bairns and they had plans to be married by Christmas time. Those plans were dashed – and almost Will Brown's head, too – when his widow-turned-wife-again brandished a griddle at him. She knew he was no ghost. He was the real thing all right and that was what annoyed her. Jacobina Twatt had to be taken to hospital on the Mainland as she became a gibbering wreck, wittering on about the phenomenon, and that if her son could return from the dead, would her long-lost husband not appear also? The returning 'dead' men were stunned by their 'welcome', which was not at all what they had expected. Life had moved on without them and an awful lot of living can happen in four months. Time waits for no man as Laurence Stout's mother-in-law pointed out.

There were so many questions to ask the back-from-the-dead fishermen. When the furore died down the men tried to explain, but the shock and disbelief were hard to overcome and their explanations fell on stony ground. Stranded and battered in their storm-buffeted yawl the men had been rescued when it capsized, plucked from the clutches of the raging sea by a passing ship from Canada bound for Norway. The ship had to continue on its course and it took the four 'lost souls' these past four months to make their weary way homewards, begging passage on many different vessels, mostly on the strength of their tale of survival. Then questions came flying at them in torrents. Why had they not managed to send home word of their rescue? Did they not have any idea about the pain and hardship they had left behind?

The first remark Anderina made on Alexander's incredible re-appearance was to point out that she did not take to his beard. She was inexplicably annoyed with him. Hellen tried to reason with her but her mind was set. As far as she was concerned she had thought of Alexander as dead these past four months and, as he had not sent word to state the contrary, dead he was, in her heart. They never spoke again. The slim second chance that Hellen had in the hopes of seeing her third born daughter married, both times to the same suitor, ended as abruptly as it had arisen.

When Jacobina died two months later, Alexander moved his home to Lerwick on the mainland of Shetland. In no time he became a popular member of that community. They found him amusing and often gave him forum, taking charge of a meeting or dominating a gathering with his tales and ideas. A new found assertiveness was born in him. The following year, Alexander was one of a leading group of Shetlanders to innovate a tradition that has carried on down the years – the burning of a model Viking galley during the festival of Up-Helly-Aa in Lerwick.

Up-Helly-Aa had been a traditional festival for centuries, a celebration of the Vikings held at the end of January. The influence of the Vikings, who had invaded in the eighth and ninth centuries, was still strong in Orkney and Shetland. From early in the nineteenth century, Christmas at Lerwick had been celebrated with noise and fires and even gunpowder. It seemed to stem back from the time of naval wars that culminated at Lerwick. An annual celebration took place, coinciding with Christmas and stretching out until the end of January for the festival of Up-Helly-Aa. Lerwick's Christmas celebrations had a reputation at one time of being the most boisterous ones in the whole of Europe.

'Tar barrels' became the main burning sensation at that time. Barrels filled with wood chip, old rope and tar were set alight and dragged on heavy wooden sledges through the streets and down to the pier, where they were allowed to burn furiously. Some of the young people of Lerwick would burn and roll similar burning barrels down hillsides and were traditionally chased by the local police constabulary. Much damage to private property was occurring through this uncontrolled practice and this prompted Alexander, as an outsider to these traditions, to come up with a better idea. He organised a group that built a large model Viking galley, which they proposed to drag along at the head of the procession to a designated place, the Market Cross in Lerwick, where they could set it alight with more measure of control. This would also mark the Viking festival with true Norse feeling.

The burning of a galley became a spectacle that people from far and wide came to view. Some wealthy Americans and Canadians with Shetland ancestry, descendants of the poverty-stricken emigrants, occasionally travelled there in January. One of these, a Canadian widow, whose husband had worked for the Hudson Bay Company, fell in love with the huge, bearded leader of the procession, impressed by his Viking regalia and striking horned helmet. Alexander had found new life and love. He married his doting tourist and the next year at Up-Helly-Aa, she, too, headed the procession, dressed in a Viking outfit that her ex-husband's ancestors would have been proud of.

Over fifty miles away in Westray and completely oblivious of their shared happiness, Anderina carried on with her own simple, uneventful but totally befitting life.

12

Summons to Black Bull Farm

It was a bright morning in late April 1879 when Hellen received her summons. The all-dominating Orcadian sky was cloudless and the wind unusually light. Hellen sat on her wicker chair by the But End door of Rabbitha', enjoying the warmth of the early sunshine. Her hands never idle, she deftly peeled and chopped some freshly picked potatoes, dropping them into a large enamel bowl of water balanced on her lap. The peace around her was broken only by the occasional faraway lamb bleating or the call of gulls overhead.

Sound travelled easily in the clear open air and Hellen's attention was alerted to the distant clopping of hooves against the dirt track. Squinting against the brightness she peered along the approach road. For many months there had been neither sight nor sound of Meg and Hellen's hopes soared when she saw the Laird's small horse-drawn wagon making its way towards Rabbitha'. But as it neared she saw there was only one figure on board. It was Seth, alone, holding the reins. Meg was conspicuous by her absence and disappointment stabbed sharply at Hellen's heart.

The Harcus children ran from their play to greet the 'pownie an geeg' as they called it, skipping and dancing close to the pony's steady, plodding gait. Seth pulled the wagon to a halt, his tall shadow falling across Hellen's seated figure. The children ran off to play and Hellen, sighing deeply, looked up into Seth's pale blue eyes. This man was the only link she had with her youngest daughter. Hellen and Seth, two people from different generations, different worlds, whose only common denominator was Meg, stared at one another for a silent moment. Meg was on both their minds.

Seth's silence made Hellen feel uneasy. A man of few words he appeared to be contemplating which ones to use, yet for Hellen he merely conjured up in her an anxiety over Meg's well being.

"Weel, out wie it, man!" she demanded of him. "Whit is it yer here fur?"

He nodded and spoke at last. "Meg Williamson requests her mother's presence." He spoke formally and firmly, his deep voiced words emitting from hidden lips, from somewhere under his long moustache. Hellen was confused by his fancy words.

"Agnes, wha's he sayin'?" she turned to her second daughter, who had appeared at the door of Rabbitha' curious as to what was taking place in the yard.

"Meg wants ye, midder," replied Agnes.

Hellen rose from her chair and handed the enamel bowl to Agnes. Standing in Seth's shadow, she peered up into the face of this mysterious bidder, who sat holding the reins of the situation. In vain she tried to glean a hint to whither he was the bearer of good or bad news. But Seth sat motionless, expressionless, and turned his gaze out to the sea ahead of him as if to some invisible interest on the horizon. His face was indecipherable.

"I'll be goin' wie ye den?"

"Aye," he said.

Hellen and Seth travelled in silence, side by side on the raised seat. Occasionally Hellen asked him the odd question, was Meg well, did he know why she wasn't able to visit them? He responded with brief nods of his head or vague shrugs of his shoulders, whilst keeping his eyes firmly fixed on the road ahead. Exasperated by his apparent aloofness, Hellen gave up, believing him to indeed be a strange and irritating fellow. Stranger things were yet to happen before the day was out.

It had been a long time since Hellen had made a journey of any distance. Life was self-sufficient at Rabbitha'. There was never a need to venture further afield. They grew their own vegetables, the chickens laid plenty of eggs, and the cows provided them well with milk, for buttermilk, whey, butter and cheese. Rapness Farm was visited regularly by tradesman with supplies. Agnes and her brother, John, were the distributors of "Ellen's Finest Fair Isle Bannocks" transported in batches to the Logie's Grocery or to the ferry on the carts or wagons of passing traders. Any other journeys were usually made on foot.

Seth's silent though strangely comforting presence allowed Hellen rare time for her own thoughts and she began to relax and enjoy the changing views of the passing landscape. At several points along the route, the cliffs and coastline were clearly visible to her where she sat high on the wagon seat. They drove by a wide bay where seals basked on tide line rocks. They were close enough for Hellen to make out their doleful-eyed faces. She found herself returning the stares of inquisitive seals out at sea as they surfaced from the dark water to watch the moving wagon. She watched the antics of the comical puffins in their scores trying to perch along cliff ledges, their brightly coloured beaks and feet sparking fiery daubs against the blue of the sky.

The road took them along the side of the peat fields where young peat boys were digging and collecting peat, the island's main source of fuel. They loaded supplies into wide baskets slung on either side of small but strong Shetland ponies. The track then skirted the edge of a loch, where wader birds delicately tip toed through the shallows, continually dipping their long beaks into the calm waters. The centre of the loch sparkled with reflected sunlight and mute swans elegantly skimmed across its surface. Westray widened as they travelled north and its western coastline sank behind the Ward Hill. In the distance ahead of them Hellen saw the harbour settlement of Pierowall and on the right overlooking another loch she noticed the high walls of the Fortress of Nilt, built some three centuries before. The road divided and Seth directed the pony to turn into the right hand fork.

A few yawls and sixerens floated in and out of the harbour as they arrived at Pierowall and in and out of sight around the headland. Seth pulled the geeg to a halt by the water trough provided by the alehouse. When the pony's thirst was quenched, they set off once more. Not a word was spoken between them. Smoothly and unremarkably they passed by the town and its people about their daily chores and came to a part of the road where a sandy beach stretched out level to them on the right. Several seals languished in and out of the surf.

Eventually they turned into a long driveway at a brightly coloured and pictorial sign that read "Black Bull Farm". Hellen was unsure reading the words, but the sign was easily decipherable. Three bold red words levitated in an arch on blue sky above a huge black bull standing stoically in a bright green field. The sign for Black Bull Farm was beautifully executed yet few folk who passed by it realised it had been painted by the Laird of Westray's right hand man, the very same unassuming fellow who sat next to Hellen.

Seth led the geeg past the main farmhouse and around to the rear, where he pulled it to a halt outside a small cottage. After alighting he came round to Hellen's side where he held out his hand to assist her down the steep step. She sighed indignantly. As far as she was concerned the man had been trying his utmost to ignore her with his persistent avoidance of eye contact and his lack of conversation. She would return the complement and, ignoring his helping hand, she slid with ease down from the high seat. Hellen, mother of five and grandmother of more, was as fit in her fifty-sixth year as she had been in her twenty-sixth.

Seth walked on down the path to the cottage and Hellen was left to presume she was meant to follow him. He entered the cottage without knocking through a door at the back. Inside it was gloomily dark and muggy. Hellen felt a tight panic grip her heart. Where did Meg fit into this strange charade?

"Midder?" A weak but recognisable voice drifted over to Hellen out of the gloom.

"Meg?" Hellen asked, instantly sensing that something was amiss.

"Aye, midder," said Meg. "I'm here on the bed."

The only light in the room came from glowing embers in a small fireplace. The heat from these embers added to the oppressive atmosphere. The curtains were drawn tightly across the only two windows, barring the entry of even the tiniest ray of sunshine that flared outside the cottage. As Hellen's eyes became accustomed to the dimness, she shuffled her way across the room to a bed in the corner. Although it was the middle of the day, Meg was dressed in night-clothes and sat slumped in the bed. Her flushed face bore an anxious, slightly frightened expression. Hellen frowned. She remembered that as a child

Meg had been frightened of nothing.

"Wha's the matter, lass?"

Hellen was taken aback by the strangeness of the situation and turned to confront Seth, but he had unobtrusively left the cottage. Hellen and Meg were alone – or so Hellen believed.

"Meg, are ye ill?" said Hellen, groping along the bed for Meg's hand, which was damp and clammy. She wrapped both her hands tightly around her daughter's, then with one hand she smoothed down Meg's flaxen hair, which was wet with sweat.

As Hellen searched Meg's face in shadow, she saw tiny beads of sweat strewn across Meg's forehead. As Hellen opened her mouth to ask if she had a fever, an ember crackled in the grate, but the noise was not quite loud enough to obliterate the sound of a muffled whimper.

Hellen's spine jolted her upright. Her brow furrowed fleetingly and her ears strained to hear a repeat of the tiny sound. She didn't have to wait long. The peace was suddenly punctuated by the unmistakable and unique sound of a new-born baby's wail. The moment was forever lodged in Hellen's memory. Only then did Hellen catch sight of the crumpled countenance of her latest bloodline. Within the crook of Meg's elbow nestled a peedie infant in swaddling wraps.

"This is William, midder," said Meg, calmly. The corners of her mouth twitched as she tried to smile. Then she tilted her head towards the rosy-cheeked baby, unmistakably conveying her love for him.

Hellen's head began to swim. The slow preamble of her ride to Black Bull Farm had too swiftly been replaced by this abstruse situation. Until that moment the day's progress had been pedantic and her mind was unready to take in this sudden change of pace. For a moment her mind felt numbed and her comprehension of the situation very confused. Was this baby Isobella Stewart's son? Was this part of Meg's child caring duties for the Stewarts?

But in her heart, Hellen knew the answer and Meg confirmed the obvious.

"Dis is yer grandson, William Williamson," she said simply.

Hellen's jaw fell as she realised what had so recently taken place in that oppressive room.

She would normally receive several months' notice before the expected arrival of a grandchild. The occasion was usually a happy one and shared with the rest of the family. Yet here they were – three members of three generations of one family alone in a cottage that was alien to Hellen yet seemingly home to Meg. For the past two years she had been unable to visualise where Meg lived and worked. Hellen now wondered if this oppressive one roomed cottage was Meg's home. Her mind raced. Was this also the scene of this baby's conception as well as his birth?

Hellen felt like some dirty laundry had been thrown to her and it needed to be sorted. Distress etched itself onto her dainty features and her heart thumped against her ribcage as if trying to jump out at Meg, to cling hold of her.

"He wis born just a few hours ago," Meg went on, "an' I wanted his grandmidder to be de first of oor family tae see him."

Hellen wrestled with her thoughts, trying to control the preaching words that sprung to the tip of her tongue. This was Meg, once happy and carefree now burdened and alone. Hellen's youngest and unwed daughter, suddenly and calmly showing her first baby. Though startled Hellen knew she must deal quickly with the shock she felt at being thrust into this anxious situation and composed herself enough to ask Meg about practicalities.

"Were ye alone at his birth?" Hellen asked, daring not to hear the answer.

"I had help," Meg said.

"Who?" said Hellen in relief.

"I canna say, midder."

"Wha'........?" Hellen wanted answers, not more mystery or insensitivity.

Meg bowed her head. William yawned, wriggling at her elbow as if to make his presence known. He opened his eyes wide yet unseeingly and thus unwittingly diffused the moment. Hellen instinctively reached out to touch him, gently stroking the soft, new skin of his cheek.

"Ye ne'er telt me any o' dis....." Hellen mumbled under her breath then looked her daughter straight in the eyes. "Ye said his name was Williamson – our name." Hellen searched in her mind for a comfortable solution. "Den I'm guessin' ye are nae tae be married– an' nae telt me anything.......?"

Her voice trailed off in shrill disbelief, that a daughter once so close could manage to keep such a secret for all these months. Hellen then understood why Meg had stayed away from them at Rabbitha'. She felt shame at this outcome. Hellen would have been upset to hear that Meg had secretly married, but was more troubled to find out so suddenly that her treasured daughter was an unwed mother with an apparently fatherless bairn, a situation that always meant poverty. Meg could see the distress she knew this caused for her mother and tried to ease the pain.

"Isn't he grand, our wee William?" she said, gently squeezing on Hellen's limp hand.

There was a poignant stillness between them as Meg watched her mother soften and warm to the now sleeping William. The baby's dark hair stuck out in jagged tufts, so different from Meg's sleek blonde hair. If it were not for the fact that Hellen's other children had this same hair colouring, she would have convinced herself that William's father must be dark haired. The embers in the fireplace sparked and whistled, a thin plume of fire rose briefly, then died. Hellen again stroked the baby's soft and downy cheek.

"So he's merrybegotten, is he?" Hellen said despondently. "Who is his faider?"

Such words were not meant to escape the sanctity of her mind, but they involuntarily burst forth. Beseechingly, she held Meg's gaze as Meg visibly stiffened, her dreamy blue eyes turning to the colour of slate.

"Ye ha' tae accept William as he is. No questions, midder." Then she added, "I'm sorry."

In Meg's gaze Hellen saw that the initial wary look of only minutes before replaced by strength and determination. There sat a stubborn young woman that Hellen was only beginning to get to know. Meg, the child, had been replaced by Meg, the young woman, who was seemingly taking control of this lost situation more so than her mother.

A make or break situation had arisen concerning the future bond of their mother and daughter relationship. Meg grasped both Hellen's hands in hers and her gaze softened though her eyes remained fixed on her mother's obvious torment.

"I won't be sayin' who the faidder is," said Meg calmly.

"But I ha' tae…."

"No."

"But I'm yer midder!" Hellen cried in disbelief.

"An' I'm *his* midder," Meg' eyes fell onto the now peaceful infant. "I take responsibility fur William."

They stared at each other for several minutes.

"I'm sorry, midder" Meg said, quietly. "I jist canna say."

"Sorry?" said her stunned mother, losing composure. "Sorry fur wha'? Sorry fur da shock ye've given tae me? Sorry fur da babby's future? Sorry fur yersel'? Which is it?"

Meg looked dejectedly away. Finally she said, "I'm askin' fur yer help."

Hellen let out a long and low sigh of resignation. "Aye, of course, lass," she said, knowing now that she would be given no more information from her daughter on this of all days. Meg's lonely predicament was at least shared with her mother at last, with all its sad and sorry implications. The two women hugged and held onto each other, gaining strength from support. They relaxed into each other's presence, relying on the comfort that their shared past history allowed them. The happy upbringing and close relationship over the years was enough to tide them in good stead at this crucial time. Baby William slept peacefully in his mother's arms, oblivious to the upset his arrival into the world was causing. The only explanation Meg would give about her situation was that there would be no wedding and that she wanted no more mention of William's father. She was undoubtedly under a lot of strain and it was not the best time to overturn the fine balance they had created so Hellen decided to go along with Meg's requests and between them they planned what should be done for the best.

The sun had set when Seth arrived to take Hellen home to

Rabbitha'. Meg and Hellen parted without tears, both feeling strong and resolute in their decision. Hellen convinced herself it was the right thing to do yet so many unanswered questions darted around in her fraught mind. Seth led the way to the awaiting wagon by flickering torchlight. To Hellen's amazement, this time he looked her straight in the eye when he offered to help her climb the high steps of the trap. Hellen suddenly found herself thinking – was Seth William's father? Or had he previously been avoiding her gaze in order that Meg alone would be the one to explain the dilemma to Hellen? In her bewilderment, Hellen frowned up at him.

"Are you feeling all right, Mrs. Williamson?"

Caring words issued from under the normally still and silent moustache. She kept a stunned silence, taking time to register that he spoke well and seemed quite educated in his ways.

On the journey home, Hellen's thoughts raced wildly. Why was Meg so secretive? Why was she unwilling to tell her own mother the identity of her baby's father? Her thoughts turned from grim to unspeakably dire, her torment made worse with each wild stab at the possible truth. Was the father already married? Was the truth perhaps too shocking? Had Meg slept with several men? Had Meg been seduced, or worse – had she been raped? Hellen felt like weeping but kept her quivering lip in check whilst in Seth's presence.

The inky blackness of night descended like a shutter across the sky. As the pony trotted on the fish oil lantern swayed and bobbed, casting distorted shadows over their faces. Hellen glanced sideways to look at Seth but his face was indecipherable. From what little she knew about Seth, she had become accustomed to the fact that his expression barely altered.

He was the only man she had met at Black Bull Farm. Surely there were plenty of others on such a many-acred farm? She had noted no signs of previous passion in the indifferent relationship between Meg and Seth. If Seth was William's father, was Meg not able to admit to this because he had perhaps refused to marry her – or was he already married? A sudden rock on the road surface jolted Hellen out of her reverie.

The inside of her head was thumping; satiated with the incessant, rhythmic clopping of the pony's hooves on the dirt track and bruised by the perpetual wild thoughts without resolutions. These continued to bounce and flit around her head, like the flaying tail of the pony before her.

Was Meg innocent or worldly? Hellen realised that she only knew Meg the child, and not Meg the woman. Her pubescent years had coincided with Andrew's death and Hellen could not recall taking time to explain to Meg about becoming a woman or any subjects of a sexual nature. Her elder daughters had been informed about such matters, because she had been determined to give them more knowledge, more preparation, than she had been given by Grizel. That had been years before Andrew died. Then Hellen had been consumed with grief, and Meg's sisters, Barbara, Agnes and Anderina had all been living away from home. It was at the most crucial time in a young girl's life that Meg had been separated from her mother to start her independent life away from parental instruction. Have I failed her so miserably, Hellen wondered in deepening despair? Did Meg know just how her baby had come about? Sitting in the isolating dark of the open road, Hellen became overwhelmed with guilt.

Yet it was of no benefit to dwell on the past. She had to look to the future now. And the future included William.

The journey home seemed to pass more quickly than the morning's trip. The activity within her brain consumed her time. She thought about the other servants and workers at Black Bull Farm, conspicuous by their absence that day. None had come to visit Meg while Hellen was with her. Outside the cottage the noise of human presence had been all around. Carts rumbled along the dirt tracks. Stable doors opened and closed. Voices were heard, yet no one knocked at Meg's door to inquire about her. Why? Did no one realise a baby was being born? Or had Meg told them to stay away – or was she being shunned?

By the time they reached Rabbitha' Hellen was mentally exhausted. She tried to imagine Meg back at that cottage, also exhausted but hopefully sleeping. Was she sleeping fitfully – or peacefully, Hellen wondered? Had a lifelong agony been created that day – or had Meg's conscience been cleared?

As Seth tethered the pony, Hellen watched him, feeling strangely drawn; wanting to reach out to him with questions he may be able to answer. She knew hardly anything about Seth and yet he undoubtedly knew more about Meg's present life than Hellen. She needed to talk to someone. She missed Andrew, her soul mate. She needed someone strong-minded to help her with her confusion and bewilderment.

A still silence flooded around Seth and Hellen as the trap stood motionless in the yard. The rocking motion and the gentle clopping of the pony's hooves had ceased.

A single muffled cry broke the peace.

For the duration of their journey, the swaddled baby William had slept contentedly in Hellen's arms. Now he was awakening from a dream of a mother briefly known, a dream he would never remember. He was awakening in the arms of a new mother, in reality his grandmother. And he had arrived at the door of the extended family to whom he would be welcomed and to whom he would belong; a home where he would be given the chance of a happy family life otherwise denied to him.

This way Meg could continue working and living in those precarious times at Black Bull Farm and the Manor House. There was no room or work for an unmarried mother, either there or at Rabbitha'.

Seth helped Hellen to climb down.

"It's for the best, Mrs. Williamson," he said, his hand squeezing hers with a fleetingly light touch.

Again he looked her directly in the eyes as if having overcome his shyness for Hellen's time of need. His gaze never fell to the wriggling bundle in her arms. Surely a father would have taken one last look, Hellen mused. She satisfied herself that Seth was merely the messenger, the manservant appointed to transportation. But he was as mysterious as Black Bull Farm though Hellen was seeing a deeper side to him. As she adjusted William's shawl, Seth turned the trap around and set off at a brisk trot, leaving Hellen standing in the yard.

The door to Rabbitha' opened and Agnes appeared in the shaft of light from within. She was full of smiles and cheerily welcomed her mother back into the fold, beckoning to her to hurry inside out of the chill of the night. She had yet to notice the bundle of mystery that had come to live with them.

The Harcus children were all asleep in their beds with only Agnes, Peter and John in need of some explanation. All three were aghast at the new arrival and stunned by the unanswerable questions that followed when they quizzed Hellen. They found it hard to contemplate their lovely sister as a fallen woman. She had always seemed the blessed one, the sibling destined to lead a special life, but her promised future seemed bleak now. There was too much deceit involved for good to prevail. Black Bull Farm held even more mystery.

13

Ella

It was early morning on the week before William's fourth birthday. He became aware of the touch of a small being resting on his arm. Although he was only half-awake and his eyes were shut, he could feel the soft breath against his cheek and sense a presence lying between him and Hellen in the boxed bed. William lay very still in a dream-like state and blinking rapidly, he opened his eyes. The doors to their boxed bed were slightly ajar and a shaft of weak, early morning light fell across the middle of the bed. Turning his head fractionally, he peeped out the very corner of his eye, trying not to disturb anyone and to see who or what was lying between them. Lying peacefully in apparent carefree slumber was a tiny baby, one that he had never before set eyes on.

This was not baby Laurence, Agnes's latest addition to her family, because Laurence had wisps of red hair and this baby had dark hair and was a lot prettier than Laurence.

Hellen was already awake and propped up on one elbow, smiling at William.

"Dis is yer sister, William," she said in a whisper.

"Ma sister?" he said aloud. His sister stirred in her sleep.

"Her name is Ella."

"*Ella?*" said William, beginning to think he was still in a dream.

He wondered how a sister could arrive, unexpectedly, in the middle of the night.

"She's a gift," said Hellen as if reading his thoughts.

"Ah," said William, pretending to understand, but his brow was furrowed.

If he had been asked he would rather have had a brother, and he felt sure he would have remembered if Hellen had mentioned this was going to happen. He decided he must be dreaming and rubbed his eyes hard with his two clenched fists. But when he looked again, Hellen was smiling as before and the vision of the sleeping baby was still in front of him, just as before. In his bewilderment, William wondered if this sister was perhaps a birthday present. Hellen had said she was a gift. Hellen was unaware that her fabricated explanation had caused confusion.

"We're adopting her," she continued, "because she needs a midder – and a brudder, too."

"Ah," he said again, even more confused.

Ella was the second of Meg's merrybegotten babies, but that information Hellen would hold back from William, forever if possible.

At this point little Ella squirmed, opened her mouth and let out a short wail. The wind gurgling in her belly made her face grimace into a quirky, smiling expression.

"Ellen, look, she's smiling at me!" said a suddenly delighted William.

William always called his 'mother' Ellen. He never called her 'Midder' and never thought it strange to call her by her first name. He had difficulty pronouncing the 'H' in Hellen's name and simply reverted to the name that Andrew used to call her. Calling her Ellen at least distinguished her from the many calls of "Midder!" for Agnes by her young brood.

"Isn't she bonnie!" said Hellen.

"She's like a wee piglet!" said William in glee.

They laughed and Hellen had to agree that the baby did look a bit like a piglet. Many times in the past, Hellen had told William that when he was born he looked like a piglet, like the runt of the litter, she said. He was amused by this image, especially as he had since grown into a fine strapping lad. An independent child, he was strong, belying the prediction of the local nurse who had visited him when he was a day old. The fact that baby Ella also looked like a piglet immediately endeared him to his sister.

The doors of their boxed bed began to slowly open, revealing one by one, the inquisitive faces of Agnes's children, who had heard the baby's wail. The sweet baby was accepted without question as part of their extended family. And William found no more immediate desire to ask other questions about Ella.

But Hellen knew that questions would arise one day and she had no idea how she would answer them.

When William had arrived four years before, Hellen's neighbours had not been entirely satisfied with her scant explanation. Hushed rumour and gossip had abounded. Many deduced that William was Meg's illegitimate child – Meg, the lost and dissociated daughter. Why else, they reasoned, would Hellen in her late fifties take in an abandoned baby? Behind shut doors the talk was that Meg must have morally 'fallen by the wayside'. When Ella arrived equally mysteriously, the rumours ran their course once more. Hellen knew of these rumours but said nothing. She could neither dispel nor disprove them. However, folk were generally kind and for the sake of the two children involved the talk ceased. As William and Ella grew they were well liked by all who came in contact with them and their true roots were incidental to their happy lives.

But Hellen became more reclusive after Ella's arrival, wishing to avoid any awkward explanations. She no longer went to social events or neighbours' gatherings. Some of the other women stopped paying her friendly visits in the belief that she had let her youngest daughter down by not showing her the decent path and 'allowing' her to have yet another bastard child. Others thought Meg had brought shame upon her family and that she was a heartless wench for abandoning her offspring. Hellen worried about how and what to tell the young William before gossip might reach his ears. She never wanted to see him and his sister excommunicated or shunned by the community through no fault of their own, but through the sins of their father, who ever he might be. She continually procrastinated on deciding what to do for the best. Fate would prove to be the best decision-maker.

The questions from William did not arise until he was around eight years old.

"Why are ye so auld, Hellen?" said William, out of the blue.

"Awa' wi' ye, ye cheeky wee piglet!" said Hellen. "So I'm auld, am I!"

She knew William's true meaning – that she was much older than the other mothers of boys of his age. Hellen was in her sixty-fifth year.

Brandished her broom at him, she playfully chased him out of the byre, then stood in the entrance, arms folded and balanced on the top of her broomstick, as she watched with pride the laughing child run across the yard.

She was rearing both William and Ella as her own. They were blessings given to her by the lost daughter treasured in her heart. They filled a void in her life left by Andrew's untimely departure and the chicks vacating the nest syndrome. As Hellen watched William she was keenly reminded of Meg as a child. So similar was he to his true mother in his movements and traits that were he to meet Meg, Hellen was sure he would instinctively feel the bond.

William ran over to help John, who was shovelling the valuable manure from the floor of the byre and piling it up on the compost heap. During the long winter months, the cows and sheep remained in the byre. As this was the first day of spring, the weather was deemed mild enough to let them roam free on the pastureland. Only the two milking cows were kept close to the But and Ben, tethered on the richer pasture.

Hellen watched and wondered for the umpteenth time if she should be telling him the truth. But what was the whole truth? Not even Hellen knew. She was of a mind that it was unnecessary to fill his young head with such confusing thoughts. He would probably not understand anyway. Hellen didn't understand. 'Better left as it is,' she always thought. William had only voiced one query before, which was more of a rhetorical question. He merely wondered how an adopted sister could look so much like him. They were practically identical, different ages and different sexes, but unmistakably closely related.

A shout broke Hellen from her reverie. Agnes stood in the doorway to Rabbitha', also watching William's antics. Time for lunch, she shouted across to them, but as they were all smelly workers she wanted them to eat outside – she said they might as well sit upon the compost heap, because everyone inside smelled pretty good that day. Hellen, John or William no longer noticed the putrid stench of the manure, having worked with the smell all morning. Hellen sniffed at her own shoulder and chuckled.

Agnes was thirty-six and the mother of eight children. After Alexina, Angus, Peterina and the twins, James and George, Jessie Anne was born and, in the following year, Laurence, just before Ella joined the family. Samuel was born three years later. Rabbitha' was bursting at its seams with so many children. John had moved in with the other male farm workers over at the main farm at Rapness. Alexina, at fourteen, also started work as a farm servant and lived over in the female servant's accommodation at Rapness.

John was twenty-two and still courting Mary Elphinstone. Hellen despaired of her son ever marrying. She thought Mary Elphinstone probably despaired, too. John would not be hurried on any matter. He was a slow, methodical worker and this trait trickled over into his private life. He saw it as being sensible to wait until he was ready to marry. He knew how Peter and Agnes struggled to make ends meet with babies so regularly being born to them. John enjoyed his freedom and was not keen to be tied down by a wife and children quite yet, but Mary Elphinstone was feeling more and more like an old maid yet only just turned twenty. Hellen thought Mary's devotion to John might not hold out as long as he presumed and that a proposal of marriage from him was required fairly urgently. She thought she really should have a talk with him about this and oh, how she missed Andrew at times like these. He would have been the person to speak to him, father to son. Would he also have been able to sort out Meg's fall from grace, she wondered? She would never know.

Agnes produced the midday meal and allowed the workers into the But end as long as they washed their hands and took off their boots. Before they supped her vegetable broth, John said Grace:

"Some hae meat and canna eat
And some wad eat that want it;
But we hae meat and we can eat –
And so the Laird be thank it."

This was the Selkirk Grace written by Robert Burns; it mattered not to John that they were about to eat a meal without any meat content. He was a fervent admirer of all Burns' poetry and Burns' songs.

As Hellen sat by the peat-burning fire supping her tankard of soup, her daydream came back to haunt her. She sat with her back to Agnes and the children, who were slurping soup up at the table. Peedie

Ella unobtrusively appeared at her elbow, pulling gently at her sleeve.

"Wud ye like sum bannock, Midder?" she said, holding up the heavy platter.

"Thank ye, ma pet lamb," said Hellen as she took one.

In the intervening years William had continued to be Hellen's 'piglet', but Ella had become Hellen's 'pet lamb'. She had tried in vain to make her granddaughter call her 'Hellen' or 'Ellen' as her brother did, instead of 'Midder'. William had no problem with that. But Ella was not of the same independent nature as her brother. She was in need of a real mother figure. Besides, Hellen's name seemed so similar to her own. Both children thought of Hellen as their mother; they knew no different. They were not aware a generation had been skipped.

Eight years before, on the night of William's arrival at Rabbitha', Hellen, Agnes, Peter and John had made a family pact to take on the upbringing of William. This might help to save Meg from shame and to give William a chance of a decent family life. Although this was the best alternative at the time, the situation had to be reassessed as he grew older. William was of an age where he had thoughts of his own and might be vulnerable to any malicious gossip, either overheard or directed at him. The family cover-up was in danger of being rousted or dragged into the community spotlight at any time. But what was Hellen to tell him? She still felt that even the partial truth would be shocking to him. Besides, none of them knew the true facts. No one knew the identity of William's father – or Ella's – or if Meg's children had the same father. To depress her bright and breezy grandchild by telling him that the person he loved as his mother was really his grandmother, that he was an illegitimate child, whose real mother had sent him away from her, was too hard for Hellen to contemplate. To tell him that he would probably never know who his father was and that it was probably best that way, was all too harsh and enough to break his happy spirit.

There was a trail of discarded souls emerging along the route of Meg's path through life. Two of those souls, William and Ella, were yet to realise they had been discarded. But there was one more, who was downhearted by her life's sad development.

Part 3

14

Hogmanay, 1889

An hour before midnight on Hogmanay 1889, there was a knock at the door of the Tulloch home, next to "Tulloch's Ironmongery" on Victoria Street in Kirkwall. Christina and Hugh Tulloch would never forget that knock for it changed their lives.

On any other night of the year the Tullochs would be in bed asleep, but it was Hogmanay and traditionally a night for revellers. 'First footers' would be out and about wishing friends and neighbours goodwill for the coming year. And the Tullochs were ready, whisky in the decanter, buttered oatcakes on a truncher, for any well wishers and customers of their Ironmongery. Christina and Hugh looked at one another with slight bewilderment at the sound of the knocking, because first footers always called after midnight.

A first footer, or first person to set foot in the home after midnight on Hogmanay, was traditionally a tall, dark and handsome stranger. A man bearing a gift of coal would be welcomed as this would symbolically ensure prosperity in the forthcoming year. It was believed that this tradition probably dated back to northern ancestors who maintained roaring fires during the shortest days of the winter in order to 'feed' the sun, to make sure of its return and hence their continued survival in the following spring. The fact that the stranger would be more welcome if he were tall and dark may have originated from northern ancestors' dislike of their Norwegian invaders and Vikings of old, who would almost certainly have been blonde or red haired.

Hugh Tulloch wondered if someone was in need of an urgent plumbing supply or some such other remedial device at that time of night. He rose from his armchair and stretched his stiff limbs before descending the flight of stairs to the front door, which was adjacent to the locked and shuttered door to their store. More urgent knocking greeted him. A flurry of hope from the past flitted over his mind....

"I'm coming, I'm coming," he said.

When he opened the door he saw on his doorstep a cloaked female figure, tall and stoutly built. The stranger's anxious face, framed with long flaxen hair, was visible from under her hood. She appeared to be trying to say something but as the wind whistled into the stairwell the partially deaf sixty-year-old shopkeeper found it hard to hear what it was she had to say. The woman smiled, lighting up her face. Hugh was captivated. The wind howled and whipped at the woman's cloak, flapping it against Hugh's legs.

"Who are you and what is it you are wanting, missus?" he said, instantly regretting his curtness.

"Please sir…"

"What's that?" Hugh cupped his hand around his ear as if this would make it easier to hear her.

"I NEED A ROOM, SIR!" the woman raised her voice to a desperate yell, which was heard by the curious Mrs. Tulloch on the landing above. She called down to them.

"For goodness sake, Hugh, will you bring whoever it is up here? – and wish them a Guid New Year, will you! But for pity's sake, shut that door! The draught's biting up here!"

The stranger lifted her head and shook off her heavy hood. Meg Williamson smiled again at Hugh Tulloch, her potential saviour.

"Aye, of course," he said, standing aside. "Come away in and just you follow me."

Christina Tulloch, woman of empathy and foresight, was at the top of the stairs. She listened to the voice inside her head that told her this lovely and distressed stranger was in need of compassion.

"You are welcome, my dear," she said. "You're not a first footer, are you? But come in, come in and have a dram with us. What can we do for you? Hugh, dear, take the lady's cloak."

As Hugh helped Meg take off her cloak, he involuntarily let out a short gasp. Meg's belly was so extended it looked fit to burst. He then realised the woman was not stout but heavily pregnant.

"My, my, that looks like two wee babbies in there!" Christina said, equally taken aback. She was confident in her diagnosis, having seen many a pregnant woman in her time.

Meg looked visibly shocked. The statement immediately explained the increased turmoil in her belly throughout this pregnancy. The presence of twin babies had not occurred to Meg.

Christina and Hugh looked at each other with the telepathic vibe that only couples long married can give. Christina reckoned Meg was about thirty and could scarcely believe that someone this mature would not have given a thought to the fact that the extreme size of her pregnancy might indicate the presence of two babies.

"I'm guessing you're in need of some help?" she said tenderly.

Within minutes of meeting Meg, the Tullochs had presumed this to be a woman in trouble in more ways than one. This newcomer to Kirkwall looked as though her journey there had been arduous; she looked drawn and needy. Christina assumed this was most likely an unwanted pregnancy, no matter if the outcome was single or double.

The kindness radiating from this couple released Meg's tension. The sigh she emitted drained her weary body of the last of its fragile strength. Her head swam just before she slithered to the floor in faint.

After more than a decade of unsettled living, emotional heartache and misuse, Meg just couldn't take any more. The shame of her ignored and unsupported third pregnancy left her in more dire straits than ever before. She had resolved to leave Black Bull Farm forever. Her lover had proved to be full of empty promises and her own duplicity sapped her self-esteem.

Looking back on why things had gone so wrong Meg's memory rested on her idyllic childhood brought abruptly to an end by the death of her father. Then she was made more vulnerable in her isolated independent life at Black Bull Farm and firmly grasped, and held onto the first chance of affection offered to her. There followed the whirlwind excitement of first love, the thrill of desire, the irrepressible feeling of being adored. But these soon began to erode into the slow decline that brought her to this present desperate plight. The illicit nature of her life style meant that she had to put a distance between herself and her mother, her family, her own offspring. She had to shut the door to a previous life. With hindsight, she knew her passionate love affair had been doomed from the start.

To discover that she was pregnant with twins was too much to bear. Twice she had endured the agony of sending away one baby then another, forced under strict instructions from her paramour. At the time she thought it was best for them all. It was best for her merrybegotten children not to know their mother. They could never understand the miscarriages of justice, the misguided trust that ruled her life. Meg knew that in Westray she was probably regarded as a miscreant, because she had never tried to explain, not even to her beloved mother. But it was he who was the wrongdoer.

She was weary and weakened by all the pain and shame. It made Meg weep to think of what Hellen had gone through for her sake, or what Hellen must think of her once bright, youngest daughter. One day she hoped to somehow be able to set her wrongs right. But in the past week any hopes and dreams had been dashed – by the true bastard who created a fallen woman and now four bastard souls.

Meeting with the Tullochs had been sheer chance. Arriving into Kirkwall harbour by ferry, Meg had been frozen with fear of the unknown and panic at the unborn within her. She was at her lowest ebb yet holding out for a new start. She had enquired about rooms to rent and a lady had recommended the Tullochs. They usually had a room to let, she said.

For Meg, the first few days of 1890 went by in a haze. After collapsing with relief in the apparent safe haven of the Tulloch's home, she found that all she wanted to do was sleep. When she awoke she was at first unsure of her whereabouts. She had been dreaming that she was a child again, wrapped in a warm blanket and lying in the heather on a summer's evening on Fair Isle. She felt the years roll back, the weariness fall away and the happy, relaxed feelings of childhood return to her.

"Hugh, Hugh!" said a voice in her dream, seemingly on a faraway hillside… "She's waking up, get the tea on!"

Confused, Meg flickeringly opened her eyelids as her dream faded away. The heather turned out to be a purple bedspread and the smell of the outdoors came from freshly laundered linen sheets. The cosy, comfortable feeling of her dream still enveloped her as she recognised the friendly face leaning over her. Christina Tulloch in her excitement had laid down her darning on Meg's whaleback stomach. Both women's sets of eyes were drawn to the darning and to the stomach.

"Oh, I'm sorry, my dear," Christina said, hastily putting the darning on a chair.

"Mrs. Tulloch…" began Meg, apologetically, but Christina Tulloch stopped her in mid sentence.

"Don't you be fretting yourself about anything now, lass. We're taking care of you."

Hugh appeared in the bedroom doorway carrying a tray. He smiled at Meg and said, "Ah, that's better!" as he set the tray down on a bedside table. Meg could see he had boiled an egg for her and made little toast 'soldiers'. Also on the tray was a steaming pot of tea and three delicate china cups and saucers with silver teaspoons.

"Really, you're…too kind," she said weakly.

"Nonsense!" said the Tullochs in unison.

Hugh poured them all a cup of tea while Christina helped Meg to sit up in bed on propped pillows. Glancing down at herself, Meg noticed she was wearing a man's over-sized and collarless shirt.

"My nightshirts were too small for you," Christina said in way of explanation.

Meg knew that the kindly Tullochs would be in need of an explanation soon, but what could she say that would ever make them accept her? Christina picked up the telepathic vibes.

"We'll just be here to help you, my dear. Don't go bothering about talking just yet. You need to build up your strength."

"Thank ye both kindly." Meg quickly blinked her tears away.

The Tullochs made conversation about this and that while Meg ate. She watched them carefully. Meg felt that for some reason these good people genuinely wanted to help her. But she was also aware that her last major character assessment had proved to be, eleven years down the line, very wide of the mark.

Hugh was slightly shorter than his wife and wore small, silver rimmed spectacles. The only hair on his head grew like a high, fluffy white collar, from behind one ear right round the nape of his neck to the other. In the gaslight the top of his head shone as if it had been polished.

Christina Tulloch was wiry and nimble looking. A scarcity of eyelashes and brows created a paleness around her eyes, intensifying the darkness of her brown irises. Her salt and pepper coloured hair was swept up high into a bun set further forward from the crown of her head than was usual. Her face was wrinkled and quite swarthy, like that of a fisherman. The thought of this kind and genteel lady being a fisherman made Meg smile. The Tullochs noticed her smile and asked if was feeling better. She nodded obligingly.

Meg had brought with her very few items of clothing, most of which would not fit a heavily pregnant woman. It was as if she was unprepared for her pregnancy and in a way, denying its existence. Christina borrowed a voluminous skirt and blouse from a stouter friend. The Tullocks noticed that Meg wore no wedding ring, but were determined to ask her no awkward questions. It mattered not to them which of the many islands within the Orkney archipelago she had absconded from, or indeed if she had travelled from further afield as Hugh thought her accent was more like someone from Shetland. The only questions they asked were about how she was feeling or what she would like to eat. They waited for Meg to proffer her history if and when she was inclined.

Their genuine desire to help the woman who had suddenly walked into their lives stemmed from twenty years before when their own daughter had just as suddenly walked out of their lives.

Meg explained how she had come to knock on their particular door. Hugh confirmed that the room they were in was free to let. She gazed around her in wonder at the contents of the room; its high single bed, its own fireplace, armchair, large chest of drawers and small bedside table, tastefully draped with a lacy cloth. It was more like a room in the Laird's Manor House. Daylight flooded the room from a tall window with a view out over the harbour at the back of the Tulloch's property. Christina pulled out the large bottom drawer of the chest and said that if it was pulled out far enough, it could make an ideal crib for the twin babies. A faint grimace flickered across Meg's face at the mention of her babies. Another knowing, yet unknowing, look passed between the long-married couple. The Tullochs believed that Meg had been jilted.

It would make a refreshing change, they said, for Meg to stay with them – *and* her babies when they arrived. The room had previously been let as short-term lodgings for a travelling salesman or apprentice tradesman. Meg's pregnancy, rather than being a hindrance, seemed to be a bonus for the Tullochs. They fervently looked forward to new life in their home. There had not been a baby there for nearly thirty years. Their reassurances eased the seemingly interminable anguish felt by Meg only the day before. Confronted by such optimism and enthusiasm Meg was beginning to smile again. She felt that for her a new life was beginning – simultaneously she felt a tiny limb move as if to remind her of the other new lives about to be born.

There had been no mention of rent and Meg had the impression they were prepared to waive it, but she insisted it would be paid. And sure enough, in her first week with them, the rent money, two months up front, arrived at the local post office for Meg to collect. She gave no explanation to the Tullochs as to where the money had come from and they didn't ask. They presumed the father of her unborn had at least seen fit to send the money. But they presumed wrong. Initially, the Tullochs were left to presume much, as Meg kept her past life sorely embedded within her broken heart. Christina and Hugh curbed their curiosity and happily incorporated their new and mysterious lodger into their lives.

In her time, Christina had delivered four babies for her sisters and neighbours. She said she would be howdie for Meg. Meg relaxed into the comfort of their care, growing happier by the day and, like a united family, they eagerly anticipated the births.

Christina and Hugh shared with Meg their greatest sorrow about the disappearance of their only child, Rebecca, when she was only seventeen. It explained the unquestioning empathy that they felt for Meg and her predicament. Apparently a neighbour had seen their daughter board a ship bound for Canada. Rebecca was never seen again. The year before a man twice her age had struck up a secret romance with Rebecca and when Hugh discovered this he had banned his daughter from seeing the man, who promptly left Kirkwall to work with The Hudson Bay Company in Canada. Rebecca disappeared two months later, without a word as to where or why. Christina said the anguish they had gone through was too terrible to describe. The worst thing was not knowing what had become of Rebecca. They were not even sure whither she had gone to Canada to be with him – or merely in the hopes of finding him. But, to add to their despair, they thought she might have been pregnant, because in the month before she vanished they noticed she had been putting on weight and wearing bulkier clothing. Devastated by the loss of their only daughter in such a worrying manner, they had hoped every day for over twenty years, that the next letter, the next knock on the door, would bring some news. They never got over the fact that their own daughter, once so close to them, could leave them without a word. Their world had been devastated.

Meg could identify with a girl so young, on the brink of womanhood, setting off on the wrong path in life, falling in love with the wrong person and make disastrously wrong decisions. She knew how easily a young girl's life could slip into a muddle, how it might have felt like the end of the world. Rebecca Tulloch's mixed-up, emotional young mind had probably thought this was her only option, to leave her loving family rather than cause them shame, but without realising that in doing what she did she had given a far greater pain to her loving parents.

Meg finally understood how her situation was so poignant to the Tullochs.

15

Twin Arrivals

The Tulloch's Ironmongery was a thriving business. The shop was busy from opening to closing time. At the top of the Ironmongery door was the shop bell, attached by a metal spring, which rang cheerfully every time a customer opened it, therefore it rang twice for every customer, once on entry and again on exit. Meg could hear the tinkle of this bell from the comfort of her new room and it was like music to her ears. In their shop Christina and Hugh were natural genial hosts. They were instinctively helpful people, who over the years had helped to solve many a domestic as well as practical problem for their customers. Occasionally Hugh would catch the ferry to the Scottish mainland and travel on to Edinburgh or Glasgow on business, but generally Christina and Hugh's lives were entwined and they spent most of their time in each other's cheerful company.

Meg's new room was like a miniature paradise of comfort and peace. The view overlooking the harbour fascinated her and she especially enjoyed watching people about their daily chores. Being a country dweller it was a novelty for Meg to see so many people and so much activity taking place in one vista. There were boats sailing in and out of the harbour, fish catches being unloaded onto the quayside and packed into boxes of ice, fish skinning, gutting and curing going on, and people buying and selling fresh seafood. The sea birds in Kirkwall seemed much more forthright than the ones on Westray or Fair Isle. They were continually swooping and squawking, demanding their share of the bounty.

The Tullochs found the prospect of twin babies being born into their home exciting and this helped Meg come to terms with the doubling of her plight. With these new friends on her side she felt rejuvenated. Her initial feelings of gratitude changed to love for the endearing couple. She suddenly had so much love to give. This was the start of a new and better life and she at last felt positive about what the future might hold for her.

She took to knitting gloves and socks to make a small income by selling these to a local shop owner. As a contribution to the Tulloch home, she baked 'mother's recipe' Fair Isle bannocks, which were much appreciated. Most evenings she would join Christina and Hugh in the parlour, where they played rummy or whist. Playing cards held a fascination for Meg, who had rarely before managed to spend leisure time in the company of friends. Other evenings she would continue her unfinished work of the day, knitting socks or gloves for sailors and seafarers, while Christina would sit with her, needles clicking frantically in her hands, knitting bootees and cardigans, layettes and bonnets, all in duplicate, for the anticipated new comers.

At midday Meg made a habit of cooking them all a pot of soup for their midday meal, either using the bones from a Sunday joint or by boiling a variety of fresh vegetables from the market. To any left-over stock she would add a handful of barley or lentils to ring the changes. After she had cleared and cleaned the dishes, Meg liked to walk along the shop fronts and around the harbour if the weather was not too wild. Had it been summer, she would have made a conspicuous sight with her enormously pregnant belly. But in the depths of winter she wrapped herself in Isobella's parting gift, the voluminously flowing cloak, whose ample folds disguised her condition. The draped hood hid her head and face, and made her feel anonymous. She was beginning to walk with the side to side rock that pregnant women often adopt and walking had become a cumbersome task. As her time neared she went out only when necessary. One such time was when she ran out of navy wool on the heel of a sock.

Christina and Hugh were serving customers in the Ironmongery as Meg set off. On the way to the wool shop, she passed a school. It was playtime and the children were out in the schoolyard with skipping ropes or playing hopscotch with chalk and pebbles. The noise level at that end of Victoria Street always increased tenfold at school playtimes. Glancing over at the children, Meg smiled with an aching heart for the memory of her two previous and 'lost' babies, who would now be children, their upbringing and development excluded from her life.

The passion of her illicit love affair had been all consuming. At a very young and vulnerable age she had lost her way and begun a life filled with uncertainties and insecurities. Her babies were merely the natural outcome of their lovemaking. She never meant to cause so much upset to so many lives, not only those of her offspring but of her mother, sister and brother. They had all been forsaken in order to salvage the sanity and sanctity of her lover's legitimate family. All along she had held out in the belief that family life for her, her man and their children would be established – sometime in the not too distant future. After eleven years of broken promises, of plans gone sadly awry, she had finally had the courage, or foolhardiness, to decide her own destiny. Pulling herself out of her naivety, pushing aside her beleaguered and deluded trust, she entered a new and more frightening phase, that of maturity and independence, reversing the bitterness and frustration.

For the two new babies that she carried inside her soon to enter her world, Meg determined she would dedicate herself to their care. They would not be denied her love and she would embrace motherhood at last. By her previous obedience to the demands of her lover she had been denied true motherhood and the upbringing of her existing children. In her naivety she had believed that her family would be united; that this was only temporarily delayed and would be established eventually. But his loyal partner and trusting family would have added a needless four more souls to the hurt list and irrevocable damage to his position in society. With hindsight she saw her own cruelty in this assumption that they might live as a family. Yet hope sprang from her lover's promises and the trust she felt in his good intentions. But when she considered fully their implication, she realised they were based upon the impending death of his wife. There could have been no other way. Therefore, in truth, Meg had been waiting for her to die. Meg shuddered at her own selfishness and duplicity.

Meg's breathing suddenly grew heavier and she was forced to rest on the school wall. She sat awkwardly with her hands under her large belly as if to hold it from falling off her body. She watched the children play as a spasm travelled around her body, making her check her forced exhalation. An uncontrollable urge to bear down came over her. Oh no, she thought, not this quick – not in the schoolyard!

The school bell rang. The noise from the playing children abated as they appeared to be sucked back into the schoolhouse in a long trailing line of little bodies. The yard fell silent, making Meg even more aware of her laboured breathing. She tried to steady it and when she felt somewhat more in control, pushed herself up from her safe perch on the school wall and set off to walk the few hundred yards home. People were walking up and down, on both sides of Victoria Street, but they were all busy with their own thoughts or chatting with fellow walkers. No one noticed her distressed, though controlled, state. And she was in no frame of mind at this stage in her calamitous life to make a fuss or ask for help on a busy main street. She was hoping to keep some anonymity in Kirkwall society, not to put herself into the local newspaper.

Waves of weakness continued to flow over her as she concentrated hard on walking. Instead of entering Tullock's Ironmongery by the back door at the harbour side of the store, Meg took the shorter route through the front door on Victoria Street. Clutching the stair handrail, she managed to climb the high steps. She was flagging by the time she reached the landing and let out a short pant of breath. Women's voices and laughter, along with the clink of china teacups, drifted out from the parlour. Although out of sight, Christina called through the open doorway.

"Is that you, Meg dear? Come away in and meet my friend, Robina. She's the lady who has lent you the clothes...."

The slumping noise of Meg's limp body passing out on the landing arrested Christina in mid speech. The introductions went no further than that moment, which was the second time that Meg had fainted on the Tulloch's landing in as many months.

Robina Williamson was an aunt of Meg's, but as the introductions on the landing had been one sided due to nature and circumstances beyond anyone's control, this was a fact that neither Meg nor Robina would realise till much later.

Before the bell tolled to announce the end of the school day,

Meg was delivered of two protesting boy babies, twenty minutes apart. Christina and Robina were howdies at the births. Robina was a large, loud spoken, rosy-cheeked woman, a complete contrast to Christina, but obviously a close friend.

"Aren't dey bonnie wee laddies?" said Robina in booming tones.

The newcomers replied to her decibels with hearty decibels of their own, wailing with scrunched up faces that made them both look anything but bonnie. Having lost two offspring, who led their lives quite separate from hers, Meg felt blessed and at last had the chance to mother her babies from their very beginnings of life. She longed to be a good mother.

Christina and Robina handed a baby apiece to Meg, each boy carefully cleaned and firmly swaddled in sparkling white wincyette sheeting. They lay peacefully in the crooks of Meg's elbows and she cradled them in her overwhelming love. The howdies surveyed the scene with admiration and pleasure. Later, they were both to agree that Meg looked innocent and vulnerable at that moment even at that advanced child bearing age.

Gazing at her children, Meg felt fulfilled at last, contented and purposeful with a job to do in bringing up these adorable babies. This was a comforting, calming thought. She would not be sending them away to a better life than she could offer. There was no better life for these two. The upbringing Meg would give them would have to do, but she was determined to do her utmost for them.

Even if she had wanted to send them away from her, Hellen would have been too old to take care of twin babies. Meg's heart ached when she thought about her estrangement from her mother. The only consolation was that those dearest to her heart were living together. She wanted no one to know where she was living – with the exception of Isobella. Meg was unaware that one other person knew of her evacuation to Kirkwall. She was also wrong in her assumption that William and Ella were still living at Rabbitha' with Hellen, John, Agnes and their Harcus cousins.

"What will you call your sons, Meg?" asked Christina, still basking in the glory of the successful double delivery.

Meg smiled on hearing the words 'your sons'. She pondered on this question while Christina and Robina, fussed over the babies, taking them for cuddles and handing Meg cups of tea and gammon sandwiches to build up her strength. When all was clean and suitable for visitors, Hugh was allowed to visit the birthing room, as if he had been the expectant father. Meg was touched by everyone's obvious happiness.

With the adult chatter and the babies snuffly noises drifting in and out of Meg's subconscious, she delved dreamily into her far off memories, where Hellen and Andrew and Agnes and John appeared to her. Should she name her sons after her father and after her brother perhaps? But what did John think of her after all the heartache she had bestowed upon them all? Would her father, were he alive to know, not feel equally let down? John might be angry if he were to know she had used his name for one of her illegitimate children. The same applied to the memory of her father. She became too tired to think. There was no rush to name them. That would have to wait...

It had not occurred to Meg, being somewhat preoccupied in having her babies, that Christina's friend had the same name as her deceased father's sister-in-law. She had forgotten that Will and Robina Williamson lived in Kirkwall. Meg had no memory of her aunt, but her uncle Will had come to attend Andrew's funeral on Westray when Meg had been twelve years old. As she began to breastfeed her little ones, one under each arm, a panic arose in Meg. The notion crossed her mind that this rousing, cheery woman named Robina could be her aunt. If this was so, her aunt had unwittingly helped to deliver her own great nephews.

Fear of discovery gripped at Meg's already spasmodic stomach. The desire to keep her mystery could be shattered all too soon if this proved to be correct. She contemplated the name Robina. It was not a common name and this lady was about the right age to be her aunt. Listening more carefully to what Christina and Meg were saying, Meg tried to catch any mention of the name of Robina's husband for verification. But, their conversation revolved solely around babies and previous deliveries attended.

That evening Hugh produced his special, dust-covered bottle of celebration whisky from the far recesses of their sideboard. Pouring a glass for each of them, he proposed a toast:

"Here's tae us, an' wha's like us.
Gey few, an' they're a' deid – mair's the pity!"

They were soon all a trifle tiddly, except Meg, who was determined to keep control of all future aspects of her life, including her sobriety. Robina, amidst spurts of merriment, tried to string her words together coherently to announce that she would have to return home to her husband.

"Will will – oh, ha ha! Will will be….ha! He'll be waiting fur me, will Will!" she guffawed.

Fuelled by the whisky, Robina and Christina were convulsed with girlie laughter. Hugh's laughter was confined to creasing up his face and displaying his letterbox, open-mouthed smile, whilst his shoulders heaved up and down in silent, uncontrollable mirth. Meg was entranced by the scene and abandoned herself to her own irrepressible laughter.

Meg had noted the mention of the name Will, even disguised in drunken laughter. It was her uncle's name and enough to convince Meg that this large lady could indeed be her Aunt Robina, wife of Will Williamson. The last time Robina had seen Meg was thirty years before, when she was a babe in Hellen's arms. There was no chance that either woman would recognise the other. Surnames had not been necessary in Meg's new life in Kirkwall and she resolved to keep hers unmentioned for as long as possible, wishing dearly to erase her troubled and shameful past and not to spoil this chance of a new beginning.

Meg's desire to keep her possible relationship with this jolly woman hidden marred the moment and made her feel uncomfortably guilty. But she reasoned that she still could not be positive that this was indeed her aunt; this lady swaying gently before her on her large and inebriated legs, only hours after delivering her own great nephews though oblivious to that fact – oblivious to any fact at that particular time. Besides, Robina was in no fit state to retain any serious information in her present state. So Meg merely offered her profuse thanks, adding that, had the babies been girls, she would most definitely have named them Christina and Robina. This simple statement caused such utter delight amidst the already delighted gathering that Meg was also overwhelmed. The three women howled and cried with joy, dabbing at their eyes with the first piece of material they could get hold of, which in Christina's case, was her husband's woollen scarf. Meg marvelled at the ease in which she had managed to spread happiness to people close to her – sharp contrast to her previously misplaced deeds.

Only recently had she become aware that, during her years at Black Bull Farm, she had spread nothing but unhappiness. Blinded by her love and the vain dreams of a future full of promise, it had taken her so many years to find her own mind, to grow wise and emerge from her fantasy to face reality. The glaring hopelessness of her aspirations had not been obvious to her at the time, caught as she was in a bubble of cherished ecstasy in which she naively believed she shared with her loved one. Yet he had drifted in and out of her life at his own discretion and it was only in hindsight that this harsh yet deniable truth gingerly arose to the surface of her clearer conscience. This conclusion was only initiated with the waning of her obsession.

The dark shadow of hurt and pain that followed her, the unsaid trauma caused by abandoning her first children, still overcame her at times. The realisation of her misdeeds, her wrong decisions, were only recently becoming apparent to her. And now, for the first time in years, she was able to convey at last, to her friends and the people that mattered to her a sense of joy. She knew she must have hurt and denied love to many of those close to her, but she had not yet given up hope of redeeming this at some point and in some way in the near future. It pleased her that she was also capable of spreading joy.

On the day of her twin sons' births, Meg felt as close to the Tullochs as she did to any of her blood family; the family banished to her past until she felt strong about her future. She felt no shame with the Tullochs, who were, as yet, oblivious of her murky past. Under the caring and attentive eyes of her new guardians, these surrogate grandparents, Meg's little family flourished and a happy year passed by, as they remained in their lodgings above Tulloch's Ironmongery in Victoria Street.

16

Uprooted

Months passed at Rabbitha' without word from Meg. Agnes wrote to Black Bull Farm but got no reply. The older Hellen grew, the less judgmental or sentimental she became. Besides, her days were too busily occupied with bringing up the next generation to sit around debating the whys and wherefores. If any harm had befallen Meg the island grapevine would have secreted the news to their door, Hellen had no doubt of that. She was left to presume that Meg was fully occupied with her independent life. William and Ella were the light of her life now. They had given her purpose and hope after the emptiness left by the loss of Andrew. They had given her happiness. And therefore it had been Meg who, albeit inadvertently, had bestowed this happiness on Hellen. Hellen would fulfil her part by bringing up her grandchildren and continue to hope that whatever circumstances Meg found herself to be in would one day be made clear to Hellen. It was obvious that William and Ella had the same father because they looked so alike. "Twa peas in a pod," Agnes said. This fact was a blessing to Hellen for she took it to mean that Meg was not being promiscuous, that these two children at least had the same father, hopefully one that Meg had loved.

The fact that a mother had lost touch with a daughter was not unusual in those times. Hellen seldom heard from Barbara about her busy life in Germany. It was not unusual for illegitimate children to be looked after by other family members, but illegitimacy was considered shameful. What was unusual was the mysterious lack of detail as to the circumstances of Meg's life at Black Bull Farm and Meg's insistence on secrecy. What was also unusual was Meg's abandonment of her own babies, coupled with the shunning of her family. Hellen had her own beliefs on what was going on, but would not want to divulge these thoughts to anyone. She would wait until she met with Meg again, never losing hope that this would occur one day.

With most families having many children it was often a relief for the breadwinner to see them, one by one, leave to find their own livelihoods. If the evacuee moved far from home, it would be difficult to stay in touch. Emigration to all parts of the globe was common practice amongst both the younger and the older generations, all in the search for a better lifestyle. Meg was in charge of her own destiny. The physical distance between their two dwellings precluded regular visits to Rabbitha'. Besides, Hellen had promised to bring up Meg's bonnie children and Meg wanted it that way. It would be confusing for William and Ella to think they belonged to an absent mother. Better as it was. Hellen frequently went over these musings in her mind and always came to the same conclusion. Then she would nod her head positively as if to close the matter and rock gently in Barbara Brown's rocker for those thoughts only came to her when she sat there.

Friday, a cold and still Friday in January: the day that one cataclysmic confrontation would prove to change the destinies of three members of the Williamson family.

William, Ella and the older Harcus children were expected home from school and Hellen was sitting in her wicker chair next to the fire, peeling potatoes for the family supper. She was imagining what they would all get up to the next day with no school to attend. Enough snow had fallen for the children to build snowmen and throw snowballs. As she smiled at the thought of the fun they would have, her reverie was broken by the distant sound of a child's high-pitched sobs. The smile froze to a grimace on Hellen's face.

Ella's sobs could be heard long before she reached the sanctity of Rabbitha'. Due to the gently falling snow, the air was still and quiet. The noise of her sobs drifted up the hillside from the track below Rapness Farm. It was too early for the normal school finishing time and a chill ran down Hellen's spine. She had an intense feeling of foreboding.

Lifting the enamel bowl from her lap and setting it down on the table, she slipped on her cloak and hurried outside. Far down the track in the distance, she spotted Ella's dishevelled figure, contrasted by its darkness against the bright covering of snow. The child wove a weary path from side to side, sobbing as she ran. Tears were blurring her vision and she tumbled into a heap on a drift of snow at the side of the track, burying her face in her skirt. Hellen hurried down the track towards her, calling out for John. He soon appeared and overtook Hellen along the track. Scooping Ella up from the snow and into his comforting arms, he carried her up the hill to Rabbitha'.

"Wha's de matter, pet lamb?" Hellen asked gently, after they had settled her into the big chair by the fire.

Ella was too out of breath and sob-worn to give any immediate explanation. She managed to calm herself only to suddenly grab hold of John's wrist and start pleading with him to find William.

"Save him from de big boys!" she shrieked.

There began a frantic and garbled story about big boys at the school persistently taunting William with nasty sounding words, shouting "yer midder was a pros-pert-stewit" or was it a "pro-post-thru-toot", she said. And they said that William and Ella were "bast-ter-hards". Ella was only nine. Their offensive sounding language shocked her, but the true meaning of the words from Ella's interpretation was fairly clear to Hellen. She put her hand across her own mouth to stop from cussing.

Ella continued, constantly wiping her streaming eyes and nose with her sleeve. She said that William had become furious, that she'd never seen him so angry. He "thwhacked dem big boys hard", she said there had been three of them and that William was "clarted in blood". Hellen and John looked at each other, knowing the collapse of the family pact was imminent as the situation turned ugly. John left immediately to fetch William from school. But William was nearly home, limping and with his arms draped over the shoulders of Agnes's twin sons, James and George.

William's teacher had not witnessed the start of the argument and knew only that William had lashed out at these boys, causing many cuts, bruises and black eyes. He had been sent home in disgrace. The splattered blood that "clarted" William was mostly the blood of the other boys. The anger William had unleashed that day reverberated on the whole family and Hellen expected some raging parents to appear on their doorstep.

But the neighbours stayed away. The expected irate knocking on the door did not materialise. Hellen believed her family was probably in disgrace and knew the time had come to make decisions. It could only get worse. The unanswerable questions would soon be asked. She made a determined decision to take William and Ella away from Rabbitha' for a time, before the tarred brush of shame ran over Agnes and her family, too. An explanation to William and Ella would follow in due course.

In the evening, during a discussion with Agnes, Hellen said she had decided to visit Uncle Will and Aunt Robina in Kirkwall. In an old letter from them, they had asked her to visit them. The last time she saw Will was at Andrew's funeral. She had not seen Robina for many a year. Will and Robina didn't know young William and Ella existed.

Agnes accepted Hellen's plan readily as she was getting to the end of her tether concerning her mother's lack of commitment to giving an explanation to William and Ella. She had been kind to Hellen's reasoning over the years as she knew the hurt it caused.

Hellen lost no more time and wrote a hurried letter to Will and Robina, hoping they were well, that they were enjoying their retirement from sea faring, and asking after Bethia, the only remaining daughter living at home with them. Bethia would be nearly forty and still unmarried. It was by now very unlikely that she ever would marry. At one time Hellen believed that the family had moved to the town in hopes of finding a suitor for Bethia. She was a big handsome lass, though truculent. She was disapproving of just about every man she ever met. Barbara Brown used to say this was because, in an accident as a baby, Bethia had been dropped on her head by one of her brothers. They said she had never forgotten this trauma and had developed an unreasonable resentment towards all males. Barbara, as her grandmother, had been in the room at the time, but had not managed to save Bethia from a nasty gash on her forehead. The scar was always visible, always reminding. Bethia's aversion to men made it a thankless task for her parents to find suitors for her, but they never gave up trying to play matchmakers.

In her letter Hellen announced to Will and Robina she would be coming to stay a while and hoped this would be convenient. She decided not to mention the existence of William or Ella just yet or to say that she intended her visit to be fairly permanent, a plan she also withheld from Agnes. Hellen had never been to Kirkwall, but felt sure that it would not be too difficult, with the help of Will and Robina, to find accommodation and she would take up hosiery knitting, like most other widows. She amazed herself at how resourceful she could be, even as an old woman in her late sixties.

Hellen, William and Ella all slept badly that night. By morning, William was still hurting, both physically and mentally, from the fight with the four bigger boys. Questions began to loom up at the back of his mind and he carefully tried to think them through before asking Hellen. He was troubled by the fact that there had been no scolding for his outrageous outburst. Both Hellen and his schoolmaster would know his violent actions were out of character and surely understood that he had been severely provoked, yet William felt there was something mysterious in their acceptance of his reaction, something hidden from his understanding. He wanted to know what it was.

By the following daybreak Hellen had decided they should leave as soon as possible and had started to pack some meagre belongings. It was then that Anderina walked into the yard. The night before, Angus Dearness, the schoolmaster, had come to supper at Ness Farm and she'd heard all about William's fracas at school. Angus had told Anderina that a relative of his, a man called Gideon McLeod, who was an elderly lighthouse keeper on the island of Sanday, was looking for an assistant to train for the eventual post of lighthouse operator. Gideon and his wife lived in the lighthouse and had done so all of their married lives. They had raised five children there, all of whom had grown and flown their nest. None of their sons had wanted to take over as keeper of the lighthouse. Although Gideon felt he was becoming too old for the work and less agile for tackling all those spiralling steps every day, he was loath to leave because it would mean giving up their home in the lighthouse. All he needed for the time being was someone willing to help and to be trained. The pay was low, but board and lodgings were offered free.

Although William was still young for such a position, Angus Dearness had recommended William apply for the post. Anderina felt this was an opportunity not to be missed and Hellen agreed. This job would help him out of this predicament by removing him from the scene of possible future conflict. William needed space, independence, and time to find himself.

They told William. The thought of manning a lighthouse instantly appealed to him. He had never wanted to be a fisherman and there weren't many other alternatives on Westray. Anderina explained that Sanday Lighthouse was stuck out on the most eastern tip of the most eastern island of the Orkney group and could only be accessed at low tide. But this only made William more attracted to the idea. She told him the Laird of Sanday kept many fine horses in his stables and William might have the chance to exercise them sometimes. A chance to learn how to ride a horse added to William's enthusiasm. Hellen was pleased to hear that the position also entailed regular trips to Kirkwall for supplies for the McLeods.

As his bag was already packed and ready, Anderina said she could accompany William to Sanday as she had a day free from work at Ness Farm and had already arranged for Sinclair Wilson to take them there in his yawl. Angus Dearness was confident the McLeods would welcome William, believing him to be a personable and honest boy, eager to learn.

As William walked down the track with Anderina, followed by a convoy of kittens, he looked back and waved to Hellen and Ella. It was then he realised it would be a while before he had a chance to talk to Hellen again. His question would have to wait. Hellen promised to visit him as soon as they could.

The snow had stopped falling but the day was bitter with cold. Hellen and Ella took the ferry to Kirkwall and, in a mailbag on the same ferry, was the letter that Hellen had written to Will and Robina the previous night. She knew they would arrive before the letter and that their visit would therefore be unexpected.

The sea was choppy and Ella was seasick. It was the most

146

confusing day she had ever experienced. Her brother's fight had begun an incomprehensible chain of events, leaving not only her stomach churning with the novelty of sea crossing, but also her head spinning with uncertainty. She wasn't sure what was going on. All in one morning, she had been told they were going to Kirkwall that very day, but no one had got around to telling her why or for how long. Then William was all too suddenly given a job and apparently extradited. Ella determined to hold onto Hellen's hand tightly in case she, too, was whisked away.

Ella had never travelled anywhere out of Westray. She had never set foot on a ferryboat or been to a town. When they at last entered the harbour at Kirkwall, Ella was amazed to see so many houses crammed together in one area, and with so many people moving out and about. The gannets swooping overhead looked the same as the ones that nested on the cliff faces at Westray, but they seemed louder and bolder.

Hellen and Ella left the ferry carrying their few belongings and clothes in a carpetbag as they ventured along the streets of Kirkwall. The town had two main streets running parallel to one another along the back of the harbour. This made it easier to locate Will and Robina's home, number seventy Victoria Street. As they stood on the front step waiting for a reply to Hellen's knock on the door, the biggest door Ella had ever seen, Hellen noted that the house number embossed on the bold brass plate was nearly the same as that of her age. She felt very old that day.

Looking sweet and pretty in her best Fair Isle sweater and red tartan skirt under her Sunday best woollen cape, Ella felt anticipation rising within her. The door was answered by a large, rosy-cheeked woman, who appeared to tower over the two dainty figures of Hellen and Ella standing on the step below her. Her large and cheery face was thinly framed by a frizz of grey hair, tied half-heartedly into a bun at the top of her head. Ella was fascinated and her eyes opened wide as if trying to take her all in.

"Hellen!" Robina boomed her greeting and flung her arms wide in welcome.

"Robina, you do look well!" The very largeness and loudness of this woman swamped Hellen's small frame and soft voice.

Robina was delighted to see Hellen and gave her a crushing hug. Ella was then introduced. She had never been introduced to anyone before. Introductions were unnecessary in Westray, where everyone knew each other. Everyone there had known Ella since she was a baby. Hellen spoke in a soft, almost incoherent voice, saying, "This is Ella, one of my granddaughters…" Her words trailed off at the end.

Robina made an instant fuss saying how bonnie a wee lassie she was, and what a braw jumper, and did yer grannie knit it, she asked. Hellen said no, no, and tried to change the subject of relationships by asking how they all were, are you well, Robina? Och, we're fine, all the better for seeing you.

Hellen had not been quite quick enough.

She pinned her hopes on the fact that Ella was still too young to pick up on everything said in adult conversation. But a sense of bewilderment crept over Ella. Robina presumed Ella was one of Agnes's many offspring and asked no more questions. But questions were bubbling up inside Ella. In the confusion of meeting a new and fascinating person, she was not initially sure she had heard correctly the words that had been said. She kept smiling sweetly at Robina until the old aunt turned her back on them to lead them upstairs. As they followed behind, Ella looked up at her 'mother', feeling disorientated. She couldn't believe that Hellen could tell Aunt Robina a lie – for Ella was now positive that Hellen had said 'granddaughter' when she should have said 'daughter'.

Hellen eyes were firmly directed forwards and upwards to the top of the staircase without a side-ways glance to Ella. This only added to Ella's feeling of unease. It was a short flight of steps, not long enough for Ella to collect her wits. At the top, her confusion was squashed into the recesses of her mind because there were more people to meet and introductions to be made. Uncle Will was sitting by a roaring fireplace, which had a carved wooden frame around it and a mantle shelf across the top on which stood some delicate china ornaments. Will stood up and shook her tiny hand in his enormous one. He, too, was a towering specimen of mankind who dwarfed the newcomers. To Ella, his shoulders seemed to be as broad as the fireplace and his full head of thick black hair sprouted from his head like that of a Troll's. A similar, slightly smaller female version of this Troll was introduced to them as Bethia, their daughter. The talk back and forth between the adults and all their joviality seemed muffled and distant to Ella's ears. It was as if Ella was watching and listening from under water. Robina was patting Hellen on the back and saying things like, 'My, my, such a long time since we've seen you, you haven't changed a bit, no, only a few more wrinkles!'

Ella's head began to swim until uncle Will roared, "Get the lass a glass of ginger beer, Bethia – she's as white as a sheet!"

After being fussed over and getting to sip the most amazingly sharp and spicey drink that she had ever experienced, Ella was tucked into a cosy, cushion-covered wicker chair by the fireside with a buttered oatcake to nibble. The chair was child-sized.

"When I was your age, Ella, that was my chair," said Bethia, putting her large smiling face close up to Ella's, completely blocking out the heat from the fire.

Ella wondered how this huge person had ever been small enough to fit into it. The rest of the evening was spent in exchanges of news and in making plans. It was decided they could sleep in Bethia's room for that night and Bethia would sleep on the sofa in the living room. That was what she always did when they had visitors and it was no trouble, they said. Ella had never seen a living room before and wondered what 'lived' there. She only knew the But and Ben style of homes, like Rabbitha' in the countryside. The town houses were very different, built sometimes above shops and joined on to other homes. They talked of getting rooms and Ella had no idea what rooms were. But, Ben or Byre was the extent of her vocabulary concerning internal housing.

That night the moment Ella's head touched the pillow, she fell asleep and although she slept fitfully, by the morning she felt refreshed. Waking with the sun's rays warming her cheek as it shone through the thin gauze curtains in Bethia's bedroom, she accepted that a new and exciting world was opening up to her. Hellen was still asleep when Ella crept out of bed to look out of the window, where she saw the hustle and bustle of harbour life; fishermen on their boats preparing for a day's sailing and sea birds squawking their continuous and unmistakable demand for food. This was the back of number seventy Victoria Street. Will and Robina's home was one flight of steps up from the main street, above the shops but it also had this view of the harbour from the back of the house. Ella found this all fascinating and longed to go out with her mother to explore. Doubts and confusion of the day before melted away in her mind, buried deep underneath a flurry of excited thoughts of this new adventure. She was only sorry that William was not there to share it with them.

17

Kirkwall and Sanday Island

As they sat by the peat burning fire Hellen told Will and Robina that she intended to stay in Kirkwall for the time being, explaining that Rabbitha' was somewhat overcrowded and Agnes had her hands full with a new baby. Perhaps, she said, when the older children moved out to start work elsewhere, she and Ella would return. Will and Robina happily accepted this reasoning and as they knew every shop owner, landlord and resident of Victoria Street, they were in an excellent position to help Hellen find a place to live. They all agreed Ella should start school as soon as possible. Hellen determined to make an income from knitting stockings like Robina. Good money could be made from knitting, especially for fast and prolific knitters and Hellen would join the body of knitters who normally congregated most days in Robina's parlour. It was a pleasant way to earn money, chatting ceaselessly to other women as many pairs of knitting needles clicked away furiously. Although she settled quickly and took very nicely to town dwelling, Hellen's days were filled with thoughts on how the rest of her separated family was faring. She had resigned herself that she would always be left to think heavily and wearily about Meg. What had become of her? The rest of the Williamson family had washed their hands of Meg because she'd abandoned her fatherless bairns and because of her treatment of their mother. Only a mother could still accept the unacceptable. Hellen despaired at the strange and secretive life her youngest daughter had chosen to lead – or had she chosen this route? Would she ever know? Since leaving Quoylet, Meg had apparently not been willing to share her new life with her family. She had left home at not much older than a child, to live an independent life. And Hellen, as a mother having already brought up her family, was back rearing her daughter's two children as her own. Her strength and energy for such a task was waning. Hellen felt old and was old, with her heart continually aching because she was being denied access to Meg's segregated life.

When Ella overheard the fireside conversation she again felt bewildered, panicked. Everything was moving too fast for her. She longed to see her brother again. She wanted to know what he was doing. This was the first time in her life she had been parted from him. And she kept overhearing Hellen saying things too difficult for her to understand.

On the second day in Kirkwall, Will found two rooms with small kitchen to rent with immediate availability in lodgings at the far end of Victoria Street. They would still have a view of the harbour area. Ella loved the harbour and Hellen promised that they would go walking there every day. When they had settled in the first thing Hellen did was to write William a short letter, her command of the written word having improved with age. She told him about Kirkwall, gave him their new address and asked him to write back with news about his new job.

Ella started her new school, which was only a ten-minute walk from her new home. A bright little girl of the same age, who had thick wavy red hair clipped back at the sides with tartan ribbons, seemed very pleased that Ella had joined the school and smiled continually at her during lessons. When the bell rang for playtime the girl linked arms with Ella and led her out to the schoolyard. Her name was Georgina, known to everyone as Gina, and her father, George, was a ferryboat man. When Ella heard this it gave her an idea. A plan to see William was hatched between the two new friends. Gina was to ask her father to take them to Sanday island with Hellen the following Saturday. With this adventure planned the start of a life-long friendship between the two girls was cemented.

Anderina sent word that the McLeods had welcomed William at the lighthouse, but no news arrived from Sanday. Hellen wondered if he was enjoying his new occupation and if the McLeods were looking after him as she would like.

On collecting Ella from her first day at her new school, Hellen was relieved to find her happily smiling and in the company of a new friend. Ella excitedly explained their plan for the following Saturday and Hellen thought it a very good idea. As she was still unused to travelling as a lone adult, it suited her well to know that Gina's father would be there to guide them on the ferry trip. The only two journeys that Hellen had made in her entire life were from Fair Isle to Orkney with Andrew and their young family and, more recently with Ella to Kirkwall. She made a mental note to buy supplies of items she knew William would like to eat and to bake some fresh bannocks.

Very early on Saturday morning, Hellen and Ella met Gina on the quayside next to the ferry stance. Gina was a spirited yet respectful child and the two wee girls giggled and talked continually. Ella was happier than Hellen had seen her for a long time since Gina had taken her under her wing, proving to be a good distraction for Ella's recent doubts. A tall older man with a beard was introduced by Gina as George Rendall, her father and ferryboat man. Apart from Will, George was the only man Hellen had conversation with since arriving in Kirkwall. She had spoken briefly to shop owners when buying food supplies or wool for her knitting work, but as for real conversations with members of the opposite sex of her generation, those had been sadly lacking since the death of Andrew. George Rendall was easy listening and very knowledgeable on subjects about nature, such as the tides, the islands and the wildlife. He pointed out to Gina and Ella where the puffins nested on some of the island cliffs and where the seals swam. The weather was sunny and breezy and the clear skies gave them excellent views of some of the other Orkney Islands as they passed by. The ferry sailed between Gairsay and Shapinsay and they could also see the small islands of Wyre and Egilsay. The jagged inlets of the island of Stronsay lay off to the starboard side with Eday opposite. The long and straggling island of Sanday loomed directly ahead of them, ten miles or so of inlets and sandy bays with the lighthouse situated at Start Point, on the far east of the island. This was the most easterly point of all the Orkney Islands and an obvious choice for a beacon to be built to warn night-travelling ships of the existence of its jagged rocky coastlines.

As George told them about the history behind this lighthouse, several of the near standing fellow voyagers on the ferry listened in. He said the original tower had been erected in 1802. Four years later the first revolving light in Scotland was fitted by the famous Scottish engineer, Robert Stevenson, who died in 1850, the very year his grandson, Robert Louis Stevenson, the Scottish writer, was born. The tower had also been visited by Sir Walter Scott. Rebuilt just over twenty years before William's arrival on Sanday, it was now painted annually with distinctive vertical black and white stripes, making an eye-catching sight for seafarers.

Start Point was right at the opposite end to the regular terminal, so George said he would set them down at an alternative pier, Kettletoft Jetty. George's elder brother and wife happened to live on Sanday and he had arranged for them to meet the ferry and then take the visitors by horse and cart up to Sanday lighthouse, which could only be accessed at low tide. George warned them to take heed of local advice to avoid being stranded on the rock overnight. William would keep them right. Ella and Gina were thrilled at how their adventure was turning out.

As they approached the island of Sanday, they could see the horse and cart and George's elder brother and his wife waiting on the jetty. The ferry only stopped at Sanday on special request and Hellen agreed with George a time when he should collect them. Gina and Ella skipped on ahead as Hellen paused to wave back at George. She hadn't felt so good in herself for a long time.

William had just finished polishing the brass instruments at the top of the lighthouse when he noticed the horse and cart with five occupants approaching the rock at the low tide mark. Visitors to the lighthouse were a rare occurrence and his curiosity made him walk round for the best vantage point. With a strong feeling of being in control, of being trusted and able for the job, William Williamson felt he was now 'master of all he surveyed,' the phrase his grandmother, Barbara Brown, used many years before when describing the pompous-looking Laird of Westray on his annual visit to Quoylet. However, William was still unaware that Barbara had actually been his great grandmother. When in charge of the lighthouse beacon, he liked to imagine himself as important a person as the Laird, never for a moment realising his close connection. Whenever William thought of a Laird, he would imagine in his mind's eye, a big man, with his nose in the air, sitting imposingly astride a high horse. The height of the lighthouse gave William this feeling of pomp and grandeur, which was lacking in life at ground level. Mr. and Mrs. McLeod were the only other residents on the rock and were often away travelling, a new pastime they had discovered since William had taken over most of the duties and he was often left in charge. Gideon McLeod had taught him much about reading signs to indicate a change in the weather and that the duties of a keeper were most crucial during the hours of darkness.

William recognised two of the visitors before they spotted him. When Hellen and Ella did look up to the top rail of the lighthouse, they caught sight of what appeared to be a wild, wind blown creature attempting to flap its wings. William was waving his arms madly over his head to attract their attention and the strength of the winds at the top of the lighthouse was sending his hair into a frenzy around his face. Welcoming shouts were lost to the ear, gobbled up by the elements in the volume of noise all around them, the howling winds, the waves crashing over the rocks.

The Rendalls bade them goodbye after making arrangements for their subsequent collection in time to catch George's return ferry to Kirkwall. By the time Hellen, Ella and Gina reached the foot of the lighthouse William had descended the long, internal, spiral staircase and appeared through the smartly painted red door at the base of the tower. Hellen noted that he looked well fed and certainly in happier frame of mind than at their parting on Westray.

The day passed happily for the girls, who spent most of their time climbing rocks, playing in rock pools, chasing seabirds or watching seals from the top of the lighthouse. Hellen and William took windswept walks around the tower and sat drinking tea at the McLeod's kitchen table. They talked about what had been happening to them both since leaving Rabbitha'. Hellen was impressed by how he had grown in maturity in the short time they had been apart and felt that she was now talking to William, the young man. Time had moved on. His job seemed to be a success. Many times throughout the afternoon, however, William reverted to his rascal self of old, playing pranks on his sister and her friend, showing off and making them laugh.

The McLeods made a brief appearance descending by the spiral staircase from their sitting room on the floor above the kitchen. They were a very together couple, seemingly not prone to idle chat. They didn't strike Hellen as being particularly sociable people, which would have stood them in good stead for living their life in isolation and cutting themselves off from any kind of society to man a lighthouse on an uninhabited rock only accessible at low tide. They said how pleased they were to have William working with them, that he had proved to be hard working and a most capable lighthouse operator, even at his young age. Their confidence in him added to his maturing process. Hellen beamed with pride as they casually sang his praises.

The basket of groceries and useful items that Hellen had brought for William were gratefully accepted, including the writing paper and envelopes, which were already written with Hellen and Ella's new address in Kirkwall and stamped ready for posting back to them. She wanted him to be able to contact her if needs arose. He told her about how he had met up with the Laird of Sanday's stable lads, some of whom were about his age. These boys didn't ask questions about his past. They lived for the present. They took him exploring and let him exercise some of their horses. When with these boys, William had seen the ruins of Pictish and Viking settlements and burial grounds, which were dotted all over the island. He had seen Quoy Banks, the site of ancient Viking boat burials, where many Viking relics had been found and carefully looked after in a nearby croft. A plan was made for William's forthcoming birthday when Hellen suggested he take a trip to Kirkwall for the day. She and Ella would show him around, he could meet Uncle Will and Aunt Robina and he would experience a bit of the hustle and bustle of town life. William promised to arrange the day off work.

It was Gina who espied the Rendalls returning with their horse and cart to collect the visitors from Kirkwall before the tide cut them off. Hellen could see that they would have to leave right away.

All afternoon William's dark thoughts, which needed dispelling, the questions grown from seeds of his boyhood, lurked fleetingly at the back of his mind. But he couldn't bring himself to confront the closest person in his world with the inner awkwardness he felt, for fear that he might forever ruin their treasured relationship. For fear his words might come across as accusations and might devastate this lovely person, his 'mother'. Had William been able to read Hellen's mind, he would have seen that she, too, was burying dark and troublesome thoughts. Not questions but revelations. Hidden responsibilities, the very ones William brooded over. Hellen's reasons for staying quiet were the same as ever before. She still couldn't justify stating the cruel truths when everything in both their lives was working out so well. There was no point in upsetting the apple cart.

Perhaps it was their genetic make-up that prevented confrontation. Both held onto the unsaid for fear of hurting the other. And so the afternoon in each other's company concentrated on their recent attainment of respective happiness found.

Yet William began to regret his reticence as soon as he waved farewell from his tall, striped tower. He resolved that the next time he spoke to Hellen he would pluck up courage to ask about his father and who he was, to ask for her real reason about leaving Westray. He wanted her to solve his confusion regarding his roots and other nuances concerning his perception of the family. These kept cropping up and troubling him at the strangest of times. In later times he would wish that he had found the courage during this visit.

On the rumbling ride back to the jetty, Hellen found herself looking forward to her ferry journey home and tried to ascertain if it was the sea crossing or the conversation with George that she enjoyed the more, but she quickly decided it was incidental.

Arriving back in Kirkwall at dusk, quite chilled and all of them in need of a hot meal, George seemed to be tardy in saying goodbye to Hellen and Ella. He kept clearing his throat as if he wanted to say something more to them. In the end it was Gina who helped him out of his predicament by suggesting Hellen and Ella came back with them for some of her father's home-made lentil soup. Gina said George was an expert at making delicious soups, which he made on Friday nights to last them through Saturday and Sunday. It was at this point that Hellen discovered there were no other members in the Rendall family; no other children and no wife. Gina's mother had died of childbed fever after her birth. Hellen's admiration for this soup making, single parent grew by the minute.

Knowing that George was an unattached widower allowed Hellen to view him differently. She felt relaxed about her feelings of comfort in his company and that evening, time passed unheeded as conversations, previously many close to the heart, were shared between them with each openly expressing their individual experiences and past histories. George was several years younger than Hellen. He was smaller in build than Andrew had been. He sported a stiff, auburn tinged moustache that looked a bit like a small scrubbing brush with its bristles disjointed. The thick, wavy hair on his head was like Gina's but streaked with grey.

Gina showed Ella and Hellen her father's delicately painted watercolours, completed from drawings he made on his ferry crossings on quiet days. Sometimes he had painted the same view but in different atmospheric conditions, with a storm dominating the sky or in the exaltation of a sunset. George framed them himself with pieces of whittled driftwood that he and Gina would find on walks along the rocks. Hellen said he should try selling some to the local craft shop, but George only smiled modestly.

On Saturdays, it became a regular habit for Hellen and Ella to journey on the ferry between the islands with Gina and her father, whatever the weather. If George was operating the ferry, they would travel on it. And if they sailed past Sanday, George would blow the horn to alert William's attention in the lighthouse, whereupon all the ferry passengers of the day would join in with ritual of waving. The day would be completed with dinner at either the Williamson home or the Rendall's cottage above the harbour, where there was more space and always a big pot of soup. Saturday evenings became extended to take in a card game or two and some time for George's teaching of the rudiments of chess to Hellen. At the end of the day, George and Gina would walk Hellen and Ella back down to their home in the town.

For Hellen, George was in no way a replacement for Andrew in her heart, but he was a comfortable companion who she looked forward to seeing. For George the relationship with Hellen was different. It was love that he felt though he kept this to himself, thinking it inappropriate to romance at their advanced stage of life. Although George was nearly ten years younger than Hellen, neither of them bothered about such triviality. In contrast, Gina's mother, George's deceased wife, had been ten years younger than him though that had not given her any advantage in the longevity stakes.

A gentle romance grew between them, based on an ideal companionship. Marriage was not an issue. The relationship worked well for both sets of parent and child, and their friendship was of utmost importance to them all.

18

Chance Meeting

With the sun shining and the high wind sending scudding puffs of cloud across the pale blue sky, Meg set off to push her boys in the perambulator down Victoria Street. Every day she took them out to fill their young lungs with invigorating sea air. Kirkwall was always a whirl of sea breezes. The perambulator was an extremely dated contraption, but it was in working order and served its purpose. Christina had kept it carefully stored in the back store of the Ironmongery since Rebecca had outgrown it so many years before. The Tullocks always hoped for another baby, but it was seemingly not to be God's will and when He took Rebecca away from them the Tullochs lost faith, rarely entering church again.

As she passed by the school, its bell rang out loudly, swiftly followed by the noise of cheering and shouting children as they poured out of their classrooms into the schoolyard. As Meg watched their youthful exuberance, one child caught her eye. It was a little girl of about nine years old with very straight dark brown hair, sleekly bobbed. She was dressed a touch more formally than the other children, in the way an older mother would dress subsequent offspring in hand-me-down clothes, somewhat dated but clean and tidy. What made this child stand out from the others was not only her attire but also her *joie de vivre* and general energy. With a friend of about the same age, who had long wavy auburn tresses, the girl started to play a hectic game of hopscotch. The pair were perpetually laughing and giggling. As close friends do, both girls wore their hair in the same style. Their hair was tied back on each side and fastened with gay tartan ribboning. The girls were happily singing, "Pease pudding hot, Pease pudding cold, Pease pudding in the pot, Nine days old!"

The child who primarily caught Meg's attention seemed familiar somehow, with her sleek dark hair and elfin features. She noticed how strikingly pretty this child was and that she was smaller and daintier than her contemporaries. The girl seemed to sense that she was being watched and turned to look directly at Meg. The child smiled as Meg was caught unawares. Meg blinked and smiled back. At that very moment the school bell again tolled to announce the continuation of lessons, whereupon all the children turned on their heels and ran quietly indoors. With their noise abated, the schoolyard again fell silent. Meg was left with a feeling of *déjà vu*.

The next day was Saturday, William's fourteenth birthday. The small reception committee consisting of Hellen, Ella and Gina waited on the quayside for George's ferry to arrive from Sanday. As the two young girls skipped off to climb the parapets and stone steps at the back of the harbour walls, Hellen paced the cobblestones, idly glancing around her at all the activity going on. The queue for the ferry was lengthening as people trickled into the quay side area from all sides, boats were bobbing around at anchor in the harbour and a dray lorry was unloading beer barrels at The Buckles Inn. The day was brightening, though there was some heavy cloud to the west. These images remained happy and clear in Hellen's mind's eye – for a while.

Idly passing time until the ferry carrying William appeared on the horizon, Hellen strolled past the entrance to the close between Tulloch's Ironmongery and Beattie's Butcher Shop. This passageway connected walkers on Victoria Street to the harbour area. Echoing footsteps of a lone pedestrian reverberated down the close towards her. They were the footsteps of a lone and purposeful woman and, somewhere in Hellen's distant memory these ladylike steps roused a familiarity within her. Out of curiosity and on a whim, she looked up.

Doused in shadows down the gentle slope of the darkened close was the tall hooded figure of a woman in a flowing black cloak. Her head was bowed against the jet of wind forced up the close from the harbour area. The woman looked to where she stepped and appeared to glide towards Hellen, her long fine flaxen hair flicking out from under her hood.

Sudden expectation gripped at Hellen's heart. As if in a dream, the sound of the woman's heels clipping against the flagstones tapped out a rhythm in Hellen's ears. Memories flashed before her, memories of a younger, smaller daughter, smiling a distinctively askew smile.

The longed for and startling sight that appeared took Hellen's breath away. Emerging from the shadows, flinging back her heavy hood, Meg stopped in her tracks as the weak sunlight washed over her tall figure. As it bathed her stunning face in sunshine, Hellen gazed in wonder at the face still more beautiful than this mother could remember though now etched with tiny lines of worry around her eyes. Meg looked directly into Hellen's tear-filled eyes. Both mother and daughter stood in stunned silence. Meg felt her heart miss a beat. Hellen thought her world had stopped.

Each had lived in Kirkwall at opposite ends of Victoria Street but not until this chance meeting had their paths crossed. Meg still believed that Hellen lived at Rabbitha' with William, Ella and Agnes. She had received no news from Isobella to the contrary. But then again, she had received no news at all. The happenings in Kirkwall had taken up all her time and all her thoughts. Her days were happily filled with the demands of her growing wee lads and her new friends. To dwell on thoughts concerning her shamed past was not a pastime she allowed time for. Christina and Hugh acted as grandparents, the best that children could have, and Meg had no need for any other family.

The passage of time was made sharply aware to Meg when she came face to face with the mother she had surely alienated. Such a well acquainted face yet so much older than she remembered. Meg's troubled conscience froze her to the spot.

Since the births of her twins, Meg had also endeavoured to avoid contact with Robina, seeing her as a vague connection with her still secret past. This only added more guilt to her conscience, because she would dearly have loved to make herself known to her Uncle Will, the closest living relative to her departed father that this world could offer. But, unlike the Tullochs, an aunt and uncle would insist on knowing what had been happening to their niece in the intervening years and would ask after Hellen. It would be all too complicated. The scandal would unfold and Meg's serendipitous new life would crash down around her.

In emerging from the close, Meg faced her past as she walked into the glare of sunshine.

Hellen also stared in disbelief. For a moment the world went quiet as they fell deep into each other's eyes, down into each other's souls, searching for their lost bonding and scrambling for words to describe the sudden feelings that arose inside them. A wealth of emotions arose and ebbed within them both. Lost years welled up as soft tears. Past cares were erased, vanished in an instant.

Tentatively they approached each other, Hellen being the first to offer open arms of welcome and discernible forgiveness. Wrapping their arms warmly around one another, the touching scene they portrayed took the attention of many passers by on the quayside. The two embracing women were oblivious to their surroundings. They appeared like the long lost souls that they were.

The ferry sidled into the harbour with William standing at the helm, shielding his eyes with his hand and visibly possessed with an aura of confidence and self-assurance. On the quayside, Ella was bouncing up and down and waving madly. She was the first person he recognised at Kirkwall. Ella stood by Gina, just the two of them, standing high on a parapet at the far end. It took him a moment or two to pick out Hellen in the milling crowd around the harbour. She was separated from the girls and further along the harbour wall. She stood opposite a tall, blonde haired woman, whose hands she held in hers. William wondered who this person could be? She was important enough for Hellen to be heedless to the ferry's arrival.

"Blow da whistle, George!" he shouted.

George was also perplexed by Hellen's lack of interest as he was usually assured of a cheery welcoming wave. Even after the whistle was blown Hellen failed to respond to them. George and William looked to one another and shrugged.

"Perhaps she's gettin' deef in her auld age…" quipped William.

Time stood still for Hellen and Meg. People walking past, seagulls swooping overhead, the ferry's arrival and the whistle blowing, were all happening a million miles from where they stood. Hellen had only the vaguest awareness of the world outside their special moment. William, the ferry, George, Ella, were only in the far, heavily veiled recesses of her mind. At the forefront was the feeling of pure joy on discovering Meg, safe and well and lovely as ever. Any words Hellen might have said were choked with the rise of pent up emotion. There was so much to be said and the thought of the eagerly expected, plausible explanations from Meg began to overwhelm her. Tiny beads of sweat burst across her flushed cheeks.

Her strength slowly drained from her head down to her toes.

Just in time Meg noticed that her mother was about to collapse. She led her mother over to the wooden bench propped against the back wall of Tulloch's Ironmongery. Their eyes were still wide and fixed upon each other. They sat and rested their weary minds while all around them bustled and jostled. Passengers alighted from the ferry and the queue of new passengers boarded, destined for the next crossing. Keeping to the timetable, George set off for his next destination with his new set of passengers, feeling keenly disappointed that Hellen hadn't approached to speak to him. He knew it was William's special day and reasoned that she must be preoccupied with relations who had come to join them.

Meg had so much to say to her estranged mother yet she felt too emotionally choked for words to form. A sudden desperate urge to see her abandoned William and Ella came over her. She had believed she would never see them again yet here was a chance, but there were no children in Hellen's immediate vicinity. Meg's throat felt constricted and her voice failed her. She tried to ask Hellen with her eyes.

Hellen read the message clearly. She knew what Meg wanted to know, but weakness made it impossible for her to physically respond. There was all too much to say and Hellen had a feeling that time was running away with her – that time was running out. Her breathing became laboured and came in short, sharp bursts. She managed to keep smiling at Meg as her heart slowed.

Meg placed her cool palm gently across her mother's pallid and clammy forehead. Hellen's hands clenched into fists and she grimaced alarmingly. Pain and terror filled her staring eyes. Realisation of her own mortality flooded over her and she turned to Meg, beseechingly, holding her in her sight because she knew then this would be the last view of her world. Hellen let out a short wail of protest at the untimely moment of her demise and slumped limply forwards onto Meg's shoulder.

Through dire necessity Meg's voice returned and she screamed for help. Grasping her mother's lifeless hands, she felt even then the chill as Hellen's blood stilled in her veins. People stopped by the bench to see what was the cause of her distress. Pushing through their throng was an elderly doctor from Aberdeen, who was in Kirkwall for a holiday with his sister. Taking one look at the elderly lady slumped on the bench, he suspected by her blue-grey pallor that he would feel no pulse in her limp wrist. There was none.

Removing his hat from his head as a mark of respect, he placed it on the edge of the bench as he set about gently laying Hellen's body along the bench. Hellen had died of a heart attack. The pain had not lasted long. The doctor would never know that this lady before him had lived with far more hurt in her heart, lasting more than a decade, more severe in its longevity than this, the swift pain of her death.

Shock and disbelief, anguish and guilt, flooded Meg's spinning head. How could this be? How could they end like this – with Meg's opportunity to make amends to her mother within her grasp then ripped away? She stared at the doctor with wild, wide eyes, which pleaded with him to somehow rectify the situation, to bring her back from the dead. But they both knew he could do nothing more. He shook his head, gently clasping his hand over Meg's shoulder. Meg groaned in mental torment and sank to her knees on the flagstones. She let out a low moan, which intensified and echoed around the harbour walls. She sat on the cold, wet ground in front of her mother's body, wrapping her arms around Hellen's knees. Their reunion had been incredibly short lived. The grey haired doctor helped Meg to her feet and sat her down on the bench. No one would ever understand the irony. No one else around them would realise that this mother and daughter were cruelly denied their first talk since the day of William's birth, exactly fourteen years before. That Meg was about to make amends for her life to date, when suddenly, Hellen's lifetime was complete.

Three children pushed their way to the front of the small

crowd that had gathered. They stood, dumbfounded and staring in bewilderment. Meg looked up. She saw a ginger headed girl with a freckled face holding hands with a pretty, elfin-featured girl. Both girls wore their hair tied back with tartan ribbons. Meg remembered them from the schoolyard. She could see now who the pretty girl reminded her of – Hellen, and yet it was also herself. Standing beside them with his arm around this girl's shoulders, was a taller, darker and handsome male version of this child. Meg's tormented mind allowed her to realise with certainty that she was looking at her own two children, William and Ella. Because she knew this, she could see herself looking back, and she could see Charles there, too. A huge smile uplifted her face as she beamed at her children.

Ella screamed a high pitched, seemingly never-ending shriek. The horror in front of the little girl was too terrible to comprehend. Hellen looking dead and a strange woman sitting beside her, stroking Hellen's hair – *smiling* at them! William hugged his sister tightly and frowned hard at this seemingly evil, uncaring woman. He knew her to be the very one Hellen had been so absorbed with as his ferry sailed into harbour. What had this wicked woman done? He had to keep strong for his distraught sister.

"Did she kill Midder, William?" Ella's voice was still shriekingly high.

Meg's mind jolted into the realisation that Hellen had brought them up to believe she was their mother. They would have no idea who Meg was. In an instant she resolved that they must never know and the smile dropped from her face as if a switch had been turned. The total confusion added to Meg's distress. The doctor stepped in to try to diffuse the mounting crisis for the children.

"No, no, lassie, your mother's had a heart attack," he said. "Nothing we could do. God must have called to her."

Meg realised how she must have looked to the children, a stranger to them, smiling a welcoming greeting when she should be giving compassion as she sat beside the body of their dead 'mother'.

"I'm sorry, I'm so sorry," she murmured.

It was as if pendulums were swaying, this way and that, on her facial muscles. One moment she was awash with grief, the next smiling at her long lost children; confused, agonised, grieving, yet at the same time, ecstatic, delirious. She must take hold of the situation. It had to be carefully managed else she would find that she was again adding to the misery of loved ones. Just when her life was going well, how could it all go so wrong again? She must think carefully so as not to ruin everything. Meg was astounded at the emotions that were hitting her from all angles on that ill-fated yet amazing day.

With the doctor's help, Meg managed to explain to the three children that Hellen had indeed died of a heart attack in the last few minutes, that nothing could have been done for her and now they must be taken home to recover from this shock.

"Children, where is it ye live?" Meg asked.

Gina was the first to answer. She told Meg this was Ella and William's mother, but not hers, that she had never seen her own mother. Meg appreciated the similarity in the backgrounds of these young friends and that William and Ella did indeed look on Hellen as their mother. Gina went on to say that her father ran the ferry.

"She usually stays with me and Midder on Saturdays," said Ella in a weak little voice, momentarily forgetting her family fatality.

No one noticed for a moment the grief that overtook William. His body felt as if it had walked into a wall as he dropped to his knees, level with Hellen's prone body and threw his arms around her neck in silent heartache. Ella burst into tears when the circumstances struck home to her. Her hand brushed against one of Hellen's, already cold to the touch, and she let out a piercing squeal, springing back and covering her mouth with both her hands in horror. Meg realised the little girl was in desperate need of a warm hug and tentatively drew Ella to her. Ella eyed her suspiciously then threw caution to the wind and howled, wrapping her arms around the evil, kindly stranger.

The weak sunshine gave up its quest and dropped helplessly behind a bank of cloud that had built up across the harbour. The crowd dispersed, many of them shocked at what they had witnessed. Two fishermen stayed behind and offered to help the doctor carry Hellen's body wherever she needed to go, wherever she was to be laid out.

The doctor had mentally noted that the grief-stricken children and their little friend appeared not to know the beautiful woman, who was equally upset at the loss of the older woman. He was confused because there was a strong family resemblance between them. He deduced they were long lost relatives and it was not his business except to ensure the children made it safely home – if there was anyone else at home for them. Arrangements became more confusing the more enquires he made. Meg listened to the answers given by the children to his questions, as they were answers she, too, wanted to know.

"I don't live in Kirkwall," William said. "I live on Sanday – at the lighthouse."

"He's fourteen today," wailed Ella, mopping her eyes with her sleeves.

William remembered another eventful birthday time earlier in his life. The day he had believed Ella was a birthday present for him. The day of William's birth came flooding back to Meg for it was the day she made her first wrong decision.

"Aah, dear me," said the doctor, peering over the top rim of his spectacles and wondering how he could salvage this calamitous situation.

He had to get the necessities over and done with, the arrangements for the laying out of Hellen's body. He asked Ella if her father would be at home.

"Never had a faider," she muttered, then she began to wail again. "I waa-nt Aggg-nesss!"

Ella was overcome with tears. She felt weak. Her eyes were blurred and as she went to sit down on the bench she found herself sitting on Hellen's hand. This horrified her and made her stand bolt upright and wail all the more.

'Agnes, dear Agnes,' thought Meg, wishing she could be with them in this tragedy. Agnes and John and Barbara would have to be contacted as soon as possible.

As the doctor heard from Ella about uncle Will and aunt Robina he decided that this was where Hellen's body should be taken. He arranged with the fishermen for this to be put into effect, but first he asked another bystander to go and give Will and Robina the bad news. Death is always a shock but he didn't want her body to arrive before the news. While this was being arranged, Meg led Ella to one side and they walked slowly backwards and forwards along the edge of the harbour wall. William followed on. He not only felt bereft but also a strong sensation of doubt was creeping over him, which he didn't understand. The situation by all accounts was very strange. Who was this blonde woman? He knew she was not just some bystander. From the ferry he had seen how enrapt Hellen had been with her and he wanted to know why.

"Who are ye?" he asked Meg directly, "an' why were you wid my midder on the quayside?"

Meg looked at him longingly, wishing the words of her answer could be simple as her name. But as she took a deep intake of breath, someone called out her name, inadvertently answering the first part of her reply yet interrupting the moment.

"Meg, Meg!"

It was Christina, still wearing her working pinny. She had heard all the commotion at the back of the Ironmongery store and came out to see what was going on.

"Oh Christina!" Meg broke down and fell into Christina's outstretched arms.

The children looked on in bewilderment and Christina looked back at them in equal perplexity from over Meg's shoulder.

"What's happened, lad?" she asked William.

"Ma midder died. Ma midder died right hear – with this wummin…"

His words trailed off and put his arms round Ella's heaving shoulders as she continued to sob.

"And who are you, wee lassie?"

"She's ma sister Ella," William explained. "Dat's her friend, Gina."

"Yes, I know Gina," said Christina, who often used the ferry to visit friends on the other islands.

"Mrs. Tulloch, you gotta help!" said Gina, becoming wrapped in the severity of this tragic event she had witnessed.

"Och, yes dearie, I will, I will," she said as she patted Meg's back, consolingly.

Meg regained some composure and they looked in a quandary at each other, Meg and Christina.

"You pose us some grand puzzles, don't you?" Christina sighed and turned around to Meg. Out of earshot she said: "I have no idea what's going on here except that these children have suddenly lost their mother."

"Their grandmother," Meg whispered for only Christina's ears to catch.

Christina stood back from Meg, holding her at arm's length by her shoulders. She looked deep into Meg's eyes, darting from one eye to the other, over and over, searchingly. It was obvious to her who their mother was.

The efficient doctor interrupted them. He knew Mrs. Tulloch from his childhood in Kirkwall. In fact, she had been in the class above him at the Kirkwall school.

"Excuse me," he said. "Can I rely on you, Christina, to look after this distraught lady for me today? Are you a friend?"

"Oh yes, a good friend," replied Christina, feeling she would be even more needed in Meg's life from that moment.

"Good," he said. "Then there's just the children…"

"I'll be looking after dem!" Meg said in earnest, whilst wiping away her tears.

"But they don't know you," said the puzzled doctor.

"But I'm a close relative. Dey just haven't met me before," said Meg taking hold of both his hands in hers then turning to the children, she said truthfully;

"I am Hellen's daughter, Meg."

They gazed up at her. Somewhere in the back of William's mind he remembered that name from somewhere. Perhaps he had heard Hellen and Agnes talk of her, though not frequently.

"I've never even heard of ye!" said Ella in disgust.

"She must be yer sister!" said Gina.

Then, shielding her mouth with the side of her hand, she whispered, "Isn't she bonnie, Ella?"

"Right," said the doctor. "We need to all go home now."

He realised that it would be better for the children not to have to stay where their mother's body was being laid out, at Robina and Will's home, so he turned to Meg.

"If you are who you say you are, and Christina Tulloch knows you well, I believe you should take charge of the well being of these poor children. At which address will you be staying that I might continue with your mother's funeral arrangements?"

"With Hugh and me at the Ironmongery," Christina answered for Meg.

"Right," he said again, scribbling on a page of a notepad that he had produced from his inside topcoat pocket. "This is where I am residing for the following week. It is the address of my sister's home. You must contact me there if you need anything or if I can be of any further help to you."

The grateful glimmer flitted over Meg's tear ravaged face.

19

Drawing Conclusions

In one eventful hour of a wholly traumatic day, two children had lost their 'mother' and a mother had found her two lost children. William's birthday was all but forgotten in the drama of the day though Meg had been aware of its significance. The coincidence of a reunion with her firstborn child exactly fourteen years to the day after she had last set eyes on him was stunning. The trauma that had unfolded during the preceding moments, however, took precedence over the day's events, with Hellen's collapse and death destroying any chance of reconciliation between mother and daughter. On the very brink of tenuously reuniting, the inconceivable had happened at such an incongruous moment, leaving Meg's emotions in turmoil. One of the worst moments of her life was followed by the best – Hellen dying in front of her eyes, the very eyes that were immediately forced to feed on the wonder of her lost creations as William and Ella stood before her. Although they were seemingly searching into her soul, they were both obviously ignorant of the fact she was their real mother. Meg felt she would burst with ecstasy at the very sight of them, wanting to let her hungry eyes linger over their handsome faces till she could remember every nuance for fear the moment would disappear. For fear their image would be torn from her, because she felt she didn't deserve her joy to last. She had known instantly this was her son, intuition had engulfed her senses. Yet she remembered seeing Ella before, the girl who had previously caught her eye in the schoolyard, and intuition had not kicked in then as it did on this day of heightened tensions.

One of the first of Hellen's friends to know of her death was Robina. After the ferry arrived, she and Will had been expecting Hellen and Ella to call round with William. They were looking forward to meeting the birthday boy and Robina had baked a fruitcake for the occasion. When she heard the slow, dull knocking on their front door, a welcoming Robina with a beaming smile on her face opened the door with a flourish. But her smile soon faded when she saw the solemn looking fisherman, the bearer of bad news, standing on the doorstep. As gravely as he could muster, the fisherman, never before the conveyor of bad news to a stranger, told Robina that Hellen Williamson was dead and her body would be immediately brought to their home. She found his words incredulous and stood deflated, dumbfounded with shock, her hands clasped over her cheeks.

This was shock enough for one day, but when she went back inside to tell Will what the fisherman had told her, there was a second knocking at the door. This time Robina opened the door in fear and trepidation, expecting the stiffening body of her sister-in-law to be carried in. But, there on her doorstep, stood the very woman whose two baby boys Robina had helped to deliver over three years before. Their paths had seldom crossed during the interim time but Robina would never forget her. Ella had her arms wrapped around Meg's neck as Meg held her close. A very dispirited William and Gina stood on either side of her. Robina's shock was compounded with bewilderment.

Settling them all by the hearth side, she had only just despatched Will to the kitchen to warm some milk for drinks when there was a third knock at the door. They all knew what would be on the other side of the door that time and Ella let out an anguished wail, nuzzling her head in Meg's neck.

Very few words were spoken over the drinking of warm milk and all of those were accompanied by the soft sobbing from Ella. Meg explained she was Hellen's youngest daughter and waited with faked innocence for Robina's stunned reaction. Meg had impulsively decided to pretend she had no idea these people were her relatives, although the moment they opened their front door to her, she had known for certain. It would not be long before they would start to wonder why she had not made contact with them, surely knowing they lived in Kirkwall and why she hadn't known Hellen was also in Kirkwall. Trying to control the panic rising inside her for the sake of her confused children, she had to act out a charade.

"But...." Robina was flabbergasted.

"Wha's dat?" said Will, Uncle Will, equally nonplussed.

"….if ye are Meg – ye…." Robina mind was speeding up, ticking over like dynamite about to explode.

Will was oblivious to the implication. Standing in front of her, he held Meg at arm's length and took a good look at her face. "Aye," he said with a smile, "ye are Andrew's bonnie one!"

The tension was diffused slightly as Will launched into a rambling speech about how long it had been since he'd last clapped eyes on Meg, the last time being at Andrew's funeral and here they all were, about to plan Hellen's. Meg remained calm, relying on the dire circumstances to excuse her behaviour.

Robina had time to observe her guests closely. As her eyes flitted from Meg to William and then to Ella, a stronger than expected family resemblance slowly emerged. The mannerisms, the expressions, even to William's hint of the askew smile when he was offered a piece of fruitcake, were so similar. Robina surreptitiously glanced at Will but he didn't appear to notice what she now saw as blatantly obvious. She knew with certainty which of Hellen's granddaughters was the mother of these two 'orphaned' children. She realised that previously she had only presumed they were Agnes's children. The reason for Hellen's delusion then came to her. It must be that the children themselves had not been told. On several occasions, she had heard little Ella call Hellen 'midder', but dismissed this as just a term of endearment for the time she was away from her real mother.

Pondering over this new and stunning revelation, Robina wondered what would be the outcome for the two children involved in this muddle. As she was not a principal player in this unravelling scenario, she determined to stay on the side stage. She decided to keep to the purely practical activities for the rest of that fateful day, leaving thought and emotion until another time. She poured three stiff drams of brandy.

Meg's fraught and raw senses were working to full capacity. Dilemmas were presenting themselves fast and furiously and she could guess the quandary Robina would be finding herself in. Whilst still wondering if there could ever be a right time, Meg prayed that no one would ruin her revelation to her children before a decent time had elapsed from this day of Hellen's death. When she saw her aunt's facial expression change with the dawning of their true identities, she beseeching looked into Robina eyes. In that private moment, the two women came to an intuitive understanding and Robina reassuringly patted Meg on her arm. It was not the time or the place. Meg should put such disclosures on hold for awhile.

Robina decided to speak to Meg in private at some point. She said nothing to Will about her deductions. The conflicting events of one day left him confused enough as it was. His life was usually quite pedantic and suddenly the pace had quickened.

The last ferry journey of the day was nearly over and as George piloted the boat into Kirkwall harbour he smiled as he contemplated the welcome he would receive when he arrived home. Hellen had invited him to join the family gathering at Will and Robina's. He knew that William planned to stay the night in Kirkwall and return to Sanday lighthouse on the Monday, there being no ferries on a Sunday. George was looking forward to his Sunday free from work. If the weather was fine, he and Hellen had decided to take their families for a ride to Skara Brae in a friend's pony and trap. As the ferry straightened and headed directly for its moorings, George became aware of the solemn-looking group waiting on the quayside. At the forefront stood Gina, uncharacteristically still. She and Ella were standing on either side of the blonde woman, who George remembered standing with Hellen earlier in the day. Ella was very close to this stranger, leaning into her, and the stranger's hands were resting reassuringly on each of the girl's shoulders. Hellen was conspicuous by her absence.

It was Gina who broke the bad news to him gently. George thought he had been punched. He felt completely crushed. Hellen had become such a big part of his life and that of Gina's and being without her now was too hard to contemplate. He looked in disbelief from face to face of the small gathered crowd, willing someone to deny his daughter's words. The stranger was among those who returned a silent nod of affirmation. He scrambled in his head for his most recent memories of Hellen, conjuring up a picture of her smiling face. Sadly, he recalled her oblivion to him that afternoon. He hugged Gina then stretched out his free arm to the little bedraggled and sobbing figure of Ella, taking her into their embrace. A compassionate smile passed over Meg's lips at the sight of his tenderness and heartfelt sorrow.

George offered to look after Ella and William for the few days before Hellen's funeral but Meg insisted they would stay with her, ignoring the fact that she still seemed like a stranger to them. William and Ella had no objections. They were numbed by grief. The secret fact that she was the children's birth mother was something Meg knew she must keep close to her heart for the foreseeable future. The time was not right. But would there ever be a right time to shatter illusions, she wondered?

As the sun began to drop behind the harbour wall, Meg took Ella and William back with her to her lodgings above the Tulloch's Ironmongery. Christina had been looking after the twins that afternoon and Meg had yet to tell William and Ella about them. She turned to face them as they stood at the foot of her stairs. She felt it only fair to warn them.

"Ye'll get anither peedie surprise when ye go inside," she said, relishing in the anticipation of having all four of her offspring together in one room. "I have twin boys for you to meet."

"Guidness me!" exclaimed William. "Whitever else will turn up today?"

Christina met them at the top of the stairs.

"Have you told them about your boys?" she asked.

"Aye," said Meg, "dey are prepared for dat."

She gave Christina a look that clearly indicated that they were not prepared for anything more at that stage.

"Well, they are both sleeping soundly and after you have had a wee look at them, children, come in and meet Hugh, then I'll show you where you can sleep tonight."

"They can sleep in my room," said Meg, positively.

Christina saw Meg's determined expression and said that would be fine. Two bedspreads and eiderdowns were carried up to Meg's room and spread out on the floor in front of her fireplace. Ella had stopped sobbing and became interested in seeing the twins. She and

Meg smiled at one another as they gazed upon the identical sleeping infants. Ella held Meg's hand. It seemed a natural thing to do. And the comforting presence of the calm little bodies in the warm room, lit only by the flickering flames from the dancing fire, helped to ease Ella's pain. William sat down beside the fire and stared into the flames. He politely refused any offers of food from Christina though he did drink and enjoy his first glass of home-made ginger beer.

That night as the children slept, Meg lovingly watched over the occupants of her room. Her offspring gathered together – all with her at last. William was a boy of independent means and would have to return to the island of Sanday soon, but for now, she revelled in the blissful sight of all four of her children together, yet all unaware of their close relationship. The ability to gaze upon them undetected gave her the greatest pleasure. One moment she felt high as a kite in a cloudless sky, but in the next instant she was down a dark, oppressive pit, bereft at the thought of losing Hellen just as she had found her.

How could she have torn asunder this unit of siblings? What would Hellen have thought of this reunion? How had Hellen planned to reveal the truth – or *had* she ever planned to reveal the truth? Would this situation ever be resolved or would it be exacerbated?

20

Catalogue of Catastrophes

As the news of Hellen's sudden death spread around the community, grief circulated like ripples, radiating wider and deeper through the hearts of all the people who had known her. She had made many friends in her short time at Kirkwall.

The formal laying out of Hellen's body in Will and Robina's front parlour was taken care of by Robina, who prepared and dressed her and laid her in her coffin. This was done in readiness for family members to come and pay their last respects, as was the custom. Meg helped William and Ella come to terms with the changes in Hellen's appearance before they went to see her by saying that Hellen's spirit was now in heaven with God, that she had been taken from her earthly body, which she no longer needed. But Hellen looked so different to the children in the state of death. They remarked on how strange it was to see her still and motionless, when she had always been active and busy. Her closed eyes disturbed them. They had never seen Hellen with closed eyes. Her eyes had always been open, animated, twinkling. In the mornings she had been the first to be awake and she never took a nap in the afternoons. After two days, the parlour was softly stifled by a sickly, sweetish smell, which hung oppressively around the room. It was the smell that accompanied death; the smell of decomposition.

To distract their young minds from their traumatic grief, Meg, the Tullochs, Will and Robina, all determined to keep William and Ella busily occupied. Bethia offered to take William fishing from the rocks, which amazed Robina as her daughter had never before shown such consideration for a child. William appeared to have been hit the hardest by Hellen's death. Ella was so taken with the twins that just to be with them kept her relaxed and happy. Gina accompanied them like one of the family.

The journey from Fair Isle to attend the funeral was too much for many of Hellen's older surviving siblings, but some of their descendants and second generation came to pay their family's respects. Mhairi

Wilson brought her son, Jerome. Mhairi was one of Hellen's sister's daughters and Jerome was the same age as William. They had never met before but from the sad occasion of a family funeral was born a friendship between the two lads, who would, from that day forth, meet every year on Fair Isle to help with the harvesting. Hellen would have said, "Some good comes from bad" because she always tried to see the bright side, to find some good in a bad situation. It was how she had coped with Meg's abandonment of her children. The addition of two more children to bring up in Hellen's middle-aged widowhood had turned out to be an advantage, lifting her spirits and giving her purpose, making her feel needed. If Agnes had ever started a tirade about Meg's behaviour, Hellen would say, "Tae know all is tae forgive all." Hellen had so eagerly waited for the day she would hear the truth from Meg and all would become clear and forgiven. But instead her heart gave out and she was denied any revelations.

Word was sent to Agnes and Peter, who arrive for the funeral with their nine children in tow. On the very day the news of Hellen's death had reached them, they were coincidentally already in mourning with the rest of the population of Westray, because two other tragic deaths had occurred in the space of as many weeks. Two deaths in one family – that of the Stewart family.

For the Laird of Westray the past few weeks had proved traumatic. His youngest son, sixteen year old Samuel Charles Stewart, had been a sickly child since birth and had suddenly taken a turn for the worse. In the space of just four days, through complications he died of pneumonia. The day before the funeral, the elder Stewart son and heir, William Bruce Stewart, disappeared whilst walking with his dog. When the dishevelled dog, badly bruised and cut, returned without its master, the Laird set up a search party, which continued throughout the night under the light from blazing torches. It wasn't until daybreak that a discovery was made. The Laird was summoned by a section of his search party to the West Cliffs where an atrocious sight met his eyes. Strewn across the rocks at the foot of the cliffs, lying spread-eagled, was the body of his firstborn son, the nineteen year old Stewart heir. William Bruce had lost a lot of blood and it appeared to the shocked onlookers that the end had not been quick. Both his severe injuries and the bitter cold of the previous night had contributed to his tragic death. The cliffs were more than a couple of miles from the Westray Manor. No one would ever know exactly what had happened to cause William Bruce Stewart to fall to his death.

Isobella, as the boys' mother, was utterly inconsolable after this second tragedy to her family. The degenerative illness she had suffered for more than fifteen years suddenly and viciously exacerbated. Her progressively disabling illness had begun with an infinitesimal slurring of her speech, only barely detectable. She complained of this before her husband, the Laird, had noticed it. Mood and temper changes were to follow, gradually increasing over the space of the first year. Then came a deterioration of her limb co-ordination and muscle weakening. She became weak and tired, her once lovely body becoming mercilessly bloated, her graceful movements clumsy and less controllable. The doctors who were called in from far and wide could do nothing to make her well or to stabilise her condition. A normal marital relationship was abandoned although the Laird still cared deeply for his tragic wife and made sure she was well cared for. Normally a man who showed little emotion, he was compassionate towards her fate, as they both knew she was unlikely to improve. Regressing over a lengthy and agonising period, she came to depend completely on the care of her servants, as she became more and more helpless. Meg had been her favourite servant and latterly her only friend.

The only surviving Stewart child was eighteen year old Catherine May. She had lacked the attention she craved with neither parent devoting much time to her. As her mother struggled with her indeterminate disease, Catherine May grew into a spoilt adolescent, the product of her over-indulgent childhood, and showed no sympathy for her mother's plight. Her father had never felt a strong interest in his children, as Meg could vouch. He was not a demonstratively loving or caring father. The early childhood of his children with Isobella was of no interest to the Laird, who had wished for more of a relationship with his children when they grew up, little realising that two of them were destined not to reach adulthood and the third would deny him hers.

A further blow was dealt to Charles Stewart only a week after his sons' funerals. Catherine Mary left a defiant note for her parents to say she had run away with a seaman she had fallen in love with. This man had been recently dismissed from duties and was someone the Laird had forbidden her to see. Her constant craving for attention and affection had been satiated with this ne'er-do-weel. Her father's disapproval only fired her defiance of him. Not a trace could be found of where the calamitous couple had gone and neither of the lovers was ever seen or heard of again.

With the trauma of losing all her children in such a short time, Isobella's illness was exacerbated. To her ailments was added a broken heart. Already bedridden she then suffered a stroke, never to speak again. Charles Stewart was left a shattered man.

The news of the Stewart family's tragedies travelled to Kirkwall on the ferry. Meg, numb from her tragedy in Kirkwall, was unable to take on board this misery. It passed over her subconscious that Charles Peter Stewart had had his fair share of disasters, too, and she resolved she must somehow contact Isobella in her time of need.

A high point arose from the depths of that catastrophic week. Meg's suppressed claim to motherhood was smoothly resolved, for the time being, by Ella's loving nature.

Ella immersed herself in the care of the two infants, Peter and Charles, for those were the names Meg had chosen for her twins. This new interest for Ella helped to satisfy her need to give and receive love for she missed Hellen, her love and her hugs so much. Meg gave Ella space to grieve, time to adjust, whilst making sure she was around for her. And Ella saw Meg, the bonnie 'sister' as someone warm, approachable and dependable. At their time of dire need, she had stepped into their lives like a guardian angel and she'd been there for William and Ella, for them to turn to. Meg was willing and generous enough with her attentions to take care of them all, and Ella began to see Meg as a likely candidate for motherly love. She followed Meg everywhere and Meg gave Ella the constant companionship she so craved at that time. The two became inseparable and, with the twins in tow, became a bonded unit.

William came around to joining in with the family activities and to accept this beautiful stranger into their lives, into the void left by Hellen. It took him a few days, a few sad days, when he frequently visited Hellen's prone body in Robina's front parlour, lying serenely and surreally in her coffin. He began to take an interest in the boys, playing rough and tumble games with them. To Peter and Charles's glee, William would allow them to ravage him in play fights. When the twins woke in the mornings to find their two new roommates ready and waiting to play, their excitement abounded and life was suddenly full of fun for them. Squeals of laughter peeled around the Tulloch home at one end of Victoria Street while at the other end of the same street, Hellen's body lay sedately awaiting burial.

Incongruous as the whole situation seemed, Meg was elated by how the week was transforming from the deep despair to a melee of unbridled happiness. She justified her obscure feelings by convincing herself that Hellen would also be overjoyed to see this heart-warming family reunion that had come about as a consequence to her death. A birth of a family had arisen from the demise of a matriarch.

On the eve of the funeral, Meg talked openly with the children about Hellen, about how much they had all loved her, about what a wonderful person she had been and that they would always hold her dear in their memories. Meg told their receptive minds that Hellen's soul would live on in their memories of her and in the way she had influenced their lives.

At this point, Ella snuggled up to Meg, riveting her with her eyes. Meg could tell she wanted to say something important but couldn't have wished to hear better words. Smiling sweetly and pleadingly she asked, "Will ye be our midder?"

Meg thought her cup had overfloweth. She hardly deserved such an easy ride to claiming motherhood – until William interjected. He jumped up, putting a stop to the reply she readily wanted to give.

"*I'll* look after ye, Ella!" he said adamantly.

"But I don't want to live in a lighthouse!" Ella replied, screwing up her face.

"I'll get a different job..." his voice tailing off and his eyes drifting out of focus as his mind mulled over this rash promise, one that he wasn't happy to make. Meg could see he would only be doing that for Ella sake.

"Ye love yer job, don't ye, William?" she asked him softly.

Before he replied, he went silent as he gazed out of the window at the lights around the harbour, the lights that saved lives by warning approaching boats of the whereabouts of the harbour walls and the shipwrecking rocks beyond.

"I do," he said.

"Do ye want to be a lighthouse keeper yerself one day?"

Meg wanted to do what was best for them all. She dearly wanted them to be happy, to make the right choices if they could.

"Aye," he said simply, still gazing dreamily into the night sky through a chink in the curtains. "I would really like dat."

"Well I would love to see ye fulfil yer dream, William," said the one person who, until that week, had failed to fulfil any of her dreams. Because of this, she knew better than most how important it was to make the right decisions.

Mother and son looked each other in the eyes for the first time with soul-touching understanding, as, telepathically, they knew what was to be done about these two dreams: William's dream to be a lighthouse keeper and Ella's dream of a new mother. William should give his blessing and allow Ella to live with Meg and the twins, where there was obvious love, and this would enable him to continue lighthouse duties at Sanday.

"Ella, ye can have yer new midder," he said gallantly.

Ella flung her arms around his neck and he laughed, swirling her around as far as the width of the room would allow. When he put her down they started playfully slapping each other on the back in a congratulatory way and the toddlers joined in with gusto.

The new arrangement had the Tulloch's full approval. It meant they had gained two surrogate grandchildren, one of which would live with them in Meg's lodgings. Ella was ecstatic. She couldn't believe her luck at her creation, a new happy family. She now had a replacement mother, twin baby brothers, and grandparents into the bargain. All she had asked for was a mother. They drank their warmed bedtime milk as a celebration toast to the agreed plan for their future – on the eve of Hellen's funeral.

21

From the Buckles Inn

Sitting alone over his untouched pint of warm ale, Seth gazed on the view of Kirkwall's windswept harbour from the bay window of the Buckles Inn. He watched the boats tied at anchor, bobbing furiously on the choppy waves. Sitting bolt upright with his hands firmly grasping his widespread knees, he peered out at the spray soaked quayside, his posture suggesting that whenever he saw what he was looking for he would be ready to sprint out of the alehouse. He shuffled uncomfortably on his wooden bench seat, which was polished to a high shine by decades of seated ale drinkers. Unless in a saddle, Seth preferred standing to sitting, but was trying to be unobtrusive. He was waiting for Hellen's funeral procession to pass by the window.

An eventful week had passed since his arrival in Kirkwall yet he was no nearer to achieving what he had set out to do. Seth had left behind the only job he had ever known, right hand man to the Laird of Westray, and the only home he had ever known at Black Bull Farm. He found that his life's direction was now dominated by an overwhelming need to follow his heart. So far, this had led him to Kirkwall harbour. Staying in lodgings at The Buckles Inn, he had made sure his room had a view of the harbour area. Everyone in Kirkwall would cross the quayside at some time, to perhaps buy fish, to walk and take the sea air, or to alight from a ferry.

The reason for his upheaval was Meg's sudden disappearance from the Manor House at Black Bull Farm. He had spent years of standing aside, watching Meg's life meander out of control and leading her further and further into a desperate situation. He had waited patiently for a suitable time to intervene only to find he had nearly lost her for good when she vanished without trace. Knowing that she was near her time with her third unwanted pregnancy he was worried for her state of mind. Meg had never confided in Seth about her affair, too loyal to her master – and to her mistress, Isobella, preserving the need for absolute secrecy in order to save Isobella hurt and despair. When the news of Meg's disappearance was reached him several days had gone by. He had suspected something amiss for he usually saw Meg at some point every day, but for over a week he had not caught even a glimpse of her. He had decided she must have gone to lodge within the Westray Manor House to be nearer her needy mistress – or to prepare for her own imminent birth. The Laird had been acting irrationally with his temper ready to surface on a whim. Meg had apparently not needed Seth's help to find release from Black Bull Farm. But he felt sure that Isobella knew where she had gone.

Seth's dilemma was that to ask Isobella outright might make her jump to the conclusion that he was the father of Meg's unborn child and perhaps also of those two previous illegitimate births that Isobella was fully aware of. This deduction would, however, do him no harm and would at least deflect any possible guilt from her husband, were she ever to have doubted him. Seth, like Meg, wanted to protect the vulnerable and innocent party.

Eventually Seth had inadvertently been given a clue to Meg's whereabouts by Isobella when she handed him a letter to send to Kirkwall. The large manila envelope was addressed to "Meg Williamson, c/o Kirkwall General Post Office". He desperately wanted to deliver the letter in person but held himself in check, because he wanted to withhold this information from the Laird. It was perhaps a chance for Seth to intervene – if Meg was indeed over her love for her master.

Over the years, Charles Stewart had obviously charmed and cared for Meg in his own inimitable way and it must have impressed Meg enough for her to have stayed in love with him. But Seth believed the big man was incapable of real love, believing that his master merely felt a strong infatuation, a compulsive fascination with Meg, coming at a time when his marriage to Isobella was following a downward spiral with the onset of her physically debilitating illness.

By the time Seth was ready to speak with Isobella, the catalogue of woes had begun to beset the Stewart family, one son's death quickly followed by another, and the doom and gloom intensified with the elopement of her one remaining child and only daughter. Devastated,

Isobella's health plummeted and the stroke she suffered rendered her speechless and partly paralysed. She lost the will to live and would see no one. The loss of her loyal maid, Meg, would only add to her misery. Charles Stewart had also to deal with these catastrophes.

An incredible crisis point had been reached and, although it was not a good time to leave Black Bull Farm or the Stewart family, what was left of them, Seth felt compelled to go – or lose Meg forever.

And so it was that Seth had found himself standing at the window of his new lodgings as the ferry sidled into harbour on that fateful day for the Williamson family. He had watched in stunned disbelief, the unfurling of the most tragic scene ever to have the misfortune to witness. Not in his wildest imagination could he have depicted his first sighting of Meg in over three years to turn out as tragically as it did.

His constant vigil over this harbour scene paid off when Seth noticed, emerging from the dark entrance to a close, a tall woman wearing a flowing cloak. Although hooded, there was everything about the figure that caught his eye. As she stepped from the shadows and the sunlight flooded over her face, Seth saw what he was sure of – it was Meg. Stunned at this stroke of good fortune, he was unprepared for the tragedy about to unfold. When Meg stopped he followed her gaze and it was only then that he noticed Hellen standing on the quayside. He noticed her at precisely the same moment as Meg. He oversaw the chance meeting of estranged mother and daughter after years of separation. He shared their feeling of joy. Yet then, happening simultaneously, he witnessed the sudden finality of their reunion as joy turned to pain. He watched helplessly, numbed with his feeling of anguish for Meg, as the elderly doctor took control of the stricken scene.

From that day, Seth continued his vigil from the window of his lodgings, overseeing many of the comings and goings of the separate factions of the Williamson family during the following week. From his vantage point he recognised William and Ella, by deduction. Like Meg, this was the first time he had seen the two children since the day of their respective births. He looked in affection at the baby boy now grown to near manhood, whom he had once held when he was only an hour or so old. He had also been with Ella when she was only hours old, again accompanying Hellen back in the dead of night to Rabbitha' to join the family saviours. The two children were so alike that they were obviously brother and sister. Seth was pleased to note that they in no way reminded him of his one-time employer.

In the days before the funeral, he watched as William went fishing with Bethia and as Meg took all the children for walks near to the harbour area. This was when he noted the two small additions to her previously disjointed family and realised she had delivered twins from her last pregnancy. What a family there had been created by one prolonged, illicit and seemingly irresistible affair. Seth thought that if it weren't so incredible, it would be wonderful. Still he was undecided as to the best time to approach Meg. He had waited so many years already that he was not in any rush.

Hellen's funeral procession passed by the window as Seth sat over his neglected pint, a mere prop needed to gain access to the highly polished seat with a view in the bay window of The Buckles Inn. Separated by the blown glass panels he could watch in anonymity. The pallbearers for Hellen's coffin were her brother-in-law, Will Williamson, her only son John Williamson, and her sons-in-law, Peter Harcus and Jon Muller. Barbara, Jon and their daughter, Elizabeth, had made the journey from Germany. Agnes, who had all nine of her children with her, walked with her sister, Anderina. As with most funerals, Hellen's death had brought together so many of her widespread family. Seth thought dolefully that Hellen would have enjoyed the gathering created by her own funeral and he hoped she was spiritually watching over them all.

As the solemn crowd of relatives and friends moved slowly before his eyes, Seth sought out William. The boy appeared to have matured and visibly aged since his grandmother's death. Seth's thoughts were full of unanswered questions. Did William think that he and Ella were now orphans? Would he ever know that both their parents were alive?

The day of his fateful fourteenth birthday had been shattering and chaotic enough without anyone divulging his true origins or an iota of the truth behind the drama. Would William ever come to realise that the mother he knew and loved was in fact his grandmother? That he was not grieving for a lost mother, because she had materialised, as if out of the blue, at the same moment that Hellen had dematerialised? If it had not been for their chance meeting with Meg at Kirkwall, William and Ella might never have met their two brothers. Did they yet know the twins were their brothers? His unsettling thoughts brought his own quandary into perspective.

Meg, straight backed and unwittingly commanding attention with her intrinsic elegance, strode out behind her mother's coffin, hand in hand with the twin toddlers and with William and Ella holding their tiny hands at either side. The family of four walked nobly and steadfastly. Charles Peter Stewart would have been flabbergasted to see the family he had created, congregated together without the need of him. Over the following years he probably would begin to feel a need for them, since all his legitimate family were lost.

Charles had been the one to insist that Meg's babies, their babies, be sent away – for their own good, he said, for the sake of everyone concerned in this affair; for himself, for Meg, and most importantly, for Isobella. She, of all people, the innocent party, must be protected from the immeasurable anguish the knowledge that a whole new family existed, issue from her husband's seed. The pain would be even more acutely felt now that she had lost all her own family. Charles Peter Stewart and Meg Williamson had always agreed on one thing, the protection of Isobella's good name. The people concerned with this forbidden love all had one thing in common, the protection of the tragic Isobella. Even Seth felt a need to protect her. Isobella, the figure in the middle of the hypothetical whirlpool, static as the others spun in a hectic spiral around her. Isobella, thankfully unaware throughout the years of the ever-growing fascination her husband had for her maid.

Charles Peter Stewart, crushed by the complete destruction of his family, his first and legitimate family, and the degeneration of his once lovely wife, felt overwhelmed, weak and powerless. All his disasters happening in so short a period of time exhausted every bit of his mental and physical strength. It had begun with the overnight disappearance of Meg, late on in her last pregnancy. This left him confused but, to his credit, anxious for her well-being. Having no idea where she had gone, or whither she had delivered safely, he was completely unaware that twins had been born. He had not foreseen Meg's abandonment of him, presuming she would always be his mistress, a constant presence in his life. But his anxieties over Meg soon paled with the furthering tragedies, leaving him meekly resolved that his future lay in the care of his devastated and neglected wife. Compassion was born though upheaval. Charles mellowed and aged. Isobella, though forevermore speechless, was consoled and appreciative of his attention at last, although somewhere in the thick fog of her mind's dementia, she knew drastic occurrences must have brought this about.

When Seth discreetly left his home at Black Bull Farm for the first time in his life, it had deteriorated into a sad and sorry place. There was nothing anyone could have done to lift the situation. Charles Peter Stewart, a shadow of his former strength, bereft and fallen, appeared ostensibly punishment for his sins.

Meg's sudden disappearance had proved Seth wrong. He had waited patiently all these years for just such a detachment and now felt that he, too, should take some sort of action. Convinced that the end of Meg's torturous affair would be effected by the Laird's eventual rejection of her in his increasingly demanding and selfish manner, Seth had been taken off guard when Meg took matters into her own hands, vanishing overnight between Christmas and Hogmanay, heavy with child once again.

Meg had made her move because she was no longer able to take Charles's inconsiderate and domineering treatment of her. She feared she might again lose the status of motherhood with her imminent unborn and the thought of this became too much for her to bear. The future held only visions of herself as a miserable old maid, childless and outcast, with no happy memories. Her principal reason for leaving Black Bull Farm was to escape the oppression of her love for the Laird and to try to salvage some sort of a life for herself, away from the unhappy one she led in Westray. She could never have predicted the horrendous sequence of catastrophes that were all too swiftly to follow her departure, resulting in the total decline of the Stewart family, the complete devastation of Charles's world.

Although Seth had nearly lost contact with her altogether, he now felt confident of success with his principal aim in life – to be with Meg. Not being a man of many words, he had no thoughts of declaring love for her, merely to be where she was, and for her to become accustomed to his presence. Over a decade had been lost to him already and he knew he would have to act soon. Nothing ventured, nothing gained, though he knew that Meg's new found love for her lost children would be uppermost in her priorities for quite some time.

He needed Meg to want him for herself, not present an alternative to her bad luck, a release from her fettered existence, an answer out of her plight. He didn't want her to see him as a way out of her desperate situation or to be with her on the rebound. The consuming love she obviously felt for her master had to die inside her before Seth could accept or realise any success in a shared future with her. He would wait, wait for Meg to want him as he had always wanted her. Seth's patience was verging on the inane, but he saw no other way. Life moved slowly and steadily in Orkney.

Part 4

22

Black Bull Farm, 1877

One day in 1855 when Charles Stewart's father, Archibald Stewart, was Laird of Westray, a fifteen-year stranger walked into the yard at Black Bull Farm. The girl said she had travelled all the way from Shetland and asked the Laird kindly for employment. Desperate for work she was also desperately concealing an unwanted pregnancy. The Laird took the girl on as a dairymaid. It was to be the first and the last job of her short life.

Seth was the issue of her premature and difficult birth. The day Seth was born was the day his young mother died. The two dairymaids who helped her with her delivery heard her last words, which were that she wanted her baby to be called Seth. The only name she had been known by at Black Bull Farm was Betsy and this was the name that a stable lad, moved by her demise, etched onto a simple cross made from driftwood. She was buried on unconsecrated ground outside the Kirk yard and this cross marked her grave.

Archibald Stewart organised a wet nurse and then a series of elderly spinsters of the parish to be responsible for an upbringing of sorts for the orphaned baby Seth. For one reason or another, his carers changed in fairly quick succession, two of them actually dying in his presence. Presumed too young to remember such traumas, he in fact remembered every detail. He remembered auld and wizened Lizzie Brown choking on one of her greedily consumed, roasting hot potatoes. Tears of pain welling in her eyes, she had clawed at her throat as her face turned puce, before beginning to claw irrationally at three year old Seth's throat in her agonising panic. He had stood terrified and clamped in her almighty dying strength till he heard her death rattle as the last breath in her old lungs expired, releasing him from her clutches.

The next spinster to take care of him was partially paralysed on one side of her body, which had left her face with a distortion and blindness in one eye. She also had a pronounced limp. Although she had been able to fend for herself well enough before Seth was brought to stay with her, she made her disabilities an excuse to treat the young boy as a slave, sitting in her chair while Seth fetched and carried for her. He knew no different and did as he was bid. One day the woman was struck by a terminal seizure. She was catapulted from her chair, foaming at the mouth, and thrown across the floor, twisting and twitching. The next day a neighbour travelled past the house twice before realising something was wrong. On his second trip he noticed that Seth was sitting in the same place on the front step of the woman's home. It was unusual to see the boy sitting, let alone for such an inordinate amount of time. The boy was usually working. As the neighbour approached, he noticed Seth was whittling and had carved a series of miniature yet exquisite horses' heads from pieces of driftwood he had found on the beach. It was as if some suppressed urge had been released with the demise of his tyrannical surrogate mother and he was free at last to do what he wanted to do. He seemed unconcerned about the fact that his 'carer' lay dead and cold on the floor inside.

Childhood was short for Seth. He matured and became self-sufficient from an early age. He was keen to do man's work by the time he was eleven years old and went to the Laird to tell him this. Archibald Stewart was impressed by the boy's indomitable spirit and made him companion to his own son, Charles, hoping that Charles would take on some of Seth's strength of character. Charles was five years older than Seth but was showing signs of impulsiveness and self-indulgence. Together the boys learned to ride, to manage the farm, and to collect rent from the crofts scattered across the Laird's island of Westray. Seth only spoke through necessity and his uncommunicative habits isolated him somewhat from his immediate community. He accepted hardships without complaint. He knew no other way. As far as he was concerned hard times were sent to try him, to make him stronger for whatever else life was going to throw at him. The other workers at Black Bull Farm wondered if all the disruption and change in Seth's childhood had contributed to his estranged attitude to their society. Others thought it was the trauma of his difficult birth that made him as he was. "What disnae kill ye, will strengthen ye" was a motto of one of Seth's more personally favoured elderly carers, who also used to say, "what's for you won't go by you". Seth believed in both these philosophies. He believed things were meant to be. This woman's most frequent expression was "none so queer as folk", which may have accounted for Seth's social detachment.

When Archibald Stewart died his son and heir, Charles Peter Stewart, was twenty-one. As the new Laird he retained the then sixteen year old Seth as his loyal and trustworthy companion. Seth's hard working trait and silent manner made him an obvious choice for Charles, who wanted all work completed swiftly and efficiently without idle chatter involved. As Laird's manservant, Seth enjoyed an active, outdoor life with a particular passion for riding horses. He loved nothing better than to exercise the Laird's fine horses and gallop freely across the scattald. He accompanied the Laird and helped with the management of Black Bull Farm and with the duties as landlord of the Westray crofts. It was Seth who rode with the Laird when he made his visits around his tenanted properties and it was often Seth who collected the rents for him. Owing to his duties of rent collecting he was set apart from the rest of the work force, just as Meg's eventual position as personal servant to the Laird's wife alienated her from the community. His preference for keeping his own company only added to his segregation. Seth was one of life's loners – until the emergence of Meg into his world.

Life had been uneventful and routine until the day Seth was given the duty of offering work to Meg Williamson. His instant and strong attraction to her awakened his inner soul and life took on a different aspect. Seth hadn't known love before and was not to initially realise that this was what he felt. He found it hard to deal with, not knowing how to show her he cared and this crucial and irretrievable hesitation allowed Meg's path in life to go down a different route, one severing her from family ties and depriving her of mothering love. The outcome could have been so different, happier for them both; the consequences less disruptive.

Seth was taller than most men of Orkney. He liked to wear his hair and moustache long. He followed a different lifestyle to his contemporaries. Although he had been born in Westray, his roots were elsewhere, though he was never to be sure quite where. The peculiarities of his upbringing caused his disinterest in idle conversation. It was a pastime he was unused to. His one passion was horse riding.

Some women workers found his smouldering looks sexually alluring. Seth had never actively searched for a woman to share his bed. Women approached him. His few lovers over the years knew they could not hold his interest and, indeed, most found that there was no more to this man; no sentimentality, no need for companionship, and no capacity for love. He was an enigma to most, though the memory of sex with Seth usually brought a self-satisfying smile to the faces of his bedded partners. But none were lasting relationships for Seth. He enjoyed being with the women he chose to bed, but he had never loved a woman – until Meg. He had never felt such strength of feeling for any of her predecessors.

Meg became Seth's main desire, but he was forced to bide his time. He wanted just one woman in his life and he had set his heart on Meg Williamson. She was the only woman he wanted to spend more time with. He was more determined than besotted. It was as if his goal – to have her as his life's partner – was indisputable, absolute. Although these feelings were unrequited, he was not unduly concerned for at that time she had still to settle in to her new surroundings before she could be expected to take heed of him. He was in no hurry. He had no set plan of how to achieve his aspiration but felt sure that fate would take its course. Determination had always been one of Seth's strong points, albeit a slow determination. The mere presence of Meg had given him hope of a better life, a life to be lived to its best potential, though it seemed that potential would take a long time in coming.

Isobella Grace Stewart, wife of the Laird of Westray, had led a charmed life until the onset of her debilitating illness. Her wealthy parents had moved to Orkney from the Scottish Highlands before she was born. From an early age Isobella's manipulative mother had groomed her only child for the coveted position of wife to the eligible Laird of Westray and had had no difficulty in orchestrating a romance between the young couple. Charles Peter Stewart's head was easily turned by Isobella's strikingly dark and handsome looks, unrivalled on Westray. When she married him Isobella was a poised and self-confident twenty year old and the people of Westray would long remember how stunning she looked in her wedding gown, the finest ever seen on the island. In those days she believed that looks were all that mattered, beauty coupled with wealth; she knew no other way. In time, circumstances would change her cosseted attitude.

Isobella gained weight after each successive birth of her three children, William Bruce, Catherine May, and Samuel Charles, and over the passing years she remained buxom and heavy breasted, though her height helped her to carry the extra weight well. She was poised and self-confident, a formidable force to be reckoned with, and a woman convinced of her unrivalled beauty on and around Westray. She was also convinced of her husband's fidelity. But as her illness slowly but surely progressed, her marital relations became nigh impossible with the increase in her disabilities. There followed a general lack of intimacy between Isobella and Charles. But, if she were honest with herself, she had always been more in love with the trappings of her marriage than with her husband – and she had lost none of those.

When Isobella first set eyes on Meg she felt slightly disconcerted by Meg's special type of beauty although she thought it lay mostly in Meg's eye-catching flaxen hair, seldom seen in Orkney. For Isobella Meg's paleness of skin and hair could never rival her own richness and creamy complexion, or her grace and grooming. Meg would always be servant class. However with Meg as her personal servant Isobella was happy to drop the air of aloofness that she extended to her other servants. Over the years she came to depend upon Meg more and more, both physically and mentally. The slow yet continual progression of her illness sapped at her confidence. But Meg was ready with reassurances and could be depended upon to be there night and morning to give Isobella's long hair the desired one hundred brush strokes.

Doctors came and went yet none could arrest the downward trend of her illness and Isobella became resigned to her fate – that of a premature death. A unique bond grew between the two women from such different walks of life.

When Meg first arrived at Black Bull Farm she was young and
naïve; an eye-catching blonde amongst a sea of brown or red haired
servant girls. She was given lodgings in a farm cottage with two other
servant girls, both of whom resented her from the start. Isolated from
family and home life Meg immersed herself in hard work, which only
created yet more ill feeling from her two co-workers. The other girls
were established workers and had their own lackadaisical yet acceptable
methods for completing tasks and Meg's enthusiastic attitude irked
them, but moreover it was her head-turning beauty that caused
them angst. They considered her to be a physical distraction to their
respective sweethearts and to them her mere presence was a threat to
their marital aspirations. Meg unwittingly made them feel inferior in
all aspects of their lives. When Isobella, the Laird's wife, commandeered
Meg's services at the Manor House, the promotion, as it was seen to be,
did not go down well with other hopefuls for the position, but Meg was
relieved and grateful for the isolation it gave her.

Seth's position as the Laird's right hand man separated him from
the other workers. From a distance he kept an eye on Meg. He saw
the rejection shown by the other female servants. He saw her constant
calming of male egos as she set aside each advance. Meg appeared to be
disinterested in any of the male workers. Seth's decision to admire her
from afar was to cost him greatly.

Friends were a thing of the past for Meg. They were memories,
memories of children on Fair Isle now grown and dispersed across the
globe, emigrated to mainland Scotland or Canada or New Zealand.
Their paths would probably never cross again. Isobella's friendship
had been unexpected. The two women were from very different
backgrounds. Isobella was well educated, an accomplished horse rider
and pianist. Meg was accomplished in domestic duties that Isobella
only knew how to delegate. So it was a surprise for Meg when, out of
the blue, Isobella announced that she considered Meg to be her dearest
friend. She sealed her statement by giving Meg one of her cast off
night-gowns, made of embroidered silk and edged with lace – it had

become too small for her but fit Meg perfectly. Meg was overawed at the gift.

The two girls in Meg's cottage married their suitors and moved to crofts outside the Farm complex. She was left to live alone in the small cottage. By that time she had decided to keep her unhappiness and homesickness buried, unwilling to burden Hellen, who was still suffering Andrew's bereavement and was proud that her daughter worked at the Laird's Manor. Her sisters were incommunicado; Barbara out of reach living in Germany, Agnes deluged by her many offspring, and Anderina too pragmatic to help with emotional problems. Meg's independent streak wouldn't allow her to rely on anyone else. She wouldn't burden someone with a worry if they couldn't actually help. Unintentionally, Meg was allowing her life to go awry. A contributory factor was the onset of her womanhood. The bonnie child was transformed into a stunning young woman, attracting the attention of a forbidden lover.

One event on Black Bull Farm left a lasting impression on Seth. There had been persistent rain for several days before the dawn of a much-appreciated dry, sunny day. The wet weather had created a quagmire at the foot of a field with poor drainage and it was into this that a pony in foal had become embroiled in a sea of mud. By the time Seth discovered the pony's plight, the animal was stuck fast and exhausted. Seth set about trying to free the pony, becoming caked in mud from head to foot. A motley crew of servants and farm workers gathered around the scene and shouted their support for Seth's exertions.

Meg had been collecting eggs in the hen barn when she heard what sounded like a fight going on in the distance. On investigation she noticed the small crowd at the foot of the field and left her egg basket by the barn as she ran down to see what all the commotion was about. From somewhere behind her she heard the low rumble of thundering hooves across the sodden field and before she could turn, the Laird himself galloped past her to arrive with a flourish at the scene of the debacle. He began gesticulating to the crowd to let him through and demanding that Seth get out of his way. He would be the one to free the panicked pony.

Two seemingly effortless minutes later the pony was free and the gathered servants cheered for their Laird. He proceeded to take pleasure in making a mockery of Seth's endeavours and the other servants felt obliged by loyalty to their employer to laugh with the Laird and at the sorry muddied state of Seth's appearance. Meg was their exception. The Laird sneered at Seth, loudly declaring that he was weak and perhaps he should cut his wages, or give him dairymaid's work, or perhaps he should be given the job of hanging out the laundry. Finally, when the Laird was satisfied that his servants were whipped up into a frenzy of ridicule towards Seth, he mounted his horse and rode off in apparent triumph.

Throughout the whole episode, Seth had remained unflinching and silent. Initially, he had seen the funny side – until the Laird persisted in his hardened and prolonged attack on him. Seth couldn't know of the Laird's inner workings at that moment, his eagerness to impress a woman he desired. What you saw was what you got with Seth. He had no desire to impress. As the galloping horse reached the brow of the rise, he saw the Laird stand tall in his stirrups and look back over his shoulder to catch the eye of the beautiful blonde bystander who stood out from the crowd. The Laird's look of power and gloating was met at a distance by Meg's glare of contempt for his unnecessary actions, yet the Laird was blissfully unaware of whatever emotions lay behind her eyes. He saw what he wanted to see – that his look was met by that of the woman he desired.

Her respect, which the Laird would have been happy to receive, was instead directed towards his unbeknown rival. As the Laird and his horse rode out of sight over the brow of the hill, Meg approached Seth at the edge of the quagmire, putting her hand on his arm and looking up into his eyes. He was never to forget that moment. She reassured him that his efforts had more than likely achieved all but the final release of the pony, thereby making it easy for the Laird to come along and impressively finish the job. She inwardly warmed to his candour as Seth stood silently seething, his blue eyes shining with anger.

"De Laird wis nearly just as caked in mud as ye were, Seth," she said, "an' he wis only here twa minutes!"

Seth's twenty minutes of struggle seemed worthwhile to him after Meg's approval. This had been the first time Meg had addressed Seth personally and the first smile that he would call his own. For Meg, her thoughts on Seth that day were uncomplicated. She felt strongly about injustices yet was unable to notice the injustices to herself in the decade to follow. It was to be the last occasion where Meg took note of Seth for her attention was soon to be distracted when she was caught up in the Laird's seduction. Yet the beginnings of brooding rivalry between the two men had hung over the surface of the quagmire that day.

23

Laird of Westray

When Meg first arrived at Black Bull Farm she caught only fleeting glimpses of her employer and usually from a distance as he directed and delegated proceedings at the Farm. Several weeks passed by before the omnipotent Laird sought out his latest recruit. It was early one morning as Meg turned the corner of her cottage that she found herself nose to nostril with sixteen hands of chestnut stallion. Both servant and horse were startled and Meg took a step backwards in alarm as she gasped and the horse whinnied. From behind the enormous animal came the sound of heavy footsteps echoing on the cobbled stones, accompanied by the clinking of riding boots. The horse shook its mane vigorously and dipped its head. In doing so the Laird himself was revealed, standing beside his steed and holding the reins.

The Laird's expression was haughty and couldn't contain his amusement at Meg's alarm. She fought to suppress her feelings of intimidation and to regain composure, uncomfortable to be in such close proximity to the imposing figure of the Laird. He and his huge horse blocked her path. There was nothing she could do but stand between the wall and the solid mass of horseflesh; the rock and the hard place. He began to remove his leather riding gloves, fingertip by fingertip, striding towards her as he did so. He stared keenly into her eyes, narrowing his own infinitesimally and at last he spoke.

"Are you Meg Williamson?"

"Aye, I am," she said calmly.

Slowly he encircled her and Meg stood unflinchingly, holding her gaze steady as she felt his eyes bearing down on her.

"Are you finding the work to your liking, Meg Williamson?"

Surprised by the question, Meg merely nodded her head and took a deep breath, which she instantly regretted for her bosom noticeably rose up as the Laird moved to the front of her stance. He took the opportunity to float his eyes up and down her body, allowing them to linger on any moving parts. Discomfort flowed over Meg like clawing treacle. Indignant at the power he could command she shot him a flash of irritation as his eyes came back to rest on her face with a soul-searching glare. She wanted to avoid his penetrating look yet the first chemical charge between them tingled through her body.

Over the ensuing weeks Meg became more aware of his presence around the Farm. She watched him deliver his orders to the workers, directing a task in hand, delegating work and instilling a sense of purpose and swiftness to his workers. She remembered the rent collecting day as the Williamson family stood in front of Quoylet and how his gaze had been penetrating even then. He had cut a dashing figure. Now, living at Black Bull Farm, in her naivety she was impressed by his high standing position - that of "master of all he surveys" as her grandmother had once noted. Believing she was inaccessible, she allowed herself illicit thoughts. He was of another class, another breed even. A pillar of the community and this all held a fascination for her. Alone in her cottage, she became obsessed with her infatuation for him. She mused about how it would be to be close to him, to be alone with him. Meg believed it to be mere fantasy.

But the fantasy became reality. It was not a rushed, thoughtless affair. It was slowly infused, hesitatingly brought to fruition. This added to the heightened intensity of the tantalisation. At different corners of Black Bull Farm at all times of the day and night, both Meg Williamson and Charles Stewart began to find that their minds were dominated by thoughts of each other, troubling them both in different ways.

Initially Charles was irritated by the fact that Meg kept cropping up in his mind. She was someone who consistently disturbed his *status quo*. His thoughts kept turning to the likelihood of when he might next catch a glimpse of Meg's beauty. He had never felt like this before. It had all been so different with Isobella. Although he now had all he needed, a wife and an issue of children, with hindsight he felt that he had been duped into his marriage. Isobella had been the most striking woman Charles Stewart had known. She was attentive and charming towards him. Their respective parents were delighted at their developing romance and as Isobella had no other competition in Westray for style, class and beauty, Charles was easily swayed in her favour. Lusting after her could only lead to marriage in his class system. Their respective parents were good friends and Charles and Isobella's betrothal seemed a *fait accompli* before he had much chance to think in depth about their romance, or marriage, which soon became the inevitable and expected outcome. Their partnership was successful, although he had never thought deeply about whether he loved Isobella.

Unlike Seth, who had fallen for Meg at first glance, Charles's fixation had been slow in dawning. On his first sighting at Quoylet, he had indeed become transfixed with thoughts of how stunningly beautiful this girl standing before him would become as she grew to womanhood. A happily married man, Charles Stewart had never been unfaithful to his wife. His exterior show of aloofness and superiority towards his workers was entirely an act in order to keep a certain detachment and maintain their respect and obedience. Although he was aware of his elevated position in the Orcadian society of the time, he felt his birth to be but a quirk of nature and that he might just as easily have been born into a poor family. This made him a fair employer, who knew his workers as individuals, their strengths and their weaknesses.

His deep feelings for Meg would not abate. She was like a magnet and his eyes were always drawn to her. He knew he was a class above, but felt somehow that it was she who was too exquisite for him. As with many affairs of the heart, this one was not meant to happen, yet it was so surely destined to be. The ensuing unavoidable but forbidden love affair between master and servant was a natural progression to the mutual attraction.

Isobella's illness gave opportunity for the illicit affair that began gingerly. As her unnamed malady worsened, Isobella took to sleeping alone in a separate bedroom. On the transitional night when her husband gave in to the overwhelming temptation he felt, Isobella slept peacefully and in blissful oblivion.

It was a bitterly cold winter's night when Charles succumbed to the aching desire within him. No moon visible and the sky as dark as ink, just the cover he needed as he was irresistibly drawn to her cottage door. He determined to take the chance and to face Meg with his torment. He felt compelled to open the door and step inside forbidden territory. The beating of his heart was so loud that he thought it would surely wake her. Closing the door silently behind him, he momentarily wondered what Meg's reaction would be, but he had gone this far and now believed this was meant. In the far recesses of his mind was a small nagging conception of the true immorality, the iniquity, of what he was about to do.

Meg's room was bathed in an amber light given off by the weakly glowing embers of a dying fire in the grate. Striding forward, he stood on the hearth and stared into the peaceful scene before him. On the lonely bed in the corner under a patchwork quilt, Meg's recumbent form gently rose and fell with the rhythmic motion of her sleep-induced breathing. She stirred – as if his eyes were boring a hole into her body. Gracefully, she rolled over in her sleep to face him. Even in her soporific state she was suddenly aware of something untoward and quickly raised herself onto one elbow, the soft firelight washing over her fear-filled face. Bewilderment enveloped her sleepy eyes.

His heart in turmoil, Charles stood silent, watching unashamedly the beauty of the woman he longed to be with. Her golden, tousled hair fell in tantalising wisps over her bare shoulders as she clutched the bedclothes tightly to her bosom. Her night-gown hung loosely, baring one shoulder and her forearm to her elbow, revealing the top of one compressed breast, its soft roundness highlighted by flickering flames from the dying embers. It had once been Isobella's night-gown. Charles remembered it well and for a fleeting moment his conscience jolted him from his adoration of Meg. The night-gown looked better on her slender frame.

As if from the dead, his loins awakened as he gazed upon the core of his desire, his only immediate ambition about to be fulfilled. Not a word was spoken, but through their facial expressions they relayed their thoughts and unspoken questions and answers moved with ease between them. Could we, should we, do you want me? Meg gave out a very long sigh as if she had been holding her breath for years.

That night was seemingly endless with only the crowing of the farm cockerel to bring the new lovers to their senses.

The out of the way location of Meg's servant cottage enabled their trysts. It provided total privacy. The door opened onto the gable end wall of Westray Manor, which had no door or window. No one could oversee the comings and goings of Meg's cottage. The path to her door led nowhere else. She was the only unmarried female servant and therefore had the cottage to herself.

Their affair began tentatively. It was inevitable that Charles would assume the upper hand and that Meg would take the dutiful mistress role, constantly waiting for her master's surprise arrival at her hearth. But she accepted this enthusiastically. It gave her dull existence sparkle, a passion and intensity. Meg didn't feel used by him, she felt cherished, which indeed she was in the way that the initial passion of a love affair is all consuming and the two people involved mean everything to each other – for that fleetingly savoured time. She knew he had held himself in check for quite a time and wanted to believe this was because he was a good person, who would not venture lightly into an affair with a defenceless and vulnerable young servant girl.

Meg's waking hours became filled with anticipation of possible after-dark trysts. It brought forth intense and heightened emotions, being needed and loved in a way she had never previously experienced. Initially she gave no thought to the future, wanting only for their special times to continue. The excitement over their obvious wrongdoing consumed her and she felt like a mischievous child.

At the beginning Meg was intoxicated by the sudden delirium and spent no time in thinking about the emotional distance she was creating between herself and her already physically distant family. Contact with Hellen and Agnes and John, the very people she had always loved, would always love, would soon fill her with thoughts of doubt and shame as the reality of the implications of her precarious and ignominious situation began to sink in. The future crept into her thoughts and troubled her. Where would this guilt-ridden liaison lead?

Their intimacy developed and continued. When they lay together naked in her bed, Meg could believe they were in love on equal terms, oblivious of class differences. She wanted more than secret liaisons, but they both knew this was impossible. Isobella was terminally ill. Her illness had caused her body to balloon, yet she was a faded image of her former self. Neither of the two people closest to her wished to cause her more pain. They both cared for her.

This was the way it had to be – until Charles's seed implanted on Meg's fertile ground and a seemingly insurmountable watershed rose up between them. "Nothin' so sure as change," Hellen used to say and she was right – nothing ever stayed the same for long and Meg's time of ecstasy seemed to have lasted a mere fraction of her life.

24

Unwanted Seed

Even before the bubble of self-indulgence burst, showering Charles with cloying dilemmas, he had begun to show signs of stress caused by the deceit of his guilt-ridden liaison with Meg. Consumed with thoughts of possible discovery, leading to unforgivable anguish to his ailing wife and innocent family, he was not equipped to handle the news Meg gave him. She said the life-changing news as simply as she was able.

"I think I have yer child growing inside me."

A silence descended over them, so powerful it was as if they had fallen mute and deaf. Charles stared into the void beyond Meg's beautiful eyes, deep into the dark pits of her pupils, down into infinity. Icy needles penetrated his skull and reality bore a hole into his cocoon of fantasy. This was an unconsidered consequence. A result of their unbridled passions reared up and demanded to be addressed. On this, their first acrimonious moment, Meg and Charles stared at one another, unsmiling; his eyes filled with denial, hers with vain hope.

"*No!*" he spluttered emphatically and Meg felt her tide of happiness ebb far, far away as he uttered that ugly word.

Charles Stewart, Laird of Westray, felt more out of control than he had ever done. Initially his anger was directed at himself and this wanton behaviour that had caused the careless implantation of his determined seed. In his ensuing ranting, he blamed Meg, blamed her naivety, her alacrity. Having three legitimate children to his credit, he had long since dismissed the necessity of any further procreation on his part.

Panic set in on the realisation that an illegitimate offspring of his was growing inside Meg's soft belly. He wanted to deny its existence. He insisted that when the baby was born it would have to be looked after elsewhere. To all intents and purposes, it was to be banished. He entertained no other plans for his love child and ignoring Meg's pleading eyes, he told her in no uncertain terms that no one must be told he was the father. Both realised Meg's name would be tarnished through this act of abandonment, but that was the least of Charles' worries.

Powerless, Meg's exhilaration rapidly dissipated. She felt she was sinking into a quagmire that swamped her thoughts and adhered to her conscience. As his verbal ranting reigned like blows to her feeble body, she had a vision of her depressing future. The situation had brought out the worst in Charles. He spat out hurtful words with sincere disaffection in their first argument. Meg wondered if it might also be their last. She felt impeached by the one person who mattered to her. The pedestal she had placed him upon was crumbling before her. It was the start of his fall from the exalted position in which she had placed him.

The cockerel was crowing boastfully as Charles slammed the door behind him. There had been no apologies for his shocked behaviour, no kiss goodbye, no usual tender words on parting.

To Meg, Charles's reaction was more shocking than the prospect of unmarried motherhood. She began to wonder at the true essence of this supposedly great man. His handsome and strong outer shell had peeled away to reveal an inner core turning rotten. Knowing him in depth was a disturbing experience. The once blissful state of cherished love that he had given to her had been ripped away. Their passion was sinking beneath the surface of a swamp of injustice and bitterness. She felt trapped with no means of escape.

For several months, Charles's ardour was cooled by the knowledge of their unplanned creation. Meg's passion for him was equally chilled by his icy and cruel behaviour of her. Any joy she had on knowing she was pregnant with her first child, a love child, had been squashed and trampled in his ensuing panic.

She knew there would have been no perfect conclusion, but the bleakest of prospects appeared to be hurtling towards her with no evasive tactics available. With the dawning of the enormity of what had befallen her, desperate thoughts disturbed her peace of mind as she realised she was now friendless and alone in her greatest time of need.

The future of her baby beyond his birth was given scant consideration by either parent-to-be. William was shunned in the womb.

The clandestine obsession, which had taken over Meg's empty life, was soured. Their secret affair was still a secret, but that was all it had become. Charles' indiscretion was merely that he had fallen in love, but his fear of a possible scandal and the heartache for a wronged and frail wife instigated a change in his character. He became deceitful and hardhearted.

It was not a rare occurrence for servant girls to become pregnant, but a wedding to a suitor generally hurriedly followed. Meg was a mystery. When the other workers heard the rumour that Meg was pregnant, most were amazed that she had taken a lover. No one was aware of any suitor therefore they could only guess at the identity of the father and the general conclusion circulated that Meg must have been with one of the many traders who delivered goods who came and went. As Westray was normally fairly devoid of newsworthy talk, Meg's state was much discussed behind closed doors.

More mystery abounded when her unborn baby vanished overnight and Meg returned to work, obviously delivered of child. They began to wonder whither her baby had died, but no minister came and there was no funeral. The other workers and servants were stunned when she continued to work as usual for Isobella. Most presumed that as an unmarried mother she would most definitely lose her job and have to leave Black Bull Farm.

Isobella for her part had not an inkling as to the identity of the baby's father. During the early days of her unexpected pregnancy, Meg's mistress had detected her shame, realising that the baby had certainly not been planned, but resolved not to pry, concluding the father must be one of the other farm workers. Meg's private life was of no interest to her. She always found it hard to believe the wanton morals of the servant classes. However, when Meg asked for her help with delivery when her time came, Isobella felt somehow honoured to be considered for such a crucial task. The fact that her favoured servant needed her gave her a very rewarding feeling. The roles were reversed. Although it was of enormous relief to Meg, she became racked with guilt at her mistress's continued kindness and at the whole hidden, sordid feeling the affair gave to her.

Any thoughts of bonding with this unwanted foetus were furthermost from her mind. The baby was barely considered. Meg's once warm and loving heart was hardening with the pressures that life was thrusting her way.

Meg was descending the two flights of stairs to the lower kitchen when she was taken with her first labour pain. The kitchen was empty except for Bessie Sinclair, the cook, who was stacking plates into a dresser having served and cleared away supper for the other servants. Meg was accustomed to eating alone. Isobella didn't require her services until mid morning, creating working hours that were out of step with the rest of the work force and contributing to her detachment from them.

Bessie set a steaming bowl of cock-a-leekie soup in front of Meg as Meg winced with pain, putting a hand to her belly.

"Whit's up, Meggie? Ma soup is nae that bad!"

The bap in Meg's clenched and white knuckled fist was reduced to a gooey ball of dough.

"Aah!" said Bessie, knowingly. "' 'Tis babbie comin', eh?"

Meg released her grip on the mutilated roll and looked up anxiously into Bessie's kindly eyes. The dreaded birth indeed appeared to be imminent.

Being another of the everyday servants at Westray Manor, Bessie knew Meg fairly well. She cooked meals for the servants as well as the Stewart family dinners. She was fond of Meg though she thought her a "queer fish" and was always telling her husband how elusive and mysterious she was. Bessie's husband was a dairyman. He provided the Stewart household with daily supplies of milk, butter and cheese. Her first husband had been lost at sea in a sudden storm, the only man to be washed overboard from a sixern. Although the sea usually delivered most of her drowned victims to the islands' shores, his body was never recovered. Bodies were frequently washed up after periods of rough weather, those of drowned fishermen or shipwreck victims. Bessie had been left with one small child to bring up. This was not dissimilar from other women in Orkney, whose seamen husbands were away from home for much of the time, the difference being that their men would eventually return with an income to pay the rent. Crofts were the property of Lairds and it was the fishermen, fathers and sons, who paid the rents, the Lairds having sole rights to sell the fish that they caught. Bessie had then needed work with lodgings and she appealed to the Laird, who took her on as an apprentice cook. She had found her *forte* and soon excelled at her work in the kitchen of Westray Manor. Ten years later, Jeremiah Sinclair, bachelor dairy herdsman, proposed to her after two years of flirting and teasing. She was forty years old and he was twenty-five. As a fifteen year old youth, Jeremiah could remember the day Bessie's husband had been swept away and he remembered her distress at that time. Their age difference didn't bother them.

"Ye are as old as the hills, Bessie Sinclair, but ye are as fit as a fiddle!" he would say, poking her in intimate places, making her squeal. Bessie's rosy-cheeked complexion made her look like she was continually blushing. Folk would say that Jeremiah and his humour kept her young. Bessie's gift of love was food; she fed him the unwanted excesses from the Stewart dinner table and he was twice the man in girth than when they first met, unlike Bessie, who remained the same size. The ever-accessible food in her kitchen didn't continually tempt her and she survived on a small intake of food. "Ye dinnae eat enough tae keep a speug alive!" Jeremiah would complain.

Meg's crumple-faced baby boy, protesting gustily, was safely delivered by Isobella and Bessie, not long after dawn the following morning. They placed the tiny washed and calmed infant into Meg's hesitant arms. With a self-congratulatory smile, Isobella admired the satisfying scene of new mother and child, then left the cottage, leaving Meg startlingly alone with her new-born son.

The snuffling and swaddled baby nestled in the crook of her arm. Only his tiny face could be seen, puffy eyelids clamped shut over unseeing eyes, his tiny mouth making infinitesimal sucking movements. A sad smile drifted over Meg's weary face. Mixed emotions washed over her. She knew Charles was right. For everyone's sake, she must continue with the plan to have her son – for it was now her son, Charles would have none of him – to be brought up by his grandmother. Meg knew that Hellen would love him as her own. He could not be allowed to grow up in the vicinity of his father for fear of any growing family likeness. Meg thought he already looked more like a Stewart than a Williamson. Her baby would have a happier life elsewhere, but the very notion deeply grieved her. Alone with her baby her feelings turned to panic. The sudden opening of the door roused Meg from her still private moment. Isobella and Bessie were talking as they entered the cottage.

"William has bin lookin' fur his midder high an' low!" Bessie announced to Meg.

"Of course," continued Isobella, "his nurse never thought to find me here, did she?"

William. The name implanted in Meg's mind. William was a name from her own family; one of her uncles, a brother of Andrew's, and on Hellen's side, her great grandfather. Perhaps it was appropriate that William was also the name of the legitimate son of her illicit lover.

The opening of the door swiped clear her mind, and like a frothing tide over a sand-covered pebble, her mind was cleansed, porous, receptive.

Bessie came over to Meg's bed and gave the baby a soft little pinch on his scrawny cheek.

"Ne'er mind, lass," she said. "He'll soon fill oot when ye fill da wee belly wi' guid mulk."

Breast milk. Meg could feel the tingling sensation in her nipples at the very mention. Yet another problem to be overcome, the cessation of her milk production.

"Whit will ye be callin' him, Meggie?" asked Bessie.

"His name is William," Meg said positively.

Bessie and Isobella shot one another a brief and bewildered glance. Conferring earlier they had thought that the baby's name might reveal the identity of Meg's mysteriously secret lover. But it appeared to be simply the first boy's name she'd heard since giving birth, as if she had given no thought whatsoever to the naming of her child.

"Good choice," said Isobella, sinking wearily into Meg's only chair. She shifted her weight around trying to find a comfortable position in the hard backed, wooden seat, lamely padded with two thin cushions.

There was a knock at the door. Bessie opened it to find Seth, who had been summoned to speak with Isobella.

"Ah, Seth," said Isobella, "I need you to go to Rabbithall directly to fetch Hellen Williamson. I must impress upon you that under no circumstance are you to tell her why her presence is required here, or to mention Meg's baby. Meg must be the one to tell her."

Seth had been exercising horses from early morning and, like the rest of the servants, was unaware of the recent delivery at Black Bull Farm. He looked over to the bed to see Meg propped on one elbow, her hair tousled, her forehead beaded with sweat. His expression was warm, kindly, and Meg's inner turmoil welcomed this sight. Something in her reached out to him.

"Do ye want tae see him, Seth?" she beckoned to him to come nearer to the bed.

Isobella tried to hurry Seth on his away, but Meg persisted. Bessie was unable to stifle her intake of breath. Seeing Seth's obvious fascination – he had never seen such new human life before – she suggested he might like to hold the baby. The feeling of wanting to share this moment so precious to her was strong. Although taken aback by her suggestion, he felt honoured to hold her child.

"His name is William," she told him softly.

"Aye?" was Seth's reply.

He was amazed that Meg thought he might want to hold the tiny being. Undoubtedly, she was unaware of his love for her and that for him to hold the love child of another man would hurt him to the core. But strangely he found the experience uplifting. He had seen dozens of new-born foals in his time, and lambs for that matter, but this was quite different. This baby boy encapsulated his own beginnings, and a sense of eternity. Never having held a baby before, let alone one that was less than an hour old, Seth was happy to participate in such a private moment and to share Meg's joy. He stood smiling down at William's squashed wee face snuggled in the crook of his arm.

It crossed the minds of the two onlookers to this scene that Seth might well be the baby's father. But why would Meg and Seth hide a love for one another? Then Isobella asserted her authority once more by insisting that Seth travel immediately to Rabbitha'.

"Be sure, Seth, not tell her the reason for her journey," she pointed her elegant though puffy finger at him, "is that clear?"

"Aye, quite clear," said Seth, reluctantly handing William back to his mother.

Seth's heart lay heavy with unrequited love.

25

Seth's Travels

Seth had a chance to become Meg's saviour directly after William's birth. At that time Meg was lonelier than ever before. Charles kept his distance, determined to rid himself of his passion for her. Her life was a sad debacle; denied the upbringing of her baby, compelled to send him away, to abandon him, and coerced into an estrangement with her own mother and family by remaining silent over her plight to protect Charles, and to protect Isobella. In so doing she also allowed cruel assumptions to be made about her by other workers intrigued by her predicament. Alone, she struggled to find strength to deal with the pain. Still in love with Charles, she was young enough to believe this was the only love of her life.

Meg felt deserted when she heard from Bessie that Charles was making plans to visit lairds and landowners on the other Orkney Islands. He had chosen to remove himself from his temptation by leaving Black Bull Farm for a lengthy period of time. Had Isobella insisted in accompanying him, his plan would have been thwarted for she would have brought along a maid servant, who, of course, would have been Meg. But, he knew his ailing wife was not strong enough to cope with the travelling involved and, as he had hoped, Isobella refused outright to entertain such an idea. Instead, she invited her parents to come and stay with her for a while. Isobella's father, retired from his working life but active and willing, would assume the management of Black Bull Farm in his son-in-law's absence thus releasing Seth of any covering duties. Much to Seth's chagrin, the Laird told him that he would be accompanying him as usual, dashing any hopes Seth had of making his presence more known to Meg while the Laird was away. Through a twist of circumstance yet another stumbling block was put in Seth's way.

However, on the morning the Laird was due set off from Bull, an opportunity arose for Seth and he determined to grab his chance.

Charles and Isobella planned to take their three young children for a pony and cart ride around their estate. Bessie prepared a picnic breakfast so that the family could stop by the side of Loch Burness, a favourite spot with the children, and watch the wildfowl, the waders and swans there. After the picnic Charles would set off on his open-ended trip around the islands.

With the dust from the departing wheels of the Laird's cart still hanging in the air, Seth made his way to Meg's door and knocked boldly upon it.

"Who is it?" Meg's voice from within carried through her open window.

"Seth," he said simply.

There was a silent pause.

"Seth?" Meg was one of the few Fair Islanders that could pronounce his name without the use of the 'd' for 'th' sound.

"Aye."

The door opened to reveal a smiling though surprised looking Meg, smoothing down her apron.

"Guid day to ye Seth," she said. "Will ye no come in?"

"Aye," said Seth. "I will, Meg."

Seth's smile showed in his eyes first. His moustache disguised any movements of his mouth. They held eye contact for a moment before she turned inside and he followed her, shutting the latched door behind him. It was a warm spring day and although Meg had lit a fire, both her small windows were flung wide to let in the fresh new season's air. She motioned for him to sit down near the fireplace in her only chair. Removing the kettle that hung on a hook above her fire, she poured the hot water into a small glazed teapot and made them both a cup of weak tea. She hadn't asked him if he wanted tea. After handing him a cup, she pulled across a three-legged stool from a corner of the room and sat at the opposite side of the fireplace.

Meg felt surprisingly at ease as she watched the tall, silent man sitting in her chair, the only man ever to have sat in her chair – Charles only ever used her bed to rest upon. She had no idea why Seth had visited her and had no intention of asking him. It was certainly not an urgent errand for he looked well at ease. The ambience he created was comforting. There seemed no need for idle speech and the silence between them was easeful. On this of all mornings, Meg was pleased to have someone care enough to call on her. The first smile in days warmed her cheeks.

"He'll be away a good lang time," Seth said at last, staring blankly into the fireplace.

Meg wondered if somehow he knew and felt a constriction around her throat. He looked directly at her and his look was soft and in no way judgmental.

"Are ye tae go too, Seth?" she asked.

"Aye," he spoke with a tangible dejection.

"But dat should be grand fur ye – travellin' – awa' frae Black Bull fur a while, eh?" Meg was puzzled by the apparent sadness in his voice and tried to sound reassuring. "I wid love tae get awa' frum here…"

"Aye," Seth's voice drifted as a thought occurred to him and before he could bury the idea he heard his own voice say, "I would like to be travelling with you…"

Straight-faced and in all sincerity, they searched each other's eyes. The same question arose within both them. Seth wondered if he really said what he just heard? And Meg, bewildered, thought – did he just say what he just said?

"I must be going,"

Seth felt he had overstepped the mark and rose from the chair. Meg sat just where she was and stared ahead of her. He let himself out and she continued to stare at the door he had just closed behind him. Then she rose and went to the small window where she watched him striding away until he turned the corner and was out of sight.

A week later a letter arrived addressed to "*Meg, The Cottage, Westray Manor*". It was not news from Rabbitha' written by Agnes, nor was it Hellen's spidery and fairly illegible hand. The envelope was of a fine quality and Meg's hopes were suddenly aroused – could it be from Charles? Before reading the letter, her eyes darted to the foot of the page. The one word signature clearly and simply read "Seth".

Strangely, Meg didn't feel disappointed to know this letter was not from her lover.

"*Dear Meg,*" she read, "*Here am I on the island of North Ronaldsay, along with the horses in the stables of Laird Bruce. I am now as far north as I can go in Orkney – the next isle to the north-east would be your homeland, Fair Isle. The heather on the hills is glowing purple in the sunlight that shines all over the island today. Travelling is a fine thing but it is not quite as grand as horse riding. I am to exercise these horses now with Hamish, a groom who comes from Aberdeen. Hope you are in good health, Seth.*"

Meg was amazed to receive from Seth such a fine letter. He had written more than he had said in all the time that she had known him. It warmed her heart to think that someone wanted to contact her like this. And it reminded her of those strange last words he had said to her before he left on the trip – "I would like to be travelling with you…"

Her closed heart felt warm around its frayed edges.

While the Laird was away, Isobella became noticeably more unwell, but her parents kept her company and Meg's duties were eased by their support of their sick daughter and with the attention they gave to their three grandchildren.

Over the following five months other letters from Seth arrived for Meg and the receipt of these helped Meg's slow recovery from despair. One was posted from Sanday, one from Stronsay and one from Shapinsay. In the first Seth told her he was very taken with the beautiful island of Sanday, which had a fine lighthouse at its most north-easterly tip, visited by both Robert Louis Stevenson and by Sir Walter Scott over the years. He said he had taken some 'grand gallops' on his horse up and down the long island. The next letter described Stronsay, its beautiful beaches and an inland, naturally-formed swimming pool. At Shapinsay he stayed at the island's castle.

"*The Laird of Shapinsay,*" he wrote, "*has taken us right around the island on horseback. A very grand day indeed.*" Meg presumed the 'us' meant he and Charles Stewart. This had been the first mention from Seth of his master. Seth wrote more about horses and riding than he did of people.

She began to think of Seth as a friend, a friend at last in her friendless environment. She longed to write a letter back to him and let him know how much she appreciated receiving his news, but this was not possible as Seth never knew where they would be heading next. Meg also found the idea of writing to her lover's companion and father of her child quite a ridiculous proposition. The last letter that she received before their final return to Westray contained some of Seth's sketches depicting the places he had visited and the route they had taken.

First stop had been North Ronaldsay to the north east of Westray. Then they journeyed south to Sanday, where they stayed for a month. Over a period of several weeks, their travels took them south from Sanday to Stronsay, west from Stronsay to Eday and Faray, then south to Shapinsay. Gairsay was next then Wyre, Egilsay and Rousay. These islands were all situated to the north of Mainland Orkney. They spent a month calling on landowners on Mainland before taking the shortest sea crossing from the southern tip of western Mainland to Graemsay. After Graemsay they went to Hoy and then to Flotta, islands that lie south of Mainland Orkney. From Flotta they sailed east to South Ronaldsay and north to Burray before returning to Mainland, where they travelled overland to Kirkwall and took the long crossing to Papa Westray, just off the north-east coast of Westray.

Meg was impressed with Seth's sketches. He appeared to be very literate for a servant with much creative instinct hidden in his silent character. Meg sometimes read books that Isobella willingly lent to her and she was sure that Seth's journal would make a good travel book detailing the islands of Orkney. He was direct, straightforward, and precise, yet he could be quite lyrical about things that held his interest. And he could illustrate with confidence.

Meg determined to tell him of her idea when he returned and found herself looking forward to speaking with this increasingly interesting man, who had shown a different side to his character through his letters. She also wished she had a sharper picture of him in her mind's eye, because her memory of him was not altogether clear.

26

Renewed

After five months of travelling, visiting, discussing farming and tenanting with other Orcadian Lairds and landlords, Charles Stewart and Seth returned to Westray Manor and Black Bull Farm. They were both refreshed and ready to inject new life into work to be done at Westray.

It was Seth who benefited more than Charles from the trip – and in more ways than one. Like a tame but caged animal knowing only confinements and limitations, this travelling had given Seth a new taste of freedom. And although he had been away from Westray Manor at a crucial time in Meg's life, a vague, barely discernible bond had been established via his letters, letters that he felt compelled to write, so strong was his desire to share his new experiences with her. A near tangible bridge had been put in place between them, one that surpassed Seth's inadequacies at person to person communications. He had at last made a connection with her. Meg saved and stashed Seth's descriptive letters in a tin box under her bed and resolved to tell him about her idea.

When the Laird's return was announced to the farm workers, Meg's heart skipped a beat. Yet she found herself also keeping watch for Seth around the Farm. Every now and again during her day's work, she would wander to the nearest window in Westray Manor and allow her eyes to flit across the panorama of Black Bull Farm. Forever illusive, Seth was nowhere to be seen. At the end of her working day, she persisted with her quest by walking over to the stable block, where the stable lad told her Seth was out riding one of the horses and that he had been gone a good long while and should be back soon. She ambled over to the perimeter of the courtyard and ran her eyes over the landscape stretching for miles to the sea on the horizon. Sunlight still glinted on the water's choppy surface.

Meg heard the low rumble of galloping hooves before she saw horse and rider. Seth and his mount rose part by part, head, then chest, then saddle and horse, above the hill before her. Each thundering stride brought them closer. Appearing as he did, by degrees as he rose above the landscape, so did Meg observe him, by degrees. She watched as silent sheep scattered every which way ahead of the horse and rider. Seth rode in a steady line towards the stable yard. She watched as the tall warrior-like figure of her recent correspondent took on his physical presence. She watched as her memory of him was jolted, yet as if she were seeing him for the first time.

When Seth caught sight of the free-flowing blonde-haired woman of his dreams, standing on top of the hill by the stable courtyard he thought she was an illusion. She appeared to be watching his approach, watching and waiting. She was smiling, smiling and waiting, waiting for him. He pulled up his horse a few feet in front of her.

"Meg," he said simply in greeting.

"Seth," she replied, a smile on her lips.

He dismounted and walked towards her, holding his mare's reins in one hand. Meg turned side on with horse and rider to walk in step with them, the mare in the middle. The heat rose in clouds of steam from the mare's body and she shook her mane, showering them both with beads of sweat. Meg laughed as she wiped her cheek clean with her long apron.

While Seth groomed his horse, Meg and Seth talked. They talked as they had never talked before. They spoke of his tour of the Orkney Isles and Meg told him she appreciated receiving his letters. When she went further and suggested her idea to have his journal published, Seth fell silent. He looked at her as if she had asked him to touch the moon. Such a plan was beyond his comprehension. Meg's plan was shelved as quickly as it had been pro-offered, but inwardly it pleased him greatly that she still kept his letters in her possession and had shown such confidence in his ability by suggesting this idea.

A fine drizzle of rain started to fall as they left the stables. They were both hungry and made their way to Bessie's kitchen to see what supper could be had. It was long after the other servants had eaten and Bessie was stacking clean crockery into the kitchen dresser. When she saw them enter the kitchen together, lost in conversation, and sit down at the long table oblivious to her or anything else, she found herself subconsciously raising an eyebrow. She ladled out two bowls of broth and set before them a platter of bread. Jeremiah arrived to walk Bessie home and discreetly winked at her when he saw the lone couple, hitherto unseen together, engrossed in each other's company. Bessie smartly nudged her bony elbow into his ribs and swiftly bade Seth and Meg goodnight.

Alone in the kitchen that night, a bond slowly formed. After a time Meg confided in him that she deeply regretted giving baby William away. Her shame and guilt were set deep, but she couldn't reverse her actions for the sakes of all concerned in her predicament. She didn't tell Seth that her priority, muddled as it was, was to protect the reputation of her baby's father, although he already knew this. Neither Meg nor Seth made any reference to the Laird in person. Meg presumed that Seth, like the others, didn't know who had made her pregnant. She couldn't return to Rabbitha'. There was no room for her anymore. The only home she could hope to retain was the cottage at Black Bull Farm.

Meg was trapped by the beck and call of her controlling master.

It was past ten o'clock when they blew the last candle out and left the kitchen. Only then did they notice the lashing rain that had been falling for the past hour. It had pounded on the kitchen windows yet they had been oblivious to its thundering noise. Seth used his overcoat as a shield, holding it above their heads and shoulders as they ran to Meg's door. Lest they stood too long in the drenching rain, they parted and Seth continued to run for cover to his attic room above the stables.

He was pleased that Meg had opened her heart to him. That was important to him. But within days he was to realise that his rival had swiftly stepped back into old habits and claimed Meg's attentions once again, embroiling her in emotional dependency.

For Charles, separation from Meg turned out to be just that, a separation as opposed to a cooling off period. It took less than a fortnight before he succumbed, allowing himself to be drawn to Meg's door, letting himself in, appearing at her bedside in the wee small hours as on so many previous occasions. Charles put the arguments of the past behind him as if time had distanced him from them and allowed him to move on. Although his cruel demands, his shirking of any parental responsibility and denial of Meg's were still fresh in Meg's mind, she was yet again charmed and seduced at a vulnerable and lonely time. Their passion for one another was resumed, although spasmodically and dependent on Charles's whims. The sour note of their last parting became a memory. The renewed intimacy was a reassurance she so badly craved. William was never spoken of. Not only rejected but also denied.

The compulsory secrecy attached to their affair heightened the purely private and physical side. Meg saw that their 'love' was purely sexual, without progressing to anything deeper. There was no spiritual companionship. There could be no discussion of a future together. No plans could be made. Their liaison was simply for the present time, for the moments they stole together.

Meg had not recognised Seth's more worthy feelings towards her, or given thought to the idea that with him she might have a bright future. She was too tied up in Charles's powerful influence. Because she despised her own despicable behaviour concerning her secret lover and the rejection of her baby, she imagined that everyone, this included Seth, thought badly of her. She wondered if the other workers thought she had secret liaisons with men, perhaps they thought she was a whore, who wilfully abandoned her babies. She was convinced no man could be interested in a good way in a woman such as herself.

Seth kept his distance so as not to cause embarrassment and confusion, or lose them both their jobs. He also felt a loyalty to his long-term employer though this was diminishing the more he saw of the Laird's ill treatment and lack of respect for Meg. Seth and Meg kept apart for different reasons yet both believed they were doing the right thing.

Different aspects of Seth's character were evolving. There were qualities that had lain dormant emerging. His growing maturity was a revelation to himself. Emotionally starved for most of his life due to constant changes in his childhood, Meg had aroused a deeper self. And before Meg, he had been fairly disinterested in what life had to offer, thinking that there would never be much more for him than Black Bull Farm and Westray. Now he was changing in readiness for a new life.

Three years later the realisation that she was again pregnant descended like a heavy haar upon Meg. She had dreaded this happening again yet hadn't known how to avoid it. Scared of Charles's reaction, she knew his inevitable solution to the problem for a second time. And so it was that one evening some months later Hellen found Seth with the familiar horse and cart in the yard at Rabbitha'. Hellen, now over sixty, only ever travelled to Black Bull Farm for the removal of Meg's unwanted children and this time she had wanted to insist that Meg return with her, but there was no room to put her up at Rabbitha' and no work for her there. Meg needed to earn her living and Hellen assumed that it must be a stipulation of her employment that she was allowed no dependants living with her, but it didn't explain why she continued to be so mysterious and withdrawn.

The handing over of Ella was a much more traumatic and emotional event than it had been with the baby William. They had been through it before and knew the hurt that was to follow. Meg again refused to divulge the identity of Ella's father. Both women were distraught when they parted, then little realising what the end result of their next chance meeting would deliver.

And so it was that Ella arrived in the middle of the night for William to discover the next morning. Again with Seth's unwilling assistance, one of Meg's babies had been delivered into Hellen's despondent arms.

Part 5

27

Endings and Beginnings, 1894

Lightly rapping her knuckles on little Peter's clammy brow, Meg began the ditty.

"Knock a' da door, peep in…" as she gently lifted one of his half-shut and weary eyelids. "Lift up da latch…"

Charlie giggled as Meg gently pushed in the tip of his brother's nose, likening it to a pig's snout. Peter smiled feebly.

"An' walk in!"

Obediently Peter opened his dry lips to accept the spoonful of appetising broth. For a week the little boy had suffered from convulsions of coughing. He was exhausted and had hardly eaten for two days. Singing the rhyme helped to disguise Meg's desperation for him to swallow some health-giving broth from her pro-offered spoon. As she blew cooling breath across another spoonful, Peter was overcome by paroxysms of coughing, so bad that he vomited. These attacks were steadily increasing.

Meg decided a trip to the doctor was necessary. Charlie went along, too.

"Whooping cough," the doctor said as gently as he dared.

This was the diagnosis Meg had been dreading.

Peter's condition worsened. He was often seized by uncontrollable successions of short, sharp coughs, followed by the distinctive deep whooping sound. These attacks became so insistent and rapid in sequence that he was frequently left, unable to catch his breath between bouts, exhausted and tear-stained.

Meg prayed. She gave him her undivided attention, but could only try to alleviate his suffering and keep him as comfortable as possible. Witnessing Peter's agony distressed those around him although the little lad seemed bravely resigned to it. Sapping at his strength, both physically and mentally, the illness wore him down; his was a constant battle with a persistent enemy.

Peter died in his mother's loving arms, his ashen face wet with her tears. It was just three weeks before his shared fourth birthday.

Charlie took his brother's death badly. They had been inseparable. He talked little, ate less, and found joy in nothing. Meg later believed that he pined so badly for his brother that he brought the dreaded illness upon himself. At first it appeared that Charlie had escaped the highly infectious disease, but he was soon coughing with a distinct whoop. His illness was not as debilitating as his brother's had been and everyone was hopeful for his recovery. But they were proved wrong.

In the middle of the night, Meg began to gently awake from the deepest sleep she had experienced for many weeks. There was a fading smile across her face as she was left with the memory of a carefree dream where both her twin sons were running towards her on a sun baked, iridescent beach, their arms outstretched, their faces shining with happiness and health. Twin bright suns shone dazzlingly from behind each of their heads, slowly darkening their features and blurring their images. Meg awoke fully. The warm and pleasant inner feeling vanished and a keen feeling of guilt flooded over her. It intensified when she rolled over to check on Charlie.

An eerie stillness drenched the room. An aura of peace swamped her senses. All was unnaturally quite. As she reached out to touch his pale face, her fingertips froze and her hand recoiled at the chill from his skin. Charlie was cold as stone.

The corners of his tiny mouth were slightly uplifted, giving the illusion of a last smile. It was as if, when no one was looking, a soothing wave of peace had drifted over his aching body as death released him from his earthly pain and led him, willingly, to his heavenly brother's side. His little face was set with a dying smile. Charlie's had been a private death.

After a futile struggle with herself for not being awake for him in his passing, for her lapse in nursing vigil, Meg comforted herself with the thought that the souls of her boys would be together again, that they had not been separated from each other for long.

The memory of her dream gave her solace. She believed absolutely that Peter and Charlie had both been with her, their three souls united, for the duration of her dream; that it had indeed been a shared experience for the three of them. Although Charlie passed away when she was asleep, she truly felt that he – and his brother – had been with her in some other world, where there was no pain; where there was only soul-nourishing aesthetics. The dream experience was reality to Meg. She would remember it vividly, how she had woken, cocooned in the warm, ethereal feelings of happiness and togetherness with her twin boys. The dream and its augmented peace, its comfort, stayed with her forever.

Twenty years before Meg remembered her grandmother, Barbara Brown, describing her strange dream, the implications of which had not been understood until her father's near drowning and subsequent death. Meg could remember her grandmother trying to make sense of it back then. Both their dreams were premonitions of impending death, but Meg's was a comfort in her double dose of grief.

As she kissed Charlie's peaceful brow, she realised what day it was. Precisely four years before, she had given life to the now departed twins. It would have been their fourth birthday. The irony was not lost to her. These were the two children with whom she planned to share her future, the children she had wanted to keep with her, to cherish and never abandon. She had borne her boys in maturity and strength without the influence or demand of another. They were the proof that she was accountable for herself. But now, was this not retribution for all her wrongs? Meg felt keenly the justice-served angle of this double-edged tragedy.

Recollections of a childhood story came back to Meg. Her sisters had told her of the time before Meg's birth and after the death of their first brother, Hellen's first son. They spoke of Hellen's deep-rooted sadness that lasted for years. Meg's existence had been the release, a new start for the family. A lesson had to be learnt from this and Meg knew it would be wrong to allow it to happen again in this next generation. Had she not regained William and Ella? She had a future to build with them. Concentrate on the living and don't dwell on the dead, had been

Hellen's motto after her overwhelming grief had lifted. And that is what Meg would do. She needed to move forward.

The whole of Victoria Street was affected by the double tragedy. Ella was inconsolable and wept copiously for days. Her involvement in the care and attention of the twins had filled the void left by Hellen's sudden departure from her life. Their presence had been a distraction and eased the pain of losing Hellen. Meg worried about so much loss for the child. It was Gina who helped to pull Ella through the difficult time by telling Ella that Meg's loss as the boys' mother must be even greater, and that they must support Meg through this. By helping Meg, Gina said, they would help themselves to get over the trauma.

In the days following Hellen's funeral, Seth saw a note on a Kirkwall notice board. It read:

HEAD GROOM WANTED.
GOOD PAY AND ACCOMMODATION.
Apply to Edward Murray of Kirk Green."

He applied for the post. Although he was by far the oldest of the applicants this fact actually went in his favour as his new employer believed that age meant stability. Edward Murray, pillar of the community, little realised that to date this was assuredly the most unstable period in Seth's life. Seth was willing and up for any challenge set before him. The lodgings offered with the post were in the comfortable attic above the stable housing Edward Murray's six fine horses. He had always preferred living above stables. With plentiful supplies of hay and straw for bedding it was warmer and more comfortable than living in a But and Ben or a town apartment. Seth enjoyed being within range of the homely smell of horses.

Edward Murray was pleased with his new groomsman and found him to be a reliable and conscientious worker, a confident horseman, who on any formal occasion, looked impressive at the reins of his carriage. Nearly in her dotage, Mrs. Margaret Murray surprised even herself by taking quite a fancy to Seth, giggling like a teenager whenever she was near him.

Seth was determined to take advantage of the many opportunities offered by coming to live in the town and another opportunity in Kirkwall, which would not have been accessible to him in Westray, was the Orkney Library. Founded in 1683, it was the oldest Scottish library.

Age and maturity had brought with them his desire for knowledge and betterment of self. Ten years before Seth would not have opened his mouth in the presence of strangers unless spoken to directly, but now, armed with the writings he had made during his travels around the Orkney Isles, and boosted by Meg's confidence in his work, he approached the librarian to ask for his advice. In rewriting the itinerary of his travels, he had relived the enjoyment of that time, a rewarding time that he was keen to immortalise. He had illustrated his draft book with pen and ink drawings as Meg had suggested, and was taking her advice in trying to find a publisher.

The librarian recognised Seth's work as a prospective best seller for travellers to Orkney. He liked the illustrations and described it as "a book of worth" to which Seth felt his first flush of pride. The librarian was a man of integrity and Seth trusted him when he offered to show it to a good publisher when he travelled to Inverness in the following week.

Although it was to take some time to come to fruition, the wheels had been put into motion for publishing Seth's book.

Ella appreciated Meg's presence and care of her, and Meg dared to hope that she could at last prove to be a decent role model for her daughter. However, Meg was aware that William's curiosity could alter the new *status quo* at any time. He was possibly already waiting for the right moment to accost her about unanswered questions, family mysteries, true parentage.

During his childhood, William had not bothered about the identity of his father as long as he had Hellen and the extended family of John, Agnes and Peter Harcus. But Meg knew that when the questions arose in his mind, he would probably not rest and it would be only natural for him to pursue the truth. Ella, on the other hand, was a simpler child to satisfy. She had only once asked who was the father of Meg's twins and Meg appeased her by saying their father had let her down badly.

Since leaving Rabbitha', her only home, Ella's life had been in turmoil, alternating between highs and lows, and Meg was a stability in an ever-changing world. The silver lining to Meg's dark cloud over the loss of her boys was that her focus was averted towards her two older children, bringing them closer. William and Ella, still stinging from the loss of Hellen, recognised Meg's loss and therein spawned a supportive bond. She hoped their futures would be connected although William was already independent. Life settled into a different routine without her twin boys to nurture. Meg found that she could devote much of her time and attention to Ella, who gave her so much happiness. The child's fun-loving nature, her enthusiasm and warmth, rose from the ashes of shock and sorrow. They enjoyed each other's company as good friends rather than guardian and child, and often talked about memories of Hellen and the love she had shown them both. Meg felt honoured to know this little girl and took secret pride in the fact that she was one of her creators. She was grateful to have been given a second chance of being with Ella, getting to know her and spending some of their lives together. Ella and Meg were soon devoted to one another and as the bond strengthened, they made one another feel loved and needed.

In the year following Hellen's death, Meg allowed her thirty-fourth birthday to slip by unannounced and, although her life was more enjoyable in many ways than it had been for years, the deaths of her mother and her twin sons in such close proximity made it Meg's saddest year. Yet to have met and bonded with her lost children made it also the most memorable.

Christina noticed that her favourite bread shop, Cursiter's Bakery, needed a salesgirl who could also bake. She told Meg. Meg jumped at the opportunity and prepared to call on the proprietors. Ella helped her to get ready by looking out Meg's best clothes, her lace-fronted blouse and her full, dark blue skirt, one that was tightly caught in at the waistband.

"How do I look?" she asked, giving a twirl.

"Aw, you look *grand!*" said Ella with her eyes shining.

"Very bonnie, my dear" Christina agreed.

They wished her luck and she set off down the street, bursting with bubble and good intention.

Meg knocked any other applicants into a cocked hat. She shone like polish on good wood. Her exuberant presence arrested the attention of the owner, eighty-nine year old Bruce Cursiter, and his two spinster daughters, Polly and Grace. The sisters managed and ran the business, a business that had been handed down from father to son for three generations, though this generation it would be handed from father to daughters on Bruce Cursiter's eventual death. The Cursiter family all agreed that Meg would make a cheerful addition to their shop and her good looks couldn't fail to draw customers. They were also impressed with her baking skills, ones she had learnt from Hellen. They actually recalled being given a packet of "Ellen's Bannocks" in years gone by and one of their regular customers had wanted the recipe emulated. Unable to satisfy his request at that time, they were delighted at the prospect of Meg being able to fulfil it now. She was hired on the spot and other applicants were turned away. Meg was thrilled and shook Bruce Cursiter's hand so enthusiastically that the old man, chuckling, had to ask her to stop.

The pay was excellent. Bruce Cursiter was a generous employer and Meg was able to contribute again to the Tulloch household coffers though they wanted no money from her. She was like a daughter to them and could not envisage a life without her. Nothing had arrived from Isobella since her stroke.

Polly and Grace Cursiter, both master bakers, baked the loaves and baps for local hotels and boarding houses as well as those sold in the shop. In order to bake griddle scones, broonies, bannocks and shortbread petticoat tails in time for the shop opening every morning at eight thirty, Meg had to arrive at around five thirty. She would return home to take breakfast with Ella and walk with her to school before returning to the Bakery, where she spent the rest of the morning serving customers, finishing work around lunchtime. She did this every day except the Sabbath.

Meg enjoyed her work. She liked dealing with the public and soon came up with an enterprising idea. It concerned the use of a spacious, unused room directly behind the shop. The room had a large bow window overlooking the cobbled walkway to the harbour. Meg suggested that it could be transformed into a small tea room in which customers and shoppers in Kirkwall could rest awhile to take tea with a cake or scone. The name she proposed for the tea room was 'Polly and Grace's Pantry'. The spinster sisters were amazed at the futuristic ideas that came from their new member of staff. "Ellen's Bannocks" had originated from an idea Meg had given to her mother. They promised to give her idea consideration.

Both Meg and Seth, having gained the courage of their separate convictions, were embarking on new lifestyles. Although they lived in the same town, for the moment circumstances determined to keep them apart.

28

Legacy

The Laird of Westray was a shadow of his former self.

He could never have envisaged the troubles that had befallen him. He felt that the course of his destiny could not have been altered through any different course of action taken by him. Left in the solitude of his present life, with neither family member nor manservant as companion, his despair frequently turned to anger. The venting of this anger at least gave him some strength at a time of abject weakness. But there was yet one more devastating blow dealt to his fragile stability, which occurred in the same year as the deaths of his legitimate sons, the elopement of his only legitimate daughter and his wife's paralysing stroke.

On the fateful morning of Charles Stewart's grim discovery, he entered Isobella's bedroom as was his usual custom at the start of every day. The dawn on this particular day was gloomily dull and oppressive. He crossed the darkened room and opened the drapes of the window overlooking the rose garden.

Charles would usually speak to his wife at this point and tell her his working agenda for the coming day. It was always a one sided conversation due to her unresponsive state, but after so many bonding years of marriage, he found this contact therapeutic as he firmly believed that the Isobella he married was still somewhere inside this unrecognisable shell of her previously lovely body. Charles would not give up on the only person left to him, convinced that her lack of interaction to external influences did not mean she was no longer able to hear or feel. He felt she had become numbed to her sad existence, but that this was nature's way of helping her to cope. Although he knew she would remain speechless, he hoped that she might at some time want to communicate through the written word. With this in mind, he had instructed the servants to ensure there was always some writing paper and a charcoal pencil within reach on her bedside cabinet.

But this particular morning Charles didn't speak. There was an ominous feel to the room.

The dim and gloomy light of the new day weakly infiltrated the darkened room as he pulled back the heavily draped velvet curtains. His footsteps reverberated on the wooden floorboards as he walked over to Isobella's bedside. As he stepped onto the tapestry rug by her bed, his footsteps became muffled and it was then that he was alerted by the complete stillness. Looking down at Isobella's calm, upturned face, he saw that her wide-open and rummy eyes were fixed, staring up to the ceiling. Her face, pale and lifeless, looked sunken, as if it had slowly melted into the pillow behind her head. Her fists were clenched across her chest, tightly gripping a sheet of the white writing paper. Rigor mortis had already set in.

Life had slowed to a snail's pace for Charles over the previous year. He could clearly remember a time when his grand and opulent home had echoed to the sounds of children and servants coming and going, and his cheery and talkative wife continually interrupted his working day. A time when he had been kept busy with a business to attend to, a farm to run and a mistress to service. His life, once full to overflowing, was grinding to a standstill at the side of Isobella's deathbed.

He stood motionless, gazing with pathos at her sad demise. Reflecting on the hopelessness of her latter years, which she had been forced to live out, needlessly and piteously, Charles mused on how her life had begun so full of promise. A good and affluent family upbringing, followed by a marriage to the most eligible bachelor in the land was graced with three children, which in Charles's belief, was the fulfilment of ambition for any wife. A large house and garden accommodated Isobella's every whim and wealth and opportunity abounded all of the days that she enjoyed good health. But, as soon as her health declined, a domino effect was set up. In the years that followed, Isobella lost the respect of her children, who were unable to cope with their mother's strange debilitation. They in turn lost stability when emotionally deprived by both parents. With hindsight, Charles acknowledged that his attraction to Meg may have been fuelled by his lack of desire for the physically failing Isobella. Had she ever known of his consuming affair? He would never know. And now, too late for him to salvage happiness with Meg, Isobella had been released from her purgatory.

Too late he yearned for the intimacy of Meg and dreamt of what life with her might have held for him. Because of the Christian morals of his time, Charles could never have publicly admitted to a love for Meg, which would have destroyed the respect he commanded in Orkney society. But by keeping their secret, he had lost his only passion in his life, the love of Meg. Once, and once alone, he had given thought to the deep social divide that made some situations impossible, such as a marriage to a person beneath his position, and he had felt anger towards the class system which did not recognise that people fell in love across the divide. Sometimes with passion, undying passion, as he had done. He was in denial that any of his misfortune, in particular the losing of Meg, could in any way be his own doing, preferring to vent his anger at others. During his times with Meg, Charles had only been aware of his passion with no commitment to make. In retrospect he had never before been so overwhelmed by his own feelings and realised the depth of his love for her long after she had left him. He had taken her for granted. He tried to remember if he'd ever shown Meg more than passion, such was the effect she had over him. Had he ever told her he loved her? He couldn't remember such an occasion, yet he continued to blame all but himself.

If Isobella had thrown off her mortal coil some years before, might he have thrown caution to the wind and declared an attachment to Meg? But these thoughts were no good to him now. From the day Meg left Black Bull Farm, he had been given no clue to her whereabouts. This was a secret Isobella saw fit to keep from him. Even returning to Rabbitha' had proved fruitless and only aroused Agnes's concern. Charles's daughter, Catherine, was lost to him forever, into the vastness of the world beyond his small island, beyond his small world, and this brought home to him the fact that he had rejected his children with Meg. And now the last remaining person dear to him, his loyal wife, had joined his sons in the other world, the other greater vastness beyond.

Time stood still and Charles had no idea how long he remained, numbed and frozen to the spot at the side of his wife's bed, dejectedly musing on the meaning of his life. Solitude engulfed him like a chilly wind.

Returning to the window, he stared out into the gloom of that misty morning. Below, the blanketing bareness of the stark winter garden spread before him. Against the greyish white of the swirling inland mist stood the stark stalks of the rose plants and their dark and brutal jaggedness appeared menacing. They pricked at his pain. He resolved to dig out all the rose plants himself, to be rid of their associated memory to that moment in time. In his confused state he would have done so immediately, but he was roused from his depressive reverie by the resonant striking of the grandfather clock from the hallway downstairs. Instead, he made his way to the kitchen, where he knew Bessie the cook would be the first servant to have started daily chores at the Manor House.

In a state of numbed resignation, he entered Bessie's domain and stood motionless in the doorway, staring ahead of him at nothing in particular. Bessie was perturbed by his appearance. The Laird very seldom visited her kitchen and just by looking at him, she knew something was very wrong.

"Laird, wha's the matter?" Bessie asked, wiping her hands across her apron.

"Isobella," was all he could muster.

"Is she nae weel, sir?"

There was an awkward silence followed by a lengthy sigh from the Laird. "She's dead."

"Och," Bessie gasped, covering her mouth with her hand.

"Dead. In her bed," he continued dolefully.

Charles continued to stare into space and Bessie continued to stare at her deflated master.

"Can you see to her, Bessie?"

"Aye, sir, I will."

As he left the kitchen by the garden door, wandering aimlessly into the courtyard and over to the rose beds, Bessie's eyes followed his slumped figure and felt his sadness. What would become of him now, she wondered, now that he had lost the last person he cared for? Bessie had never been aware of any other woman in the Laird's life.

Climbing the stairs, she approached Isobella's room with trepidation. Tentatively, she opening the door and listened to the only sound audible, the creaking of the door hinges. Tears filled her eyes as she surveyed the pathetic scene. The sheet of paper in Isobella's clenched fists caught her attention and after she had gently closed her mistress's eyelids, she tried to prise open her fingers to release it, but the paper tore in two, though it was a clean tear. It was then she noticed the lettering across the surface, "Charles I…." She wondered. Perhaps the Grim Reaper had cut short Isobella's message to her husband. Bessie felt angry that Isobella had latterly been forced to live a useless and pathetic existence, yet her final demise had been so untimely as to curtail her last wish, a love note perhaps to her husband. She tucked the two pieces of paper into her apron pocket and resolved to give them to the Laird when he returned. It was then that she noticed a carefully folded bundle, something wrapped in a sheet of the same paper, lying on the bedside cabinet. It was marked with one barely decipherable word, "Bessie." Her mistress must have been writing her last thoughts with whatever strength remained in her. Carefully Bessie unravelled the folded outer paper bearing her name, which was a wrapper to a smaller, more tightly folded package. This package was marked with four words, words that were only to add to Bessie's confusion that morning, *"To Seth for Meg."*

The words were written in Isobella's shaky handwriting, the charcoal's imprint smudged but still distinct. They made no sense to her. Why would Isobella be thinking about Seth of all people on her deathbed? And why would she have wanted Bessie to be in control of the package? Curiosity got the better of her and she found herself unwrapping the inner package. Its contents astounded her. There, startlingly beautiful against its background of pure white paper was Isobella's favourite gold ring, a central deep purple jewel set between two pearls. Before Isobella's fingers had become sore and swollen, she used to wear the ring constantly. Bessie had vague memories of being told it was an heirloom from her parent's side of the family. Was Isobella's last request to give this precious item to Meg by way of Seth, Bessie wondered? But why? What had Seth to do with Meg? Bewildered, she tried to discern the true meaning of her mistress's last instructions, not wanting in any way to misconstrue them.

Bessie sat down on an ornately carved high-backed chair at the opposite side of the room. She took the liberty of sitting in this privileged position through necessity, because her body felt suddenly weak and drained. She needed to concentrate in order to think out the problems arising from these simple yet veiled messages. She knew that the heirloom could no longer stay within Isobella's family. Isobella had no other siblings. There was no family to leave it to now that Catherine had vanished and Isobella's other two children were dead. The Stewart family lineage had come to an abrupt halt – or so she believed. But it appeared that Isobella had decided she wanted the ring to go to Meg and this, to Bessie's way of thinking, did seem befitting, as Meg had been Isobella's closest and most favoured servant for many years.

But why should it go primarily to Seth? What was his connection to Meg? And why should Bessie be given the task? Was this because Isobella had not trusted her husband with this job? Perhaps Isobella didn't want him to know about it. Bessie thought he was in no fit state to undertake any errands at the present time and that it had not been addressed to him so she decided that the Laird should remain ignorant of this request. Bessie began to take her responsibility in this matter very seriously, realising that one wrong word to the wrong person could foil Isobella's ultimate plan.

The meaning of those four bewildering words, *"To Seth for Meg,"* were tasking her simple brain but slowly the dawning of an explanation filtered through to her.

29

Bessie and Jeremiah

Bessie found the dilemma she faced nearly too big for her to cope with. The undertaking of Isobella's last, though veiled, request took top priority. She was determined to rise to the occasion, having never before been given such enormity of responsibility.

"Jeremiah! Wha' am I tae do?" she wailed to her husband as they sat together by their fire with a dram of whisky apiece. Whisky was only usually consumed on birthdays or holidays in the Sinclair cottage, but Bessie had deemed this a necessary requirement to steady her nerves at the end of her exhausting day.

"Isobella wantit me tae gie this ring tae Seth fur Meg!" she carefully deliberated over the words and continually shook her head slowly form side to side. "Why? I dinnae ken. An' I've nae idea where 'ither Seth or Meg have gang tae!"

"Weel, we will find oot, lass, and dinnae fret yersel'," Jeremiah reassured his wife by putting his arm around her shoulders.

"How?" she wailed. "How on earth do we find that oot?"

Jeremiah remembered that since Meg's hasty disappearance from Black Bull Farm, Isobella had surreptitiously and with regularity, sent for Seth to post a package for her. He thought nothing of it at the time, but now with this strange and short written instruction for his wife, he was realising a connection. Bessie sat on the edge of her stool, eyes wide with amazement as he continued. He particularly noticed Seth being summoned by the Laird's wife because he always seemed to be passing by the stables with the morning's milk delivery at the time of Seth's departure. This usually took place when the Laird went riding and was the only time that Isobella met up with Seth. She could have sent any other servant, but she always asked for Seth. Was this not an indication that not only did Isobella know of Meg's whereabouts, but also that she wanted Seth alone to also know this? Who else would it be that Isobella secretly started to correspond with?

"Ah, ye see!" said Bessie getting quite agitated at this discovery. "That does mean the mistress didnae want the Laird tae know summit."

"Aye. An' have ye thought aboot why she wantit Seth tae gee that ring tae Meg?"

"Naw, naw, that's whit's wurrin' me, ye daft egit!" Bessie was flaying her arms around and spilling precious droplets of whisky across the face of the fire, causing embers to spit and hiss at her and fine threads of flame to leap into the air.

"Calm doon, wummin!" said Jeremiah, who couldn't take hysterics, even in a mild form. "Ye are the daft egit!" he retorted, to which Bessie took extreme umbrage. She shot up from her seat, allowing Jeremiah's arm to drop heavily to his side, and she stared angry daggers at him.

"That whisky's gang tae yer heid, sit doon, sit doon, fretty wummin," he said patting her stool and taking her whisky glass from her hand.

"Aw richt then!" Bessie stood in front of him with her hands on her hips. "Why did Isabella want Seth tae gie that ring tae Meg, smart Alec that ye are?" she said, one eyebrow raised to nearly touch her hairline.

Jeremiah smiled smugly and waited for his conclusion to dawn on her. The awakening of Bessie's reasoning visibly rippled across her tensed face and the irritation she felt towards her husband eased. Her irate eyebrow sank in line with its neighbour and her eyes opened wider to meet them. Jeremiah allowed himself a smirk of triumph.

"Becus' Seth must be the faider o' Meg's bairns!" she squealed.

"Aye! Yer richt this time, lass."

Jeremiah drained his glass dry in smug triumph.

"So," he continued with an air of importance, "I'm thinkin' they are noo in the same place, becus' Seth left Bull nae sae lang efter Meg did. They were the only workers tae leave this year."

"Ye think Seth went tae follow her?"

"Aye."

"So where did they go?"

"Ah, weel, that is the question."

"Och, man," said Bessie sitting back down onto her stool with a bump.

Jeremiah stroked his chin as he thought deeply about this.

"Where did the Laird's wife keep her writing stuff, Bessie?"

"Beside her bed."

"Well let's go see if there's anything in her bedside cabinet."

"Wha' – the noo?"

"Naw time like the present," he said rising from his chair.

They were both the worse for the whisky, but couldn't contemplate holding onto their curiosity till the morning. Neither had given due thought to the fact that Isobella's body was 'laying out' in her room, ready for burial and the arrival of her coffin the next morning. It wasn't until they opened Isobella's heavy bedroom door and stealthily crept into the room that the sudden fear of the dead overcame them both. They had failed miserably in trying to avoid the creaking of the door and its eerie noise filled them both with dread. They need not have worried about waking the Laird in the next room, because that evening he had consumed a much larger amount of whisky than both of them put together and was out for the count.

Gripping onto each other for solace and support, the little and large couple groped their way in the dark to Isobella's bedside. The Laird had left the curtains open and this allowed the moonlight to flood across Isobella's bed, highlighting her dead body, carefully washed and dressed that very afternoon by two of the local howdies. Isobella lay as if neglected in the gloom. Neither Bessie nor Jeremiah had the presence of mind or the wits about them to bring a candle and the scene soon dissolved into bedlam. Jeremiah had to remove, piece by piece, all the paper from the drawers of the bedside cabinet and take them over to the window, where he strained to decipher any writing and see if any clues could be gleaned. Bessie clung to his elbow, wide-eyed and shaking with fear. Their panic calmed with the discovery of an envelope marked "Meg Williamson", which had been tucked away in the furthest recesses of the top drawer.

"Let's git oot o' here, Jeremiah. Come on!" Bessie whispered, tugging at her husband's sleeve.

They made a hasty and bungling retreat back to the sanctuary of their cottage for another dram of whisky to steady their nerves, which proved to have the exact opposite effect and destabilised them both. The morning light found them both huddled in their chairs, fully clothed and fast asleep.

The writing on the front of the envelope was faint, but after Meg's name, they could read the words "Tulloch's Ironmongery, Victoria Street, Kirkwall." Inside the envelope was twenty pounds, more money than either Bessie or Jeremiah had ever seen in one place. They decided that this had been meant for Meg and they would deliver it to her with the stated ring, the heirloom. They also discovered a poignant letter, obviously written by Isobella a long time ago, just before her stroke, yet after her family tragedies. She had never managed to post it. Perhaps as Seth had already gone. It read:

"Dear Meg,

Terrible times for me here. My delicate one, my Samuel Charles, has died before his seventeenth birthday. My healthy lad, my William Bruce, has fallen to his death only days after his brother's death. And now they tell me Catherine Mary has run away with her scoundrel. Wicked child.

I feel there is nothing left for me. I feel devoid of emotion. I do not even want my Charles near me now. I just want to fade away.

Meg, you have been a good friend to me and I want you to know that it is only now, after you have gone, that I truly appreciate the care you gave to me over the years. I know I have been a hard taskmaster, but we had some good times, did we not?

I will never see you again, I know this, and it hurts me deeply, but you have a full life ahead of you, a better life than can be had here at Bull, tending to my depressing ailments. It gives me vain pleasure to think that I may in my small way be able to help you attain a life suited to your talents. I feel I am at last giving something back after all the taking I have done in my sad life. You will fulfil some destiny better suited to your character and I feel for your future as I would a favoured child. My children were all a disappointment to me. I have no qualms in saying that now.

I do not know why you and Seth wanted so much secrecy surrounding your love affair, but hope that now at last you can feel free to be together and settle with the children blessed to you both.

I am sure you never suspected that I knew about your love, did you, Meg? If truth be told, I have only deduced this on reflection – being too wrapped up in my own follies over the years. Something at Black Bull Farm obviously drove you and Seth apart, but I hope – now that you are free from its ties – you can start afresh. I hope your problem was not my hard and unfeeling husband with any possible threats of loss of employment due to your merrybegotten babies.

Be good to Seth for I see he loves you deeply.

Good Luck and God Bless.

Isobella."

The signature floated confidently across the foot of the page. Bessie was in tears.

"We were richt then, wern't we, Jeremiah?" she sobbed. "Aboot Meg wi' Seth?"

"Aye, lass, seems so."

"Wha' does she mean, aw' that bit at the end there?"

"Dunno, lass."

When their hangovers eased the following day, Bessie and Jeremiah made a plan to contact Meg at the address on Isobella's letter. They would summon Seth to return to Black Bull Farm and take possession of the ring for Meg. They decided that the Laird should know none of this.

Bessie wrote a letter and despatched it to: Seth, c/o Williamson, Tulloch's Ironmongery, Victoria Street, Kirkwall." She, too, assumed that Meg and Seth would be together. In her imagination she saw them as happily wed, living with their three children, for she also assumed that Seth must indeed be the father of Meg's bairns, the outcomes of her three pregnancies. She imagined them all living above the Ironmongery where Seth probably worked. Bessie's romantic idyll was far from the truth.

30

Sanday Stables

It was horses that brought Seth and William together.

Sanday's wide, open spaces made perfect horse riding country. During his travels with the Laird, Seth's time on Sanday had been primarily spent riding along the beaches and pastures. His favourite mount at that time had been a jet-black stallion called Noah, whose name derived from his proclivity to manoeuvring his rider onto the nearest beach and to the sea's edge in order to freely gallop along the surf. Seth was engulfed with a yearning to ride again across the sweeping white sandy beaches of Sanday and decided to visit the stables of the Laird of Sanday the following Saturday.

Saturday was a mild but blustery day. The clouds above Kirkwall harbour were constantly changing their tone, their shape and their speed. When the ferry sidled into the quayside Seth recognised the ferry boatman as one of the pallbearers at Hellen's funeral. But George Rendall knew nothing of Seth, the tall, fair-haired stranger, who moved along to the helm of the boat and stood looking skywards at the antics of the swooping gannets.

The noise of the seabirds' consistent calls was not enough to muffle the sound of the most memorable voice in Seth's life, a voice that never failed to strike a chord in his heart.

" Mornin', George." Meg's soft and lilting tones drifted lightly on the sea breeze.

Keeping his head down, Seth side stepped behind a group of voyagers and glanced furtively towards the sound of her voice. His eyes rested on her loveliness and his heart skipped a beat.

Meg was boarding the ferry. All his buried emotions for her rose up swiftly and he was stunned at their intensity. The nearness of her left him in a sudden quandary as to what to do for the best. This vulnerability irritated him, but it was what had driven him all these years. His feelings were so powerful they would not be ignored and were the reason he had left his known world for wider horizons. Meg had set the trail and now he could set the pace.

The instant he heard Meg's voice he knew this would be the day when they would speak. This is not what he had planned. The fact was he had planned nothing. But he knew it was only a matter of time before Meg noticed him amongst the dozen or so passengers on board and resolved to leave the outcome to providence and, for the time being, he slowly turned his back on his fellow travellers to gaze seaward.

As the ferry left Kirkwall harbour, Meg was lost in conversation with George. He was showing her one of his watercolour paintings of a view of Westray from the sea. On a calm crossing he still enjoyed to sketch from the ferry, drawings that he would complete with a wash of watercolour when he returned to his home. Surreptitiously Seth turned his head to see Meg and George had their backs turned towards him and Meg was holding up George's painting for a better view. Her flaxen hair blew dreamily around her head and shoulders. Glinting highlights reflected the morning's hazy rays of sunlight.

Seth's eyes were then drawn to George's picture, a fine landscape painting which possessed far more life and colour than the stilted portraits Seth remembered hanging in the halls of Westray Manor House. It was painted in nature's colours and was full of depth and atmosphere. Seth's eyes drifted to the standing figures within the happy group of Meg, Ella, Gina and George and his gaze somehow bore a path into Meg's subconscious.

Until the sensation came over her, Meg had been unconcerned with the other passengers. But a connection was being unwittingly attempted, something unspecified. From behind her she felt a beam of empathy flowing her way. She turned her head slowly and her eyes alighted upon Seth.

As they stood at opposite ends of the ferry, a history of past life floated between them. Meg saw flashbacks of a time long gone. Their eyes collided and held. Her lips moved as she uttered one inaudible word, which was drowned in the sound of the seawater rushing past under the ferry, but Seth could clearly see his name hanging in the air.

The strength of their gaze drew him towards her across the deck. He moved determinedly through the other passengers until he stood but a few feet from her. George, Gina and Ella were oblivious to the moment, this moment so longed for by Seth.

But Meg looked haunted and her arms hung limply by her sides. Drained by weary memories of her past life that the sight of Seth brought back to her, Meg felt as if a ghost had reappeared.

She pulled herself together and became aware of her own too candid facial expression and how it would be conveying a confused message to this old friend. It was not Seth she was upset to see; it was the place and era to which he belonged. She gave a little shake of her head as if to toss asunder the sad thoughts and she smiled quietly to him. Seth took a step forward as she raised a hand to tame her wind blown hair and was surprised as Seth gently took hold of it. Her eyes darted from their hands to search his face. With rapidity an understanding flitted between them and Meg felt reassured, comforted. Then their frozen moment of oblivion was interrupted audibly.

"Will ye no introduce us, Meg?"

George had spoken and initially he made no sense to Meg. She had momentarily forgotten where she was and who she was with.

"Wha' s dat?" she said, confused.

Ella and Gina giggled, bringing Meg back into the present. She wondered how long she had been standing staring into Seth's honest eyes that were so firmly fixed on her. Seth in turn wondered how long he could gaze unchecked upon the object of his life's desire.

"Och, I'm sorry," said Meg, flustered. She slowly removed her hand from his warm hold. "Dis is Seth. He's from Black Bull Farm on Westray."

Seth shook his head infinitesimally.

"No," he said.

Meg threw him a puzzled look. Was this word of contradiction to be the first word spoken to her after all these years? Searching his eyes, she saw from the warmth within them that he was smiling. The length of his moustache still managed to hide his mouth yet the moustache had grown wider as he smiled.

He hadn't changed much over the years; a few grey hairs mingling with his fair ones, a few crow's-feet on his temples etched there by years of screwing up his eyes against the expanse of Orcadian sky.

"I'm not at Black Bull Farm any longer," he corrected her and turning to the three bemused onlookers, George, Gina and Ella, he said, "I'm a groom at Kirk Green, working for Edward Murray."

"Edward Murray!" repeated George, who had heard of this important member of Kirkwall society. "Weel, he's a good man to work fur."

Meg was pleased to hear that Seth had also managed to escape the clutches of their taskmaster, the Laird at Westray; that he had moved on.

"Are ye, Seth? Dat's grand den," she said. It was good to see Seth again, especially as he no longer had a connection with the man who had broken her heart. It gave her a sense of relief to know this.

The ferry arrived at Sanday and its passengers alighted onto the jetty. A horse, cart and driver awaited any passengers who required a ride to more distant parts of the island. Seth offered to carry Meg's picnic basket. She explained to him that they were travelling up to the lighthouse at the most north-easterly tip of the island to visit William there. He declined her invitation to join them as he felt it an imposition on their family outing. He told them he had horses to ride. The Laird of Sanday's stables were within half a mile of the jetty and Seth set off on foot. They arranged to meet again later that day for the return ferry to Kirkwall.

Neither Meg nor Seth noticed George watching them from the departing ferryboat. Watching body language was another of George's pastimes. With constant noise from sea and wind on the ferry it made sense to lip-read or watch body movements in order to understand people. Watching Meg as she sat in the moving cart with the two young girls and amongst other visitors to Sanday, he noted the warmth in her departing smile to Seth. While on the crossing George had noted her ease of movement in this man's company and now he noticed the way her eyes lingered longer than expected upon Seth's diverging figure as he strode up the gentle rise towards Sanday stables. He saw the tall, angular stranger of few words, turn at the top of the slope and gaze after the disappearing cart. George had a good feeling from what he saw. With Hellen gone, there was nothing he would like more than to see her lovely daughter happily involved with a man special enough for her. Was Seth special enough, he wondered? He had felt honest vibes from the stranger and some strong feelings of warmth from Seth towards Meg, though he wasn't sure if Meg had been aware of those. Feeling protective of her in a fatherly manner, George resolved to discover more about Seth. He knew another servant of Edward Murray of Kirk Green and would ask that man's opinion of Seth on the next occasion they met over a pint of ale at the Buckles Inn. George would have been stunned to know this intriguing man from Meg's hidden past had harboured feelings for her for nearly seventeen years.

When Seth reached the top of the Ward Hill, the island's highest natural vantage point, he stood and surveyed his surroundings. Sanday Island, ragged and spindly, ravaged by centuries of torturous elements, sprawled nonchalantly across the sea. As with all the islands of Orkney, Sanday's landscape was dominated by sky, its wide horizon supporting neither tree nor mountain to interrupt the panorama. The winds across the islands were generally so strong that trees found it near impossible to take seed on the open ground. As far as Seth was concerned this allowed for uninterrupted gallops. It was warm and he removed his leather jerkin, flinging it over one shoulder as he made his way onwards to the stables. This was a day to be savoured, especially for his chance meeting with Meg. And now he had the anticipation of meeting with her again for the return voyage to Kirkwall.

Arriving at Sanday Stables he found only one of the original grooms there. He was a wiry, slightly built man called Jeem, who had a badly broken nose of old, which he had more than likely received in a fight, for Jeem was known for his quick temper. Jeem remembered the horse called Noah that Seth loved to ride. A horse called Jonah was stabled there now.

"Ye canna keep dis yin awa' frae the waater," Jeem said as he breathed hard on the horse's nostrils, making Jonah shake his mane. "Take a ride on him, man! Gang doon da waater wie him, git him on da shore an' gie him a gallop."

"Aye," said Seth. "I will."

Seth rode Jonah over the gently rolling hillside then sloped down to the sandy beach at Backerskill Bay, over to Otterswick Bay and along to Quoy Banks. They met few people on their ride; the occasional crofter about his work, some peat boys and a woman collecting eggs with her children. The wind grew stronger, helping to keep Jonah cool. Hours passed by but they seemed like minutes to Seth. When he returned, a stable boy approached him offering a tankard of ale and a platter of crusty bread with cheese, which Seth carried out to the sun-dappled courtyard. As he sat on the mounting steps a distant rumbling sound could be heard and he looked east towards Start Point Lighthouse. The horse and cart was ambling along the dirt track towards the jetty. William was sitting next to the driver with Meg and the girls behind him. The cart stopped at the foot of the track to the stables, but William was the sole passenger to alight and start to walk up the slope to the stables. Seth watched and waited.

"Ye bin ridin' on Jonah?" William asked in an indefinable tone.

Seth looked at him warily and nodded. For a time William's face was indecipherable. Then he suddenly shot a broad smile at Seth.

"He's a grand ride, is he no?" he said.

Seth laughed in quiet relief.

"Aye, he is, lad."

William sat down beside Seth and told him that he often came to help with the exercising of the horses in exchange for a bite to eat. He had watched Seth riding Jonah over at Quoy Banks from the top rail of the lighthouse. Seth and William had something else in common besides Meg. They had a love of horses.

Meg, Ella and Gina had gone on to watch the seal pups off the Holms of Spurness until it was time for the ferry to arrive. William wasn't prepared to tell Seth that Meg had brought up his name in just about every conversation they'd had that day and therefore he had wanted to meet Seth alone to try and assess this stranger's appeal.

William felt protective of his 'sister' in much the same way as George. The fifteen-year-old had grown taller than Meg and was nearly as tall as Seth, though heavier in build. Seth was lean where William was broad and muscular, like his father.

William and Seth talked until the time came to walk down to the jetty. Seth liked the boy, not just because he was Meg's son or because he had played a part in the day of William's birth, but because he enjoyed his company and their common bond, the love of horse riding. They walked together in comfortable silence as Meg stood watching and waiting for them by the jetty. Ella and Gina were running around playing tig when Meg produced a crumpled paper bag full of boiled sweets, which she offered to everyone. The girls shot their hands into the bag and ran off with a sweet each.

"Cheeky monkeys!" Meg smiled after them.

For some strange reason this comment reminded William of something said in the past.

"Helen used tae call me a cheeky piglet," said William. "She said I looked like a piglet when I was born."

"Aye, ye did," said Meg – too quickly.

William looked at her. "Why? Were ye dere?"

There was a short pause before Meg calmly replied.

"Aye," she said, looking sideways to Seth for visual support. He nodded infinitesimally to her.

"Here's the ferry," he said with relief.

31

Post

" 'Tis strange indeed that I should meet wi' ye again, Seth."

Meg had to raise her voice above the sound of rushing sea against the side of the moving ferry. She had set her gaze out to sea, far over the starboard rail of the ferry. Seth stood beside her, leaning on the rail; his eyes also fixed on the seascape in front of them.

"Ye see, I have a letter fur ye back at my hame," She went on.

"For me?"

Seth was bewildered. He couldn't think who would send *him* a letter to *Meg's* address. The expected news of his travel book was due to arrive in the post, but certainly not via Meg. He had not told anyone about Meg.

"Ye'll ha' tae come back wi' me tae get it," Meg said.

This plan inwardly pleased them both.

On their arrival at Kirkwall harbour, Meg explained to Ella that Seth would return with them for a while. Ella liked the idea of visitors. She liked the rigmarole that Christina went through when visitors stopped by; the making of tea, the bringing out of the best china cups from the sideboard and the way Christina lifted her pinkie finger in the air when she delicately supped her tea.

Christina and Hugh had shut shop for the day when their extended family arrived home with Seth in tow. And as expected, when Christina saw that Meg had brought a guest with her, she started to rummage at the foot of the parlour sideboard and Ella heard the chink of china cups being set out on their best tray.

Meg introduced them to Seth, the rightful recipient of the envelope she had recently received. The arrival of the mysterious envelope had puzzled Meg as much as it had the Tullochs, because Meg had not seen or heard of Seth for such a long time and, until the letter arrived, Christina and Hugh had never heard of Seth. Meg could not imagine why a letter to an old acquaintance had been sent to her and to Kirkwall of all places. She had no idea why it was addressed "c/o Williamson". It was unquestionably the Seth she knew. They all presumed there must be some mistake and it was decided that Meg would post it on to Black Bull Farm in due course, not realising that Seth no longer lived at there. The envelope had been slipped into a drawer in the sideboard, where it had remained out of sight, out of mind. Luckily, she had procrastinated long enough after their decision for its rightful recipient to appear in person.

Hugh was despatched to the kitchen to brew the tea, while Christina rose to the occasion, ready to enjoy conversation with their guest. But she soon deduced Seth was not for small talk, but was nevertheless quite taken with his tall, good-looks and his determined, yet calm expression. It seemed an amazing and uncanny coincidence for Meg to come across Seth in the same week as the arrival of his letter. Here sat a link with Meg's undiscovered life at Black Bull Farm.

"You both worked at Black Bull Farm, did you?" Christina took the opportunity of plying an innocuous question in the hopes of an answer of some description might be forthcoming.

With Meg so settled in her new life in Kirkwall, Christina felt she would no longer feel sensitive to a mention of her past. But one look at Meg proved her wrong. She watched as despondency dropped heavily across Meg's face, a heavy curtain descending at the mention of Black Bull Farm. Her eyelids drooped, nearly closing altogether. Hugh, who had poured them all a cup of steaming hot tea and a milky one for Ella, noticed this discomfort and changed the subject before his wife received her awaited reply, much to Christina's chagrin.

"Ah, this reminds me," he interjected. "Something else arrived in the post, Meg. It's a parcel for you."

"Fur me?"

Now it was Meg's turn to be bewildered. Hugh had achieved his aim because Meg's bewilderment quashed her melancholy.

"Ye *both* have sommit tae open!" said Ella in glee, to which everyone smiled.

Hugh handed Meg the parcel. Isobella's flowery script stared back at her, conjuring up memories of the little notes she would leave for Meg if she was sleeping or out with the children; lists of chores to be done, clothes to be mended, or pewter to be polished. Meg knew Isobella had suffered a stroke. No letters had arrived from her ex-mistress since then. It prayed on Meg's conscience that she couldn't visit Isobella at her most desperate time of need without risk of running into Charles.

Shock had taken the place of melancholy. Hugh again came to Meg's rescue.

"How about giving Seth his envelope, Meg?" he said gently.

"Yes, Meg, you'd better do that," agreed Christina.

The Tullochs wanted to give Meg some privacy in opening her mail and time to be alone with this new man. Although Seth did not seem to be an old sweetheart of Meg's, the couple appeared to be comfortable with one another and Christina felt that time together should be encouraged. She made her way to the kitchen and Hugh followed, calling to Ella to come and help with the clearing up. Ella frowned. She was excited at the prospect of opening the packages, curious as to their content, and now she would miss the occasion, but dutifully she did as she was bid. Hugh made a point of thanking Ella for her discretion on the matter, which made her feel quite grown up about it all.

Meg and Seth looked at each other. They both felt a little wary about the contents of their envelopes. Seth took the initiative and began to unfold the crisp white paper. Meg recognised the writing paper to be Isobella's, but knew the handwriting on his parcel belonged to someone else. Without scanning the contents, he launched into reading aloud the letter he found inside.

'Seth, I hope this finds you well. We need to tell you that Isobella has died....'

Seth broke off and looked up at Meg, who gasped. He continued.

"She left something for you here to give to Meg. You must return soon to collect it from us. The Laird does not know about it. He is too sad and drunk these days to care. Give our best wishes to Meg. From Jeremiah and Bessie Sinclair, Black Bull Farm, Westray.'

Seth and Meg stood in stunned silence and stared at one another. Meg's jaw had dropped slightly. Seth revelled in these moments, and there had been several that day, when Meg was totally attentive to him, looking only to him for guidance. And their eyes would lock. He took a deep breath to steady himself. Meg spoke.

"Isobella, dead? But *Isobella* has sent me this parcel..."

Gingerly, she untied the string and opened one end of the packet, as if it contained a frightening object that might burst out at her. She peered inside and saw the money.

"It's rent money agin!" she said with a puzzled look. "But Isobella hasnae sent any since her stroke!"

"Open it up and see what it says," said Seth.

Inside were two pieces of paper. Meg pulled out only one and began to read it to Seth.

"It's frum Bessie, too!" she said aghast. "But the envelope..."

"Read what Bessie has tae say, Meg."

Jeremiah had written Seth's letter, but Meg's was written and signed by Bessie, whose command of the written word left much to be desired.

'Der Meg, 'I wus goin to giv this muny to Seth when he cams up to see us but I want yo to hav it now in case yo needs it. The mistres wantit yo to hav it, see. I hop Seth got his letter frum Jeremiah aboot the erlom. Its very spesul. Tel him to cam see us soon. This ither letter – she must hav rit it long time ago. Yo shud hav it, too. We ar very well. I hop yo ar well. My best wishes, Bessie.'

Meg had to read it through again to make full sense of it, then she looked up at Seth and said,

"What's an *'erlom'* – what's a special 'erlom'?"

Seth shrugged his shoulders.

"Ye'd better read Isobella's letter," he said. "Maybe that'll tell us."

Meg had struggled to read Bessie's letter and wanted, calmly and privately, to take in Isobella's news so decided to read it to herself then pass it over to Seth. Meg was sad at the news of Isobella's death, yet felt a certain amount of relief that her old mistress had been freed at last from her miserable life.

258

To read Isobella's letter was like reading a letter from the grave, but Meg realised it had been written a long time ago, before Isobella had the stroke. The compliments about Meg written in Isobella's letter, statements from her heart, had never been said directly to Meg. She was relieved at the way Isobella had perceived Meg's circumstances as a servant whilst at Black Bull Farm. She handed the letter to Seth, pointing to a part she wanted him to read.

'*I do not know why you and Seth wanted so much secrecy surrounding your love affair...*'

Seth's eyebrows shot up in stunned disbelief and he stared at Meg for a moment.

'*but hope that now at last you can feel free to be together and settle with the children blessed to you both...*'

Meg clasped her hand to her mouth in astonishment. Seth was equally astounded. Meg took the letter back from him and continued to read.

'*I am sure you never suspected that I knew about your love, did you, Meg?*'

This line brought Meg to a gasping halt and she stared speechlessly at Seth. A terrible dread overwhelmed Meg, who feared that Isobella's next words might confirm she had known of her husband's infidelity with her favourite servant. Yet that did not seem to be the way the letter was heading.

'*If truth be told,*' Seth had gently extracted Isobella's letter from Meg's other hand and continued to read. '*I have only deduced this on reflection – being too wrapped up in my own follies over the years. Something at Black Bull Farm obviously drove you and Seth apart, but I hope – now that you are free from its ties – you can start afresh. I hope your problem was not my hard and unfeeling husband with any possible threats of loss of employment due to your merrybegotten babies...*'

Seth couldn't bring himself to read aloud the very last lines. Isobella's words were incredibly astute. Cruelly chained to a limited existence within one room, she had spent much of her time observing the comings and goings of others on Black Bull Farm from her bedroom window. Her thoughts in that time deliberated on the few happenings around her. She had seen what Meg could not. He handed the letter back to Meg. She read the last line to herself, *'Be good to Seth for I see he loves you deeply.'*

Seth studied her facial expression as she read. He saw her mystified, incredulous expression as she looked up from the letter then back down to read again Isobella's incomprehensible words.

"She got it all wrong, Seth, all wrang – God bless her soul."

Meg gently shook her head from side to side with her forehead furrowed and her eyes fixed on Seth's. He gave her a strong, steady look as if relaying to Meg the question, 'Did she?' Confused by his visual message, Meg needed confirmation.

"*Didn't* she, Seth?"

Yet somehow deep within her, a denial was desired. Her mind began to race, backwards in time, receiving flashes of moments in each others presence, looks exchanged, fragments of conversations that had passed between them over the years. Her thoughts ran away with her and she had a hard time trying to keep up with the discoveries, the revelations and assumptions, flying around inside her head. A strange new feeling, that of hope, arose within her. It was a strange, but welcome feeling.

"Not *all* wrong, Meggie,"

Meggie. Meg liked that. Seth called her 'Meggie'. It felt warm, close. His words were intense yet softly spoken. Could there really be truth in Isobella's words? Had Isobella seen something to which Meg had been oblivious? Was Seth really implying at this moment what she thought he was implying?

Such an opportunity as Seth could never have hoped for had arisen from Isobella's letter from the past – and Seth had to grasp it. Meg's quandary was all too transparent. Seth took newly found confidence from what he read in her beseeching eyes.

Like a charging horse, the revelation hit Meg full on, knocking her inner being sideways. It was as if, all at once, she had been plucked from the dust of the past, shaken gently into the present, and given a glimpse of what the future might hold. A feeling of exhilaration tingled through her body from the tips of her toes to the roots of her hair.

Seth's eyes, unblinkingly set on hers, were full of care, full of – love. She realised it all of a sudden. Looking back she could see missed opportunities, brief times they had spent together, and the way Seth used to look at her; all these gone unheeded because of her obsession to her unworthy master; because of both their loyal commitment to him.

Tears welling up in her eyes began to roll down her rosy cheeks flushed by the spinning activity of her brain, still registering the revelations, affirming the knowledge of hope. Deep, soul-searching smiles passed between them. Meg held out her arms to him and he instinctively moved forward. With a dream-like quality they melted into each other's embrace, oblivious to all else around them.

The warmth of Meg's tears seeped into the shoulder of his shirt. Seth's accompanying sigh was as long as the years spent standing on the periphery of Meg's life, as if he had been holding his breath for that time.

For the first time in both their lives, Meg and Seth could feel the strength within them created by their forces joining together. Meg stood cocooned in Seth's welcoming arms. The unspoken knowledge that Seth had loved Meg from afar and throughout the worst episode of her life was a testament to the endurance of his worthy love. The feelings of warmth she felt towards him were strangely not new to her; more like the release of something suppressed. She had always felt at ease and comfortable in his company over the years. This was not a sudden attraction for Seth, but one denied, due to her persistent infatuation for Charles.

Meg stepped back, still holding Seth's arms, and looked at him with new eyes. Seth's pale blue eyes smiled, a gentle creasing at his temples. A tamed mane of fair hair framed his strong, tanned face.

"Do you like what you see, Meggie Williamson?"

Meg tossed her head to one side and laughed. "Aye, Seth, I do," she said, suddenly assured of her answer. Since breaking free from her dependency on Black Bull Farm, a new confidence and a new wisdom had been born within her. Her old naivety had been shed like an unwanted coat. She enjoyed her new maturity, her freedom.

Ella burst into the room ready to ask about their letters. Realising the intimacy of the moment and how unwanted her interruption would be, she stopped at the edge of the sideboard and was about to turn and tiptoe back to the kitchen, hoping she hadn't been heard, when Meg looked over and beckoned to her. Meg dried her eyes on Seth's shirtsleeve whilst giving a cheeky glance up at him.

"It's alright, pet lamb," she said. "Come away in. I'm fine. I've jist read a sad letter."

Ella was much more interested in how Meg and Seth had come to find themselves locked together.

At the end of that evening, Meg and Seth found it hard to say goodbye. In silent but comfortable company, they faced one another on the harbour doorstep of the Tulloch's home. The night was still and dark; clouds flitted across the moon. The only noise to be heard was the gentle lapping of seawater against the harbour walls. Meg stood on the top step, where she was level with Seth's eyes. She could reach his shoulders with straight arms. They smiled simultaneously, the sort of smile that transcends the physical, connects with the soul. Seth measured the day's outcome as the best that he could have hoped for, the most rewarding day of his entire life. Meg felt her day, with its troughs and its heights, had left her happy and full of future promise.

Reluctantly, Seth bade Meg goodnight.

This triggered the ultimate reward of the day. Meg moved her face closer to his, her eyes lightly closed, her soft lips parted. For Seth, it was the cherry on the cake. He gazed for one amazed moment at her beauty in the dim harbour lighting before again taking the opportunity presented. He placed his lips lightly over hers. She responded with a soft kiss of acceptance.

In his lonely Manor House on the island of Westray, Charles Stewart drained the last drops of his malt whisky into a crystal tumbler. His head was numb and devoid of thought. Raising the tumbler unsteadily to his lips, he swiftly tipped it back, greedily gulping down the golden alcohol. He had no way of knowing that, at that very moment in time, his unbeknown rival of so many years was gently kissing the lips of his own lost mistress.

Part 6

32

Quandary

It was Ella who notified William about the budding romance between Meg and Seth. She wrote a letter to her brother at Start Point Lighthouse on the day after she suspected the growing alignment between them. It was at a time in Ella's life when romance featured high on her list of interests; her letter was full of girlish excitement that caused William to chuckle. He received it on the morning of his free day from work, a day he had promised to spend with John, Mary and their family on the next island. On the ferry crossing to Westray he found time to reflect on past unions within the family, and he realised things did not add up.

Hellen would have been fifty six years old when he was born, and although he was not fully conversant with the procedures and functions of the female body, he had never heard of any other mother that advanced in years giving birth. There were other mysteries; the fight with the older boys at Westray School, for instance, which had never been discussed, and Hellen's immediate decision to visit relatives in Kirkwall. All this had coincided with the offer of an assistant's position at the lighthouse at Start Point. There were questions for Hellen that he had never had the chance to ask.

Hellen had always done her best for him and Ella and he would never think ill of her, so whatever her choices had been William was convinced the reasons behind them must have been good ones. It was only with the curiosity of a pubescent that a vague feeling of some sort of cover up had occurred to him. For some unfathomable reason it was best for him to know no more than he did. The dilemma concerning dates and ages began to prey at the back of his mind and these re-emerged on Westray when he came across Andrew Williamson's headstone.

Two of John and Mary's children had persuaded William to take them for an exploratory walk, which turned out to be more revealing to William than to the children. They passed by the Kirk yard with its adjoining cemetery, which was always a fascination for the children. The graves proved an irresistible draw and they began to wander around idly reading inscriptions on the headstones. One of the children grabbed William by the hand and pulled him towards a small stone, nearly hidden by undergrowth under a tree.

"Dis is ma grandfaider's grave," she said proudly.

Her brother called to her and she then ran off to find him, leaving William to face the sudden mystery of his roots as he read the short inscription: "Andrew Williamson of Fair Isle. Born 1816 Died 1872". He tried to take in the implications behind those simple words – the headstone stated that Andrew Williamson had died seven years before William was born.

Just what and when William had been told about his father was hazy in his memory. Had he always presumed his father was Hellen's husband, Andrew? That his father was dead? He knew that the family had once lived on Fair Isle, but how did he know this? It was just one of those inherent assumptions that a child accepts as truth. He had no memory of Hellen relating stories about the past. She had never been one to speak of those who had departed – either though death or through circumstance. With a furrowed brow William continued to stare at the gravestone. If Andrew was not his father, and from this inscription this was clearly the case – then who was his father? The question seemed too pertinent to ask an aunt or any other member of his family. He wished to do the impossible – to ask Hellen.

As he stood alone in front of the buried bones of this ancestor, whose precise relationship to him was a mystery, William's feelings swung up and down like the waves on a troubled sea. Throughout his childhood years at Rabbitha' with Agnes, Peter and their children, he had never felt the need of a father and never lacked a fatherly presence. His Uncle Peter had been a constant presence and there had always been John. John, his brother – or the person William had always believed to be his brother – but he was Andrew's son. This inscription proved that William was not Andrew's son.

William rubbed his forehead as if to clear his muddled thoughts. He had been kept in the dark about some family secret and it was an uncomfortable feeling. Who was being protected, he wondered?

John's two children returned, skipping and chasing around

William before dragging him off to continue their walk. Strong gusts of wind bearing a smattering of drizzly rain accompanied them on their return to John and Mary's home. The weather helped to refresh and cleanse William's mind.

Whatever his roots, and if ever his true parentage were to surface, he had to agree that there had been no adverse effects from not knowing the full facts. The identity of his actual parents was not an issue that he would allow to hold him back or to upset his life's balance. But his curiosity was aroused. Then there was the question of Ella's parentage. When she arrived as a baby at Rabbita' Hellen had said she was a gift, which William readily accepted, a kind of adoption of Ella. Any additional information was never pro-offered and seemed unnecessary. But as they grew older, a family resemblance between William and Ella had become more obvious. Whilst left to his own devices on duty at Start Point Lighthouse, William had began to pick out discrepancies in his family history.

If Hellen was not his birth mother then why, he thought, would she lie to him? But had she lied to him? He took this for granted. He had always happily called her "Ellen" – had she told him to call her this? He remembered when Ella was very young that Hellen had wanted her to call her Ellen, too, but that Ella insisted on calling her "Midder". Had Hellen adopted him as well as Ella? As Ella grew older, he knew she would also wonder the same things. There were three people that he could ask; John, Agnes and Meg. He vowed to approach John about this quandary. After their midday cup of mutton broth and freshly baked bread, William took John aside.

"It's naw fur me tae say, lad," John said, stunned by William's query.

He scratched his head as he contemplated William's predicament. He felt it was certainly not his place to implicate Meg. For John it was something so far in the past and so accepted in the normal run of things that he had forgotten the details. He had been but a lad himself when William arrived as a baby at Rabbitha'. Until that moment John had not put himself in William's shoes.

"I reckon ye hav' tae ask Agnes or Meg aboot dat, William," was his advice.

There was no time that day to seek out Agnes at the other side of the island for he had to catch the last ferry back to Sanday. In Ella's letter she had said that they would be visiting him on Sanday in a few weeks' time so he would have to wait and ask Meg then.

During that week as William wrestled with his need for answers, a person unrelated to him was also wanting him to be enlightened; a person who would never know his own roots, other than that his mother's name was Betsy and she had died giving birth to him. Seth had never worried about what might have been, though occasionally he felt sadness that he was the cause of his young mother's death. He believed it unnecessary to waste time on something you couldn't change, and that nothing could be gained by dwelling on tragedy. And these were sentiments he wanted William and Ella to realise. It was the only cloud to hang over Seth, the delusion concerning William and Ella's family relationships.

Seth could foresee that if William and Ella were not told that Meg was their natural mother, there might be a breakdown in trust with other family members, because sooner rather than later the children would begin to put two and two together. He was not to know that William had already begun the process of backtracking through his history. The family secret initiated to protect the children was increasingly unnecessary as they grew up, yet the shock might prove insurmountable as Seth felt William would not take kindly to feeling duped. There was only one way and that was to tell them the truth, or at least some of the truth.

Like her mother before her, Meg remained adamant that it was unnecessary to tell them. She felt the hitherto false assumption that Hellen had been their mother was in no way a bad assumption. But it wasn't the truth, and that's what concerned Seth. The children's belief was on borrowed time. There would never be a perfect time to divulge the information, Seth was well aware of that, but he knew the later it was left, the worse it would be. In fairness to William and Ella, Meg should be the one to tell them and he would support her. They had lived with this deception for so long, but it was a deception only acceptable to children. The chance came on their planned trip to Sanday.

33

Return to Black Bull Farm

It was decided that Seth would return alone to Black Bull Farm to discover what it was that Bessie and Jeremiah were holding in safe keeping for them. The mysterious special "erlom" beckoned. For if Meg were to suddenly appear back at the Farm, they could envisage trouble from the Laird. In his letter Jeremiah had stated that Charles was frequently drunk. Seth was going in order to fulfil Isobella's final wish. He would only be gone a day or two at the most.

On the evening before his trip the sun began to set over Kirkwall harbour in glorious pink and orange hues. Christina encouraged Meg to take a walk by the shore with Seth and the girls, who often accompanied them on their walks as a courting couple around the town. Ella and Gina walked several paces behind them and after much whispering between themselves, Ella approached them with a cheeky expression on her face.

"Are ye two in love?" she asked and both girls began giggling.

"Oh, ye scallywags!" said Meg blushing.

Seth laughed and pretended to chase them along the path. The girls ran off down the path to the pebbled shore, leaving Seth alone with Meg, both standing braced against the wind.

"Grand wee girls," he said, watching them slide and scramble onto the shore.

"Dey are dat," said Meg, pulling locks of her hair away from her mouth where the wind had lashed it.

Seth turned to face her.

"You do know, don't you Meggie...?" he began to fumble for the right words – the simplest yet most meaningful words in the world.

"Whit is it, Seth?"

Meg hoped that the words she wanted to hear were the next ones he would say. There was a stillness, a comforting pause, and the wind calmed as Seth said:

"…I do love you, Meggie Williamson, with all my heart."

To hear his words was ecstasy for Meg. Happiness engulfed her like warmed silk. She reached up and draped her arms around his neck, feeling like a child again. Seth held her lightly around her waist. She wanted to shout from the cliff tops – "I love ye, Seth, I love ye, too!" though the words remained within her.

"Will you go forward with me, Meggie Williamson – to wherever our path may lead?"

At that moment Meg knew she had assuredly found her partner for life.

"I *will* go with ye, Seth."

Their faces grew closer until their lips met and they were lost in a kiss. Standing above the stony beach, above the lapping waves, they were oblivious to the incessant wind, which wrapped Meg's shawl around them both like a cocoon. They kissed – a long and lingering kiss. A kiss that awakened their senses yet numbed their awareness of the world around them. The sun was setting and from along the beach Ella and Gina caught sight of the embrace and started to whistle and whoop.

For Meg the shock of losing Hellen was softened by the love she found within herself for her first two, once deserted children. Now a fresh new love had sprung into her life; the comforting, deep-rooted love that Seth revealed to her. She was left reeling at the speed in which her life was turning around; intoxicated by the sincerity of Seth's commitment to her. To be cherished was a new feeling – and to be suddenly cherished was incredibly moving.

For Seth, it had only been a matter of time, because his quiet inner strength and the confidence he had in his own convictions would never have allowed him to give up on Meg. For him it was his ambition achieved; a coming home. For Meg's part, it was a discovery of true love with freedom from restrictions in which she felt pride, not shame, and could acknowledge the difference between a stagnant, oppressive infatuation and a future based on an open love. Seth told her he felt he was the richest man in Orkney, and she understood what he meant. For

Meg there was new air to breathe. Meg felt comfortably respectable, a part of society. She could hold her head high for there was nothing secretive or hidden about their feelings for one another.

It was noon by the time Seth arrived at Black Bull Farm. Nothing much had changed and the farm appeared to be operating as usual. Some farm workers were making their way towards Bessie's kitchen for midday sustenance. Seth followed them. He stood in the open doorway of the kitchen and looked around the familiar room. A few workers nodded an acknowledgement; others whispered or stared. By the stove, Bessie was stirring a cauldron of broth with a large wooden spoon. The first person she saw when she turned around was the tall, shadowed figure blocking the sunlight from the doorway.

"Weel, weel, jist look whit the cat brought in!" she said, smiling.

Spoon in hand, she made her way across the kitchen. Seth noticed that around her neck there was a short, collar length string of pearls, incongruous with her working dress and apron.

"Sit yersel' doon, Seth, an' I'll get ye a bowl o' my mutton broth."

Detaching himself from the rest of the workers, Seth sat down at the end of the long wooden table as Jeremiah entered the kitchen. They shook hands and Bessie brought them each a bowl of broth. She spoke to Seth in hushed and furtive tones.

"The Laird is awful bad."

"He's taken tae the bottle awright," Jeremiah added.

"He gave me these pearls!" Bessie ran her fingers lightly over the string of polished gems around her neck. "They were Mistress Isobella's, but he said she would have wantit me tae have them – he insisted, an' he said I should wear them a' the time I was working so he could see them every day – so I feel I have tae!"

"Drunk richt noo, he is," Jeremiah went on. "Ye'd better gang alang tae see him, Seth."

Seth knew they were right. He had to see his old master. They had been companions for most of their lives and it was, after all, Charles's father who had rescued Seth as a baby, given him skills and work. Circumstances had changed so drastically over the past year for Charles, with his world fallen apart around him. He would know nothing of Seth's connection with Meg, but Seth was not looking forward to their meeting.

"Ye go an' see him an' we'll see ye efter," said Jeremiah.

"We hav' tae gie ye the 'erloom, Seth," Bessie added.

"Ah!" Seth's curiosity awakened, "– what is this 'erlom' you're talking about, Bessie?"

But before she could reply everyone's attention was diverted by a curious cacophony from outside. Workers left their seats and went out to see what was happening. A rumpus was coming from the stable yard and Seth went to investigate. As he crossed the courtyard he heard the sound of raised voices and the erratic clopping of horse's hooves on cobblestones.

" 'Tis the Laird agin," said one worker to another as Seth strode past them.

"Aye, drunk as a Laird – agin!" another jested.

"He'll come a cropper one o' these days, so he will."

Muffled comments rippled through the gathering, but the workers appeared to be accustomed to this type of disruption.

Cumulative clouds rolled over the sun, carrying with them a strong feeling of foreboding. Seth entered the gloom of the main stable and gave his eyes time to adjust. He instantly recognised the silhouette of the Laird, framed by daylight in the far end stable doors. Charles Stewart was moving erratically. Beside him a young stable lad held tightly onto the reins of the Laird's horse. The Laird, obviously the worse for drink, was in irascible mood.

"I *will* ride today, lad," he boomed. "Let go of the reins this *instant*, do you hear me?"

"No, Laird, I canna, I jist canna let ye!"

The tall young lad, not much older than twelve, was panicked, agitated and under strengthened for the task in hand. Seth realised he would have to intervene at this most inopportune moment; an awkward time for a reunion. But the Laird in his drunken state must be stopped from mounting the horse.

"Laird!" Seth shouted across the yard.

Both the stable lad and the Laird swung round, the latter a lot more ponderously and hesitatingly than the former. But it was the stable lad who was to be caught off guard, loosening his grip of the reins.

"Oh please, sir, 'elp me stop him!" he pleaded.

Suddenly, the Laird's ponderous movements became sharp and controlled as he seized his opportunity, along with the reins of his horse. Grabbing them free from the lad's hands, he took swift control of his fidgeting horse, hooves clacking loudly on the cobbles. Deftly, he manoeuvred the horse's rump in an arc around the boy, cutting him off, and before Seth had time to run forward, Charles's foot was in the stirrup. He threw his lumbering frame across the horse's back and the confused horse quietened under his master's firm hand. Seth stood his ground, blocking the stable exit.

"So!" said Charles, high in his saddle. "You have deemed fit to return, have you, Seth? Fallen on hard times, eh?"

A distant memory hurtled to the forefront of Seth's mind, brought back by the Laird's present mocking tone, his dominant attitude. Time was of the essence in controlling the situation yet its unwelcome vision rushed in and froze in Seth's mind. He saw again the pony in foal stuck fast in the quagmire on the day that jealous rivalry reared between Seth and his master. As on that day, the Laird had gained the upper hand.

The Laird's horse remembered Seth and strained his head forward to nuzzle his shoulder, but Charles tugged harshly on the reins, yanking his head out of reach.

"Laird, ye must not ride in this condition!"

Seth's voice was loud and edged with anger. His hand shot forward to take hold of the horse, but Charles moved quicker, his body driven by the rush of alcoholic euphoria. Since downing his last goblet of whisky, he had alternated between spasms of strength and weakness, sharpness and sloth.

"Get out of my way, you ne'r-do-weel!" he sneered.

Then he turned his horse around to face the open stable door and, setting off at a gallop, horse and rider charged passed Seth, raising a cloud of dust and straw in their wake. Seth jumped back against a stable. Charles's face looked bloated, his hair unkempt and his eyes were bloodshot.

Workers walking in the courtyard scattered in alarm as the horse and rider shot out from the gloom of the stable, across the courtyard and over to open pasture. The Laird's face was ruddied with anger. As he galloped across the courtyard, his bleariad eyes were set upon the distant horizon. Within moments his horse had taken him far out into the open countryside.

"Give me a horse!" yelled Seth to the stunned stable boy. "Quickly, lad!"

The lad darted to the first occupied stable and untethered a horse. Seth grabbed reins from a peg on the wall and deftly fitted them over the horse's head. The stable lad started to lift a saddle down from its hook, but Seth had already set off, riding bareback.

Farm servants ran around the courtyard in a chaotic manner, shouting for horses to be saddled up ready for the chase, and the stables were soon in turmoil with the most competent riders commandeering all the available horses and setting off at a gallop. The Laird, with Seth in pursuit, was far out in front of the other riders. There was a strong wind behind them and clouds raced across the sky following their direction. The pace of the chase, dictated by the Laird, took its toll on the suddenly worked horses forced into a hard gallop and many of them flagged. Seth noted that Charles appeared to be heading in the direction of the high tracks along the western cliffs. Seth knew this to be a dead-end and the thought disturbed him. His horse was not as fast as the Laird's, but enjoyed the rush and kept a steady pace.

Charles suddenly changed direction. Aghast, Seth saw him set a course no longer parallel to the cliffs, but at right angles – heading towards the sea. This was one of the highest points on the western coastline and there was a sheer drop to sharp rocks below. Is the man mad, Seth thought? Was he so blind drunk – enough to have a death wish?

Ahead of Seth, the Laird's flagging horse had sensed the danger and was trying to pull away from the course set for him. Charles Stewart looked over his shoulder, a manic look in his eyes, his teeth barred. Seth pulled his horse up a little, hoping that Charles, his anger vented, would do likewise, but he raised one arm in a defiant, straight-armed salute, like an ancient warrior intent on war damage, and kept his horse on course for disaster. Seth tried to head them off, circling to the side, but Charles dug his heels into his horse's sweating flanks and galloped on. Adrenaline and hot blood pumped through all veins.

Charles's horse tried repeatedly to veer away from the cliffs, but every time the Laird spurred him onward. Seth could hear shouts from behind and the sound of horses' hooves rumbling across the ground. The other farm workers were nearly upon them. They would all be witness to the drama that ensued.

Watching in horror, they saw the Laird's horse, nostrils flaring, confused and panicked, halt suddenly and dig his hooves into the soft turf, refusing to obey his master's command. Horse and master were silhouetted at the top of the cliff when Charles became unseated. Seth and the mounted onlookers pulled up their exhausted horses and watched tensely from a distance as the Laird was catapulted into the air, over his horse's head, to land heavily on rocky ground at the very edge of the cliff face; Charles's surge of energy dissipated, his world-weary mind blurred. Seth dismounted and his horse stood quietly as he raced forward. He was still some distance from the Laird's motionless body.

With a sudden surge of strength, Charles Stewart hoisted himself up from the earth. Seth ran hard, his heart blood on fire. Charles dragged his weary frame up until he stood, slumped, one arm hanging limply by his side; limp and distorted. The arm was broken, certainly, but Charles ignored it and began stumbling towards the cliff edge, his body stooped, his broken arm dangling uselessly. His horse paced in a circle, unwilling to leave his doomed master. His loyalty was deep.

Running hard towards the fated spot, Seth was hit full on by a defiant glare over Charles Stewart's shoulder. Seth's heart pounded and his thoughts raced. He stopped to shout a warning. The Laird looked back again, this time with disdain. He looked gaunt and wasted. The distance between the two men, physically and mentally, was infinite. Seth couldn't stop the Laird from his intent.

Charles turned his back on Seth and the other riders – on Black Bull Farm and on Westray – to face out over his chosen future, out to the wind over the sea that buffeted the cliffs. His horse whinnied and sauntered closer to him, but he ignored the animal and kept his gaze on the sea's horizon, standing still for a moment. It gave Seth time to steadily approach, close enough to speak without shouting. But Charles was oblivious to Seth; he was lost to another place far inside his head. He drew himself up suddenly, and standing erect he appeared to follow some silent order. Without warning, he took two sharp strides forwards, taking him to the edge of the world, where he leapt, free falling into another.

Seth gaped in disbelief as time stood still for him. The image of the fallen, falling Laird would be indelibly etched into his memory. Time stood still yet it raced headlong as Seth flung himself forward to the very cliff's edge, his arm outstretched in the vain hope of catching a wasted woebegone. Seth's torso dangled precariously into the turbulent air beyond the cliff, as he lay prone and rejected. Beside him on the cliff's grassy coat were the depressions of Charles Peter Stewart's last footprints; this, his last stand still visible until for a moment until the blades of grass recovered, stretched and stood tall again. As the grass sprung back to life, the Laird's life was hurtling into oblivion.

His body, though still suspended in the air, seemed lifeless. He was only minutes from certain death on the jagged, sea-drenched rocks under the cliff. Seth grimaced and shut his eyes tightly.

For an instant the wind appeared to calm and a silence descended. It was as if Nature was in awe of this bizarre act of man. The eerie stillness was broken by a distant heavy thud. Seth opened his eyes and focused in on Charles Stewart's twisted and broken body sprawled across the boulders below as if spewed up by the raging, foaming waves.

"Nnooooohhhh!"

Bellowing, protracted pain escaped from Seth's mouth and the word hung on the windless air before it reverberated around the rocks and the cliff face. It was the last human sound Charles Stewart heard. With the breath of this once great man crushed from him, the tie between Charles and Meg was also crushed. Far below Seth lay the empty shell of the man in whose company Seth had spent most of his life and who had affected so much of Meg's life.

The crowd of servants ran up to Seth, pulling him back from the edge, where he gripped the turf with white knuckles, his eyes still fixed on the incredulous sight below. Earthly sounds resumed, swamping the silence with the noise of crashing surf; the same surf that lapped at Charles's broken limbs and threatened to float his crushed body from its precarious perch to deliver it into the sea's abyss. Charles's inner being died the instant he stepped off the cliff into oblivion, but his outer shell lived a while longer. The injuries he sustained rendered him immobile and forced him to watch through rigidly open eyes the relentless sea's treatment of him. He watched his life ebbing away as he felt the salty water flood in and out of his eyes and deep into his nostrils, the same water that would drown him. By the time his servants had climbed down the cliff face, his body had vanished and was nowhere to be seen. The sea had taken his drunken, drowned corpse.

34

The Merry Dancers

That night, Seth made a bed for himself in the hay of the attic above the stable. His restless sleep tallied with that of the Laird's fretting horse in the stable below. At the other end of the attic, also sleeping fitfully, was the stable lad, troubled by the nightmare of his past day's experience and occasionally sobbing in his sleep. Seth could recall when he had been the same age as the lad and how he, too, had used this same attic for his sleeping quarters for many years. In the past it had been Seth's only home. But it no longer felt like home, more like a previous existence, a distant memory. The only home Seth wanted now was wherever Meg was to be found.

As dawn broke Seth remembered the small package secreted inside the top pocket of his shirt. After an exhaustive and futile search along the coastline, Seth and the other servants had returned to Black Bull Farm, when fading light had forced a stop to the search. Bessie sought out the despondent Seth and gave him the small package, the "erlom" as she called it. On the paper wrapping, Isobella had written, "To Seth for Meg" and on receiving it, Seth had neither the will nor the energy to examine its contents and pushed it into his top pocket.

In the strengthening light, Seth unwrapped the parcel and inside he found the exquisite ring of delicate gold and jewels. Turning it around in his hands, he realised that never before had he handled gold, let alone an intricately crafted piece of jewellery. He examined the exquisite design. Two lustrous part pearls were set on either side of a deep purple jewel. Tiny gold beading surrounded all three stones.

Bessie's "erlom" was one of Isobella's family heirlooms. With no one left in her family to whom she could bequeath it, Isobella had instinctively and determinedly made other provision for its future, her gesture being both thoughtful and instigating. Instigating because Isobella's simple, four worded, accompanying note had indicated a connection between Seth and Meg. This connection had been confirmed and plainly set out in her last letter to Meg. These tangible despatches across the divide, between Isobella's locked mind, now departed, and Meg's secret existence, had imparted to Meg what Seth had been trying to convey for years – his deep-rooted love for her.

With simplicity and ease, Isobella had managed to open Meg's eyes and unhinge the door blocking her way from an entrapped world to a more worthy one, where true love did exist and where the prospect of a better life awaited her. "To Seth for Meg." Those were the only words necessary. Possibly her last words, written with her last ounce of strength. Seth pondered on her reasoning and on her determination to have her last request fulfilled. It was clear that Isobella thought highly of Meg. As for Seth, she had astutely perceived his love for her servant from afar and, although in reality any declaration of love was still in the offing, she had presumed it was an established love, little realising her role as matchmaker. Mercifully, thought Seth, this had thrown her off the scent that led to the hurtful truth – that it was her own husband who made trysts with Meg, her own husband who impregnated Meg with merrybegotten babies and created an illegitimate family, blood-related to her own children.

With the sun barely risen above the horizon, Seth re-wrapped the ring and tucked it safely back into his top pocket. He climbed down the ladder to the stable yard and saddled up the first horse he came to. Leaving the stable on horseback, he crossed the courtyard and out to the open pastureland, where he began to canter towards the western cliffs, to the fateful spot where the Laird had leapt off the world. The dawn was glorious and a crisp fresh breeze from the sea helped to calm his inner turmoil. Mother Nature appeared pleased with this fresh start, the new beginning yet also unrepentant to the wild theft of the Laird's body on the previous day. Seth scoured the rocks and the tide line below, but saw no sign of Charles Stewart's body. Sooner rather than later, the sea would cough him up on a none-too-distant shore. Seth felt a duty to find him and to bury him.

It was not until low tide the following afternoon that the Laird of Westray's body, bloated and barely recognisable, was discovered, carefully deposited by the bored sea inside 'The Gentleman's Cave', a mile or so from its last sighting. This hidden cave had been used as a refuge in 1745 by the Orkney Lairds who supported the Jacobite Uprising. It seemed an apt resting-place, however temporary, for the last Laird of Westray. Seth contacted Isobella's parents and Charles's younger brother, who worked on the farm of an uncle on the island of Hoy. He must take over the reins of Black Bull Farm. The minister was summoned and Charles Stewart was buried in due course in the family vault alongside Isobella and their two sons.

There was another dilemma for Seth. Not all the Stewart descendants were dead. Two of his illegitimate offspring were alive and well. But, of course, only Meg and Seth knew this. Only Meg and Seth knew the Laird had other children, outwith those of his marriage. Catherine Stewart's fate might never be known and as long as there was a chance she was still alive and perhaps given birth to children of her own, William could never have any claim to his father's estate, a father still unknown to him. But the thought was mind-boggling; that William was an heir. There could never be any proof of this. No one would believe Meg even if she did declare it, which she never would. What advantage would it be to William to know that his father was the wealthiest landowner in Westray? William had no illusions of grandeur. Like Seth, he enjoyed the simple life. Complications such as position and wealth were not for them to deal with. Seth reasoned that there was no advantage whatsoever in his knowing. William would do better in finding his own feet, his own destiny. But Seth was the privileged keeper of a secret shared with Meg – something pertaining to William that William knew nothing about. Did he and Meg have the right to keep him oblivious to such personal information?

Gales caused the ferry crossings to be cancelled; it was three days before Seth, in sombre mood, returned to Kirkwall. Back in the town, people were stunned to hear about the latest disaster to annihilate the Stewart family. It was an unparalleled spate of tragedies to happen to one family in the duration of less than two years. If indeed Catherine Stewart was still alive, it was unlikely that she would ever know the full devastation that befell the family she deserted.

Seth took a long walk alone with Meg so that he could explain the fate of the father of her children, and his part in overseeing the tragedy. They walked arm in arm along the bay.

"It's all over now, Meggie," he said. "The past is gone, a closed book."

She stared at the lapping waves, persistently, rhythmically, washing the shore.

"Life goes on regardless," he continued, assimilating his remark to the sea's perpetual motion, to the setting sun's promise of a good day to follow. The evening sky was clear and tinged with vibrant pink and amber.

"Pink sky at night, shepherd's delight," Meg smiled up at Seth.

For a time, they sat in silence, eyes fixed on the calming, dependable horizon. The island of Shapinsay lay away in the distance to their right with the landmark towers of Balfour Castle protruded jaggedly up into the twilight, catching the last rays of the sun. Seth remembered Isobella's gift and in the fading light he produced the small package and handed it to Meg. The beauty of the ring and its delicate craftsmanship were well known to her, its familiarity gave her comfort. In the past her eyes had always been drawn towards it when it adorned Isobella's finger. Its every tiny nuance was known and loved to her and evoked memories of the kindness of Isobella.

"Oh – my – wonder!" she said. "So dis is what Isobella wanted me to have? Me? Is it not truly beautiful?"

Seth nodded.

"Isobella loved dis ring," she continued. "It reminded her of her childhood and of her grandmother. It used to be her grandmother's ring. I often admired it and she would say she thought 'twas a shame dat I would never own such a lovely piece of jewellery, dat she could see I appreciated its beauty."

"She must have felt it was right that you should have it after she died," said Seth.

"Aye, perhaps."

Wistfully, Meg gazed at the otherwise unobtainable wealth nestling in her cupped hands. The Williamson family had never owned jewellery of any description. The only adornments they had known as children were daisy chains they made themselves. Mother Nature's jewellery. Yet now she found herself in possession of a gold ring set with gems. Her mind wandered back to the times when she and Isobella had commented on its beauty, and to one particular time when Isobella had wanted Meg to try on the ring.

"Put it on, Meg, put it on," Isobella had insisted, and it fitted Meg's finger perfectly.

As she gazed in admiration at the ring, she remembered that day and the same words came back as if to haunt her. But this time she realised it was Seth who spoke them.

"Put it on, Meggie," he said, unwittingly reiterating Isobella's words.

Meg looked up and smiled at him and at the memory of Isobella. For a second time in her life in response to the same request, she did as she was bid. Slipping the ring over her knuckle, she straightened her arm and held it out in front of her, the heel of her wrist bend backward for them both to appreciate its beauty. The unique quality of this handcrafted ring made her feel special. Its presence seemed to soften and gentrify her work-worn hand. Seth placed his palm against hers and their touch was gently electrifying.

As if to emblazon that moment in their memories one of Nature's rare and wondrous displays appeared to them. An astute change in light, a subtle change in sound, created an arrestingly eerie atmosphere, encompassing their unity. Sitting motionless, Meg and Seth turned their heads to look at one another. All around them an aura of awe and intrigue prepared them to witness without distraction, an *aurora borealis.*

Meg was first to notice the lights.

"Look, Seth!" she said. "It's da Northern Lights!"

As if for their eyes only, a magical performance commenced within the deepening gloom above the horizon. A dancing spectrum of lights began to ripple like a curtain of changing colours across the wide panorama of sky. As Meg and Seth watched, spellbound, the colours of green, blue, yellow and amber capriciously undulated before them. Intermittent flashes of brightly coloured light streaked across the darkened sky, occasionally spinning in smooth spiralling effects of green and silver, like oil on water. A moment later these would glide across the heavens, their effect almost audible. The sky was filled with this iridescence panoply. The experience was to be binding and everlasting for the newly realised couple.

Seth's mind recalled his last sighting of the "Merry Dancers" as he called the *aurora borealis*. It had been in the gloaming of the night after his first sighting of Meg. Meg and the *aurora* were inextricably intermingled, both dazzling to his senses. A full circle seemed complete. A feeling of unity engulfed him and he ached to hold her. Meg sensed his yearning and gently turned her face to his. They locked eyes and he put his arm around her shoulders. He could smell her sweetness, could feel her soft breath on his cheek. In the dim light her eyes shone out at him with an unmistakable assurance. Irresistibly drawn, Seth held her close to him and their bodies sighed with age-long relief. The bubble that seemed to contain them was dreamlike, yet drifting on a wave of certainty. His ultimate goal, to be together at last; this was all he had ever wanted to achieve.

Seth moved his lips closer to Meg's then paused. Their breath mingling, unifying, her lips parted slightly as she welcomed his intent. Their kiss was lingering, sealing. The canopy of Merry Dancers swirled and spun in approval above them.

35

Revelation

William and Seth became close friends despite their age difference. They had much in common, particularly their sense of humour, and their joking and pranks caused much amusement. It warmed Meg's heart to see them get along so well and she could not have wished for a better relationship between them. When Meg thought back to their days at Black Bull Farm, she remembered Seth as a lone character, whose only company was that of his master, but she realised that he, too, had been unwittingly under the Laird's influence. His loyalty to the Stewart family had also set him apart from the other workers.

For Seth his narrowed life had opened up though his interest in Meg; in realising his ambition to be with her, he had not only attained his desired life partner, but also in William, a most compatible friend. By a strange quirk of fate, Seth had found both life partner and friend within the same family, and he realised that this would not have been possible if he had intervened in some way at the start of Meg's disastrous affair with her master. If he had, William would not exist. It helped him to accept that he had missed out on fathering children with Meg. But he was still uncomfortable with the fact that William and Ella would soon want questions answered and could foresee a disastrous end to the lovely relationship that Meg was building up with her newly acquainted children if she refused to be prepared for this. William was no fool and would soon come to some conclusion – if he hadn't done so already. Truths would have to be revealed, to be smoothed and pacified before they became rough and destructive.

William was standing on the jetty when the Saturday ferry from Kirkwall docked at Sanday carrying Meg, Seth, Ella and Gina to visit him. Although conversation flowed freely, Seth picked up on William's subdued and introspective mood. The usual banter between them was stifled and William seemed distracted. Seth sensed the boy had things on his mind.

When Ella and Gina asked William to take them for a ride in Gina's uncle's pony and trap, Seth found the opportunity he needed to speak alone to Meg about William. Seth took Meg for her first ride on a horse. In no time she had mastered the reins and felt in command of her horse. On the return to the stables, Meg's mood was lively. Seth was loath to spoil her buoyancy, but his urgent inner voice was forcing him to confront her. For the good of all those involved, this skeleton in Meg's cupboard must be aired and laid to rest.

"Meggie, we have to tell William."

"Umm? Tell him what, Seth?"

He turned and looked at her directly. Realisation fell over her, melting her smile into a frown. She felt the weight of a leaden blanket.

"Och, no, no... Must it come to this?" she wailed beseechingly.

Seth caught her by her elbows, supporting her numbed weight as the strength ebbed from her legs. He held her close and gazed into her pale face, drained of its recent rosy euphoria. He had destroyed her happy mood, but this was an issue that had to be addressed; it was what she had always dreaded. Just as she was enjoying the anticipation of a bright future, her past reared up and faced her head on. Seth sat Meg down on a wooden bench outside the stables before he continued.

"Meeting up with your children again was something you never expected, but I know that you wouldn't want to lose them now. Before doubts arise, before they start to ask questions – before this bond is destroyed..." he paused. "If they were to discover the deception on their own, it would surely destroy the trust you've built up with them."

"Ye judge me harshly! Ye hate me for what I did!"

Meg's voice began to rise in panic. She felt that her elated hopes for the future were being dashed, ripped away in his simple speech of truth.

"How could I hate you, Meggie?"

He lowered his head and kissed her forehead reassuringly.

"You were young, you fell in love with the wrong man ..." he said, waiting for her to catch his meaning.

She smiled and felt her panic ease.

"Your loyalties were misplaced. When your babies were born you did what was best. Look how well your children have turned out..."

She nodded meekly and fixed her tear-filled eyes on his.

"But what can I say dat won't ruin what I've got wid dem now? It'll spoil everything! My bairns will hate me!"

"Think carefully," Seth hesitated. "They shouldn't need to know the full circumstances of their..."

"Abandonment!" added Meg, burying her face in her hands.

"Listen to me, Meggie," he said as he cupped her chin in his palm, turning her face to look at him. "You need to be strong about this."

Meg dragged her sleeve across her eyes to wipe away the tears and gave him her reluctant and despondent attention. He convinced her that Charles Stewart, Laird of Westray, need never be mentioned again. There need be no connection made between the Laird and Meg, because only Meg and Seth knew of their relationship. Not only was Charles Stewart dead, but so too were all but one lost member of his legitimate family. There had never been any proof, though perhaps a little hearsay.

When William and Ella assimilated the fact that Meg was their birth mother, they would undoubtedly want to know who their father was. Meg didn't want to be labelled as a loose woman. The fact that William, Ella, Charlie and Peter all shared the same father, was something she wanted to make clear.

"We will tell them the truth," said Seth positively.

"Truth! But ye just said we didn't need to mention..."

"The truth is – their father is dead."

Meg frowned as she contemplated the truth in this statement. "Aye, dat's true – but would dat be enough tae say to dem?"

"No," admitted Seth. "They *will* want more."

After a pregnant pause, he took a deep intake of breath and said, "Well – I love them both – and I'm prepared to say they are *my* children."

Meg's jaw dropped in stunned disbelief.

"Ye would do *dat* fur me, Seth?"

Seth smiled. "I would do anything for you, Meggie Williamson."

Her heart sang as she tilted her head and lovingly placed her palm along his cheek.

"Ahh," she said, "but ye're no deid yet, are ye, Seth – an' we must say deir faider is deid?"

Meg stood up and playfully ruffled her hand through his hair. Seth's suggestion was no solution, but it helped to release some of their tension. His idea would create more problems than it solved. It would mean that both William and Ella's parents had deserted the babies. Then a reason would have to be concocted for the secrecy, for the long delay in legitimising the children. How would the chance meeting on the ferry be explained, or the mystery of the parcels from Black Bull Farm? Seth and Meg both wanted to be as truthful as they dared yet believed there must be a way to re-write this family's history.

Laughter drifted on the wind as the pony and trap, bearing Meg's children, in ignorance but soon to be enlightened, approached the stables. Meg and Seth steadily watched the three happy occupants, aware that what they were about to explain was sure to burst that bubble.

The ferry was due in less than an hour so it was first decided that the party should make their way down to the jetty. Seth and William led the way with Meg and the girls following on. William was in more forthcoming mood. Time with his sister had lifted his spirits. When they reached the jetty, they discovered that they were the only passengers waiting for the ferry. Ella and Gina sat down at one side of the wooden platform, dangling their legs over the side and began singing, "My love is like a red, red rose...". They often sang together and their young voices harmonised well. Meg, Seth and William stood nearby, leaning on the railings and facing out to sea, towards the islands of Eday and Stronsay. When they finished their song, Ella and Gina laughed and

Meg and Seth looked to one another; Meg with fear in her eyes, Seth with determination. Their opportunity had arisen and, as if to signal her to begin, he squeezed her hand.

"We have something very important tae say tae yees," she said, trying to keep her voice steady.

"Och dis looks serious, eh, Ella?" joked William. "Better listen up!"

"We don't know what your reaction will be, but things need to be said," Seth added. "Remember though – this news doesn't change anything now. It shouldn't affect your happiness – unless you let it. This only concerns your past – and that's gone, right?"

Meg moved closer to them, looking one to another as she spoke.

"You must understand, William and Ella, dat ye have both always been loved, so very much loved – and ye always will be."

It was William and Ella's turn to look to one another, perplexed.

"Wid ye want me tae go away jist noo, Meg?" Gina's soft voice interrupted.

"No, no, Gina dat's not necessary, but thank ye," Meg patted Gina's shoulder and gave her a warm smile. "Ye're part of the family right enough an' ye'll need tae know."

William pushed himself slightly away from the railings and drew himself up to full stature. He sensed that answers to his buried but ever-surfacing questions were forthcoming. Ella scrambled up to stand beside William. The children looked to Meg in expectation as she took a deep and shaky breath.

"Hellen was yer midder because she brought ye both up." Meg sighed deeply, then continued. " – But I am da midder who gave *birth* to ye both…"

Meg's words tailed off, meandering into the recesses of her children's minds, sinking through a fog of incredulity. All three children stared wide-eyed at Meg. Her throat felt constricted after releasing a truth so deeply buried in her heart. Her heart felt as if it was on fire within her fragile chest, as if flames might escape through her breastbone at any moment. So few words had been spoken yet so much had been said.

William watched Meg as a metamorphosis occurred within his mind; the absent sister transformed into his birth mother in one smooth, transitory move and without any visible alteration to Meg's physical being. Ella found the news far more difficult to take in.

"But ye are too young!" said Ella, confused as she remembered how much older 'midder' Hellen had been.

"I was too young at the time," murmured Meg.

"Aye, Hellen *was* too auld…" William said, almost to himself.

A stunned silence swooned amongst them. Gentle sounds began to intrude their privacy; the lapping seawater over the rocks, seabirds squealing far above, a distant ship's bell resounding.

"But Charlie and Peter were your bairns," said Ella.

"Aye, but ye were their big brother and sister alright."

William's face took on its frequent unfathomable mien. Ella stood dumbfounded.

Seth felt it was time to tell them his side of the story. He began by coming straight out with the fact that he had always been in love with Meg. He went on to tell them that before he could declare this love, the man who was their true father swept Meg off her feet and Meg had continued to love their father for many years. But he was now dead. He had been a good man – but a married man, and that was why their love was forbidden and kept a secret.

"Aye, dees things happen, don't dey?" said Gina.

"Aye, that's right, Gina," Seth agreed.

"I never knew *ma* midder, Ella," Gina said, turning to Ella and putting her arm around her friend's shoulders, "and ye have had two, ye lucky wee devil!"

Gina had a knack of saying the right thing in times of duress.

After one bewildered smile, tears rolled silently down Ella's face. Meg's gut reaction was to pull Ella close and hug her.

"I was only thinking of…Hellen," Ella said, stopping herself from saying 'Midder', "and how I never got to say to her how much I loved her."

"Oh she knew, pet lamb, she knew well enough," said Meg

reassuringly.

William said nothing. He gazed out to sea for what seemed an eternity. In his wildest dreams he could not have come up with that story. Yet it had to be true. Everything seemed to fit into place.

When George arrived with the ferryboat, the girls hugged William goodbye. William turned to Ella, wondering what to say to his sister, who looked lost and yet excited. Ella was a constant presence in William's life. She shared his memories. Words came to him out of the blue, comforting words that might help her, though he wasn't sure he believed them himself. No matter what, he said, Hellen would be in their hearts forever and since Meg's revelation they had actually gained, rather than lost.

He turned to Meg. She stood looking shamed, frightened. He smiled. She didn't suddenly fall into the role of his mother. She was no different than a moment before. William would soon be a man. He had done with all the mothering he would ever need and, in his heart, Hellen was still his true mother. There wasn't an instant lifelong bond between him and his birth mother. She had cut that tie and it wasn't possible to knot the two ends together again, but it might be possible for Ella. She was young and impressionable. She needed a mother and who better than her real mother. William felt a surge of relief, a reassurance that life was on an even keel, that he wasn't going mad from the lack of knowing.

"Mind, I haven't taken it all in yet," he said to her, "but I appreciate ye telling us. Dis does answer a lot of questions dat's been praying on my mind."

Meg searched his eyes and found no anger there. Tension, like taut wires strung every which way inside her body, slowly released. The burden and pressure of her deception, weighing so heavily on her for so long, was lifting. There was still a wariness within her, an expectation of some rebuke, but this far no angry words had been thrown.

"He must've been a good man, my faider, for ye tae have stuck by him fur so lang," William said to Meg, "but I have never needed him in my life and I won't be needing him now so put yer mind at rest – *Midder!*" He emphasised her title.

"Kind words – *son!*" she retorted with relief springing from her as a laugh.

Meg's long-standing fears were now addressed and William appeared to have taken the news well.

"*My* Midder!" Well, well!" he spoke as if he was talking to himself. "Mind, I won't be calling you 'midder' – I'll still be calling ye 'Meg'!"

"Dat's grand by me, William," said Meg.

Seth watched mother and son reunited, hopefully for a lasting relationship, and knew they had done the right thing.

William stood on the jetty as the others boarded the ferry. He stood alone, older and wiser than when they had arrived that morning, and as he watched their departure, he succumbed to a calming immobilisation, which allowed this new knowledge to infiltrate his deepest thoughts.

He stood motionless until they were far out of sight.

36

Toasts to the Future

After dinner Meg took a walk with Seth from the harbour out to the east. Slate rocks by the sea glistened with sea spray and became shimmering mirrors to reflect the glow from the setting sun, whose fragmented trail skimmed across the sea's surface towards the shore. As they looked out to sea Meg and Seth became bathed in the all-encompassing amber aura. Good weather continued to bless them.

Deep-rooted words suddenly escaped from Seth's mouth.

"What do you think about marriage, Meggie Williamson?"

The words surprised Seth as much as Meg. But once said, he resolved to hold to their intention, determined to take his dream as far as it could go. Too much time had been lost over the years and the events of the past few weeks had taught them both that Life was all too short for more procrastination. Meg appeared unfazed by the sudden question.

"Marriage... aye, it must be a grand business..." she pondered. "But I've never had de pleasure to try it myself." Her heart danced within her.

"I think you should give it a try," he said.

"Ye do, do ye?"

"Aye, Meggie, what d'you think?"

"Ah, but who would want tae marry me – an auld spinster wumin wie a shocking past..."

Seth leant over and planted a soft kiss upon her moving lips.

"Does dat mean ye want tae marry the likes o' me?"

"Aye, I'm up to it, lass."

She reached out to hold his hand, her face shining in the diminishing light.

" – Den so am I!"

"That's settled then!"

"I reckon it is, Seth, I reckon it is!"

The sunset danced within Meg's eyes. Her heart fluttered with unfettered wings, like those of a dove liberated from its cage, and she longed to try out those wings. They kissed again, a kiss of promise. Her heart soared.

"Meggie," Seth whispered her name and gently held the back of her head in his cupped hand. "These past years I have longed just to be close to you."

Seth's attentions stirred at Meg's very core.

"An' now ye are, Seth."

The sun dropped below the watery horizon, leaving a cloudless sky flooded with amber light. They made their way back to the Tullock's home, knowing that Ella would be waiting up for Meg, and Meg was desperate to announce their good news.

"Dere's one problem," Meg said, as they walked arm in arm in the dark.

"What! What problem?"

"Who will I *be* after we're wed?" she asked him.

"You'll be my wife!"

"I mean – what *name* will I take? Mrs. Whit-will-I-be?"

This was the first time Seth's lack of surname caused him a problem, albeit a trivial one.

"Now there's a thing, eh?" said Seth. "What d'you fancy? Mrs. Seth? Mrs. Wife-of-Seth…?"

As they hurried into the parlour, Christina emerged from the kitchen carrying a wooden tray with a supper of oatcakes, Orkney cheese, a pot of tea, and a glass of buttermilk for Ella. She sensed their intensity and was aware something important had happened. Meg's face shone with *joie de vivre* and Seth appeared to glow with positive attitude.

Setting the tray down on the sideboard, Christina placed her hands on her hips and leant towards them, a comical, quizzically look upon her face as she eagerly anticipated their explanation.

"Oh, Christina, guess what?" said Meg excitedly.

"Well, it's something good, Meg, I can see that."

Ella in her crisp white night-gown, appeared in the doorway.

"What is it, Midder? Tell me, tell me!"

Meg turned to her daughter and wrapped her arms around her shoulders. She swivelled Ella around within her embrace so that they both faced Christina. Sensing a forthcoming family-orientated declaration, Christina called out to Hugh, "Come in here, Hugh, I think you should hear what Meg has to say!"

With the exception of William, all the important people in Meg's life were gathered before her. She turned to Seth, proudly looking at the new man in her life, yet the man who had always been there, waiting and wanting to be with her. Now she needed him to declare his intention to her loved ones.

"Tell them, Seth," she said, taking hold of his hand.

In true Seth style he kept his message simple, "I want to marry Meg," he said.

With one accord everyone cheered and their happiness rippled around the room, like the northern lights across a night sky. Ella clapped her hands. Christina and Hugh gave each other one of their knowing, long-married-couple looks. They were delighted.

"So – does *Meg* want to marry you, Seth?" Hugh asked frivolously, looking over the top of his glasses at Seth.

"Better ask her yourself, Hugh."

Meg grabbed Ella's hands in hers and, like two school children in a playground, she began to twirl her around the room, *"Yes I do, yes I do…!"* she sang and Ella joined in the chant. *"Aye she does, aye she does!"*

Christina sank back into her favourite chair and folded her arms across her bosom in satisfaction. She had not imagined that Meg, so devastated and abused in the only love affair of her life, would find such happiness and the prospect of sharing a bright future with this obviously devoted, long term suitor.

They celebrated well into the night, with the aid of many tots of Hugh's whisky and made a game of taking turns to recite drinking toasts in what developed into a competition between Hugh and Seth. It was Hugh who started the contest.

"May the best ye've ever seen
Be the worst ye'll ever see;
May a moose ne'er leave yer girnal
Wi' a tear drap in its e'e.
May yer lum keep blithely reekin'
Till yer auld enough tae dee;
May ye aye be just as happy
As I wish ye now tae be!"

Seth took over.
"Here's a bottle and an honest man!
What would ye wish for mair, man?
Wha kens before his life may end,
What his share may be o' cares, man?"

And Christina managed to add the occasional Gaelic or Highland blessing.
"May the Lord keep you in his hand,
And never close his fist too tight on you."

Hugh, fou as he was, solved the dilemma concerning a surname for the happy couple. He suggested that Seth should adopt Meg's surname. Under the 'affluence of incohol' everyone thought this the perfect solution. And so it was decided, yet forgotten until late on the following day, that after their wedding they would be known as Seth and Meg Williamson.

When Ella fell asleep on the rug by the fire, Seth gently scooped her up and carried her to her bed where Meg tucked her in, then they returned to the parlour for some more toasting.

"A guid wife and health is a man's best wealth!" Hugh recited in a loud and raucous voice.

He held his dram high above his head and kissed Christina on the cheek, unintentionally showering her forehead with droplets of the amber nectar. When Christina shrieked with laughter, he proceeded to lick her forehead. The Tullochs' parlour reverberated with noise and laughter that night until fatigue overcame the party and the toasts became shorter and less coherent. Seth fell asleep draped across the sofa and Meg covered him with a tartan blanket before heading for her bed.

In the days that followed Meg would occasionally turn to find Ella mesmerised, staring and smiling at Meg, and they would laugh and hug, with Meg so heartened to see how well her daughter had accepted her stunning revelation with its follow-up proposal of future changes.

The escaped pieces of Meg's disjointed life, flung far and wide over the years, were being drawn together as if by a magnet. There was only one piece missing – the piece containing William. There had been no word from him since their visit to Sanday. On that day he had appeared to accept their explanations about his past, but Meg wondered if time might have altered his perspective, and that on reflection, on fully absorbing the circumstances of his existence, he might choose to reject Meg. Did his silence indicate a change of heart, she wondered?

The day of his birth was always clear in her mind. How could she ever forget her absolute rejection of her firstborn? At most vulnerable, she was dominated by the pressure put upon her by her illicit, omnipotent lover and ordered to obey his demand for the only course of action open to her. How could William, now an adolescent boy, understand such a time? He would be justified in rejecting Meg as his mother; the mother who took no part in his life. Seth was right – William and Ella were owed their birthright, yet in endeavouring to reunite her fractured family, she might irreparably rip it asunder. Meg withheld her agonising doubts from Ella, who had welcomed with open arms her true role as Meg's daughter and taken on board the given facts with complete trust and acceptance. Hellen's death had occurred when Ella was still at an age when she needed a mother's love and she wholeheartedly grabbed the chance of having Meg's love to sustain her. She had many questions for Meg, who answered with as much clarity as she could muster, though Ella soon realised that Meg was saddened by talk of the past and accepted the family philosophy that everyone would do better to concentrate on the future.

Only Meg and Seth knew the true parentage of William and Ella. In Kirkwall it was generally accepted that Meg was their surrogate mother. The people of Kirkwall were tolerant of most relationships as long as they worked well for the society as a whole.

37

Never Too Auld

On the following Saturday William arrived in Kirkwall and Meg went to meet him from the ferry. He was one of the last passengers to alight and as he approached her she was filled with apprehension. For a moment they stood facing one another. She immediately noticed that he was now taller than she was. When his face broke into a smile, relief flooded over her.

"I'm auld enough tae ken that Life is nae a bed o' roses," he said sombrely. "Ye had hard times, but ye're making a new start, settin' yer life in order."

Meg hung on his words.

"What ye did – "

William was interrupted by the sound of gulls squawking loudly overhead. Within a frozen moment Meg and William stared at one another. The need for forgiveness shone pleadingly from her eyes.

"All I wanted tae say was – it worked out right for me and Ella. We were loved. We were happy. I hae nae complaints."

Meg sighed and clasped both her palms lovingly over William's cheeks, playfully rocking his head from side to side until he laughingly pulled himself free. It was the first time since the day of his birth that she had held his face. Pride replaced the shame of previous years. This fine and handsome character existed because of her. His life had evolved through her wrongdoing, but his character had developed without her oversight. William was now a source of pride.

William continued, "Maybe no a bed o' roses – but it's turning into quite a garden, eh?"

And they laughed.

"It feels good to make ma auld Midder happy!" William joked.

As they walked back to the bakery, Meg told him about Seth's plans to marry her. William was silent for a time. Polly and Grace greeted them as they walked in the door.

"I've just told William about my plans to be married," Meg said with a blush of pride at the very thought of being a respectable married woman. "But he's bin awfae quiet aboot it…"

She turned to William, who looked at her thoughtfully before he spoke.

"Meg," he quipped, "are ye no too auld to be getting' married? Is there no' a law banning such things fur auld folk?"

"Och, away wie ye, ye scally!" Meg elbowed him in his ribs as Polly and Grace burst out laughing.

Marriages usually occurred between young couples. Meg was nearly thirty-five and Seth was in his fortieth year. Between older couples re-marriages were common enough following the death of a spouse, but a first time marriage where both parties were over thirty was unusual. To some of the older community, however, to people like Grace and Polly Cursiter, Seth and Meg's betrothal was more meaningful.

"It's never too auld to marry, of that I'm sure," Polly remarked reassuringly. "*I* still live in hopes, I do!"

"Ha!" clucked her sister. "You'll be hoping a long time, Polly dear!"

Both Grace and Polly had lost sweethearts in their youth. The only man Polly had ever loved drowned during a squall in the Pentland Firth, along with two horses that he had been taking to market on the Scottish Mainland. Grace's suitor had sailed to Canada in search of work, promising to return and marry her when he had saved enough money. While he was away two good suitors were spurned due to Grace's belief that her beau would hold to his promise, but she never heard from him again. By the time her trust in him finally faded, the spurned bachelors were securely betrothed elsewhere. During their suitor-less years the sisters had formed an impenetrable bond and a companionable spinsterhood existed. There was an unsaid vow between them that they would stay together. Polly and Grace were both devoted to their father and to running his business.

Seth appeared at the door.

"Ye'll be havin' a wedding den?" William said, heartily slapping him on the back.

Seth was all for the simple life. A wedding celebration was not something he wanted. He nodded, amiably resigned for Meg's sake to participate in a grand ceremony that the word 'wedding' conjured up to him. He knew how much it would mean to Meg. And the way her friends were rallying round with offers of help indicated that the wedding would be anything but simple. She tried to reassure him that it would be a simple occasion, simple as baking a cake, she said, yet no sooner had she declared this than Polly and Grace announced they would bake a two-tiered wedding cake, which was a very grand item for a simple wedding. Meg was thrilled with the idea. Seth rolled his head, wagging it at Meg.

"So simple," he muttered.

But whatever Meg wanted was fine by him, because he thought she deserved to have a fuss made of her after all the years of closet living. And he, too, wanted to mark the fruition of his quest.

The day after Seth's proposal Meg wrote letters to all her sisters. She took Seth to visit Agnes, Peter and their children at Rabbitha' and arranged for Anderina to be there that day. Her sisters were amused when they met Meg's new partner for they immediately recognised him as the Laird's rent-collecting manservant. But could this really be the same silent, dour-faced man they remembered from all those years ago? He still resembled a Viking warrior, but it was the change in his demeanour that amused Agnes. Seth had always commanded a presence, but now he possessed a touch of poise, the *je ne sais quoi* that being in love brings to a person. In Meg's company, Seth was attentive, even spirited. Agnes sensed he had been in love with her sister for many years and told Seth he must be a dark horse, which made him laugh out loud, taking Agnes by surprise and making her laugh, too.

A joy to behold, Agnes and Anderina saw the new energy in Meg. The couple were in love, no doubt about it. The traumas of their youngest sister's past were inconsequential. It sufficed that Meg had survived them and at last had the prospect of a happy future. During a quiet sisterly moment together, Agnes's curiosity drove her to ask

Meg about the father of her merrybegotten bairns. After all, she had contributed much to their upbringing and she wondered now if they might be Seth's children, but she was quickly corrected.

"Der faider is dead," Meg said, turning away from Agnes and Anderina to look out the window at the children playing. To speak of Charles still caused her pain. "He was married, ye ken, dat was de problem..."

Though she kept her assumptions to herself, Agnes realised more than Meg cared to think, yet would never divulge. It had no relevance to the present.

Barbara wrote to say that she would not miss the occasion for the world; that she had all but given up ever seeing the day that Meg might marry. When Barbara returned to Orkney for Meg's wedding, not only did she bring with her Jon, and their daughter Elizabeth, but she also came laden with fine materials and laces. In Frankfurt, Barbara was a renowned dress designer and she wasted no time in fitting Meg for her wedding dress, using the most up to the minute European designs. Following Orcadian tradition, Meg herself would hand sew her groom's finely tucked and pleated wedding shirt.

Anticipation spread amongst Meg's close community and everyone found a part to play in her special day. Both Ella and Gina were to be Meg's flower girls, carrying identical posies, and Aunt Robina offered to sew identical dresses for them to wear. For Ella it was a dream come true to have a wedding in the family. Agnes and Anderina said they would undertake the organisation of the wedding supper, contributed towards by everyone attending. Bessie was on hand to do much of the cooking. A whole sheep and several chickens would be spit-roasted on the day. Hugh was in charge of finding and borrowing a huge collection of glasses and tankards for the drinking of the Bride's Cog, the traditional mixture of alcoholic beverages, which would be passed around the guests during the feast. In addition to the two-tiered cake, Polly and Grace would bake bread and baps aplenty.

Christina crafted a tartan plaid for Meg to wear around the shoulders of her dress. And the rift between Meg and her brother John was healed, with Meg's request for him to give her away at her marriage ceremony in lieu of Andrew. John had learnt through the untimely death of his father that life can be all too short, undoubtedly too short to hold unhappy grudges. Whatever Meg had done in the past she was now trying to make amends and would always be his dearest sister.

In total contrast to her life at Black Bull Farm, Meg's life in Kirkwall had enabled her to develop in her own right. In previous years her circumstances had isolated her, not only from her own offspring, but also from her mother, siblings, and even from the other workers. Her all-consuming notion that the Laird of Westray loved her was the only thing that made her clandestine life bearable. In Kirkwall the hidden nature of the child she once had been returned; lively, carefree, gregarious and warm-hearted. She was a part of a community and revelled in that fact. And with Seth's redemption she had been given the chance of a fresh start, to re-invent her life. The love of Seth was more than the toffee on Meg's apple; it was the very core.

And his was an unrequited love at last fulfilled.

One day a package arrived at Kirk Green Stables addressed simply "To Seth". Bewildered, Seth stared at the package long and hard as if somehow its content would become apparent to him. The Inverness postmark gave him a clue. He untied the string and tore away the brown paper wrapping to find a publisher's copy of "Travels through the Orkney Islands. Written and Illustrated by Seth of Westray".

The hard evidence of his accomplishment in all its fresh glory, tangible proof of Meg's innovation, took him by surprise. In the anticipation of his marriage to Meg he had quite forgotten his other acquisition. His eyes idled over the line, "by Seth of Westray". This had been his publisher's suggestion months previously and his agreed pseudonym. Reading the title of his alternative persona made Seth grin proudly. He was now not only head groom and stableman, but also author and artist, and soon to become a husband and stepfather, too. On opening the book he found a sheet of the publisher's headed notepaper on which was a letter promising a handsome amount of money for advance of sales. Seth's moustache stretched into a wide grin as he stared and stared at the crisp new, polished copy of his work. His pen and ink sketches looked well in print.

Meg appeared at the entrance to the stables, sunlight framing her slender frame.

"Whit are ye grinning aboot, Seth?" she asked, curiosity adding extra lilt to her dulcet voice.

Unlocking his eyes from the book he raised his head and winked at her.

"Just another reason to celebrate, Meggie Williamson!"

38

Starting Over

Neighbours of George and Gina announced their intent to emigrate to Canada, where there was work to be had at the Hudson Bay Company. The neighbour's home was a thatched longhouse named "Sunnybrae" and it was a stone's throw from the Rendall's home. The house was long and narrow, its rooms leading through from one to another. There was also a room in the attic with a window to the back of the property, which looked out towards Gina's home. Its large parlour had a panoramic view to the sea. It was Gina who begged Meg to consider renting it as their new home.

Meg's room at the Tullochs' home was not suitable as married accommodation. Even more unsuitable were Seth's lodgings above Kirk Green Stables. So there was not much discussion to be done over the suitability of Sunnybrae. It was arranged that they would move there with Ella after they were wed. Ella's bubble of happiness seemed to inflate with each passing day. Christina and Hugh's home on Victoria Street was only a ten minute walk away. The Cursiter Bakery, the school and Kirk Green Stables were all within easy reach.

The start of a new and positive future was also the end of a comforting era. Living with the Tullochs had been a happy time for Meg. In accepting their kindness towards her, she had been able to rise out of the depths of despair. Christina and Hugh were like members of her close family.

On the dawn of her wedding day Meg awoke to find an all-embracing blue sky stretching over Kirkwall harbour as far as the eye could see. A thin trail of wispy cloud, like the delicate veil of a bride, floated gently across the peaceful scene. The glow of sunrise shone low in the autumnal horizon, warming the wide, low, Orcadian panorama. Meg gazed at the familiar view over the harbour from the window on this, the last morning she and Ella would spend at the Tulloch's home.

The morning was a frenzy of flippancy for the assembly of

women at the Tulloch's home. And within the men's camp at Kirk Green Stables, there was much slapping of backs and raucous laughter. Throughout the town wedding guests prepared themselves for the afternoon's rejoicing and when the bellringers began tolling the church bells loud and clear over Kirkwall, people emerged from their homes, dressed in their Sunday best, and headed towards the Kirk. Outside on the Kirk steps, all those dear to Meg gathered in cheerily chattering clusters, eventually taking their places on the pews inside. At the agreed time and not a moment late, Meg's brother, John, arrived at the Tullochs' home, ready to play his part in Meg's day, to give her away in lieu of their father. As Meg stood before him, meticulously decked in her finery, happiness radiating from her, John thought she looked ten years younger and told her so.

"Och, awa' wie ye!" Meg blushed, but she was ready to accept all reassurances for her biggest day.

John proudly escorted his sister on their walk to the Kirk. He nodded and doffed his cap to pedestrians encountered on the way. Greetings were exchanged and compliments given to the bride.

The Kirk was small, peedie, yet ample to accommodate wellwishers that day. On entering the Kirk, Meg's eyes were drawn to the magnetism of Seth's presence as he stood tall and firm by the altar with the minister to his side. Their eyes locked. Their images of one another developed like photographs within their minds, portraits that would never fade. Meg and Seth would forever remember how the other registered at that precise moment.

Meg was still the most beautiful woman Seth had ever encountered – but on this occasion he was bedazzled by the vision of loveliness. Her hair had been dressed in such a way that she looked nothing less than exquisite; shining blonde hair, immaculately brushed and drawn high to the crest of her head, where a delicate lace veil hung from the back of a small muslin cap. The cap was festooned with miniature silk flowers and wisps of ribbon. Spiralling tendrils of hair fell from her temples. The buttermilk silk dress that she wore fitted where it touched. Meg's figure was still youthful and slender. Loosely draped around her pale-skinned shoulders was Christina's tartan plaid, pinned with a silver brooch. Meg's face, smiling and devoted, was framed by the veil, which lay in soft ripples.

Meg absorbed Seth's presence, locking it in the recesses of her memory. She smiled to see him looking uncomfortably resplendent, dressed in a well pressed dark suit and the crisp white shirt that she had neatly hand-sewn with fine tucks and pleats at its front. His normally windswept hair was brushed back off his tanned face and his moustache groomed into two tapering swatches down to his chin. She saw clearly on this her most special day, what a handsome man he was.

Guests lined the Kirk pews. With so many children included in the congregation it was not a hushed or silent scene. Happiness and exuberance filled each and everyone gathered there. Christina and Hugh sat in the front row with George Rendall and Meg's sisters, Anderina and Barbara, Barbara's husband, Jon, and their daughter, Elizabeth. In the pew behind them Agnes and Peter sat with their children, unintentionally in height order though in perpetual motion with their fidgeting. On the opposite side of the aisle, Robina, Will and Bethia sat with John's wife, Mary, and their children. Behind them Polly, Grace and Bruce Cursiter were alonside with Bessie and Jeremiah. Other pews were filled by Edward and Margaret Murray of Kirk Green, with the other groomsmen, and many customers of Tulloch's Ironmongery and Cursiter's Bakery.

The organ player stuck up his first chord, long, loud and commanding, and the wedding ceremony commenced.

Hugh's thoughts centred on their lost daughter, Rebecca. He wondered where in the world she might be at that moment, whither she was happy or sad, indeed alive or dead. He would gladly have given his right arm to see her as happily wed as Meg was to be that day. Christina shed a tear or two during the ceremony, her tears accompanied by a sweet smile of wholehearted approval. Ella and Gina picked petals from their posies and stroked their dresses with lady-like grace, coyly giggling when the minister asked Seth to kiss his new wife. A communal sigh drifted in a whisper around the Kirk, followed by a rash of smiles on the gathered faces, their shared pleasure melting along the pews.

After the service, Meg and Seth turned to face their friends. An aura of unity surrounded them, a tangible binding. The Kirk Warden opened the Kirk doors and dazzling sunshine fell in a zealous shaft upon the aisle at their feet. They walked arm in arm along its golden path as loud music resounded cheerfully from the organ. Ella and Gina, their eyes alight, followed the wedding couple out of the Kirk.

Outside two very old ladies stood together to the forefront of a crowd of wellwishers. These ladies were uninvited wedding overseers. They needed no prerequisite to be acquainted with either bride or groom, the irresistible draw of any wedding being simply the sense of occasion. Wrinkled and gnarled, one was tall and stood hunched, whilst her companion, short and portly, leant in the opposite direction, leaning backwards in order to uphold her belly and bosom. Both were dressed in their Sunday best clothes and each held a large white paper bag at chest level.

Meg's all-seeing eyes alighted upon them, this odd and conspicuous couple. The euphoria within her had heightened her senses. Alert and aware, she was keenly tuned to everything going on around her and absorbed all like a sponge. These two ladies were unfamiliar to Meg and she felt sure that Seth felt likewise. She swiftly surmised that the old spinsters were regular attendants to occasions such as weddings and funerals, that this was perhaps one of their favourite pastimes. She smiled sweetly at them, showing tiny crow's feet at the corners of her bright eyes. The ladies' faces remained devoid of expression. As Meg and Seth neared the odd couple, the taller of the two dipped one white-gloved hand into her white paper bag and pulled out a large handful of good-luck rice, ready to scatter over the newly weds as they passed by. Before doing so she bent over sideways to speak into the ear of her companion and, speaking through the side of her mouth, she said in a loud whisper, "She's bonnie, is she no? – *Fur her age,* that is...." Meg overheard her remark.

Both ladies continued to stare haughtily. The facetiousness of the remark combined with the ladies' unwittingly comical expressions made Meg want to giggle. Like a schoolgirl frowned upon for smiling at assembly, Meg felt the onslaught of an irrepressible fit of the giggles. Not since the days of her childhood on Fair Isle had she felt like giggling, let alone the need to suppress the feeling. Giggling always occurred when either the venue or the timing was completely wrong. But in Meg's new found confidence no emotion was allowed to be suppressed and like a startled seabird, she burst out with a sudden guffaw.

A chain of events unravelled before Meg and Seth, like dominoes positioned to collapse. An impromptu performance was involuntarily performed before them, an event insignificant to most other onlookers.

It began as the taller of two, still clutching her large handful of good-luck rice, became startled by Meg's sudden and unladylike outburst. Like a frightened chicken, the genteel old spinster clucked and stepped sideways onto her companion's foot, at the same time as the hand clutching the rice jerked skywards and released multitudinous particles from her clutches up into the air, above the heads of the two old ladies. Propelled towards the heavens, free-moving molecules released into the atmosphere, the grains of rice jumped for joy at their release and somersaulted over each other, until gravity caught hold of them, dragging them down, free falling, to scatter and tumble in all directions across the two old ladies' hats. Grains of rice raced each other along the brim of the portly lady's hat, like a flurry of tiny insects. The brim dipped heavily at her forehead, weighed down by a gathering of rice, suddenly to collapse in a steady stream down her ample cleavage. She winced, writhed, and let out a squeal, plunging her chubby fingers into her soft, wrinkled bosom to retrieve the offending particles. The taller lady was dealing with her own irritations, trying to dislodge grains that had whistled down the nape of her neck. She strutted on the spot like a flustered hen.

Their enjoyment of a pleasant afternoon viewing and commenting on a wedding procession was spoilt for the two ladies, who were now conducting a less than genteel game of retrieving the numerous and tiny offenders about their person, detectable only by feel as neither lady could see without her spectacles. The grains continued to wriggle and worm their way into all manner of crevices and folds. The ladies, contorted into positions unknown since childhood, were driven to gyrate and stomp, hell bent on eradicating every last nestling grain.

Meg was well aware that the strange behaviour of these two prim and proper old ladies was due to her moment of wild abandon and soon both she and Seth were laughing. Meg's laughter, like jets of sparkling water, continued in a stream, all but drowning the sound of organ music from inside the Kirk.

The guests made their way in a long ambling column towards the Kirk Hall, where victuals and ale were aplenty, set out on long trestle tables against the walls. A cheer greeted the newly weds when they entered the Hall. The wedding feast was attacked from all angles and the Bride's Cog, full of a ripe mixture of brandy, whisky, ale and herbs, was handed round the room for one and all to sup. The festivities then commenced in earnest. Fiddlers gathered at one end of the Hall and struck up a merry and frantic tune. Any man who could play a fiddle well was welcome at an Orcadian wedding. Their music was all the entertainment needed for dancing, singing and foot tapping. Some guests immediately took to the open floor to jig and those standing to the side gave way to the irresistible urge to tap their feet to the rhythm. Speech was only audible at a shout.

Mingling with their guests, Meg and Seth became separated in the throng. Sipping on her glass of ale, Meg's eyes continually drifted around the room over the heads of revellers in the hopes of catching a glimpse of her unpredictable firstborn. She was taken by surprise when William did materialise – at her elbow, and later wondered how long he had been standing there before she noticed him. Seth noticed him, too, and, with tankard in hand, crossed the room to be with them. William turned to greet him.

"An' now – at last – I have a man in da family!" William shouted above the noise of the fiddlers. "I could nae have asked fur a better yin either, an' dat be true!"

William shook Seth vigorously by the hand and slapped him about the shoulder. They laughed as precious ale was spilt from Seth's overflowing tankard. Ella was quick to notice their tomfoolery and ran over to join in the bonding.

Meg's heart sang. She could never have foreseen this outcome, this second chance for them all. In Seth, she knew she had a good man. His love for her had already stood the test of time. Her love for him was an increasing and enduring love. Before, she had clutched at straw happiness savoured in intense but small doses with only pain and loneliness to fill the interim. Grasping the concept that Seth had loved her for so long had been difficult, but immeasurably satisfying. The knowledge that someone she admired and respected, a man of integrity, who knew her shameful mistakes, could love her, and for such a long time, was all she needed to build faith in herself again. She knew that he had loved her throughout those disastrous times and that she would never have to explain them. He had been there. And he was there for her now – and always.

Meg stepped back from the whole picture, allowing her mind's eye to take images for her soul, memories to hold dear until her dying day. It was as if she was floating above the scene yet seeing herself within it and for a moment she hovered over her circle of love. The essence of a happy life was fully apparent to her in that moment. It was to love and be loved in return. To Meg, the love that flowed round her nearest and dearest was proof of a life well lived.

The fiddlers struck up another enrapturing tune, jolting her back into happy reality.

By Christmas of that year Meg told Seth he was to be a father. She announced to the family at Sunnybrae that she was expecting his baby.

Printed in the United Kingdom
by Lightning Source UK Ltd.
102343UKS00001B/367-369